LONG LIVE EVIL

Time of Iron: Book One

SARAH REES BRENNAN

orbitbooks.net

Copyright © 2024 by Sarah Rees Brennan
Excerpt from *These Deathless Shores* copyright © 2024 by P. H. Low
Excerpt from *How to Become the Dark Lord and Die Trying* copyright © 2024 by Django Wexler

Cover design by Ben Prior | LBBG
Cover illustration by Syd Mills
Map by Rebecka Champion (Lampblack Art)
Author photograph by Edel Kelly

Orbit
Hachette Book Group
1290 Avenue of the Americas
New York, NY 10104
orbitbooks.net

First Edition: July 2024
Simultaneously published in Great Britain by Orbit

Orbit is an imprint of Hachette Book Group.
The Orbit name and logo are registered trademarks of Little, Brown Book Group Limited.

The publisher is not responsible for websites (or their content) that are not owned by the publisher.

The Hachette Speakers Bureau provides a wide range of authors for speaking events. To find out more, go to hachettespeakersbureau.com or email HachetteSpeakers@hbgusa.com.

Orbit books may be purchased in bulk for business, educational, or promotional use. For information, please contact your local bookseller or the Hachette Book Group Special Markets Department at special.markets@hbgusa.com.

Library of Congress Control Number: 2024934967

ISBNs: 9780316568715 (trade paperback), 9780316568722 (ebook)

Printed in the United States of America

CCR

3 5 7 9 10 8 6 4 2

For my brother, Rory Rees Brennan –
a real hero, better than in any book.

Every tongue brings in a several tale
And every tale condemns me for a villain.

Richard III
SHAKESPEARE

CHAPTER ONE

The Villainess Faces Death

Ours is a land of terrible miracles. Here the dead live and
lies come true. Beware. Here every fantasy is possible.

Time of Iron, ANONYMOUS

he Emperor broke into the throne room. In one hand
he held his sword. In the other, the head of his enemy.
He swung the head jauntily, fingers twisted in blood-
drenched, tangled hair.

A scarlet trail on the hammered-gold tiles marked the Emperor's
passage. His boots left deep crimson footprints. Even the ice-blue
lining inside his black cloak dripped with red. No part of him was
left unstained.

He wore the crowned death mask, empty of the jewel that
should adorn his brow, and a breastplate of bronze with falling stars
wrought in iron. The red-gleaming metal fingers of his gauntlets
tapered into shining claws.

When he lifted the mask, fury and pain had carved his face into
new lines. After his time in the sunless place he was pale as winter
light, radiance turned so cold it burned. He was a statue with a splash
of blood staining his cheek, like a red flower on stone. She barely
recognized him.

He was the Once and Forever Emperor, the Corrupt and

Divine, the Lost and Found Prince, Master of the Dread Ravine, Commander of the Living and the Dead. None could stop his victory march.

She couldn't bear to watch him smile, or the shambling dead behind him. Her gaze was drawn by the hungry gleam of his blade. She wished it had stayed broken.

The hilt of the re-forged Sword of Eyam was a coiled snake. On the blade an inscription glittered and flowed as if written on water. The only word visible beneath a slick coat of blood was *Longing*.

The girl with silver hands trembled, alone in the heart of the palace. The Emperor approached the throne and said—

"You're not *listening!*"

"That's a weird thing for the Emperor to say," Rae remarked.

Her little sister Alice sat on the end of Rae's hospital bed, clutching the white-painted steel footrest as if she'd mistaken it for a life raft. Alice was giving a dramatic reading from their favourite book series, and Rae wasn't taking it seriously.

Life was too short to take things seriously, if you asked Rae. Alice's rosebud mouth was twisted in judgement. Rosebuds shouldn't get judgemental.

When Rae was four, her mom promised her a beautiful baby sister.

Alice came to her in springtime. The apple blossoms in their yard were snowy white and tinged with pink, dawn clouds in front of Rae's window all day. Their parents carried baby Alice over the threshold, wrapped in pink wool and white lace that made her seem another curled blossom. Under Rae's eager gaze, they drew back a fold of blanket with the reverence of a groom unveiling his bride, and showed the baby's newborn face.

She wasn't beautiful. She looked like an angry walnut.

"Hey funnyface," Rae told Alice throughout their childhood. "Don't cry. You're ugly, but I won't let anybody tease you."

Life turned out ironic so often, fate must have a sense of humour. As Alice grew, the bones in her face clicked into the perfect position, even her skeleton shaped more harmoniously than anybody else's. She was beautiful. People said Rae was pretty too.

Rae wasn't pretty any more. Even before, Rae knew pretty wasn't the same.

Beauty was like a big umbrella, both useful and awkward to handle. Three years ago, the sisters had gone to a convention for fans of Alice's favourite books.

Time of Iron was a saga of lost gods and old sins, passion and horror, hope and death. Everyone agreed it wasn't about the romance, but discussed the love triangle incessantly. The books had everything: battles of swords and wits, despair and dances, the hero rising from humble origins to ultimate power, and the peerless beauty who everybody wanted but only he could have. The heroine overcame her rivals, through being pure of heart, to become queen of the land. The hero clawed his way up from the depths to become emperor of everything. The heroine was rewarded for being beautiful and virtuous, the hero for being a good-looking bastard.

Alice attended the convention as the villainess known as the Beauty Dipped In Blood. Rae didn't understand why Alice wanted to dress up as the heroine's evil stepsister.

"*I'm* not the one who gets confused between costumes and truth." Softening the words, Alice had leaned her newly darkened head against Rae's shoulder. "The truth is, she looks like you. I can pretend to be brave when I look like you."

At the time Rae hadn't read the books, but she wore her cheer-leading uniform so they'd both be in costume. A line formed asking Rae to take their picture with Alice. The guy at the end of the line stared, but another guy carrying the First Duke's double-bitted axe told jokes and made Alice laugh. It was nice to see her shy sister laughing.

When Rae held up the last guy's phone, his hand strayed to Alice's ass. Alice was thirteen.

"Hands off!" Rae snapped.

The guy oiled, "Oooh, sorry, m'lady. My hand slipped."

"It's fine." Alice smiled, worried about his feelings even though he hadn't worried about hers. "Everybody say 'cheese!'"

Alice was the nice sister. Rae considered the guy's smirk and his phone.

"Everybody say 'Fish for it, creep!'"

Rae tossed her ponytail, and tossed the phone into a trash can overflowing with half-eaten hot dogs. Being nice was nice. Being nasty got shit done.

The guy squawked, abandoning underage ass for electronics.

Rae winked. "Oooh, sorry, milord. My hand slipped."

"What are you dressed as, a bitch cheerleader?"

She slung an arm around her sister's shoulders. "*Head* bitch cheerleader."

The guy sneered. "Bet you haven't even read the books."

Sadly, he was correct. Sadly for him, Rae was a huge liar, and her sister was obsessed with these books. Rae shot back with one of the Emperor's lines. "'Beg for mercy. It amuses me.'"

She strode away, declining to be quizzed further. Usually she remembered every tale Alice told her, but Rae was already worried about how much she was forgetting from classes, conversations, and even stories.

That was the last time Rae could protect her sister. The next week she went to see the doctor about her persistent cough, and the weight and memory loss. She began a battery of tests that ended in biopsy, diagnosis and treatments spanning three years. Part of Rae stayed in that final moment when she could be young, and cruel, and believe her story would end well. Forever seventeen. The rest of her had skipped all the steps from child to old woman, feeling ever so much more than twenty.

Rae was past the time of hoping for magic, but Alice fulfilled every requirement for a heroine. Alice was sixteen, beautiful without knowing it, and cared more about her favourite book series than anything else.

Sitting on Rae's hospital bed, Alice pushed her glasses up her nose and scowled. "You claim you want a refresher on the story, but you get surprised by key events!"

"I know every song from the musical."

Alice scoffed. Her sister was a purist. Rae believed if you were lucky your favourite story got told in a dozen different ways, so you could choose your favourite flavour. None of the musical's stars were hot enough, but nobody could ever be as hot as characters in your imagination. Book characters were dangerously attractive in the safest way. You didn't even know what they looked like, but you knew you liked it.

"Then tell me the Beauty Dipped In Blood's name." When Rae hesitated, Alice accused: "It's as if you haven't even read this book!"

That was Rae's guilty secret.

This was her favourite series, and she *hadn't* really read the first book.

Rae and her sister used to have book sleepovers, cuddled together reading a much-anticipated book through the night or telling each other tales. Alice would tell Rae the stories of all the books she was reading. Rae would tell Alice how the stories should have gone. Back then, Rae hadn't believed Alice when she said *Time of Iron* was life-changing. Alice was a literary romantic, falling in love with the potential of every story she met. Rae had always been more cynical.

Reading a book was like meeting someone for the first time. You don't know if you will love them or hate them enough to learn every detail, or skim the surface never to know their depths.

When Rae was diagnosed, Alice finally had a captive audience. During Rae's first chemo session, Alice opened *Time of Iron* and started to read aloud what appeared to be a typical fantasy adventure about the damsel in distress getting the guy in a crown. Rae, certain she knew where this was going, listened to the fun parts with blood and gore, but otherwise zoned out. Who cared about saving the damsel? She was astonished by the end, when the Emperor rose to claim his throne.

"Wait, who's this guy?" Rae had demanded. "I love him."

Alice stared in disbelief. "He's the hero."

Rae devoured the next two books. The sequels were wild. After his queen was murdered, the Emperor visited ruin upon the world, then ruled over a bleak landscape of bones. The books were grim and also dark. The series title might as well be *Holy Shit, Basically Everybody Dies*.

Under the eerie skies of Eyam, monsters roamed, some in human form. Rae loved monsters and monstrous deeds. She hated books which were like dismal manuals instructing you of the only moral way to behave. Hope without tragedy was hollow. In the strange, fascinating world of these books, with its glorious horror of a hero, pain meant something.

By the time she finished the sequels, reading began to make Rae feel sick, adrift on a sea of words. Even listening to the books led her mind into the fog. She did want to find out the actual events of the first book, so she tricked Alice into reading it aloud as a 'refresher'. If any voice could hold Rae's attention, it would be that best-beloved voice.

Except they were now at the end, and Rae had still managed to miss a lot from the first book in the *Time of Iron* series. She feared her super-fan sister was catching on.

Time to play it cool. Rae said, "How dare you question me?"

"You constantly forget characters' names!"

"The characters all have titles as well as names, which I find greedy. There's the Golden Cobra, the Beauty Dipped In Blood, the Iron Maid, the Last Hope—"

Alice gave a scream. For a minute, Rae thought she'd seen a mouse.

"The Last Hope is the best character in the book!"

Rae lifted her hands in surrender. "If you say so."

The Last Hope was the losing side of the love triangle, the good guy. If you asked Alice, the flawless guy. Alice's favourite wasted his time longing for the heroine from afar, too busy brooding to use his awesome supernatural abilities.

The parade of guys professing love for the heroine was a blur that bored Rae. Anybody could say they loved you. When the time came to prove it, most failed.

Alice sniffed. "The Last Hope deserved Lia. The Emperor is a psychopath."

The idea of deserving someone was wrong-headed. You couldn't win women on points. Alice must be thinking of video games.

Rae overlooked this to defend her man. "Have you considered the Emperor has great cheekbones? Sorry to the side of good. Evil's just sexier."

Rae wanted characters to have tormented backstories, she just wished they wouldn't be annoying about it. The Emperor was Rae's favourite character of all time because he never brooded over his dark past. He used his unholy powers and enormous sword to slaughter his enemies, then moved on.

Alice made a face. "The thing with the iron shoes was creepy! If a creep is the true love, what does that teach girls?"

What thing with the iron shoes? Rae decided it wasn't important. "Stories should be exciting. I don't need to be preached at, I can do literary analysis."

Rae was supposed to be valedictorian and get a scholarship. Instead Rae's and Alice's college funds were gone. Rae was twenty and never going to college.

They didn't talk about that.

"If the Emperor were real, he would be horrifying."

"Lucky he's not real," Rae snapped back. "Everyone who thinks books will make women date assholes underestimates us. If stories hypnotize people, why isn't everybody terrified movies will turn boys into drag-racing assassins? I don't want to fix the guy, I want to watch the murder show."

She refused to have another argument about the Emperor being problematic. Clearly, the Emperor was problematic. When you murdered half the people you met, you had a problem. Stories lived on problems. There was a reason *Star Wars* wasn't *Star Peace*.

After Lia was killed, the Emperor put her corpse on a throne and made her enemies kiss her dead feet. Then he ripped their hearts out. 'Now you know how it feels,' he murmured, his face the last thing their fading vision ever saw. Villainous characters had epic highs, epic lows, and epic loves. The Emperor loved like an apocalypse.

In real life, people let you go. That was why people longed for the love from stories, love that felt more real than real love.

Alice's sigh could have blown a farmhouse away to a magical land. "It's about troubling patterns in media, not a specific story. Specifically, you're basic. *Everyone* likes the Emperor best."

That was ridiculous. Many appreciated the Last Hope's chiselled misery, the Golden Cobra's decadent antics, and the Iron Maid's cutting sarcasm. Few liked the heroine best. Who could be as good as the perfect woman, and who wanted to be?

Fewer still liked the wicked stepsister. The only thing worse than a woman being too innocent was a woman being too guilty.

"*Nobody* likes the Beauty Dipped In Blood best," Rae pointed out. "I don't need to remember her name. That incompetent schemer dies in the first book."

"Her name is Lady Rahela Domitia."

"Wow." Rae smirked. "Might as well call a character Evilla McKinky. No wonder the Emperor liked her."

"Not the Emperor," corrected Alice.

Right, the king didn't become emperor until later. Rae nodded wisely.

Alice continued, "Rahela was the king's favourite until our heroine came to court. The king was dazzled by Lia, so Lia's stepsister went mad with jealousy. Rahela and her maid conspired to get Lia executed! Any of this ringing a bell?"

"So many bells. It's like a cathedral in my brain."

Her sister's voice grew clearer in Rae's memory. Rae always appreciated a big death scene.

The chapter started with Lady Rahela, wearing a signature snow-white dress edged with blood-red, realizing she had been imprisoned in her chamber. The next day the king had Rahela executed before the entire court. Everybody enjoyed seeing the bitch sister get hers.

Rahela's maid was offered mercy by Lia, who was always saying 'I know there's good in them,' as the people in question cackled and ate the heads off kittens. The heartbroken former servant became an axe murderer known as the remorseless Iron Maid.

All great villains almost got redeemed, but instead plunged deeper into evil. You kept thinking, *they might turn back! It's not too late!* The best villains' death scenes made you cry.

Alice offered, "Want to read more? We need to be prepared for the next book!"

The next book would be the last. Everyone expected an unhappy ending. Rae was dreading one.

Hope without tragedy was hollow. So was tragedy without hope.

Rae had always told her sister this was a story about both. Darkness wouldn't last for a grim eternity. People wouldn't keep getting worse until they died. She'd believed the Emperor could resurrect his queen and snatch victory from the jaws of defeat, but her faith was fading. Fiction should be an escape, but she suspected nobody was getting out of this story alive.

"I'm not ready for an ending." Rae feigned a dramatic swoon. "Leave me with the Emperor in the throne room."

Alice turned toward hospital windows that went opaque as mirrors when night drew in. Rae was startled to see a tell-tale gleam in Alice's eyes, reflecting the shimmer of the glass. This wasn't worth crying over. None of it was real.

Alice's voice was low. "Don't act as if what matters to me is a joke."

Rae should be able to transform into who she'd once been, for her sister. She should be smart and strong with sympathy to spare. She used to be overflowing. Now she was empty.

Her voice went sharp as guilt. "I have other things to worry about!"

"You're right, Rae. Even when you get everything wrong, you believe you're right."

"It's just a story."

"Yeah," Alice snapped. "It's just imagined out of nothing, into something thousands love. It just makes me feel understood when nobody in my life understands me. It's *just* a story."

Rae's eyes narrowed. "Has it never crossed your mind why I might not want to reach the end of these books about everybody dying?"

Alice launched to her feet like a furious rocket, spitting sparks as she rose. "You don't even realize why the scene when the Flower of Life and Death blooms is my favourite!"

Rae was speechless, with no idea what happened in that scene.

In this hospital, doors had metal loops set in the white doors. You could grab onto the loops if you were feeling unsteady, and ease the door open. The door swung behind Alice with a force that made the squat water glass beside Rae's narrow bed shake.

Her sister leaving was no surprise. Rae had already driven everyone else away.

Rae turned her head on the pillow and stared out of the silver-blank window, pressing her lips tight together. Then she heaved herself out of bed like an old woman emerging from a bath. She tottered towards the door on legs skinny as sticks that tried to slide out from under her and skitter across the floor. Sometimes Rae felt it wasn't her legs betraying her, but a world that no longer wanted her tipping her over the edge.

When Rae opened the door, Alice was standing right outside. She fell into Rae's arms.

"Hey, ugly," Rae whispered. "I'm sorry."

"*I'm* sorry," sobbed Alice. "I shouldn't make a fuss over a dumb story."

"It's our favourite story."

Rae was the organized sister. She'd colour-coded their schedule at the convention to optimize their experience. She'd helped Alice make her costume. The story was something they did together.

The story wasn't real, but love made it matter.

Alice pressed her face into Rae's shoulder. Rae felt the heat of Alice's cheeks and the tears sliding from under her glasses, leaving wet spots on Rae's hospital gown.

"Remember how you used to tell me stories?" Alice whispered.

Rae used to do a lot of things.

For now, she could hold her sister. It was strange to be skinnier than reed-thin Alice. Rae was withering away to nothing. Alice had grown more real than Rae would ever be again.

She pressed a kiss to her sister's ruffled hair. "I'll tell you a story tomorrow."

"Really?"

"Trust me. This will be the greatest story you ever heard." She gave her sister an encouraging push.

Alice hesitated. "Mom will come by if she manages to close the deal."

Their mother was in real estate. She worked long past visiting hours. They both knew she wasn't coming. Rae did the cheesy pose from their mother's posters and delivered the slogan. "'Live in your fantasy home!'"

Alice was almost gone when Rae called, "Funnyface?"

Her sister turned, trembling with dark beseeching eyes. A fawn lost in the hospital.

Rae said, "I love you."

Alice smiled a heartbreakingly beautiful smile. Rae staggered back to bed, and lay on her face. She hadn't wanted Alice to see how exhausted she was from simply raising her voice. She reached for *Time of Iron* beside her bed. The first grab failed. Rae gritted her teeth and grasped the book, then found her fingers shaking too badly to open it. Rae hid her face in the pillow. She didn't have the energy to cry long before she passed out, still holding the closed book.

When she woke a strange woman sat by her bedside, Rae's book in her hands. The woman wasn't wearing a white coat or a nurse's uniform, but black leggings and an oversized white T-shirt. Box braids were twined into a bun atop her head, and her gaze on Rae was coolly assessing.

Blurred with sleep, Rae mumbled, "Did you get the wrong room?"

The woman answered, "I hope not. Listen carefully, Rachel Parilla. There is much you don't know. Let's talk chemotherapy."

Shock dragged Rae into wakefulness. There was a lever on the side of her bed that propped it up on a slant. Rae pushed the lever so her mattress jerked upward and she could glare from a better angle.

"What is it you think I don't know?"

Rae gestured to her head with one chicken-wing arm. She got sweaty in her sleep and knew the sheen of moisture on her bald scalp gleamed in the fluorescent lights.

The woman leaned back as if the hospital chair was comfortable. She traced *Time of Iron*'s cover with a fingertip, her golden nail polish a glittering contrast to her deep brown skin and the glossy book jacket.

"The tumours in your lymph nodes have grown more aggressive. Your prognosis was always grim, but hope remained. Soon the doctors will tell you hope is gone."

Rae's head spun, leaving her sick and out of breath. She wanted to sink to the floor, but she was already lying down.

The woman continued, relentless: "The insurance isn't enough. Your mother will re-mortgage. She will lose her job. Your family loses their house. They lose everything, and their sacrifice means nothing. You die anyway."

Rae's breath was a storm shaking the wreck of her body. She scrabbled for any emotion that wasn't panic and clutched at anger. She grabbed her water glass and threw it at the woman's head. The glass smashed onto the floor into a thousand tiny sharp diamonds.

"Do you get a sick thrill from torturing cancer patients? Get out!"

The woman remained composed. "Here's the last thing you don't know. Will you save yourself, Rae? Would you go to Eyam?"

Had this lady escaped from the psychiatric ward? Rae hadn't even known there was a psychiatric ward. She stabbed the button to summon the nurses.

"Great suggestion. I'll buy a plane ticket to a country that doesn't exist."

"Who says Eyam isn't real?"

"Me," said Rae. "Bookstores who put *Time of Iron* on shelves marked *fiction*."

She stabbed the button repeatedly. Come save your patient, nurses!

"Consider this. You say 'I love you' to someone you don't know. Is that a lie?"

Rae regarded the woman warily. "Yes."

The woman's eyes were still in a way that suggested depth, much happening below the tranquil surface.

"Later you learn the heart of the person you lied to. You say the same words, and 'I love you' is a great truth. Is truth stone, or is it water? If enough people walk through a world in their imaginations, a path forms. What's reality, except something that really affects us? If enough people believe in something, doesn't it become real?"

"No," said Rae flatly. "Reality doesn't require faith. I'm real, all on my own."

The woman smiled. "Maybe somebody believes in you."

Wow, someone was getting the good drugs.

"It's a story."

"Everything is a story. What is evil? What is love? People decide upon them, each taking a jagged shard of belief and piecing the shards together. Enough blood and tears can buy a life. Enough faith can make something true. People invent truth the same way they do everything else: together."

Once Rae led her cheerleading team. Once her family worked as a team, helping each other, until Rae couldn't help anyone any longer. Once upon a time was a long time ago.

"What gives a story meaning?" the woman pursued. "What gives your life meaning?"

Nothing. That was the insulting truth of death. The worst thing that had ever happened to Rae didn't really matter. Her desperate struggle made no difference. The world was moving on without her. These days Rae was all alone with death.

That was the true reason she loved the Emperor. Finding a favourite character was discovering a soul made of words that spoke to your own. He never held back and he never gave up. He was her rage unleashed. She didn't love the Emperor despite his sins, she loved him for his sins.

At least one of them could fight.

In Greek plays, catharsis was achieved when the audience saw treachery, twisted love, and disaster. They purged through impossible tragedy until their hearts were clean. In a story, you were allowed to be wracked by feelings too terrible for reality to hold. If Rae showed how furious she felt, she would lose the few people she had left. She was powerless, but the Emperor shook the stars from the sky. Rae shook with him, in the confines of her narrow hospital bed. He was company for her there.

Rae refused to be a hopeful fool. "I can't go to Eyam. Nobody can."

A real country would have a map, she wanted to argue, then remembered the map of Eyam that took up the best part of Alice's bedroom wall. Rae had seen the jagged peaks and pencil-thin swoops of the Cliffs Cold as Loneliness, the sprawl of the Valerius family's great estate, and the palace's intricate secret passages, grand throne room and greenhouse.

Rae had never been to Eyam. She'd never been to Peru either. She still believed in Peru.

The woman gestured. "I can give you an open door."

"That door leads to a hospital hallway."

"Does the door lead, or do you? Walk out of this room and find yourself in Eyam, in the body of the person most suited to you. A body the previous occupant is no longer using. In Eyam, the Flower of Life and Death blooms once a year. You get one chance. Discover how to get into the imperial greenhouse and steal the flower when it blooms. Once you have the flower, a new door will open. Until then, your body sleeps waiting for you. If you get the flower, you wake up, cured. If you don't get the flower, you don't wake up."

"Why are you doing this?" Rae demanded.

There was a serious note in the woman's voice. "For love."

"How many people have taken you up on your offer?"

"Too many." The woman sounded a little sad.

"How many woke up cured?"

"Maybe you'll be the first."

The button to summon the nurses was obviously broken. Rae could stick her head out into the passage and yell for help, or stay here getting ranted at.

Rae chose action.

She swung her legs over the side of the bed, setting her feet on the floor. Moving through the world when sick took focus. Every step was a decision Rae made while weighing her odds. It was like being on top of the cheerleading pyramid. A wrong move meant a bad fall.

The woman's voice rang at her back. "When the story takes and twists you, will you beg for mercy?"

Desire flew through Rae sharp and bright as a burning arrow. What if the offer was real? Her lips curved at the wild sweet notion. Imagine a door could open as a book does, right into a story. Imagine a big adventure instead of hospital walls closing in and life narrowing down to nothing. Being not an escape artist but an art escapist, running away to imaginary lands.

Behind a bathroom door while Rae threw up bile and blood,

she'd heard a teacherly voice tell her mother, *Time to let her go.* Rae couldn't let herself go. She was all she had.

Once she believed her future would be an epic. She hadn't known she would only get a prologue.

She no longer had a ponytail, but she tossed her head and fired a wink over her shoulder. "By the time I'm done with it, the story will beg *me* for mercy."

Rae grabbed the loop of the door handle. She pushed the door open with all her remaining strength.

Light broke like sparkling glass in her eyes, followed by rushing darkness. Rae looked over her shoulder in alarm. Colour drained from the world behind her, leaving her hospital room black and white as ink on a page.

Rae took her waking slow. These days she fainted whenever she stood up too fast. She usually regained consciousness eyeballing linoleum.

Now Rae found herself drowning in the broken pieces of a world. Fragments blue as the earth seen from space, with cracks running through the blue as if someone had shattered the world then fitted the pieces back together.

She scrambled up to stare at the ground. Blue mosaics depicted a shimmering pool the richly draped bed beside her seemed to float upon.

As Rae gazed incredulously down into the deep blue, rubies winked scarlet eyes up at her. Blood-red jewels, adorning softly rounded hands. Rae's hands were claws, the hands of an old woman with paper-thin skin stretched over bones. These were the hands of a young woman.

These weren't Rae's hands.

This wasn't Rae's body. She had been accustomed to suffering so long that pain wasn't something that happened to her, but was part of her. Now the pain was gone. She spread her fingers before her face, the easy turn of her wrist a wonder. A heavy bracelet in the shape of a snake slid down her arm, red light striking the metal coils like bloodstained revelation.

Someone might kidnap her, but they couldn't change her body.

She lowered ruby-ringed hands to her sides, and for the first time noticed her clothes. Her skirts poured over the floor, white as snow, the edges dyed deep crimson. As though the immaculate white had been dipped in blood. This was the dress Alice had worn to a convention, the costume she believed made her brave.

Rae bolted from the bedroom into the tiny hall beyond. Walls and floor were white marble, gently shining as if Rae was caught inside a pearl. When she tried the door, it was locked. Through the single stained-glass window she saw a sun sinking into smoky clouds and a moon already reigning over obscured night. The moon was cracked like a mirror that cut reflections in two, broken like the window of a house in which you were not safe.

She knew this sky. She knew this scene. She knew this *costume*.

A laugh forced its way from the pit of Rae's stomach, coming out as a cackle. Her beautiful hands clenched for a fight.

She was in the land of Eyam, in the Palace on the Edge.

She was Lady Rahela, the Beauty Dipped In Blood. She was the heroine's evil stepsister. And she was due to be executed tomorrow.

CHAPTER TWO

The Villainess's Plot Begins

As Lady Rahela swept into the throne room, her new guard held the door for her. Proud as she was beautiful, Rahela sneered.

Her sneer turned sweet for her king. "The evidence proves my stepsister a traitor."

"And how should I punish a traitor?"

"A traitor must be executed by pit or gallows."

"May the court bear witness," declared the king. "Lady Rahela deserves the drowning pit, with iron shoes on her feet to drag her down."

"She deserves a worse end than that." Rahela's guard moved from her shadow, a lean youth with a hungry smile. "Let me suggest a *most* unhappy end. Even commoners praise the lady of snow and flame's dancing."

The king listened.

Soon iron shoes smoked on the fire, metal so hot the slippers glowed like twin suns.

"Favour me with a last dance, my dear," urged the king.

Lady Rahela's face twisted with fear, no longer beautiful. She turned from her king to the Last Hope's icy judgement, to the guard's sinister smile. There was nobody to help her.

Time of Iron, ANONYMOUS

esperate calm descended on Rae. She made a mental to-do list. Number one: escape with her life. Number two: work out the rest later!

She swept the billowing red-and-white skirt over her arm, returning to her bedroom and seizing an ornate golden candlestick. It had a flared base and was elaborately carved with twining gold snakes. Most important, it was heavy.

Clutching her candlestick, Rae crept back into the vaulted marble hall. Her bedroom was windowless, but beside the locked door was the small arched window. The embers of sunset burned behind crimson glass. Opals in the latticework shone like the whites of watching eyes.

Rae hefted the candlestick, taking aim.

The impact was immediate. Rae's breath was knocked from her lungs as she went tumbling onto the marble floor.

A man lay on top of her, solid weight of muscle pinning her down. His arm, heavy with leather and knotted cords, rested against her breast. Fear turned her body into a bridge of silver needles, sharp chills forming an arch. A lock of his black hair fell into Rae's eyes. Cold steel drew a hot line against her throat.

Someone was holding an actual knife to her throat.

Her body jolted up under his. "Holy shit, Jesus, *Batman*, don't kill me!"

The stained light of sunset turning his eyes red, he asked: "Do I have a reason to kill you?" An old leather glove, rough as a cat's tongue, scraped her neck as he shifted his grip on the knife hilt. "I'm a palace guard, not a palace assassin. They pay assassins more." He paused. "At least I hope they do."

Being inside a book was an intensely surreal experience, but so was enduring a hospital visit that involved a huge curly straw inserted into her veins as though Rae was a giant milkshake. Over her last three years, Rae had learned not to fuss and scream that 'this couldn't be happening'. If you woke up in a nightmare, you dealt with it.

"You got me. It's the wicked stepsister, in the barred chamber, with the candlestick. Let me up."

"I can't let you jump out the window."

The guard's sing-song voice turned serious. Rae was briefly touched.

He added: "Have you no consideration for others? I'll be in trouble if you jump on my watch. Go take some nice poison in your bedroom."

Rae's eyes went shock-wide. The guard's eyebrows, going up at the ends like raised swords, lifted in an eyebrow shrug.

"I want to live," Rae whispered.

"That's not really my problem."

"I'm profoundly moved by your concern," said Rae. "What if I bribed you to let me escape out that window?"

The guard simultaneously rolled off her and rolled his eyes. "My lady, at last! I thought you'd never offer to bribe me."

He shoved the window open with an elbow. Rae rushed forward and looked down. And down. Below the window stretched a silvery stone wall, sheer as a cliff. Beyond the cliff wall lay the blackness of the void, broken by a single fat red spark drifting up from the sullen fire burning in the depths of the dread ravine.

Rae had totally forgotten about the fathomless abyss crawling with the undead. Eyam was an island surrounded by sea on all sides, except the side where flames and low moans rose. The dead were their only neighbours.

The Palace on the Edge was an extremely literal name. For religious reasons, the kings of Eyam had carved a palace into the very edge of the cliff overlooking the ravine.

"Will you be departing now, my lady? Or have you changed your mind?"

"You've made your point, no need to underline it with sarcasm!"

The palace guard was idly flipping his knife from hand to hand. Rae eyed him critically.

"I thought guards must approach the ladies-in-waiting as if we were fragile swans sculpted from priceless crystal?"

The maidens in the tower were the ladies-in-waiting-to-be-queen. Since nobody knew which lady-in-waiting the king would choose from among his favourites in the tower, all were treated as potential queens.

The guard shrugged. "Your pardon, lady. I've only been a guard twelve hours."

"That's weird."

The system in Eyam had five levels. On top, shiny as his crown, was the ruler. Below were noble families who owned lands and objects of power. Under aristocrats were the serving class, called 'noble servants' because they got to live in the palace and use the magical artefacts, though they could never own them. Below them, living in the city outside the palace and occasionally allowed within its walls, were merchants: basically peasants who'd dared make money though they couldn't have real power. At the bottom were peasants, who grew food and carried away garbage. Society would collapse without them, so they were treated horribly.

A palace guard was a noble servant. Like aristocrats, their positions passed down through family lines. You couldn't simply get a job at the palace. Rae was having a hard enough time without world-building inconsistency!

"My lady, they explained about me."

The guard sounded incredulous as Alice explaining plot details. How dare he suggest she hadn't done the reading?

"I had a lot on my mind," Rae snapped.

Another voice rang out in the marble hall. "You're new to the palace. Allow me to inform you about nobles. We're the mud beneath their feet, and they only see what shines. Lady Rahela is blind and deaf to anything that doesn't concern her king or her precious self."

On either side of the marble hall was an alcove, the type you found marble busts of politicians or dead kings in. These particular alcoves, screened with beaded curtains, held people. Her guard must have bolted from his alcove when he saw her at the window. Every lady-in-waiting had a bodyguard and a maidservant.

On the far side of the room a woman's hand parted the curtains, white beads catching the dying light with a seashell shimmer. The pearl-pale veil parted to show a cold face and burning eyes. As the woman turned, her left cheek was revealed. There was a mark upon her bone-white cheek, the same colour and irregular shape left by a splash of port wine on the floor. A girl in Rae's middle school had a birthmark. She got it removed over one summer. Rae thought it looked cool and was sorry to see it go, but that wasn't Rae's face or her decision.

There were no lasers to remove a birthmark here. People said Emer wore a mark of divine punishment for sins she had yet to commit.

Emer, Lady Rahela's maid, raised with her from the cradle. Emer, who had always done everything Rahela asked.

"Just checking . . . " said Rae. "We already had that big scene where I told you I was only using you?"

The future Iron Maid's voice was cold as the edge of an axe. "You made yourself very clear earlier, my lady."

"It wouldn't do any good to say I didn't mean it?"

"Say whatever you like. You usually do."

The maid's hands were folded in her lap and her voice emotionless, an empty hole where feeling had once been. You couldn't sound this devoid of caring, unless you'd cared a lot once.

Rae had always enjoyed the Iron Maid's unimpressed commentary on the aristocracy, but she didn't enjoy Emer's current attitude. It was obvious Emer hated her deeply.

In this place, Rae didn't have to feel pain. Emer's hatred didn't matter. Even Emer didn't matter. She wasn't real.

What mattered was digging herself out of the hole Lady Rahela had thrown her, Rae, into. If she was truly in Eyam, in the glass heart of the Palace on the Edge was a plant that would save her. Rae had to live until the Flower of Life and Death bloomed. Which meant Rae had to live past tomorrow.

The palace guard coughed. He was leaning against the windowsill, watching Rae and Emer's face-off. "You two obviously have a great deal of history. Which is awkward for me. I don't know you."

He didn't know the Lady Rahela. So he couldn't hate her yet.

Rae had to bond with him immediately.

"What's your name?"

That seemed the obvious first step in the bonding process.

"I'm Key."

Which was, if Rae recalled correctly, a peasant name. The lower classes named their children after objects, since objects in this country could be powerful. It hadn't occurred to Rae before now that this naming convention was disturbing.

Except Key's mother hadn't named him, had she? The writer must have chosen 'Key' because he was a guard – and guards held the keys to the places they guarded.

"*My lady,*" Emer snapped at Key.

"There's no need to address me as 'my lady'," said Key the peasant guard. "In fact, I'd prefer you didn't."

Emer scoffed.

"So why are you a peasant?" Rae instantly regretted her question. You couldn't go around asking people why they were peasants! "Ah, how did you become a palace guard?"

Emer the grim maid seemed tired of their nonsense. "The king rewarded him for a great deed. The court's calling him the Hero of the Cauldron."

Key the irreverent palace guard didn't seem like the hero of anything.

"Titles are for nobles. The Beauty Dipped In Blood?" Key flicked a mocking glance at Rae. "I could call myself Key the Irresistible, but people would make hurtful jokes."

He *was* tall, dark and handsome, which Rae found suspicious. Normally when fictional characters were good-looking, they turned out to be important. Were side characters allowed to be randomly handsome?

Maybe they were. Key's face suggested no dramatics, only casual good humour, with an easy grin, ironic eyebrows and cheekbones so angled they were almost hexagons. His eyes were grey, not the emerald green or summer-sky blue of a main character, and his nose was too long for symmetry. He looked about twenty, Rae's age and several years younger than Emer. He had black hair, but not a menacing mane of midnight. Chopped-uneven locks sprang straight from his head with the ends flipping down as if he were a cheery goth daffodil. He had a lean and restless look, and a general air of being charismatically untrustworthy. Rae felt she could work with this.

"So you did a great deed?" Rae prompted.

'Hero of the Cauldron' rang a bell so faint she might be hearing the sound wrong. If the guard had a title, he must have a role to play. Since Rae didn't remember any details about him, he probably wouldn't last long. Poor minor character. Rae bet he died.

Key snorted. "A bunch of ghouls crawled out of the ravine. I stabbed them."

Ghouls were the walking dead who would one day become the Emperor's unconquerable army. Rae didn't have to pretend to be impressed. "And you asked the king to make you a palace guard as a reward?"

Many characters in *Time of Iron* cared about duty. Maybe Key would feel honour-bound to serve her.

"I asked the king to give me one thousand gold leaves."

Coins came in four shapes and four different metals in Eyam. Rae couldn't remember what the other shapes and metals were, but a thousand sounded like a pile of cash.

Faintly hopeful, Rae inquired, "Were you happy to be made a guard?"

"No," said Key. "I would be happy to get *one thousand gold leaves*."

So the dude was in it for the money. Mercenary minor villain, check.

Emer's voice grew a shade less harsh, as though she pitied Key. "You distinguished yourself, so the king must honour you. However, the aristocracy don't want a peasant defiling the palace halls."

Rae began to understand. "The king and the nobles made you a palace guard, then assigned you to a lady who'd be executed in the morning."

Key was still smiling, close-mouthed. "Such an honour."

"Wow," murmured Rae. "Eat the rich."

The Hero of the Cauldron bared his teeth. "Think they'd taste good?"

His light tone held the faintest trace of bitterness, candy laced with poison. Despite his smiles, Key obviously wasn't amused by his current situation. It was becoming clear Rae was locked in a room with two extremely angry people.

A stress migraine threatened.

How did Lia get out of her near-death situations? Right! The damsel begged for help in a whisper that smote men to the heart.

"You tried to stop me from throwing myself out the window." Rae's voice emerged more purr than whisper, but she reached an appealing hand to Key anyway. "Say you won't let me die."

Key took her hand. Rae was shocked to feel as though his hand was a burning match and her spine a candle. She guessed the rumours about Rahela's wanton ways were true, but Rae had different priorities. Lady Rahela's body could cool it.

"My lady, if you're trying to seduce me . . ." Key leaned forward, gazing into her eyes. "I'll still let you die in the morning."

Rae snatched her hand back. "I'm not trying to seduce you!"

Key lowered his own musical tones into exaggerated sultriness. "Then why did you put on that voice?"

Rae winced. "Damn it."

She should have known trying to act the heroine's part was ridiculous. Rahela and her stepsister were built different. Evil minx Rahela wasn't able to get Lia's results. Rae herself wasn't the type anyone loved at first sight. Or any other sight.

In Rae's life before, she'd had a perfectly nice boyfriend. She made out with him on her bed when her parents were away, and debated with her best friend how to signal she was ready to go further.

Then Rae got sick. Her best friend took her spot on the cheerleading squad and her boyfriend. They had more in common with each other than her. Nobody had much in common with Rae any longer. She drifted away from her friends on a sea of pain and strangeness.

In hospital, Rae would chat with older women in chemo. One woman's husband always brought her breakfast in bed and took her wig to the hairdresser's. 'Some people are special,' another woman told Rae. 'Some people are made to be loved.' That woman's husband had left her the day she went into hospital.

Only special people were saved. The rest had to fight their own way through.

At least now Rae had a chance to fight.

"Why do you think you're going to be executed in the morning?"

Emer's voice flew through the air, sharp as a hurled weapon. "You said Lady Lia would be the one executed. What's changed?"

Great question.

Thankfully, Rae remembered the lead-up to Rahela's big death scene. Their guileless heroine told Emer she was visiting peasant huts to care for sick children.

An ancestral knife was discovered in one of the peasants' humble huts. The hut was promptly burned down with the peasants inside it. Any item of power was a cherished possession of either the king or the nobles, guarded and marked with the family seal. The knife was an heirloom of the Felice family.

Only Lia Felice and Rahela, Lia's stepsister, had access to the family heirlooms. Both were confined in their chambers, awaiting the king's judgement. Emer had already reported Lia's visit to the humble hut. Lia could have smuggled the knife out in her medicine basket. Lia was the obvious suspect.

Except when Lia laboured in the palace kitchens, she whispered her tragic secrets to the ashes she swept on the hearth. The hearth was directly connected to the chimney in the palace library, where the Last Hope sat wrapped in scholarly pursuits. The Last Hope, the king's childhood friend and the most incorruptible man in the country. He told the king Rahela had stolen Lia's family heirlooms and must have planted the knife. The Last Hope's evidence led directly to Rahela's death.

Rahela shouldn't know any of this. How could Rae possibly explain what she knew?

"I know I'm going to be executed because of him!" Rae gestured wildly to Key.

He pointed to his heart, or possibly his jerkin, and mouthed 'Me?' His fingerless gloves were made of ancient black leather that didn't go with the blue and steel of the palace guard uniform. This was Rae's first time seeing a jerkin in real life. It was basically a leather waistcoat.

Rae concentrated on Emer, willing her to believe. "Key was assigned to me because when a noble is executed, their servants are presumed guilty and killed along with them. The king wants Lia, not me. If he was planning to kill Lia, he'd have assigned Key to her. They want to get rid of me, they want to get rid of Key, and they want to get rid of you because you're loyal to me. One stone, three birds. We must help each other."

Thinking of it that way cheered Rae. By definition, there was only one fairest of them all, but it was different for villains. This world was against them. So they should conspire together.

"Sorry to contradict, my lady." Emer didn't sound sorry. When she lifted her chin it became clear Emer was tall, dark and handsome as well. She looked as if she would scorn beauty. "While traditionally servants are executed with their master, the rules are waived if another noble asks for them. Nobody has an eye for hair and dress like me. I have the skills to make a lady the king's favourite. I can get out of this on my own. Everything you possess will be confiscated if you're executed, so you can't bribe me. You're a liar, so I won't believe any promises. Why would I help you?"

A long-ago teacher had told Rae stories were created by villains. Their desires and evil deeds ignited the plot, while the hero only wanted to stop them. At least to begin with, villains were in charge.

Once Rae had a list of fifty colleges, and no idea what to major in. She ruthlessly organized every extracurricular activity, ending up head cheerleader and student council president. Rae had variously imagined she might be a lawyer with killer instincts and killer suits, an editor who put stories into perfect shape, or run a real estate empire alongside her mom. She'd never known what she wanted to be, except in charge.

She must seize control now, and execute her scheme quickly. The timing had to be perfect.

Rae, the head bitch cheerleader, offered an evil smile. "I'll make the oath of blood and gold."

Emer's birthmark blazed against her suddenly ashen skin. "That's forbidden."

"So what?" asked Rae. "I'm wicked."

Key blinked, expression suddenly intrigued.

Encouraged, Rae continued, "I'm a heartless monster with a strong character and stronger eyeliner game, and I intend to get away with my crimes. What about it? Why should you care about my personal failings?"

Key seemed impressed by her insight. "It's true, I *don't* care."

Emer's gaze stayed stony. Rae swept across the marble floor, skirt a darting red snake behind her, and launched into a villainous monologue.

"I'm a treacherous, power-hungry bitch, and honestly? It feels amazing. Don't listen to stories encouraging you to be good, telling you to shine in a filthy world and patiently endure suffering. Screw suffering. It's too hard to be good. Do the easy thing. Do the evil thing. Grasp whatever you desire in your greedy bloodstained hands."

By now they were both paying close attention. She'd never given a motivational speech for the dark side before, but surely these villains would see things her way.

"The other choice is to accept fate, and I won't. I scheme for power because I refuse to be powerless. I would break this whole world to get what I want. Most people die without mattering at all. If they curse your name, at least they remember it. Don't you dream of the forbidden? Choose wrong. Choose evil. Let's do it together."

Rae brought her jewelled hands together in a lavish thunderclap.

"Villains," she announced. "Let's unionize."

If she hadn't convinced her minions, she'd convinced herself. Determination crystallized as she spoke, her goal more real with each word. Heroes might be reluctant to accept a call to adventure. Villains had to intercept the call and steal the treasure.

On a mission, Rae dashed into her bedchamber. The Beauty Dipped In Blood had a mahogany dressing table crowded with ceramic perfume bottles, drawers inlaid with mother-of-pearl.

Rae wished for that moment where a character gazed into a mirror, so the audience learned what they looked like. Unfortunately, mirrors in Eyam were made of bronze. The nuance of Rahela's features were lost in a bronze lake, but she made out one surprising detail. There was a beauty mark directly over the left corner of Rae's mouth. Rae had always liked it. Everybody prepared cancer patients for losing the hair on their head, never for the rest of their hair. Having no eyebrows changed your whole face and having no eyelashes made you resemble a lizard. The beauty mark let Rae know, no matter how strange her reflection, that this was still her.

Lady Rahela had the same mark.

It was disorienting to have hair again, a weight pulling Rae's head back and lying warm against her neck. Rae had never had hair this long, or curves this curved. The reflection she beheld was the image of a temptress. Rae had experienced many things, but she'd never had a healthy adult woman's body before.

Adulthood must be different for normal people. Surely everybody didn't spend their whole lives feeling like both a howling child and a weary ancient.

Rae shook her head, heavy with unaccustomed weight, and pulled open the top drawer. She didn't need to find herself. She needed a knife.

In the recesses of the drawer lay a knife, and a snake uncoiling to strike. Rae screamed.

Her maid and bodyguard came running. When Emer saw what had startled Rae, she stilled. "Why are you shocked seeing your own pet?"

Rae searched for Key's reflection in the mirror. He leaned against the arched entryway of her chamber, arms folded. Without his ready smile, his face seemed different. Vacant in a disturbing way, a crucial factor missing.

Emer's gaze was steely as a trap. Rae remembered how cruel Emer's mistress had been to her, and the axe murders Emer would commit in the future. Across the room was a cabinet containing enchanted gauntlets Rahela had stolen from her stepsister. Wearing those, she would have the power of a dozen warriors.

If Rae could get to the cabinet fast enough, theoretically she could kill them both.

Lady Rahela was destined to die slowly and horribly. Rahela's death was the first step in the prophecy coming true. Rae had escaped her own destiny. Surely she could escape someone else's. But how?

Nobody would help her. They were all villains here.

Emer's unforgiving voice asked, "My lady. What are you hiding?"

CHAPTER THREE

The Lady Does Dark Magic

"The blood oath is the most solemn thing between sky and abyss," said the Last Hope. "It is the sword that cannot be broken, the word that cannot be unspoken. It is placing your shivering soul into someone's palm, and trusting they will not clench their fist. The oath says for all my days, your life is dearer than my life, and if I can be true to you past death, I will. Anybody who makes this oath lightly is lost."

Time of Iron, ANONYMOUS

mer's mistress had lost her wits.

The evidence was in every word and gesture. Her lady was the most graceful creature in the court, but she was taking ginger steps the way little girls did the first day they donned long gowns. She was using outlandish turns of phrase and twisting her face into unwary expressions, though a lady must not betray her feelings or risk premature wrinkles.

Not to mention Rahela's wildly promiscuous behaviour.

If you asked a courtier, that wasn't new. Emer knew better. She'd heard the lessons given by Rahela's lady mother. You didn't get far throwing your virtue over the windmill for every handsome face. Rahela might let a lowered voice or swaying hips make a promise, but she never fulfilled it. Unless behind closed royal doors.

A peasant had manhandled Rahela and now entered her bed-chamber. Emer's lady should have screamed, fainted and on waking ordered the man whipped in the Room of Dread and Anticipation. Emer felt like screaming herself.

Ladies had the privilege of fainting. Maids did not.

Apparently ladies also let their minds break spectacularly under strain, leading them to give melodramatic speeches and offer to per-form forbidden rituals.

Rahela seemed genuinely startled by her own pet snake, but today Emer had learned she was no judge of her lady's sincerity. Was this an act? What purpose would it serve to fool servants? Emer had no power save that of her own will, but she concentrated the force of her will on Rahela now. At least, at last, Rahela could tell her the truth.

Rahela held her breath until Emer feared she was trying to induce a swoon.

Lady Rahela let her breath out in a rush. "I'm calm! Others may lose the plot but I have a firm grip on it. The truth is, I have the amnesia."

"You have the what," said Emer.

She'd been told her voice was flat, but she didn't think it had ever been so flat and dry before. Considering Rahela's claim, Emer's soul seemed to shrivel away into a desert.

"Yes, Emer! The amnesia," Rahela repeated with gathering confi-dence. "Surely you've heard about it. People are struck upon the head or have a shock, and they forget their whole lives or only remember certain interesting details?"

"I have heard of it," Emer admitted.

She didn't believe a word.

Rahela beamed. Emer hadn't seen her make such unguarded expressions since they were children.

Emer's head hurt. Extremely badly, but servants weren't permit-ted migraines. Emer was used to gritting her teeth and working through pain.

"Which is it?" demanded Key of the Cauldron. "Have you forgot-ten your whole life or only certain details?"

He was a mannerless peasant, but he wasn't a fool.

Rahela drew herself up haughtily, every inch Emer's lady once again. "How should I know what I forgot?"

Over the years, Emer had become aware that in emergencies she was far quicker on the uptake than either Lady Rahela or her mother. Nobles weren't used to their lives going wrong. When their luck turned bad, they floundered in outraged confusion.

Watching Rahela respond nimbly to disaster was disquieting. Perhaps Rahela had been forced out of complacency by sheer desperation. Perhaps.

Rahela leaned forward with a conspiratorial air. "That's why I need you two. Correct me if I make any mistakes. If you see I don't know something, tell me."

Emer shot the peasant a venomous glance. Rahela had never needed anybody but Emer before.

"He doesn't know anything, my lady. He's from the gutter!"

As if their situation wasn't dire enough, they were afflicted with a ruffian from the slums as Rahela's new guard. The last guard was an old man, appointed to Rahela because – before he grew tired of her – the king was jealous of Rahela's favours. This peasant was younger than Emer, and from the Cauldron, so the gutters might be a step up for him. Naturally, as a decent woman, Emer had never been to the Cauldron herself. She visited the Day Market outside the palace walls to buy luxuries for her lady and necessities for herself, going no farther. Gossip belowstairs said the Cauldron was the vilest cesspit in the city.

The gutter guard shot Emer a look sharp and dirty as a cut-throat's blade. Men didn't enjoy being insulted. Emer knew this, as she insulted them often.

Vile as the cesspit he'd crawled out of, Key blew Emer a kiss and returned to watching Emer's lady closely, though not in the usual way. His avid face was hungry not for flesh, but ruin.

"I don't care where he's from," announced proud Lady Rahela. "The point is, I'm totally evil, and I want you to be my evil minions."

"I'm not evil!" snapped Emer. Rahela seemed unconvinced.

A whisper in Emer's mind, soft as Lady Lia murmuring secrets at night, asked Emer if she were sure. She refused to listen. It wasn't Emer's fault. A servant had no choice but to obey her mistress's commands.

Oh, but she'd known betraying Lia was wrong. All along she'd known. Rahela was right.

Key raised his hand. "I'm evil? I think."

Rahela applauded. "That's awesome!"

The gutter scum seemed pleased. "I kill people all the time."

Emer's mind howled like the ghouls in the abyss.

"You kill people? Serially?" Rahela blinked. As though banishing reason with the blink, she smiled. "Great. We may need a series of people killed."

"*My lady!*"

Rahela made a soothing motion, as if Emer were a child and Rahela rocking her invisible cradle. "Think of this as a story. There are many fun murderers in fiction! We're all just trying to survive. He kills people, you do your wicked mistress's bidding, I flounce around in revealing dresses framing innocent people for crimes. Time to take evil to the next level."

Emer's lady turned her attention back to the drawer, where her snake was wrapped tight around the knife of the Domitian family. The small viper was a mirror of Lady Rahela's bracelet, dark amber-green when her bracelet was orichal gold, the diamond-shaped markings along its coils such a dark brown they seemed almost black. Atop its flat head, ridged at the sides, the diamond pattern formed a black heart.

Rahela dropped a kiss on the viper's head. "I'm calling you Victoria Broccoli."

Seemingly Emer's lady had confused a viper with a lapdog.

Slowly, the viper unwound from around the knife. Rahela slid the knife free of its gold-and-pearl sheath. The gleam of the iron was tinged with crimson, as though Emer were staring at it through a red mist.

This was the birthright reserved for nobles. Rahela was offering it to them.

The words fell from Emer's lips soft and shaken as winter leaves. "You mean it."

"You're *out of your mind*," breathed Key of the Cauldron. His smile turned impish. "That's fun."

In days of old, nobles used to swear loyalty to their kings or their lords with the blood oath. Aristocratic lovers pledged to each other. Even nobles had ceased swearing the oath centuries ago. Nobody dared make a promise that could not be broken.

Nobody until now.

"What do you say?" Rahela's eyes danced. "Pledge to be true to me for a year and a day. If you keep faith, you receive the weight of my body in gold."

"Each?" Key sounded ravenous.

"Each," confirmed Rahela. "And I'm not padding this dress. Everything they say about Lady Rahela's enormous ... tracts of land is true."

Shock reached Emer only distantly, as though someone scandalized was shouting from a long way away. Close as cloth against Emer's skin was naked greed.

Emer had served her lady faithfully all her days. Much good it had done her.

If she served Rahela for one year more, she would have enough gold to start the new life she dreamed of in her narrow bed, shut up in a cupboard as though a maid was a piece of crockery.

A cottage. A companion who was her equal. Never having to bow her head and say 'my lady' again. Perhaps she could keep goats, though she'd never seen a goat up close. When Emer's head ached, she could lie down in soothing darkness, and her companion would murmur sweetly, 'Rest.'

Emer couldn't be loyal to Rahela any longer. She should be loyal to herself.

If she turned away, she would never have a chance at real magic again.

Rahela plunged the knife towards the snowy skin above her ruched bodice.

"My lady, *no!*" exclaimed Emer, with new and stronger horror.

Evil was one thing. This was a matter of professional pride.

"Right." Rahela's mouth twisted with ready comprehension. "The king won't want me if I'm scarred. I'll leave the girls alone."

Her lady's dark eyes slid to the mirror and widened, seeming as surprised by her own image as she had by the snake. They widened further when her gaze slid down into her own bodice. She shook her head in wonder. "I can get used to this. I've been a stranger to myself before. After the whole world and your own body changes, you know you're not safe. The world can always turn on you."

Her own body? Emer remembered Rahela being upset when she had a bosom years before all the other girls. Rahela tried to cover her bosom up. When nothing worked, she started showing it off.

The memory provoked something like tenderness, and something like misery. Emer shrugged both off. Rahela rose from her stool and almost tipped over sideways. Key moved too fast for Emer's eye to follow, reaching to steady her. Rahela patted his hand. With her bare hand.

Emer's lady smiled. "Sorry, I'm top-heavy as a double scoop ice-cream cone over here. Where was I?"

Key waved lazily to the knife, as though her life-changing offer affected him not at all. He showed only relaxed curiosity to behold what Rahela might do next.

Emer's heartbeat clanged in her ears like the servants' bell ringing at dawn.

She would never do it. Emer's lady was a soft-handed, pampered creature who had never suffered a moment's physical discomfort.

Standing in the arched doorway, Rahela rolled up one trailing sleeve, exposing a rounded arm. She drew the point of her blade along her arm. Skin parted under sharp steel. Key's eyes brightened as the blood welled.

Her lady's smoky voice was famed in the capital. When Rahela said 'good morning' men heard her promise a *very* good night. Now her husky voice promised magic.

"First cut for gods lost in the sky, second for fiends in the abyss."

She made two slashes on the inside of her arm, near the elbow. Blood beaded on the thin lines, tiny rubies glittering on pink string. She cut another, longer line, this one perpendicular to the first two. Forming the hilt of the sword.

"Third cut for me, Rahela Domitia."

"Fourth cut for you, Key . . . " Rahela waited expectantly.

"Just Key," said Key.

"Nothing else?"

Key's gaze was fixed dreamily on the blood. "I don't have a family name. It's not a family if there's only one of you."

"Okay, just Key. Like Madonna or Rihanna."

Key frowned. "Who?"

"Doesn't matter, not important!" said Rahela. "First cut for you, Key, and for you."

She looked expectantly at Emer, and Emer gazed back without speaking.

Even if Lady Rahela was executed tomorrow, Rahela's mother would redeem her oath. The Domitian family weren't rich, but they were famous for turning out beautiful schemers. Ladies of the Domitian clan could get what they needed. If the mark of an unfulfilled oath was left on a body, the body would be thrown into the abyss. Any family would pay to save their name from desecration. This was an opportunity Emer couldn't refuse.

Desire overcame caution. Emer's teeth clenched, trying to keep the words in her mouth. "Emer ni Domitia."

It was pathetic that Emer's name meant 'belonging of the Domitians.' Even more pathetic to be Key, and belong to nobody.

"Emer ni Domitia," Rahela repeated softly. Emer's lips curled at the sound coming from her lady's lips. She'd never bothered to feign sympathy before. She needn't pretend now.

Rahela cut another stripe down her arm, longer than the rest, so the hilt now had a blade. The mark of a sword, made by magic and drawn in blood.

"Sorry," said Rahela. "Could someone remind me how this oath goes?"

Emer and Key stared. She shrugged.

"This is a stressful time and I'm a delicate lady. The exact wording slipped my mind."

Key's gaze lingered on the blood staining the white marble. His sudden smile was sunset on a jewel. It made Emer fear the coming dark.

He produced a strange-looking knife with distressing rapidity, cutting his own arm as carelessly as a man cutting bread. The knife disappeared like a magic trick.

"'By the sword,'" Key sang out mockingly, "'I swear to be loyal and true, to love all you love, and hate all you hate. You will feel no rain, as I will be a shelter for you. You will feel no hunger or thirst while I have food to give or wine in my cup. When my name is in your mouth, I will always answer, and your name will be my call to arms. I will ever be a shield for your back, and the story told between us will be true. Everything agreed between us, I will carry out, for yours is the will I have chosen.'"

Rahela reflected the wicked gleam of Key's smile. Emer's heart sank below the red horizon as Emer's lady sang the vow back to this outsider. Sealing their pact to be sinful and sacrilegious together, they grinned at each other like children playing a game. Wicked, irreverent children, committing sins and sacrilege without a care.

The ravine's flame illuminated the stained glass, pale red as a drop of blood dripped into a glass of water. The wound on Rahela's arm seemed to catch alight, becoming a fiery sword. The window turned the colour of rich red wine.

Clasping Key's hand, Rahela's face blazed like the windows. The conspirators stood outlined by eldritch radiance.

Rahela declared, "This is our first team meeting. My bedroom is our evil lair, and we're a nest of vipers. From now on, we're evil together."

Have you been availing yourself of the special herbs, my lady?

"Just as you say, my lady," Emer mumbled.

"Beats being evil all by myself," Key murmured.

They stood in a circle, reflected in the bronze mirror. Emer's lady, the poisonous viper, the woman of snow and flame. Her gutter guard with his insincere smiles and cracked leather gloves. Her maid with her stiffly starched apron, turning her face away. Emer didn't like to see the mark. Growing up in the countryside, everyone said Emer was stained with wickedness. It seemed everyone told true.

Rahela laughed. "Let's go, minions! Take me to the king."

"We can't take you to the king," Emer said flatly. "Don't call us minions."

Key made a dissenting sound. It appeared he wished to be an evil minion. He might be desperate to belong, but Emer knew better. Betray desperation, and you invite cruelty.

Rahela had the gall to fix Emer with an accusing stare. "Did you or did you not swear loyalty to me?"

She hadn't. But she wouldn't draw attention to that.

"I didn't say I won't take you, I said I can't!" protested Emer. "He can't either."

Key's smile was a knife pointed directly at Emer. "I'm a gutter brat. I don't know how to behave."

"A servant can't demand an audience with the king!"

The gutter guard's gaze returned to Rahela, calculating. Emer realized with mounting outrage that he was *measuring* her. And not the worth of her character.

He came to a conclusion. "For her weight in gold, I'd steal the lost god's lost eyes."

"You speak wicked blasphemy," hissed Emer.

"Fluently," said Key. "Follow me, my lady."

He reached for his broad leather belt, tooled with crown shapes in cornflower blue. On one side of the belt hung the scabbard for his sword, and on the other a ring of keys. Lady Rahela spun in a gleeful circle as Key unbarred and unlocked the door. It swung open to reveal stone steps winding into the dark. Key set off down the spiral staircase. Emer's lady cast a single look behind her.

"Coming?"

Emer turned promptly back to her alcove. "You will both be executed. When you are executed, your family will give me your weight in gold. Meanwhile, your heads shall be on spikes atop the palace walls."

"That's it," Rahela encouraged. "Think positive."

Emer's treacherous heart clenched like a fist. "My lady. You can't do this."

"Watch me. This is my villain origin story."

Emer's lady winked, twirled, and went dancing into the shadows to her death.

CHAPTER FOUR

The Villainess Commits Blasphemy

When she of snow and flame dances through dreams
When the white knight's heart strays to lost queens
He is coming. He is coming.
When the abyss opens, when the dead bow down
The curse is come upon us, he will claim his crown
The ravine calls its master up above
He goes to tell lost souls he died for love
He is coming. He is coming.
The words run wild, escape if you can
The pearl will be his or belong to no man
His sword is ruin, his eyes are fire
All the worlds are his empire.
The child of gods is dead and grown
He is coming, he is coming for his throne.

Everyone in Eyam knew the Oracle's prophecy.

Time of Iron, ANONYMOUS

ae and Key got lost on their way to cheat death. The tower of the ladies-in-waiting was set apart from the palace proper in a small circle of trees. They followed a winding garden path to a great door, then inside to the labyrinthine passages of the palace. The passageway floors were smooth grey riverstone and deep green malachite, giving the effect of a network of rivers. Rae felt carried away by strange currents. She almost walked into the great glass case housing the crown jewels.

"Sweet," Rae said under her breath. "The cursed necklace." The hungry mouths of two wrought-gold serpents formed a clasp. In glittering chains, elaborate loops and lines shaping a golden cage for a future fragile throat, hung a great black jewel. Ominous red gleamed along its facets like lethal fire waking in dead embers. Legend said this jewel was the lost god's eye. People called the necklace the Abandon All Hope Diamond.

"Looks valuable," commented her new minion. "But difficult to pawn."

"A king of Eyam sent a hundred men down into the ravine to find this jewel for his bride. Only one returned. The queen wore it for a year before she died young. A king gives this diamond to his queen to display that she is beloved above crown and kingdom, worth a hundred lives and a thousand sins."

"So *definitely* hard to pawn," said Key. Rae laughed. "Did you think the king would give it to you?"

"I know better. I'm not the one who gets adored." Rae held up the injured arm bearing the snake bracelet. "This bracelet means I'm the king's favourite. It doesn't make me queen material."

Stories sneered at shallow women who cared for vain adornment, but women used to hoard gems when they couldn't have bank accounts. Jewels were for survivors. Rae's mother had given Alice her great-grandmother's pearls, not Rae. Alice looked better in them. Alice might have children to pass them down to. Half the value of jewels lay in their meaning. Real treasure held a story, and stories were for heroes.

Key's was a face of contradictions, his eyes hollow as the sockets of a skull, his full mouth either insouciant or serious as the grave. The snake bracelet wasn't worth the solemn attention he gave it.

"At least you did something to get that."

Rae arched a brow. "*What* are you implying?"

A sword-straight eyebrow flicked up, Key returning the gesture. "You schemed. Better than getting adored while other people do all the work."

One day the Emperor would fasten this around Lia's neck, saying if the jewel did not please her she could hurl it back into the abyss. The Emperor had a darkness in his heart and all, but he didn't care about money.

Only minor villains had petty flaws like being greedy. Rae gave her minion an approving glance.

"I think we'll be friends."

He tilted his head, with the air of a scientist beholding a new specimen. "I never had one of those before. Might be interesting."

"High five," proposed Rae.

Key's smirk tilted smile-ward. "No idea what you're saying."

Rae's hand was already lifted. "Hit my hand."

"How hard?" Key asked obligingly. "Should I break it?"

Rae started back. "Do *not*! Tap my palm with your palm. Gently! Gently!"

Key frowned as though gentleness required ferocious concentration. She watched with suspicion as he touched his palm against hers as instructed, a brief brush of cracked leather against her skin. Unexpectedly, the touch sent a pang through Rae.

In a year and a day, Rae wouldn't be here to fulfil her vow and give Key and Emer the gold she promised. Nor was she saving them from execution. Lia would beg mercy for Rahela's maid and guard.

Memory hit Rae harder than Key had. Emer wasn't grateful, but Key was. The lady's golden beauty and even more golden heart left a deep impression on the humble palace guard. Like many guys in *Time of Iron*, Key ended up with a hopeless crush on Lia.

Everything made sense now, including Key's looks and why Rae didn't remember him. Lia was constantly wringing her hands going, *why must handsome men persecute me with their love?* Except for the Emperor and the Last Hope, her suitors blended into a chiselled haze. They always sacrificed themselves so Lia could live, especially wicked ones who reformed for her sake. Perishing for love of Lia was one of the major causes of death in Eyam, up there with being eaten by monsters, torn apart by ghouls, and plague.

Terrible news. Key was doomed. Rae must use her minion while she still had him.

The memory served as a useful reminder these were fictional characters. Rae didn't have to care about their feelings, and as a villain she wasn't supposed to. What mattered was her own life.

Key gestured her forward. "So, my scheming lady. Which way to the throne room?"

"I don't know. I have the amnesia, remember?"

The way Key rolled his eyes hinted he wasn't buying her genius cover story. "Well, I got here yesterday."

Hunting through the palace they passed several pairs of guards, posted at intervals. The guards were mainly middle-aged men, hair close-cropped, military figures going thick beneath blue-and-steel palace uniforms shinier than Key's. Every guard gave them the side-eye. Lady Rahela, with her snowy, red-dipped drapery, was a memorable figure. The fact she should be imprisoned was probably memorable, too.

Most gave Rae a wide berth, their air suggesting, A *criminal on the loose, but accompanied by a guard? Above my paygrade. I do not see it.*

Inevitably, one guard decided to make it his problem. He sidled up to Key, and Key seized the opportunity to ask for directions to the throne room. As the guard gave directions, his eyeballs rolled like panicking marbles, glance after uneasy glance slid at Rae.

"Is that Lady Rahela?"

"No," said Rae. "I'm her evil twin."

This dress was great for sweeping off disdainfully.

"You're her evil twin?" Key repeated.

Rae had never realized before how much pop culture featured in day-to-day conversations. *In soap operas, when a twin shows up they're usually evil. In horror movies, if someone keeps their double in the attic, it's because their double is evil!*

"There are many evil twins in stories," she mumbled.

Key seemed contemplative. "The songs say Lady Rahela is heartless. If both twins are evil, I blame the parents."

Rae dimly recalled Lady Rahela had a pretty typical backstory for a wicked stepsister. "Both my father and stepfather died mysteriously young. On a totally unrelated topic, my mother is gorgeous and poisonous. I take after her."

"Does your mother also make bad jokes?"

Rae shoved Key, grinning, as they walked into a room white as a blank page. She recognized it immediately. This was the Room of Memory and Bone. The floor and the gleaming-pale panels on the walls, the twisted chandelier and the little white side table, were all made of bone china. Each man must die, and sometimes their bones were ground up to make china furnishings. Rae annoyed her sister by calling it the Bone Room.

Seeing the room, very much not in the flesh, wasn't amusing. Set in the wall under glass, like an insect on display, was a child's skeleton wearing blue and black regalia. The floor was worn smooth as an old woman's single remaining tooth. This was not the king's throne room, but next door to it. Nonetheless a pale stone throne was set against a wall, its gilded bone wings carved for a beloved queen who died young. Dead rulers were placed there, so subjects could bid them goodbye. The farewells took a long time. The bodies decayed. The arms and seat of the chair were stained faintly where the fluids of rotting royals had seeped into the stone.

Rae suppressed a shudder. "Wrong turn." They left behind the bone-white death chamber, heading for the throne room doors.

The doors were ten gleaming feet tall, beaten gold that shone with red light flanked by ridged columns beginning and ending with flourishes shaped like acanthus flowers. Two guards stood before the entrance of the throne room. Each held a long spear, dark cherrywood with iron leaf shapes at the tip. Rae saw the spears up close since the guards crossed them before the doors, barring her way.

"The king's period of receiving petitioners has concluded. You may not enter."

The guard spoke by rote, staring into the distance. The other guard nudged his spear slightly against his. Both guards' eyes widened on recognizing Lady Rahela. She saw them struggle with the conundrum of whether to let her pass or arrest her.

She didn't want them coming down on the wrong side of that decision. Rae shot Key a glance, hopeful he would be helpful.

Key said brightly, "I challenge you to a duel."

This was not problem-solving. This was creating an entirely new problem!

The guard's face darkened in response to Key's smile. "I won't duel with peasant scum."

The bright smile didn't dim. "I'm not peasant scum any more. I'm a guard. Our status is equal, so if you refuse a duel, you're a coward. First blood, and the vanquished must withdraw. What do you say? Are you a coward?"

The guard lowered his spear a fraction.

Key punched him in the nose with enough force to send the guard spinning in a half-circle, clutching a pillar so he wouldn't fall. Blood sprayed onto the smooth gold of the doors.

The guard on the other side of the doors dropped his spear and hurried over. "Lost gods, are you all right?"

"Let me make a quick point." Key brought back his elbow efficiently, driving the man's lip against his teeth so blood guttered from both nose and mouth.

The guard howled.

Key beamed. "First blood! Twice. In you go, my lady."

A pool of blood spread at Rae's feet. Horror movies had led her to expect the colour pop of fake blood, startling and almost cheerful. This was the same dull shine of the blood they took from her in vials at the hospital, red diluted with black. Real blood was always darker than expected.

Tone surprisingly analytical, Key said, "I thought the king would overlook a scuffle, but not a murder at the throne room doors. I can kill them if you like?"

Rae edged back from the blood. "No."

The blaze of Key's grin went out. He regarded her with disappointment, but no surprise. "Did I not please you, my lady?"

Her team member needed positive reinforcement!

"You're doing great. I have issues with other people's blood. Not my own, I'm used to that."

The weariness shadowing Key's expression faded, and he nodded with resolve. The next moment, he stood before Rae, close enough that his unruly lock of hair brushed her forehead as he bent and slid an arm around her waist.

"What are you doing?" Rae murmured.

"Let me help." The last shadow on his face was cut away by the knife of his smile. "Wasn't that our deal?"

He swung Lady Rahela's not-inconsiderable weight easily into his arms, stepped lightly over the blood puddle, and strode through the golden double doors.

Rae was currently stacked like the library of Alexandria! Nobody had this kind of upper body strength. Fiction was absurd.

Despite the absurdity, Rae appreciated the gesture.

"Thank you," she murmured in his ear.

Key's step checked, as if startled. Then he set Rae down. "Thank me by ensorcelling the king. I hope you have a plan."

Her arm still around his neck, Rae asked: "What do they say about me in the Cauldron?"

Conspiratorially, Key whispered, "That you're an evil witch."

Even in a world with magic, people acted as if being sexy was dark enchantment. That would come in handy.

Rae purred, "Wouldn't it be fun to be a witch and curse people?"

"Yeah," Key agreed, with not a moment's pause.

It was like seeing a twisted face by a single flash of lightning, an illuminated instant of instinct that said: *You're awful. Just like me.*

Rae smiled. "Consider this. A witch who curses you is just telling the future you don't want to hear."

Courtiers turned towards them like flowers towards a wicked sun. Rae took a deep breath.

"Nervous?" Key asked.

"Well. Yes. But I can't wait to see the king."

Key seemed vaguely surprised. "Isn't he about to execute you?"

"I love him despite the death sentence. He's the handsomest man in the world, he's funny, he has an enormous menagerie—"

Key smirked.

"—He has an enormous collection of cool monsters," Rae explained. "He makes epic speeches, he wins unwinnable battles, he's loyal past death, and he's lonely."

"Aren't we all," Key murmured.

The throne room was treasure laid out before her. Court officials lined up against the walls, but in her excitement Rae perceived them as simply gold-braided blue-uniformed wallpaper. The riches of Eyam had only been words to her, but now they were more than words.

A divine tragedy had occurred in this land. The very earth here was strange, and strange jewels and metals could be mined from it. Metal from Eyam could be wrought into enchanted weapons. Though few visitors travelled here, merchants came offering fabulous prices for what was known as orichal steel and orichal silver. The pillars of the throne room, as outside, were ruddy orichal gold. The walls and domed ceiling were lined in green crystal, facets tinged crimson, shimmering as though they were all trapped in a broken mirror. The floor was hammered red-gold mosaics, showing the lost goddess disappearing into the sun.

The master of all these riches waited to meet her. Even the air between her and the throne shimmered. Rae prepared to be dazzled.

She quoted the Emperor in the future. "Love is the song that wakes us from the grave. Death cannot stop *my* heart."

Key sounded impressed but doubtful. "Love survives execution?"

She recalled an internet manifesto on why villains were better lovers. "Love burns down the world for a kiss."

"Did you say, burns down the world for kicks?"

"Hush, minion," Rae murmured. She only had eyes for the Emperor now.

The king's throne stood on vast golden talons holding rubies big as dinosaur eggs. A minister stood on either side. One must be the prime minister and the other the commander of the king's armies, though Rae couldn't tell which was which. The throne was backed by a representation of raven wings, jet and red-gold feathers fanning out. The bird's rapacious beak was enamelled with human bone. Diamonds and rubies trailed after the wings to signify sparks cascading against a lapis-lazuli sky.

Against the gold and glitter, the black of the king's clothes made him stand out like a void opening up in the sun.

Rae hit Key's arm in high excitement. "It's him! I love him!"

"So you keep saying." Key started to laugh. "Don't strike me, I stab when startled."

Here he was. The most powerful and merciless man in the world. The future Emperor. Rae's favourite character. The master of the Palace on the Edge and all within it, including the Flower of Life and Death. The Emperor had the power to heal, but the flower could save someone on the very doorstep of death. Every year when the flower bloomed the Emperor's dead army would search for someone past saving in the city slums, and the Emperor would ride out and save them. Perhaps he could be convinced to save her.

An anti-hero was just a villain with good PR. The Emperor might sympathize with Rae. She'd always sympathized with him.

Rae savoured the big reveal, from tall leather boots like polished midnight, to close black garments and the heavy black cape with a deep blue lining. His bronze breastplate shone. His gauntlets were finished off by black and iron vambraces, the criss-cross of laces ending in elaborately looped bows. The wrought iron patterns over the leather, birds with wings outstretched and snakes baring fangs, were exactly as Rae had imagined. On the king's broad, crown-embellished belt hung a set of keys and a sword. The blade's hilt was a coiled silver snake. This was Longing for Revenge, the sword that would be broken.

Her eyes continued their epic journey to the king's face.

On ceremonial occasions, kings of Eyam wore the crowned mask, a blank death mask to stand in for he who would come. There was a hollow in the centre of the crown where a dark jewel should be set: the twin of the Abandon All Hope Diamond. It was the end of the royal hearing. As Rae watched, thrilling with anticipation, the king drew off his mask to reveal eyes of emerald green, a pouty mouth and great hair, silky-dark and falling softly in place. He was the most beautiful man Rae had ever seen.

As expected. Yet seeing the king felt like calling a familiar name on the street, disoriented when they turned and showed themselves a stranger. He sat the throne in regal fashion, but the Emperor sprawled with insouciant grace, one leg hooked carelessly over the throne's arm.

Other characters had descriptive titles. The Emperor, as supreme overlord, needed no further introduction. Only now did she remember the Last Hope, when they were boys together, called his future ruler Octavian. His full name was Octavianus, Eighth King in Waiting for the Emperor.

This wasn't Rae's favourite character. Not yet.

This was before Octavian returned from the edge of death for his throne. Before he changed into somebody unrecognizable and unfathomable. One day, nobody would call him by name. His subjects would forget he ever had a name. One day, the Emperor would be terrifying as an eclipse.

Right now, King Octavian demanded: "Where are the guards?"

The books said the Emperor's voice was deep and dark as the ravine itself, rasping like a vast snake upon the earth. The king's voice was deep in a way that suggested he'd give great proclamation, but the rough gravel of the disturbed grave would come later.

Key glanced over his shoulder. "The guards aren't feeling well, Your Majesty."

Octavian's eyes narrowed. "The Hero of the Cauldron? Hero or not, I do not appreciate this intrusion."

Lady Rahela advanced. "Forgive me, Your Majesty. I insisted."

A snicker came from the sidelines. "Was the Harlot of the Tower *very* persuasive?"

Rae couldn't tell where the voice came from, but the whole crowd surged with laughter. Ministerial uniforms of blue and gold made the court seem a censorious sea about to drown her.

Until a voice cold enough to freeze the ocean commanded, "Silence."

Rae's heart slammed against her ribs like a boat hitting an iceberg. She felt a crunch, as if this boat was going down.

At the far end of the throne room was the ebony stand where witnesses gave evidence. On high stood Lord Marius Valerius, the Last Hope. Unconquerable in battle, peerless among men, the icy paragon of justice who would never tell a lie or break a vow. The white knight responsible for Rahela's execution.

Rae had timed her arrival carefully for several reasons. One was that she didn't want to be anywhere near the Last Hope, the scholar with a face beautiful as a god and a heart cold as a blade. The only man the Emperor ever feared.

She'd thought Lord Marius would have given his evidence and

gone by now. Instead he towered before her, and even the king hushed at his word.

The line of Octavian's mouth and the chill emanating from the Last Hope suggested to Rae that Lord Marius and the king had been arguing. No need to ask about what. Lord Marius had come to bury her. He had a personal reason to want Rahela dead.

"Only the gods can judge," the Last Hope informed the crowd. "In Lady Rahela's case, I am certain they shall."

His white cloak snapped behind him as he departed the stand, filling Rae's vision like the blind blank sky after a winter storm. Strong men cowered. Women, for various reasons, trembled. The ducal line of Valerius was famous for their beauty, their skill in battle, and their ancestral curse.

This was true main character page presence. Unlike the Emperor, Lord Marius didn't need and wouldn't get character development. He was what he was made to be, unyielding to the end.

Lord Marius wasn't a disappointment. He was an awful revelation. The man was tall as a tree, with shoulders broader than most doors. His mane of black curls, shot through with ice white, was worn long enough to brush those shoulders. No real human had white hair that only started halfway down. His hairdresser appeared to be Jack Frost. His every feature was stern perfection and his sheer size was terrifying. This dignified scholar was built for brutality.

Rae cringed against Key, who casually caught her arm to steady her. He regarded Lord Marius with interest. Rae had a vision of her wicked bodyguard trying to break the Last Hope's nose and being instantly slain. She gave her head a warning shake.

Lord Marius spared them a single glance, then turned away. "I will take my leave, Your Majesty."

Rae was taken aback. "Don't you want to hear what I have to say?"

Lord Marius was magnetic, which meant he was cold as well as compelling. "Utter what lies you choose. Nothing can save you."

Breathless with fear, desperate to be believed, Rae asked, "What if I don't lie?"

"Then I hope you enjoy that new experience, madam." The Last Hope's voice was frosty enough to sting.

Rae's instinctive response was a cutting smile. "I always enjoy myself. My family motto is *He came, he saw, I conquered.* I'm the woman who can bring any man to his knees."

She regretted it instantly. She knew, better than any soul in the story, what he was capable of.

Scorn curled Lord Marius's perfect mouth. "And I am the man who can bring an army to its knees. I suggest throwing yourself on the king's mercy. For I have none."

When Lord Marius left the throne room, silence reigned until even the echo of his steps had faded away.

With the twist of sarcasm the Emperor would be known for, King Octavian asked, "Is the flinging yourself upon my mercy to commence now?"

Key volunteered, "Lady Rahela demanded to see you and tried to hurl herself out a window. Since I'm new to my duties, I wasn't sure if I should let ladies throw themselves out of windows?"

"You should, as a member of my guard, effectively subdue criminals," snapped the king.

His emerald eyes skimmed over Rae with as much warmth as though they were truly jewels. Rae's frail hope she could win over the king died. Clearly, Octavian's heart had already turned against her.

A terrible weight of knowledge pressed down on Rae. She knew what happened tomorrow, if she failed to stop this now.

The scene had seemed harsh justice when Alice read it aloud. Lady Rahela crawled in her torn silk gown like a butterfly with her wings ripped to shreds, begging for her life. The court laughed. The king denied her, decreeing the wicked woman must suffer a worse death than drowning in iron shoes. And, Rae recalled with a shock like walking down steps she relied on at night only to find air instead of stair, a new guard suggested how the lady should be punished. Thanks to Key's suggestion, Lady Rahela was whipped in the Room of Dread and Anticipation as iron shoes were heated on the fire until they were the colour of burning rubies. The whips had hungry steel teeth. Rahela was already a carved-up ruin when they placed the ruby slippers on her feet and made her dance, howling as her flesh crackled and smoked.

It was a horrible way to die.

Fixed by the emerald pins of the king's gaze, Rae could finally admit her sister had a point that Lady Rahela's punishment was messed up. At least Key was a stranger. He wasn't the one twisting private intimacy into public brutality. Lady Rahela was the king's ex.

Of course, Rahela was the king's *criminal* ex. Kings must give commands that turned warm once-loved bodies into cold food for crows. The Emperor was born to be relentless and remorseless.

Denying the evidence laid against her wouldn't work. Begging for mercy wouldn't work. Time for her new scheme.

"Lady Rahela?" King Octavian prompted. "What couldn't wait until morning?"

Rae made an announcement. "I'm guilty."

The king froze, an ice sculpture upon his jewelled throne. Beside her, Key made the swiftly controlled expression of a man re-evaluating his life choices.

Rae continued, "But you knew that. Right, Your Majesty? The Last Hope gave his testimony. All that's left to do is sentence me and watch me grovel in terror. If that's your idea of a fun time."

Despite seeming shaken by the prisoner's unusual attitude, the king kept his cool. "Are you suggesting the court should not punish traitors?"

Rae smiled. "You're asking the wrong question. Ask me how I know. I spent the last twelve hours in a locked chamber."

There was a pause.

"Tell me quickly," the king commanded.

Rae's mother said a saleswoman was a storyteller. Once people took the first step into belief, they would be swept along with your story. The trick was giving them something they wanted to believe in.

"When I laid me down upon my bed, the guilt of my evil deeds came upon me and I repented my sins," Rae declaimed, giving deliberate weight to each word. Octavian drummed his fingertips against the golden arms of the throne, so Rae hastened to conclude, "*Then,* I entered a trance, and the gods came to me in a vision!"

She spread her arms, shut her eyes, and willed herself to emit an aura of holy light.

When Rae opened her eyes, Key and the king were staring as though she'd grown several heads.

Oh well. Worth a shot.

"To atone for my sins, the gods made me a vessel for prophecy," Rae continued firmly.

Her announcement continued to go over like a lead balloon attached to an elephant.

Rae cleared her throat. "For your information, guys, once I saw through a glass darkly, but now I see plain. I've been both blessed and cursed with true sight that perceives the secrets hidden deep in men's hearts, and the future."

There was another pause.

"Lady Rahela, do you think we will spare your life because you feign madness?"

The king's hand lifted to summon his guards. Rae didn't want him making any such gesture.

"Wait! Let me tell your future."

Octavian gave the signal. "Enough lies. Guards! Execute her now."

Before the guards reached her, Rae shouted, "You are the godchild. You are the future Emperor. You will rule the world!"

The king hesitated, then gestured again. The guards halted. He was listening.

"Great news, the prophecy is about you," Rae continued. "You know the one. *His sword is ruin, his eyes are fire, dun dun!* Surely you recall the ominous prophecy."

"We all know the prophecy, Lady Rahela," snapped one of the ministers flanking the king's throne. "This is absurd!"

Rae ignored that.

"All your life, people whispered about the mysterious circumstances of your birth," she declared. "The truth is, you're not the king's son."

The throne room fell utterly silent.

Rae had stopped listening to her sister read at the point when Lia met her obviously fated lover, the guy with the crown, but she vaguely remembered Alice discussing the Emperor's humble origins. 'Being a king' obviously didn't qualify. She'd needed to dredge the precise origins from the back of her mind. Once she did, she recalled the king was sensitive about this subject.

Noble ladies must stay pure until marriage, so a king shouldn't sleep with any of his ladies-in-waiting-to-be-queen. Octavian was raised in the countryside, birth not proclaimed, not crowned prince until he was four years old. Gossip said he'd been born to the queen too early, proving the previous king was indiscreet with his ladies-in-waiting.

Alice told Rae that speculation raged among readers on whether the current king was sleeping with his ladies-in-waiting. Except Lia, of course. Lia would never.

There was no speculation on whether Octavian was sleeping with Rahela. He totally was.

Rae talked fast, before she was executed for foul insinuations about the king.

"Mystery surrounds your birth because you were born from the abyss. The Palace was built on the edge of the dread ravine, waiting for the time the godchild would be reborn. Two decades ago, the ravine yawned wide, smoke rose, flames roared, and the sky changed. That was a sign from the gods. That was—"

"The year I was made crown prince," Octavian said slowly.

Using the king's instant of hesitation, Rae seized her chance and her scarlet-trimmed skirts, dashing up the steps of the throne. The guards at its base moved to intercept her. Key slid between them smooth as a shark in the water.

Extreme violence exploding at her back, Rahela knelt before the king.

"I see the past, as well as the future," Rae whispered in Octavian's ear. "I know the truth of the day your father died, and the blood on the stone of the tomb. Do you believe me now?"

She hoped he believed her, and had no follow-up questions. She was quoting the Oracle from the third book, and didn't know what the father or the tomb stuff was about. It obviously made sense to Octavian.

"You say I will be Emperor." His lips curled like the edge of a page about to catch fire. "Is that why you looked at me as you did, when you entered the throne room? You never looked at me like that before."

The delighted expectation Rae had felt, waiting to see her favourite, illuminated her again. Her mouth curved in a returning smile, and the king's fingers curled warm around hers. "For the first time, I recognized my Emperor."

A roar cut through their moment of hushed possibility. Octavian snatched his hand away.

"Your Majesty," thundered the minister on the other side of the king's throne. "By the lost god's teeth, I hate to say it, but I agree with the prime minister! This *is* absurd." -

A ripple went through the court. Everyone knew the king's two chief counsellors never agreed on anything. The general was quick to anger and the prime minister slow to forgive. The general was a family man, the prime minister a confirmed bachelor. The general waged war, the prime minister urged peace. Possibly one always told the truth and one always told a lie.

The roarer with long grizzled hair and the aspect of an angry badger must be Commander General Nemeth. Which meant the man sporting a fancy gold hat and fastidiously neat goatee was Prime Minister Pio. At any other time, Rae would be pleased they had identified themselves.

At this moment, pleasure was not the emotion she was experiencing.

"For centuries those seeking to flatter kings have proclaimed their monarch the coming of the Emperor." Prime Minister Pio had the voice of a man who preferred paperwork to speeches. "Each was exposed as a false prophet. Every time, the people of Eyam were reminded: *He is coming* . . . but not yet."

Right. Everyone expected a king of Eyam to become the Emperor. Rae had to prove that this was the king, and this the time. Or else.

"The punishment for false prophets is the same as for traitors," bellowed General Nemeth. "Death. Who believes the wicked?"

The prime minister's eyes flicked to Lady Rahela's most notable assets. "Who would ever believe the Harlot of the Tower?"

People acted as if a first sexual experience must be saved, then spent at the precise right time. Virginity as stocks and shares, precious then abruptly worthless. In the real world, Rae was embarrassed to be an adult virgin. In this world, Rahela was expected to be one, and it was all ridiculous. Nobody could even tell the difference.

She wished she'd got the chance to be a harlot. She hadn't slept with her old boyfriend, but she'd intended to. Getting sick didn't make Rae virtuous, it disrupted her plans. Now the prime minister was calling her a harlot. Oh no, whatever you do, don't accuse me of being cool and sexy!

Rae smirked. "My prophecy-giving mouth is up here. What, the chosen of the gods can't have fantastic tits?"

When she turned back to Octavian, a knowing look had crept into the king's eyes. Specifically, the look said, *I know you, Rahela, and I know what you're after.*

In the future, the Emperor was a famous cynic. It seemed the king was cynical already. "I will be emperor, and you by my side always, I suppose?"

"Forgot to mention," Rae said calmly. "The gods say my stepsister Lia is your one true love."

This pause felt personal.

"Tomorrow when you condemned me to a horrible death, you would've announced after too many years wasted with an ice-hearted viper, finally you beheld radiant truth. Wouldn't you? Don't lie to your prophet."

Octavian sounded lost at sea, and floundering. "Something like that?"

Rae nodded wisely. "You would die for Lia, you would kill, you would commit complicated murder-suicide. Those who fate has joined together, let no criminal put asunder. Happy ending! Now the gods have enlightened me, I regret my jealousy. And the treason. And the frame job." Rae patted the king's arm. "Sorry about all of that. I support your love."

"Thank you . . . ?" Octavian didn't speak as though he said those words often, and he didn't sound as though he meant them. He seemed to be grasping for logic in the universe. After a moment, he took a deep breath. Kingly dignity fell over him like a mantle. "I cannot picture someone of your rapacious nature dedicating yourself to divine purity. You *are* an ice-hearted, murderously selfish viper. Hardly material for a holy prophet."

There was a pause.

"Ah," said Key. "One of those epic speeches people love so much."

Rae nudged Key hard. The Emperor was vicious towards those who wronged him. Rae loved that about him. In her experience when people hurt you, you got hurt. They got away with it. Revenge was a fantasy as beautiful as true love.

Still, even her favourite character wasn't allowed to talk to her like this.

"Your Majesty. You declare a woman an ice-hearted viper, every word on her forked tongue a lie. But you believe she meant 'Baby, I want you'?"

"*What?*"

The king's eyes went poison green with insult. Rae had no desire to be out of the 'execution for treason' frying pan, into the 'execution for insulting His Majesty's game' fire. This was the future Emperor. He could doom or save her.

Rae had always judged the ladies-in-waiting desperately scrambling for the Emperor's favour. Now she realized there was a lot of pressure to win his favour. This was a reality TV show, with a dozen girls who wanted to be chosen by a single bachelor. Except this bachelor possessed the power of life and death over his subjects.

What had Rahela done that was so wrong?

Other than framing her stepsister for treason.

She was unexpectedly saved by the prime minister. "The Harlot wouldn't dare speak so if Lord Marius was here."

The king was the Last Hope's friend. When Lord Marius became his rival in love and Octavian rose as the Emperor, that would change.

She saw the tension that would become hatred when Octavian snapped, "*Lord Marius* is not the king."

Rae snatched the opening. "And he won't be the Emperor. You will. When danger comes to our land, you climb down into the ravine for the sake of your beloved. Any mortal would have died, but you are divine. The abyss unlocks your potential, and you assume control over the living and the dead. Seriously, you will be powerful A.F."

The king's brow wrinkled. "A.F.?"

"As *foretold*," Rae intoned hastily. "I watched you climb down the sheer cliff into the abyss. I saw you rise, death at your back, your crowned shadow stretching across the mountains to claim first this land and then all lands. You will pluck the sun from the sky without burning your hands, so only the cold moon remains to witness your power. Your sword will be broken, reforged and renamed, and driven through the heart of the world. You will be invincible, irresistible and unforgivable. The future is sure. The future is glorious." Rae risked a wink. "Sounds good, right?"

She left out the part where Octavian would have to fight the legendary immortal guardian of the abyss. He would refuse the dark jewel the First Duke of Valerius offered, despite the evil power it promised, for love of Lia. Afterward, he and Lia would reunite when he stormed the throne room carrying the First Duke's head, in a scene Rae found deeply romantic and Alice found deeply disturbing. The climax of the first book was too complicated to explain right now. Best save it for a surprise.

Octavian leaned back against the jet-and-jewel wings of his throne. There was no belief in his eyes, but a new gleam of appreciation woke in the chilly green. Apparently guys enjoyed hearing about their destined glory.

"That sounds very fine, Lady Rahela, but you have no proof of these incredibly wild claims."

"Ah, it's proof you want?"

"Yes?" said the king.

"That would be proof I can see the future?" Rae pursued. "To be clear, once you receive irrefutable evidence that I can predict events yet to come, you will pardon me and make me your official prophet?"

Long ago, a lord had killed an Oracle and died immediately after. If you killed a prophet, the gods would strike you down.

If Rae was declared a true prophet, she was safe.

The king smiled, sending a ripple of amusement through the court. His smile fed on the response to become a sneer. "In that case, my lady, I will promise anything."

"Great!" said Rae.

There was another silence, this one expectant. Everybody had settled into being smugly entertained by her raving.

Everybody, with a single exception. As the seconds ticked by Key murmured, "Why are you doing this to me?"

The throne room made voices echo. Key's whisper wasn't as discreet as it could have been.

"I'm amazed you risked your new promotion to aid her," remarked Octavian. "What *did* she offer you?"

"*I'm* amazed nobody understands I'm in this for the money!" Key snapped back.

If Key kept this up, he'd get whipped in the Room of Dread and Anticipation alongside Rae.

"I'm waiting on the right moment for the dramatic reveal," Rae informed Key quietly, and raised her voice. "My king. On the count of three, a messenger will burst through the throne room doors. He will announce for the first time in a hundred years, royal guests have come to us from a land across the sea. They hail from . . ."

Shit, she'd forgotten the name of the other country. In fantasy novels, names were often a bunch of random syllables strung together, easier to write than say, and tough to remember. Rae eyeballed the court wildly for inspiration. The court stared in a collectively hurtful way.

"A land of ice," Rae decided. "They come from a land of ice to make Eyam their allies. A princess will join the ranks of your ladies-in-waiting-to-be-queen. She is known as Vasilisa the Wise."

"After this display, a wise woman would be wondrous to behold," Octavian murmured.

A ripple of laughter followed his witticism.

Rae waited for the laughter to subside. "Remember, there's absolutely no way I could've known this. One."

An anticipatory hush failed to materialize. Every time silence began, it was broken by a snicker.

"There's a merchant who always said I was born to be hanged," muttered Key. "I suppose he too received holy visions of the future."

"Have faith," Rae muttered back, and called, "Two!"

Key shook his head. "I never have faith in anything."

A disturbance sounded in the halls of the palace. The crowd stirred. When no new event followed, the excited stir became murmurs of speculation. Rae was pretty sure the ministers were laying bets on what the king would do to Rae, once she was proved a blasphemer as well as a traitor.

It couldn't be worse than red-hot iron shoes.

Could it?

Rae shouted, loud enough to drown out her own fear, "Three!"

Silence filled the room, ringing like a bell and roaring like the sea.

The king didn't restrain his mocking smile. Rae supposed kings weren't in the habit of restraint.

She'd been sure the timing was right. This was why she'd made the deal with Key and Emer, to reach the throne room fast. The messenger was due to arrive when the king and ministers were still assembled, after the Last Hope gave evidence for Lia.

People said, *don't shoot the messenger.* If the messenger didn't want to be shot, he should be prompt!

"Guards," began Octavian.

The doors of the throne room burst open.

"Announcing a messenger from the northern shore," intoned a guard.

The messenger entered, clothes and hair windblown.

"My king, I bear tidings. Visitors hail from a land across the sea!"

If the messenger expected that his words would cause a sensation, his expectations were fulfilled. If he'd anticipated everyone would hang on his next words, he was disappointed.

The court turned as if the king and his ministers had but a single head, with a single neck for it to swivel upon. King Octavian's court focused on the Beauty Dipped In Blood, who had confessed to treason and predicted the future. They stared open-mouthed, with disbelief so profound it was becoming faith. Except Key the guard. His expression lit with incandescent wickedness, sharpening into something vicious and gorgeous and for the first time truly engaged. Flicking still-wet blood off his leather gloves, he gave a single admiring nod.

Lady Rahela punched the air in triumph.

"Boom," declared Rae. "Holy prophecy."

CHAPTER FIVE

The Lady and the Tiger

"I never had a friend before," whispered Lady Lia. "Did you have many friends?"

Only one. Emer had been cast off as a child, picked up on a whim, and placed in Rahela's crib. They had been together ever since. Betraying Rahela would be betraying herself.

"No," murmured Emer, the wicked servant of a wicked mistress. The vile lie felt true and clean in her mouth. "I never had anyone, until you."

Time of Iron, ANONYMOUS

er wicked mistress and the guard from the gutters were both alive. Emer wasn't relieved. She wasn't disappointed. She was too stunned to be either.

When Emer fetched the hot water for her lady's late-night bath, she heard a guard with a broken nose saying Lady Rahela had passed herself off as a prophet. He claimed Key had carried Lady Rahela into the throne room before His Majesty's very eyes. That couldn't be true, but the mere fact it was believed belowstairs showed how unbelievable the spectacle had been.

When Emer returned with her last vase of lemon water she found Rahela singing a bizarre song as she splashed in her bath. She seemed delighted to have plunged the court into chaos.

Once emerged from the bath, Rahela's shoulders relaxed as Emer drew a silver-heavy brush through her wet hair, though in this position Emer could have cut her throat easily as buttering bread. Oblivious, Emer's lady leaned her chin in her hand. The viper crept across the dressing table and wrapped itself around her forearm.

Key leaned in the doorway, watching Emer's lady wet from the bath and in her wrap. In a minuscule mercy, while he certainly noted Rahela's outrageous state of undress, his gaze wasn't licentious. He didn't seem to know that in permitting this, Lady Rahela was hurling her virtue to the wind.

Of course, her lady claimed to have amnesia. Perhaps she didn't know either. Perhaps, faced with death, the mind of Emer's lady had irreparably broken. Perhaps she'd been cruel to Emer because she was crazed.

Tell me you didn't mean it. Tell me you wouldn't have thrown me away.

If Rahela was telling the truth about her amnesia, she didn't even remember what she'd said.

No, Emer wouldn't be tricked again.

A cynical, low-bred voice broke in on her thoughts. Key addressed her mistress. "How did you know the messenger was coming?"

A servant should not question their master, but Emer wanted the answer too.

"I can't reveal my sources," Rahela answered, with a mysterious and faraway air.

Emer lost patience. "What sources? Why are you referencing rivers? Did a message come for you by boat?"

"Uh. No."

"You are talking gibberish, my lady!"

Rahela appeared to have a spasm. "Does it matter? What you care about is the money. We'll all be villainous, vile and mercenary, and get away with it, too. Deal?"

Key shrugged. "I already swore your oath."

Emer pressed her lips together and fell silent, braiding Rahela's hair. She hadn't sworn any oath. Rahela, that arrogant fool, hadn't even noticed.

"What trouble will we get into tomorrow, my lady?" asked Key.

Her lady was lying to the whole court as she'd lied to Emer. Unlike Emer, the king had the power to punish her. All Emer must do was keep quiet, and let her lady construct an elaborate plot that would become her pyre.

Rahela stretched, indolent and self-satisfied as a cat. "I'm glad you asked, my minion. Have you heard of the Golden Cobra?"

"Sure," Key said casually. "He's famous."

Emer dropped the hairbrush and all her lady's ribbons on the floor. "He's infamous! He owns the most expensive den of sin in the city. He pays spies. He hires *actresses*. Decent women shouldn't even speak to him. A moment in his company is ruin. He's a filthy, debauched and irredeemable villain."

"I know!" Rahela beamed. "We've got to have him on our team."

The wicked Marquis of Popenjoy, the spymaster and libertine also known as the Golden Cobra. The richest and most sinful man in the kingdom.

Her lady's madness was more serious than Emer had supposed.

"Don't look at me like that," Rahela chided Emer. "I may be in a temporary break-up with reality, but I'm rocking this fantasy. Once we assemble our band of well-dressed villains, our evil adventure can truly begin."

Emer heard a soft patter off to one side, on the roof of the spiral staircase wrapping around the tower. It must be raining hard. A storm was coming.

Key's head tilted. "Sweet nightmares, my lady. I hope you never see reason." He headed, not to his station in the hall but out the door.

Emer's eyes wanted to narrow. She kept them wide and calm as she urged her lady to lie abed, easing the silk wrapper off her shoulders.

"Serve your country by getting your beauty sleep, as your lady mother always said," Emer soothed, from habit not gentleness. "Tomorrow will be more peaceful than today."

Rahela turned her face against her pillow, yawning into the red tracery of flowers and thorns. "I'm here to fight," she mumbled, tumbling to sleep in a tangle of silk.

Once Emer heard her lady's breathing even out, she checked on the gutter guard. Key stood at the top of the stairwell, lounging against the curve of the rough stone wall and filing his nails with his knife. It wasn't one of the regulation weapons issued to palace guards. This wicked weapon's blade was made up of twenty small horizontal blades with barbs on the end, a knife with teeth. Key's gaze rested on the window atop the cupola, a delicate tracery of wrought iron on glass with a four-petalled iron flower in the centre. The circular window splashed a cupful of moonlight down on his face, turning it white and black and grey, a picture done in charcoal and ashes. He was always grinning, but that didn't fool Emer. Skulls were always grinning. Nobody thought skulls looked kind.

"I'm not interested." Emer should get that out of the way.

Guards and maids frequently paired off to produce a new generation of servants, and men expected Emer to be grateful for their attention. Every man who accosted her believed they were the only one who would overlook the mark on her face. Emer wished they were right. If there was only one man in the world willing to have her, she could kill him.

Key laughed. "Understood. You'd rather die than surrender your virtue."

"I'd rather *you* die. Try anything, I'll cut your throat. I heard what you did in the Cauldron, villain. I'm sure you could overpower me, but you have to sleep some time."

The gutter brat threw back his head and laughed. "Let's be friends."

"Because I talked about cutting throats?"

"Makes me think we have common interests," said Key. "Besides our lady."

The edges of Key's sparkling smiles wavered, a shallow gleam on waters dark and deep.

A lady's maid must see if even a fold of a garment or a strand of hair fell out of place. Emer's eye was trained to notice when things went wrong, and Key of the Cauldron had gone wrong long ago.

"Let me ask you a question, friend," said Emer. "That knife's too fine for any Cauldron guttersnipe. Where did you get it?"

Key mimicked Emer's low voice, modulated to please aristocratic ears. "I acquired it from a charming blacksmith."

"Shall I tell my lady you're a thief?"

"Do. I wish her to know I have many talents." Key glanced at the closed door to Rahela's chambers. His smile grew a fraction less chilling. "She isn't like people say."

The court must seem another world to him. He definitely didn't fit in. Emer suspected he hadn't fit in the Cauldron either. The capital held many different types, but she hadn't seen anything like the cut of his features before. He looked as if he was from everywhere and nowhere at all. No doubt his mother was a woman of the night, and his father a filthy sailor.

"She isn't behaving normally. Must be the shock of being thrown over by the king."

"Oh, him." Key paused. "She seems fond of him. Did he … hurt her?"

Something in the way Key spoke signified more serious harm than heartbreak. "Why do you ask?"

No emotion showed in those bitter-ash eyes. "Isn't that how love works? You open your heart for the knife." Key shrugged. "If you ask me, she's too good for him."

"He's the supreme monarch of our land, and she's a treacherous witch whose sins scream to the sky for the gods to strike her down."

Key nodded approval. "I do like her. Is the amnesia an act?"

"Everything nobles do is an act. The longer you survive at the palace, the more clearly you'll see that. *If* you survive in the palace. I doubt you will."

The window above broke silently, glass falling like rain. Key shoved Emer into the doorway with the hand not holding his knife. When the first assassin leaped like a descending shadow, Key gutted him before his feet touched stone. Innards spilled out, a thick red tangle on the floor. Key tossed a bloodied knife in the air, and a wink at Emer.

"Maybe I'll surprise you."

He knew, Emer realized. He heard what she mistook for rain on the roof, and he knew.

Two more men dropped on either side of Key, blades bared. Key crouched and spun, his knife kissing one blade and his sword forcing up the other. He disarmed one assassin, then threw himself to the ground, striking like a snake. Emer heard a stifled gasp of anguish. Key hamstrung a man casually as he rose to meet the other assassin's blade. The clash of swords at close quarters was intense, abrupt, and over soon. Key fought dirty, sword training combined with street tactics.

No, not street tactics. These were gutter tricks.

Key stepped over the corpse to stab the remaining assassin, still whimpering and crawling on the floor, in the back. Three dead men, in as many seconds.

When the fourth assassin dropped, Key grabbed him casually by the throat and held him against the wall. "Who hired you?"

The man turned his face away and whimpered into the stone. Whoever it was, they scared the assassin more than death.

Key sighed. "Tell them not to send less than ten men at me ever again. This is boring."

He let the man drop and stagger down the stairwell. Then Key gave a thoughtful hum, leaned over the man's shoulder in a parody of affection, and cut his throat.

"On second thoughts, a murder is worth a thousand words. This sends the message."

The easy way he slaughtered made Emer think of the legends of warriors long ago, whose hands were magical as if they wore gauntlets beneath their skin. Human beings made for murder. But the berserkers of old had died out. This scum was a talented killer, nothing more.

Emer held her dress up. Real blood didn't stay a pretty scarlet like the dye on her lady's skirts. Real blood dried ugly, and stained.

"Cutting a throat is the surest kill, but it gets messy. Ring the bell for the chambermaids," Key drawled. "My lady doesn't like blood."

Emer didn't move. "You knew assassins were coming."

Key shrugged. "I saw the ministers in the throne room. They want her dead."

That made sense. "If the king believes his advisor can prophesy the future, it changes the balance of power."

Even if Rahela was truly the voice of the gods, nobody would care. The gods were already lost. Power was not.

"This place isn't called the Palace on the Edge just because it's built on the edge of a ravine crawling with the undead," Key mused. "Though no doubt that's also a factor."

Key seemed pacified as though bloodshed was his lullaby. The dark around them was edged with silver, night itself held captive in gleaming chains.

Emer's sense of crawling dread intensified. "Who knows how well you fight?"

"Hundreds of people." Key almost sang his answer. "They're dead."

"Who living?"

"Only me."

His meaning was clear. *Not you.* What Emer had seen was nothing. He was capable of far worse.

"You took a sacred oath to serve my lady."

Blood dampened Key's wild hair, red droplets dripping from choppy locks to slide down his face like tears. "Nothing is sacred to me."

"Then you won't protect her for a year?"

He paused as if sincerely considering the idea, then shook his head. "Seems unlikely."

"How long will you keep your oath?"

His smile revealed teeth stained crimson. Not the cat who got the cream, but the tiger who got the child. "Until the lady stops paying, or starts boring me. Fun and gold. What else is there to live for?"

Cynical amusement shielded against the terror threatening to overwhelm Emer. Key was just another traitor. The world was full of them. She was one herself.

"I thought you liked my lady."

Key's laugh was a gleeful peal in the bloodstained dark. "As much as someone like me can like anyone."

His laugh was the final horror that chased Emer from the stairwell. She ran from him into the clean white marble hall, pressing back against the door as if she could keep the young monster out.

Her mistress was doomed. The stay of execution wouldn't last. Half the palace was trying to kill her. The king was tired of Rahela's beauty and sick of her schemes. The king's new favourite had reason to hate Rahela worse than poison.

Thinking of Lia was like touching a hot stove. Emer's mind wrenched itself away without her own permission.

Emer had been wise not to take the blood oath. She must be ready to save herself when disaster came.

Lady Rahela had struck a deal with villains, and failed to consider villains did not keep their bargains. Emer had tricked her. Rahela's untrustworthy guard might gut her for laughs. And there was no hope for fools who tangled with the vicious, notorious Golden Cobra.

CHAPTER SIX

The Cobra's Spy

"See the building that dominates our capital, brilliant as the sun come to rest upon the earth? That is the Golden Brothel. He built it higher than our temples to the lost gods. He wrote the truth of his character in gold on our skyline. Stay away from the Cobra. Do not trust a sweet word or a warm glance. He is the most degenerate and wicked man in Eyam. I should know," Lord Marius told Lia. "He is my closest friend."

Time of Iron, ANONYMOUS

ong past midnight, the Cobra was still at his piano. He scrawled reams over sheafs of paper, occasionally tugging an ink-black braid in absent-minded despair. He'd shed his hair ornaments, leaving golden stars and snakes scattered carelessly across the fragments of his new play. The Cobra said everybody had their own creative process. His was writing frantically, chasing art down rather than creating it.

Eventually the Cobra made a dramatic gesture and swept half the pages off the piano. He reached past the papers for a vial, cut-glass and purple, tipping oil into his palm.

"I can't remember the right words," he declared in laughing mourning, more to the gilded surface of his instrument than Marius.

Since the piano was unlikely to contribute to the conversation, Marius rolled his eyes. "Is a story worth fretting over?"

The Cobra glanced up as though startled Marius was there, then smiled as though he were welcome. "Have you never considered art grants us the impossible? Art opens a door into someone else's imagination and lets us walk through. Art is the dreamed-of escape. Art lets the dead speak and the living laugh. Art takes you away from pain when no medicine can save you. Art is the first and last word. Art is the final consolation."

Typical of the Cobra, to hope he could keep talking past death. He and his set always chattered about philosophy and poetry, music and art, never anything real. Lies were the fabric of his soul.

"Why would you dream of escape?"

The Cobra raised an eyebrow, working oil through his long braids. "Why would you dream of prison?"

Once he'd mixed up his oil and his inkwell, sending both flying. When Marius attempted to assist, the Cobra flicked ink at him and laughed. *Stay clear of me, Last Hope, or be stained.*

Marius was born of the Oracle's mountains. His bones were cold stone and colder truth, and he found the Cobra's nonsense intolerable. "Make something up and write it down. If you don't like it, improve it later."

"You think storytelling is that simple?" The Cobra made an ill-bred face, then picked up the quill he'd flung down. "Perhaps I can imagine a bridge between two scenes that don't connect. That's how bards told stories when nothing was written down and memory failed. That's how stories transform."

Abruptly, Marius was sick of the sight of the Cobra, luminous with gold and inspiration. The man wasted his mind as he wasted his time.

"I do not care for stories. Someone is dying tomorrow."

"Someone's always dying," the Cobra said casually. "Stories go on."

This conversation turned Marius's stomach. He shut his mouth. The Cobra, who filled every silence, began to sing. He wrote at the piano in order to provide himself with musical interludes. What the Cobra called a piano was an unearthly contraption, a perversion of a clavichord. The instrument was carved and painted with golden-green scales that coruscated in the brilliant illumination the Cobra insisted upon. Every surface was crowded with golden candelabras wrought in serpent shapes, and the chandelier was a crystal-dripping sun. He taught the torches to burn bright, and filled the room with chaotic melody. The reflection of flame turned the window behind him into a golden lake.

Marius's father claimed merchants cheated their lords with false gold. It might shine, but tested against real gold would never ring true. Once Marius had a friend who could charm birds from trees to cages like the Cobra could, a brother in arms he trusted with his life, but Lucius was dead. Now, all Marius had was this illusory brightness, fool's gold over the hollowness of a wooden statue long rotted away. The Cobra was barely a real person. Marius had never seen him angry, grieving, or revealing any genuine feeling.

He was the ideal companion. Emotions were dangerous for Marius.

The golden lake of glass was disturbed by a movement in the dark. Marius lifted a hand to arrest the song. Catching the Cobra's attention, Marius pointed.

At the window lurked a creature dripping blood.

As they watched, the blade of a knife was inserted between the edge of the window and the sill. The sash window lifted with a sound like teeth grinding.

Marius found this mildly interesting, until the Cobra flinched.

The whole court knew the Cobra was a coward. The Cobra freely admitted it. He wouldn't touch a weapon. But he didn't flinch.

A youth rolled into the window and landed on the tiles, soundless as the light striking his bared blade. A knife wouldn't save him. Marius hurdled the Cobra's elaborately carved sofa and went for the intruder.

The bargain between them was a filthy one, but Marius kept faith. He had no intention of letting anybody touch the Cobra.

Unlike most when faced with the charge of a berserker, the youth didn't falter or retreat. He stilled, wary as a wild thing. Beasts recognized each other, but there was a difference between a caged beast who belonged somewhere and some hungry stray who belonged nowhere at all. No man at court could stand against Marius. No man even presented a challenge.

Another knife appeared in the youth's free hand, twin blades spinning. A feral smile sprang to his face as he leaped for Marius. He wore the livery of the royal guard while he broke the king's laws by trespassing. He'd scared the Cobra. Marius needed no weapon to strike this insolent whelp down.

At the last possible instant before bloodshed, there was light.

A note of command rang through Marius's body, as if his bones were bells. "*Stop.*"

Two fingers pressed against Marius's shoulder, not even a full hand, with no pressure behind the touch. The Cobra didn't need to exert himself.

"No murder in my parlour, boys."

When Marius fell reluctantly back, the Cobra slid between them.

"Thank you," murmured the worst man in the world, sent by the gods to punish Marius for his sins. The thanks was mockery. Marius had no choice but to obey.

Even though the Cobra's order was rank foolishness. This was an armed intruder with an eerie smile, and the Cobra's thoroughly indecent dressing gown made it clear he was unarmed. On many occasions Marius had spoken to him strongly about his attire, but the Cobra pretended Marius was joking.

The Cobra's glittering attention turned to the blood-soaked criminal. "Loved the entrance."

Marius said coldly, "If you are on a mission from the king or your master, use the door."

"I'm not on the king's or my mistress's business," drawled the guard, in a low-born accent. "I'm here on my own business."

The Cobra arched an eyebrow. "I haven't had the doubtful pleasure of your acquaintance. I'm the Marquis of Popenjoy, the Golden Cobra. This is my friend Lord Marius Valerius, the Last Hope."

The boy tilted his head, fresh blood dripping from his rough-cut hair. Judging by the splatter, Marius calculated, he had recently killed at least four men.

"Lord Marius and I met in court earlier."

"I do not recall every servant I encounter at court," said Marius.

He doubted the guard had been drenched in blood at the time. Marius found blood memorable.

The Cobra shot him a quelling glance. Strange wariness still clung to the Cobra, who had once hummed a tune as the city burned. "Forgive him. Too much aristocracy affects the brain," claimed the wildly hypocritical Lord Popenjoy.

Charm was a weapon Marius had never possessed and the Cobra always misused. Contrary in all things, the Cobra wasted it now on a common thug.

The guard grinned. "Do *you* know me? I hear you know everything."

He heard true. The Cobra knew when ships wouldn't return and where fires would start. Now his gaze went brilliantly intent, as though distant flames reflected in his eyes. Marius had learned this expression from years of familiar contempt. The Cobra saw this boy, and anticipated disaster.

"You're Key. People called you the Villain of the Cauldron."

The cur's teeth were too sharp for his smile to be sweet. "They call me something different these days. I don't think the new name will stick."

The Cobra sounded almost amused. "It won't. Tell me your business."

Disbelieving, Marius wheeled on him. "You cannot hire a treacherous cut-throat! I forbid it."

"Really? Thank you." The Cobra sounded definitely amused. "I love to do the forbidden."

Suddenly young and hopeful, Key of the Cauldron asked, "I hear you pay spies?"

The invitation to villainy seemed to please the Cobra. "Lavishly."

Encouraged, the guard proceeded: "This is about Lady Rahela Domitia."

"We know the lady is to die." Marius's voice sounded harsh even in his own ears.

Testifying to the lady's crimes had been a grim business. His king was rightly furious at her perfidy, but that didn't mean she should be butchered. When Marius urged she be swiftly and mercifully put to death, Octavian said she did not deserve mercy. Marius couldn't talk to Octavian as he had when they were boys. It was Marius's fault.

He only wanted justice. He didn't know why justice was so painfully difficult to achieve.

He'd given evidence. Her fate was his responsibility. He hated the woman, and hated the thought of her wretched death. Cold misery had driven Marius to the Cobra's house. There was no true light or comfort here, but Marius had nowhere else to go.

Key of the Cauldron smiled as though he knew an evil secret. "The lady will *not* die tomorrow. She's been declared a true prophet."

As Marius froze the Cobra's laughter spilled into the air like a shower of counterfeit gold coins, bright and false as hell. There never was anyone so radiant, or so vile.

"A surprise twist!" The Golden Cobra applauded. "Now that's interesting."

CHAPTER SEVEN

The Villainess, the Spymaster and the Secret

"Everything has a price," said the Golden Cobra.
"Show me your worth."

Time of Iron, ANONYMOUS

he didn't have to open her eyes to know she was in another world. Rolling over usually woke Rae with a jolt of sick pain. Here, miracles like monsters, magic, and a good night's sleep were possible.

In the real world, she wasn't waking. Alice would worry, but she'd be so happy when Rae did wake and was well.

Sunlight slanted through the marble arch, making the blue mosaics gleam with life. Emer walked in with a silver tray holding a cup of hot chocolate and a buffet breakfast for one.

"Luxurious," sighed Rae, sipping the chocolate. She hadn't had an appetite for a long time. Savouring food felt like wild indulgence.

One dish seemed to be a sweet omelette with currants. It was delicious, but Rae felt suspicious about the meat covered in fragrant fruits and spices. "What is this?"

"You have breakfast amnesia?"

Emer sounded tired. Rae wasn't a morning person either. Which confirmed it was right Rae had been cast as a villain. Villains were never morning people. They had to stay sharp for midnight plotting.

With a rich spread like treasure in breakfast form before her, Rae could afford to be choosy. She pushed away dishes she didn't recognize as fundamentally unsafe.

"If you're not going to eat the roast hedgehog . . ." said Emer.

"Be my guest."

Rae proceeded to fall on the hot buttered toast, pheasants' eggs and grapes glowing in the bowl like jewels. Eating toast used to make her lips and gums bleed as though toasted bread was more resilient than flesh.

Now Rae made the toast her bitch. As she munched, she schemed.

Six years ago, the Golden Cobra appeared from nowhere to dazzle the court as a leader in fashion and a patron of the arts. He possessed a wide network of spies and thieves, and a wealth of information. He also had a wealth of actual wealth, and owned a golden brothel. Some people loved bling. And ladies of the night.

The Cobra was Rae's key to getting the Flower of Life and Death. The trick was making Lord Popenjoy believe she'd be useful.

Being plunged in warm water eased the wracking pains, so Rae was used to frequent baths. She wasn't used to baths in Eyam, where jasmine water, orange water, lemon water and rose water were sprinkled over her head and breasts from silver vases. There was no hot and cold running water, so Rae bathed in sadly lukewarm bathwater while plotting her costume. The Cobra believed in presentation, so Rae had Emer put on her best day dress. The difference between day dresses and evening gowns was evening gowns showed even more bosom. Her best day dress still showed plenty. It was stiff white satin, scarlet threads trailing up the skirt in blooming roses, thorny briars and vines that circled Rae's waist.

Rae felt evil and cute as she stepped out of her chambers. Key waited in the stairwell. His face lit when he saw Rae, oddly sharp canines glinting. Her first friend in Eyam.

Rae purred, "Let's catch a cobra."

Emer led them into a courtyard with a huge marble fountain. A statue stood in the centre, a woman with her face in her hands and water circling her head like silver hair. Someone was brutally killed in this fountain, Rae recalled, a bloodstain left on the white marble that never washed away.

Except the marble beneath the rippling water was clear as a stretch of new snow. The murder must not have happened yet. Rae wished she could remember who died.

They climbed a flight of steps to reach the walkway wrapping around the palace walls. Rae plucked excitedly at Key's sleeve and craned her neck to drink in Themesvar, capital of Eyam. City of many colours, set between the abyss of despair and the mountains of truth. A city that was wonderful all the time as every city could be occasionally. When you visited the city, and saw a flash of how you'd imagined it proved true. Or when you lived in the city, and a rare sense of wonder visited you.

The walled palace lay within a walled city like two rings of a tree trunk. The palace wall was warm sandstone and the city wall and barbican beyond were tall grey limestone. Beyond grey walls and city gates was the deep green horseshoe of the Waiting Elms forest and the snow-capped curve of the mountain range. This land was a matryoshka of circles: rings within rings, wheels within wheels, and plots within plots. Sunlight gleamed through Eyam's smoky, shrouding clouds onto copper domes gone minty green, laid by sloping roofs of rust red, slate grey and bronze. A broad paved path stretched from the palace gates to the barbican. Lined by guild houses, the Chain of Commerce was interrupted by squares like jewels in a necklace. The Tears of the Dead River cut knife bright and the Trespasser river snaked a silvery path through the city's colours. In that riot of colour, a single sprawling gold building stretched out like a lion among cats.

"Wow, the Golden Brothel is hard to look at without sunglasses," remarked Rae. "Was it necessary to build a massive gold building for ladies of the night?"

"Actual ladies don't mention those words," Emer said in a chilling voice.

"Why are words more important than reality?" Key sounded genuinely curious.

"Words change reality," snapped Emer. "Anyone who hears her won't think she's a lady, and she doesn't know how to be anything else."

Key nodded thoughtfully. Maybe Emer being older and wiser than Rae was why getting along with Key was easier. Or maybe it was that Rahela had never betrayed Key.

Wait. Emer wasn't older than Lady Rahela.

"Hey, how old am I?" Rae demanded.

"You're twenty-four."

Emer's announcement was funereal. Rahela was the same age as Lord Marius and the king, young for a man but too old for a woman to marry.

Great news for Rae. She hadn't expected to live to be twenty-four.

"I'm nineteen," contributed Key. "Counting by the Death Day."

The Death Day was the date legend said the dread ravine was created. Amid gratification she'd guessed Key's age right, Rae had a realization about his easy familiarity with her. Key thought Rae was in her mid-twenties, so he probably looked up to her. She'd been good at leading a team once, before her team discarded her. Prophet, vixen, traitor: this world was forcing her into a bewildering array of roles, but Rae knew how to take care of her friends.

"An abyss foundling!" muttered Emer, as if her darkest suspicions were confirmed.

Only Rae knew what her scorn masked. Emer was an abyss foundling too, an unwanted child abandoned on the edge of the dread ravine. Most of those children fell. A few were saved. None were loved.

People in Eyam said, *the sparks fly upward*. On the edge, children breathed in fire and darkness that stained them forever.

Real life didn't work like that, but this world went by different rules. Emer would be the axe-murdering Iron Maid one day. Key was a various-implements murderer already.

Emer walked demurely behind Rae, but gave the impression of stalking. Emer was a towering cliff with a warning sign, and Key should wear a nametag reading 'Volatile and Unreliable'. Rae could handle this. Carefully.

"A little help, minions. I can't remember what my relationship with the Golden Cobra might be."

She and Key both looked expectantly at Emer, who sighed.

"You hardly have one. The Cobra didn't favour you, and you have no use for those who aren't admirers."

"All that's about to change," Rae told her. "Evil wins again!"

"When did evil win last time?"

Key had a point. Evil didn't win often in stories. Usually good triumphed, but that meant the forces of darkness were statistically due a win.

Rae made an expansive gesture to Themesvar, snake bracelet catching the light. "Let's take the city. Evil wins at last."

The cynicism in Key's voice relaxed, as if he didn't believe her but might like to. "Lead the way, my lady."

The Cobra's house was shaped from the same cliff stone as the rest of the palace. New buildings in the palace weren't allowed, but the established aristocracy all owned townhouses within the palace walls. The Cobra must have acquired the dwelling from an impoverished courtier.

The maid who answered their knock wore the palace uniform and a cobra symbol on her breast. The court objected to the Cobra giving his servants valuables, but the Cobra insisted his people required large golden identification pins in addition to lavish salaries. Among nobles, Lord Popenjoy had many friends and many enemies, but he was universally popular with his staff.

The maid tried to shut the door in their faces. "My lord does not rise before noon."

Rae gave her a winning smile, and the maid's eyes widened. It seemed 'winning' read as 'sultry' on Rahela.

"I am Lady Rahela Domitia, and I am burdened with glorious prophecy! Also a glorious bosom, but that's not relevant. I should have been executed today, yet I stand before you as the king's prophet. Ask Lord Popenjoy if he wants to know how I did it."

The maid nodded slowly. Rae let her close the door.

For a time nothing happened except Key prowling back and forth in front of the manor. Apparently, Key got restless if ten minutes went by without an act of violence. Rae wondered if he might have ADHD like Alison in junior high who had a hard time staying in her seat. Though Alison wouldn't dream of breaking anybody's nose.

Rae sat for hours in chemotherapy, only rising to drag her IV into a bathroom. The first time you went to the bathroom during chemo you pissed red, the colour of horror-movie blood. Waiting outside a door was no problem.

Eventually, the doors opened. "Lord Popenjoy will receive you."

The maid led the way up a flight of stairs, past a large frame empty save for scrawled graffiti reading 'IMAGINE AN ANCESTRAL PORTRAIT'.

Glass was everywhere in the Cobra's house. Glass broke more easily in Eyam and – if Rae had the timeline right – the glassblowers' guild had recently been destroyed in an incident with the undead, so the Cobra's windows were more expensive and ostentatious than gold. All the great houses in Themesvar had grand balconies from which to contemplate the dread ravine. The Cobra's balcony was decorated with stained glass in a blaze of orange, lemon and strawberry shades, turning even a dim morning into a sunrise. The maid led them down the radiant passage towards a pair of double doors. The door handles were in the sinuous shapes of snakes. Torches with winding scarlet tongues burned on either side of the doors. The flames leaped, and both doors opened without a touch.

"Dark magic," muttered Emer.

"Hydraulics?" whispered Rae, under the sound of music surging.

These books weren't set in any actual historical time period, given the enchanted weapons and the restless dead. Still, Rae hadn't expected club music.

Nobody had electronic instruments or computers, but a band was attempting to create the same effect on a piano that looked almost like a keyboard, plus bass guitars and vigorously beaten drums. Two women in slinky mermaid gowns sang through artfully muffling veils, with a lavishly embroidered tapestry as their backdrop. The whole room was rich fabrics and a profusion of light. Except for what lay in the elaborately carved display case. The long orichal steel knife didn't quite fit.

Across the room, another set of doors burst open. The singers crooned, "*Wooh.*" The beat picked up.

A young man entered, glittering from head to toe. He wore a herigaut, a costume Alice had looked up when they read about it and Rae was interested to see in person. It was a full-length robe of amber silk with hanging sleeves. The scalloped edges of the curtainlike sleeves were thick with gold thread. More gold thread twined through his rope braids, piled high on his head and falling in jet-black twists to a belt of shining gold links. Ornaments were thick as summer wildflowers in the black crest of his hair, star-bright trinkets suspended at intervals in his braids and jingling like wind chimes as he moved. Gold paint traced delicate shapes around his eyes, shimmering against his dark brown skin and inscribed along the angle of his jaw. He swayed to the beat of the music, arms an unselfconscious curve over his head. His hanging sleeves became a glittering waterfall pouring back from those arms, where gold bracelets circled the muscle around both forearms and biceps. Jewellery on men was illegal in Eyam, so the Cobra was a rebel with his hidden bracelets. He kicked up his feet as he danced through the room, shoes soled with crimson.

Directly beneath a chandelier coruscating with light, crystals set like rattles on the ends of golden snakes' tails, was a red velvet conversation sofa. The man in gold threw himself down onto the red velvet, crossed one long leg over another, and gave Rae a little wave.

"Welcome to the House of the Cobra."

"Uh," said Rae. "Hey. Do you always greet your guests in such style?"

The Golden Cobra's richly amused drawl wrapped around her like a velvet blanket embroidered with glittering thread. "If you want to make an entrance, make the whole scene."

Rae nodded. "So, I hear you have a lot of spies."

There was a hitch in the music as the musicians' playing faltered. Lord Popenjoy didn't flicker a gold-tipped eyelash. "I'm modestly well-endowed with spies. Not to brag."

"Sure," said Rae. "Like Key, right?"

The Cobra's lounge became less sprawling.

Key's smile jolted briefly out of place. "How did you know?"

Rae shrugged. "You want money, the Cobra's the richest guy in town. I ain't saying you're a gold digger, but—that is in fact what I'm saying."

"I was electrified to hear Key say that when distressed, you call on the names of your lovers," drawled the Cobra. "Jesus and Batman?"

Holy sacrilegious misunderstanding.

"I do not have a romantic relationship with those individuals!"

"Are you angry with me?" Key sounded guilty, and rather delighted to be so.

Rae winked. "Nah. You're my evil minion, vile treachery is part of the deal." She turned back to the Cobra. "You heard what happened last night?"

The Cobra yawned. "I hear about what happened last night every morning. So you're a holy prophet? Congratulations. Are you here to tell my fortune? Please say I'll be swept off my feet by a tall dark stranger. Tell me she's a pirate."

Lady Rahela sashayed forward with purpose. Swagger was the first step to being confident. She knew the rules of a villainous stalk. Head high, neck long, think *murder*.

"I have important information. In return, I want something from you. Are you willing to trade?"

"Could be. I hear you told His Majesty tales of a glorious future. What have you got for me?"

Lines of gold paint forked around the Cobra's eyes. He was more of an eye smiler than a mouth smiler, but it was a nice eye smile.

This was going to be a hard sell. Rae had to deliver it convincingly. "If someone read your story in the book of fate and it had a sad ending, would you want to hear the tale?"

"What a very interesting question," murmured the Cobra.

"Someone's going to kill you," proclaimed Rae. "Wanna know who?"

The books contained much discussion of the Cobra's cowardice. He refused to fight duels, and lived in fear of the Emperor. Rae expected a big reaction.

The Cobra tugged idly on a braid. "Let's continue this conversation in private."

Emer snarled as she sprang forward. "Any lady left alone with the Cobra would be ruined!"

The Cobra turned to Rae's minions. "I must insist. No offence, but you both terrify me. If made nervous, I come over all shy and quiet."

He batted shimmering lashes in Emer's direction. She stood unmoved as an oak tree.

The Cobra sighed. "How about a compromise? Everybody exits the room, except me and Lady Rahela. I leave the door cracked open. I whisper a secret. Lady Rahela decides if she wants to shut the door."

Over the dozen hours she'd spent in Eyam, many had made insinuations about Rahela's past. The Cobra, with whom no one's virtue was safe, hadn't mentioned it. When Emer brought up the matter, he hadn't sneered at the idea Rahela had any reputation left to protect.

Rae decided. "All right."

"You heard the lady. Take five," the Cobra told his band. "You guys sound great."

The band dispersed. A singer in a purple mermaid gown trailed a hand down the Cobra's bright sleeve before she left. Their boss shutting himself up to conspire with strange women appeared to be business as usual.

The singer also dropped a wink at Key as she swanned by. Key and Emer didn't depart until Rae nodded to them. Even then, Emer left the door conspicuously ajar.

The Cobra motioned for Rae to join him on the sofa.

A conversation sofa was two attached seats facing in opposite directions so you could whisper in someone's ear. The winding spine of this sofa was serpent shaped, the wood carved with a pattern of scales. The Cobra rested on his elbows, one hand loosely clasped over the sofa snake's mahogany head. Its forked tongue peeked between his fingers. The Cobra watched as Rae joined him. He was all glittering brightness, except those dark, steady eyes.

Rae waited to hear salacious gossip about the court, or the king. Instead he murmured, "Girl, where are you from?"

Rae gestured vaguely. "The palace?"

The Golden Cobra leaned forward. This close, Rae saw tiny

painted dragons spreading gold wings on his cheekbones, dragons' tails curling in the slight hollows beneath.

"That's not what I'm asking. Where did you live, before you walked into the story?" The wicked Marquis of Popenjoy dropped his voice even lower. "I'm a New York City boy myself."

Rae got up and shut the door.

CHAPTER EIGHT

The Villainess Strikes a Bargain

The sword slid home to his heart, giving him a cleaner
death than he deserved. It was over quickly, but the
memory of his expression in the last moment lingered like
an obstinate ghost. In that instant he was simply young
and caught off guard. The Golden Cobra, who knew every
secret, looked very surprised to die.

Time of Iron, ANONYMOUS

hen Rae turned back, the Cobra was placidly gleaming
under the chandelier after throwing his bombshell.
"You're kidding! You're real too?"

The Cobra's teeth flashed, smile less guarded now they were alone.
"I wouldn't put it that way."

She waved that aside. "You're from the real world! I'm from
Oklahoma."

"I won't hold it against you. When did you get here?"

Rae glared at him for insulting her homeland. "Last night."

He whistled. "Right before the execution. That must have been a
nasty shock."

His tone was light, but Rae caught the sidelong concerned glance.
She needn't conduct herself as a proper lady with a boy from New
York. She hopped on the conversation sofa, hugging her knees to her

chest with her scarlet skirt pouring off the seat, and eyed him with fascination.

"Are there many real people here?"

"I've never met anybody else like us. I've only heard of one."

That was a relief. Less competition for the flower.

"When did you wake up as the Golden Cobra?"

His laugh was warm and bubbling as a hot spring. "I didn't. I invented the Golden Cobra."

"Wait, how does that work?"

If Rae could escape being executed, it made sense someone else could change the story too. Still, creating a whole new character? She'd heard of being a self-made man, but this was absurd.

"I was near death. A strange woman offered me a chance to go into the story and save myself. I assume it was the same with you?"

Rae nodded. "I wish I'd got her name now. Do you think that woman wrote the books?"

Time of Iron's author went by 'Anonymous' to create an air of mystery, and presumably because everybody was onto writers who used initials to conceal their identity. Rae had always assumed Anonymous was a woman trying to avoid being pigeonholed. Sometimes women writers got discussed as if they ran a fictional vampire dating agency, while clearly men writing green bare-breasted tree women burned with pure literary inspiration.

She'd heard people often asked writers 'Do you put real people in your books?' Rae had never thought anyone meant it literally.

The Cobra shrugged. "Nobody knows who wrote the books. Do writers have universe-travelling superpowers? I didn't have the chance to ask her any questions. I was in a bad way, and I woke up as a young thief on the street who never scored a name on the page." The Cobra made a face. "You know where that leads. Offed by starvation in the snow, or executed after pickpocketing a plot-relevant item. I didn't find either outcome acceptable."

So he'd written himself a different story. Now the Golden Cobra was the brightest part of a room that contained a chandelier.

"Are you telling me you read a totally different book than I did?"

"Oh no," the Cobra demurred. "I'm sure it was basically the same story, with perhaps a few minor adjustments. The Emperor rises, the lost gods are found and everybody loves Lia, right?"

Rae nodded, though she felt the Cobra had made more than a few adjustments. He was involved in crucial parts of the plot!

Light dawned on a particular plot point. "Everybody wonders how you know everything that happens in the palace. You *don't* have the most extensive spy network in the country. You read about it in the books!"

The Cobra had a suddenly sheepish air. "Actually, it's both. I needed to explain where I got my information, so I lied I had many spies. Real spies approached me. What could I do? Rejecting their hopeful little spy faces seemed cruel. And wasteful. One thing led to another, until I had the most extensive spy network in the country."

He sounded slightly embarrassed, but proud as well. He hadn't been able to show off all he'd accomplished before. He couldn't tell the truth to anybody in this world.

Rae, a big believer in positive reinforcement for the team, said sincerely, "You're amazing."

The Cobra shrugged, one-shouldered. "Go big or go home. I can't go home, so I go big every time. Am I really in the book now? Do readers like me okay?" he hoped. "Do they think the name is cool? I came up with it myself. The plan was to fit in and keep it low-key."

Rae considered the manor and the electronic dance music. "This is low-key?"

The Cobra's smile was guilty, but not even a little sorry. "I was a theatre kid. Aren't you? From what I heard, the scene where you claimed to be a holy prophet was high drama."

Judging by his tone, the Cobra thought she'd gone too far.

He hadn't seen anything yet.

"I'm a cheerleader, which is also a performance art. Listen, I had to escape being executed for crimes I didn't commit. Unlike you, I didn't decide to be a villain."

"Wait, what?" The Cobra's eyes went wide as gold-fringed lakes. "I'm a *villain*?"

"You own a brothel."

The Cobra said mildly, "You have something against brothels?"

"Working in one, no. Owning one? That building is made of gold. Are you saying you made that much gold doing *good*?"

The Cobra glanced at his hanging sleeves as if searching for something hidden up them. "No. I can't say that."

He started humming as if he required background music to reorient himself in the narrative. Rae remembered trying to find herself in her bronze mirror.

"You and I have a whole villain song together in the musical."

"There's a musical now?" A spotlight of sheer joy illuminated the Cobra's face, then dimmed. "I can't believe I'm a villain."

"*I* can't believe you thought you could have a snake theme and be a hero."

That was so naive. At least seventy per cent of villainy was the aesthetic.

The Cobra threw up his hands in protest, which due to his sleeves created a mini golden whirlwind. "I was going for 'minor comedic character'. I'm not looking to make waves."

"Why not? Someone should organize things properly around here, and that someone is me. Securing the help of the Golden Cobra is number three on my list."

Rather than offering her aid, the Cobra gave Rae a funny look. "You're kind of Type A, aren't you?"

What of it? Whenever projects or events went wrong, Rae made a plan to fix them. Until something went wrong she couldn't remedy. Every thought had turned to formless mush, but now Rae's mind was clear. It felt so good she was almost giddy, as though she'd been trapped in a tiny airless room for years and finally escaped. She was dizzy and drunk on her own expanded abilities. She had come to conquer.

Rae eyed the Cobra censoriously. "This lax attitude is what made you accidentally become a villain."

He laughed as if it was a joke. "What can I say? I like improv."

Someone had to take control of this narrative. The Cobra was lucky she'd got here when she had. Things were about to go very wrong for him.

Rae bit her lip. "Sorry if this is tactless, but I have to ask. Are you and the Last Hope involved? Romantically?"

The Cobra's face went blank.

Rae made a delicate gesture in which both hands wound intricately together. The Cobra's mouth quirked. He repeated the gesture less delicately, as if wringing out an invisible bath towel.

"Or is it Lia?"

The Cobra had showered Lia with attention ever since she arrived at court. Some readers believed his intentions were nefarious. Others believed he was smitten. Lia was, after all, irresistible.

"Frankly, my dear," the Cobra drawled, "I'm insulted. What gave you the impression I'm the type of fool who romances a main character?"

Rae blinked. "Main characters do tend to be good-looking."

The Cobra lounged so hard he was almost horizontal. "Sure. Hot singles are in your narrative. They're so cute, and they're so much drama. The dating records of main characters are extremely cursed."

The man made sense. Rae conceded with a nod.

He sighed in disgust. "I like many people, but not protagonists. You know where that leads. High-speed chases, epic speeches, buildings collapsing, torment and betrayal. Possibly a dragon. No thanks! I'm not down to fight a dragon."

Rae felt misled by ambiguities in the text. "Why are you always hanging out with the Last Hope? People draw art! There are essays on the internet!"

"Whatever, I'm sure there are essays about Marius and his boyhood companions as well. The internet is full of overthinking perverts." The Cobra looked wistful. "Wow, I miss the internet. For your information, I'm keeping Marius company until he can be with Lia, his one true love."

The Cobra sounded almost shy. Rae scoffed. She'd crossed worlds to find somebody with the same terrible pairing preferences as her sister.

The Cobra's eyes narrowed. "The Emperor is a terrifying murderer."

Rae scoffed with increased conviction. "The people the Emperor murders aren't real. What is real is my belief he's awesome. The Last Hope? Not so much."

"I won't hear Marius slandered! He's my little cupcake who never does anything wrong."

"Well, your little cupcake kills you," Rae snapped. "So there."

There was a puzzled silence, as though Rae had spoken in a language the Cobra didn't understand. Rae had intended to break this news more tactfully.

"My Marius," the Cobra said at last. "Murders an innocent person?"

"Executes an evildoer," Rae corrected. "No offence meant."

"He wouldn't do that."

"Main characters kill off minor villains all the time. Obviously, not great from your perspective, and I can see you're not finding this plot development believable—"

"That's not who I am," the Cobra announced with sudden startling intensity. "That's not how he thinks about me. I'll show you."

For a guy who relaxed into a lounge so fully, the Cobra could move fast. He knocked three times on the half-open door.

"Be a jewel, Sinad. Send a message asking Lord Marius to attend me at once."

The maid whisked off before Rae could protest.

She protested anyway. "Please reconsider! This man comes from a long line of frenzied spree killers."

"That's why he took vows to become a scholar," the Cobra argued. "At his age his grandfather had already collected five corpse brides in a secret chamber. His parents are basically Bluebeard and Ms Manners. Marius is doing great so far."

"I'm not throwing him a 'no corpse brides' parade," Rae said flatly. "He's a ticking time bomb."

"He's my best friend!"

The Cobra was a fanatic like Alice, who wouldn't hear a word against their definitely-not-problematic fave. Rae had figured this attitude would collapse if the favourite character was in a position to actively murder you, but it seemed the Cobra was ride-or-die-mad-about-it.

She shook her head slowly. "Except you're not really friends, are you? We both know what you did."

Everyone in the palace believed the Golden Cobra was a minor noble the Last Hope had encountered on the journey back from his studies at the Ivory Tower. Despite the drastic difference in the two men's personalities, they'd hit it off. When the Cobra arrived in the capital, the Last Hope introduced him as his friend and the Marquis of Popenjoy launched his notorious career. The Last Hope, who coldly condemned men for far less, tolerated every excess. The Cobra was the only stain on the Last Hope's reputation.

Only readers were aware the Cobra knew the Last Hope's most scandalous secret, and the Cobra's silence had a price.

"I'm a *supporting character*," the Cobra claimed. "I'm supporting him."

"You're blackmailing him!"

"In a supportive way!" The Cobra waved off Rae's accusation. "I'm *not* a villain! I'm someone whose thoughts and desires conflict with those of the main characters."

Rae snorted. "Same thing."

The Cobra's suddenly lost expression struck an unexpected chord with Rae. He'd believed he knew where the story was going, and now he'd hit a narrative dead end.

In a subdued tone at odds with everything else about him, the Cobra murmured, "I expected to part ways after the blackmail. When Marius kept showing up around me, I thought, here's a chance to truly be on a character's team. If you're lucky in the real world, people are real with you. Who gets to be fictional with someone, become part of their extraordinary world? Maybe I got it wrong. His mother and little sister came to court a couple of years ago. His mom gave me a friendship knife to thank me for showing them around, but Marius's sister barely spoke to me. I figured she was a shy kid. Maybe she was scared."

For a famous coward, the Cobra seemed oddly unconcerned about the threat to his own life. Instead he chose to be overly invested in fictional characters' feelings. Media was meant to be consumed, not consume you. The Cobra's priorities had got twisted.

Rae humoured him. "He's sorry he killed you."

"I'm touched," muttered the Cobra. "No, wait. I'm dead."

"In his death scene – you could interpret it different ways, but I read it as him regretting—"

The Cobra's head spun so fast a hair ornament struck the door with a sound like a bell tolling. "He *dies?*"

"Yeah," said Rae, disconcerted. "Did he not die in your version?"

"No."

The Cobra's voice was hollow and distracted. She was surprised once again by how hard the Cobra was taking this. His gaze was absorbed in a book that didn't exist any more.

"You don't get it. I changed the story. So he dies because of me. What if when we change the story, we only make things worse?"

It should be good news that changing the story was so easy. They could shape the narrative to suit them.

Yet the Cobra had seemed taken aback by the idea of his own demise, but not horror-struck the way he was now. Maybe the Last Hope would die because the Cobra changed the story, but the Cobra would die because the Last Hope stabbed him with a sword. Cause and effect were a lot more direct in the sword situation.

"Why did you blackmail him?"

In the books it seemed obvious. The Cobra was a social-climbing bad guy who deserved what he got. The pure and simple truth was pure and simple evil.

The Cobra's face went helpless as a pair of empty hands. "To enter the palace, you need a noble to speak for you. I was desperate to get to the Flower of Life and Death."

Before, Rae saw the blackmailing situation through the Last Hope's eyes. It was uncomfortable to consider how much heroism was based on point of view. Like Rae, the Cobra needed the flower. He was fighting for his life.

Rae hesitated. "Were you sick in the real world?"

"I was in an accident. Kids, look both ways before crossing the street. What can I say? It was dumb."

When he smiled this time, it didn't touch his eyes.

She'd faked so many smiles. Seeing his, Rae decided to risk trusting a fellow villain. "I have a plan to get the Flower of Life and Death."

The Cobra twinkled. "Thought you might."

Despite his lousy priorities, Rae believed the Cobra might be a kindred spirit. "Here's my evil scheme. At first I thought, let's off the henchmen guarding the royal greenhouse."

"Then you thought, that's murder?"

Rae said patiently, "It's okay to slaughter nameless henchmen."

"They have names! You could ask their names."

The Cobra seemed strangely agitated. Rae soothed, "I agree it could get messy. That's when the scheme came to me. The king will throw a ball to celebrate the arrival of Princess Vasilisa from – er – across the sea."

"Tagar?" said the Cobra.

"Okay, *that* name sounds made up."

"All names are made up," muttered the Cobra.

Rae focused on her goal. "Most of the palace is left unguarded when they need extra staff for official functions. The ball is a prime opportunity."

"The ball happens in my version of the book as well," the Cobra said enthusiastically. "At the ball, Octavian officially makes the princess and Lia ladies-in-waiting, then Marius and Lia share a dance, right?"

Probably? If there was a murder at the ball, Rae was certain she would remember the ball more clearly.

"Definitely," said Rae.

"I'm so glad I didn't wreck my favourite scene. Marius and Lia on the romantic balcony after their dance! Fate in the moonlight!"

Apparently distracted from the issue of his own demise, the Cobra's twinkle became a glow. This guy was a closet romantic. Surprising, for someone who owned a golden brothel.

Rae ignored fate in the moonlight. "Listen. There's a set of keys on the king's belt. One is the key to the greenhouse where the Flower of Life and Death blooms. You have thieves in your employ. Let's pay a thief to lift the keys at the ball."

There was no way her plan could fail.

The Cobra's voice usually meandered, easy as a slow-moving river under the sun. Now it froze. "If a commoner is caught coming at the king, they'll be killed."

Imagine getting this worked up about the wellbeing of book characters. Couldn't be Rae. She had real problems.

"You have another idea?"

The Cobra said, "I'll do it."

That didn't strike Rae as the best idea. "You're going to steal from the king? I wouldn't describe you as inconspicuous."

"I was a street thief. I can get the key. Then I'll get it copied."

"Why?"

The Cobra's brows drew sharply together as he considered their problem. Rae was glad he was finally focusing on reality. "The Flower of Life and Death doesn't bloom for a month. If you have a copy of the keys, you can stroll down to the greenhouse when the time comes."

A month. Rae had a timeline.

"That makes sense," she admitted. "Sometimes I miss the details."

"I'm not a big picture thinker," confessed the Cobra. "We're a perfect team. Let me suggest making a scene at the party. If you make yourself conspicuous, people never realize you're being sneaky."

"Any suggestions, theatre kid?"

"Just a few, cheerleader."

She'd come here expecting to manipulate a character to her side. Instead she'd found a friend. Rae beamed, and saw a cloud cross her new friend's face. His eyes wandered back to the door. She knew who he was thinking of.

The Cobra warned, "My expert assistance doesn't come free."

Rae was prepared for that. She scrambled off the sofa and towards the window, reaching out. "Of course. We'll share the Flower of Life and Death. We'll both get out."

The Cobra shook his head. "Flower's all yours."

"No—" Rae faltered.

"How old are you in the real world?" the Cobra asked.

"Twenty," Rae whispered.

"I was fourteen, bleeding in the street," said the Cobra, his voice light as sun-warmed air. "Then suddenly I was eighteen, starving in the street. I needed to eat. I needed an identity to enter the palace. I needed to work out how to break into the greenhouse. It took a while. Someone I trusted got scared for me, and made a run at the flower. It didn't end well. Some stories don't. I missed my chance. I . . . I did try."

She felt as though someone had seized hold of her chin, forcing her to face what she didn't want to see. *In Eyam, the Flower of Life and Death blooms once a year. You get one chance,* the woman had said.

When the flower bloomed a month from now, if Rae didn't seize her chance, she would be trapped.

The Cobra was suddenly further away. It took Rae a moment to realize she'd moved back. She'd reached for him, but now both her hands were outstretched, trying to keep her own balance.

The gold paint had lost its lustre. All Rae could see were his eyes, dark and sad, but not self-pitying.

The Cobra was calm. "It's too late for me. It's been too late for years."

A neighbour had taken Rae aside when news of her diagnosis spread, counselling her to take a blanket to her first appointment. Rae didn't understand until she found herself on a reclined chair having chemo, every warm organ in her body turning to frozen grapes. She clutched her blanket as the last rope to a warmer world. When she got home, she plunged into a scalding hot bath, but once you knew such cold existed it was impossible to ever really be warm again.

Icy realization pierced through Rae as if she was in the hospital with her blanket stripped away, no illusions left to cling to.

Ruin came for the Cobra when he was only a boy. That boy had blackmailed the Last Hope and fought his way into the court. He'd built up the whole identity of the Golden Cobra, the character with bright treasure and dark secrets. He'd tried so hard.

It hadn't worked. He hadn't woken up. There was a word for people who closed their eyes and never woke up.

Desperation crushed Rae's voice. "What do you want in exchange for helping me?"

Did the dead want anything?

It seemed they did. The Cobra leaned forward, intent. "Let me tell you what I believe. This world is as real as ours, but those who walk into the story have an advantage because we know the rules."

"The real world doesn't have rules."

The Cobra scoffed. "Ever felt like someone else got the key to make the world work for them? Our world has rules. We just don't know them. Here, we have the manual! My manual is just out of date. Help me fix the story I broke. Tell me what happens in the book, so I can see where it goes wrong."

He wouldn't take her seriously if she confessed she'd only heard someone else read the first book, and she hadn't always been listening.

Rae faltered, "I don't remember the first book."

Lord Popenjoy jolted from his place by the window. "What do you mean?"

"I didn't read . . . all of it."

There was a silence. At last, the Cobra said carefully, "That is not great news. Which parts did you read?"

Rae tried to turn the question aside with a laugh. "Don't be the fan who requires a secret password to let people inside the gates of loving a story. Let people enjoy things."

Marble reflected his movement as a restless gleam. "Sure. Except in this specialized situation, where lives depend on you remembering key details!"

He didn't need to tell Rae that. *Her* life depended on her remembering. She still couldn't.

The Cobra's insistence made Rae think of the friends she'd had when she was seventeen. Her team. They teased her when she started forgetting things. At first affectionately. Then they got annoyed. She tried to pass off weakness with jokes, but everyone stopped laughing. Rae grew desperate, knowing she was losing facts, dates, stories, her friends, her family. Herself.

"I was so sick." The words came out like jagged metal from a wound. She slammed her mouth closed, slapping on a bandage so she wouldn't see how badly she might be hurt.

It was true she'd tuned out when Alice read her the first book, believing she knew exactly where the story was headed. Still, her mind should have retained more. The truth was, unless she concentrated with all her considerable force of will, her mind failed like her body. Terrifying gaps loomed in Rae's memory, plot holes becoming traps she could fall into. The story felt like a wild horse she was fighting to control. At any moment the reins might slip from her hands.

The Cobra's restless pacing stilled beside her. Rae felt the warmth of an almost touch. His hand hovered ready to cup her elbow in a silent offer of support.

Rae jerked back. She could stand on her own.

The Cobra fixed Rae with a meditative gaze. The book said the Cobra was cunning. That was villain speak for clever.

"I won't add to the confusion by talking about my version. Tell me everything you remember."

Relieved the Cobra had fallen in with her brilliant schemes, Rae felt she must prove he'd made the right decision. Retrieving memories was looking back with sharp vision at a fogged-over landscape. She might recover some details, but so much stayed lost in the mist. Still, Rae had concentrated ferociously on the second and third books, once she was following a character she loved through his world. She knew enough to put this together.

"Lia enters the palace, winning the hearts of the Emperor and the Last Hope."

The Cobra's nod encouraged her to continue.

"Much drama follows," Rae guessed. "Including my execution, until the abyss opens at the end of book one. The foreign princess falls for the king, but he prefers Lia, so that doesn't end well. In the first battle scene, a group of ice raiders invade the city to avenge the king's insult against their princess. To save the city, our heroine's true love enters the ravine and slays the ravine's divine guardian, the First Duke. Octavian unlocks his power, fulfilling the prophecy by becoming Emperor. That's the first book."

"Sorry, who does what now? Are you sure about this?"

She reassured, "I remember the other books much more clearly. Power over the living and the dead unbalances the Emperor's mind and the Last Hope becomes his deadliest enemy, but they must make peace when real war breaks out. The princess, now the Ice Queen, leads the whole army of raiders across the sea to destroy Eyam! That's about when the Last Hope stabs you."

The Cobra made a sad face.

"Lia comforts him. When the ice raiders attack, the Last Hope swears the blood oath to serve her."

The Cobra brightened. "The kiss scene!"

"Uh, no. They never kiss." Alice would definitely have mentioned that. "Didn't the Last Hope take vows of chastity?"

"It's hot because it's forbidden," the Cobra explained.

That checked out. Rae would have liked Lia and Marius together more if they did engage in sexy taboo behaviour. Relationships with no mistakes and no obstacles had no bite. Reading them was like consuming soggy salad for every meal and calling that healthy eating.

Sadly, Lia was too pure to be interested in taboo behaviour with any of her gentlemen friends. Other characters had sex scenes on the page, but even though Lia married, the wedding night remained unclear.

Rae dismissed forbidden love with a shrug. "The Last Hope battles a hundred ice raiders to protect Lia, wins but receives a mortal wound, and perishes beneath a tree. It's a hollow victory. Lia is stabbed in the back by a courtier she trusted. After Lia's death, the Emperor rains down destruction on the world."

The tale had flowed as she talked, the gaps of the story filled in by telling it. She thought all that hung together pretty well. Rae took a moment to preen.

The Cobra's expression was revolted. "I can't possibly have caused this freakshow. Lia what? Octavian what? My favourite character dies alone and unkissed under a random *tree*? I hate nature! People should quit buying these books."

Rae remembered the desolate feeling of reading along and remembering the Cobra was dead. It was much worse now she'd met him.

The Cobra continued delivering his disgruntled book review. "Relentless tragedy is misery porn. The perfect form for a story is an exciting beginning, an angsty middle, and a happy ending."

"I agree," said Rae. "So you want to set up Marius and Lia?"

"No!" the Cobra snarled. "I want them to *live*."

There was real distress in his voice, and he was a real person. It was sweet he cared so much, but ultimately misguided. If fictional characters had to die so Rae could get home, so be it. He might not be ready for villainy. She was.

It was clear what Rae must say to persuade him.

"Nobody gets a happy ending, unless we steal one. We can do it. We're villains. I'll put this story right. Deal?"

They stood framed by the window overlooking the city of many colours. She offered her hand, sunlight making her ruby rings gleam red as blood. The gold paint around the Cobra's eyes shone like the sun on a river as he shook.

"Deal." He let out a steadying breath. "Let's save Marius and Lia. And you."

Rae nudged him. "Don't get too upset. What happens to the characters doesn't actually matter. They're not real."

He gave her a look that made her shiver in sunshine. "They seem real when they die."

The Golden Cobra stood by the window. Storybook sunlight poured over his gilded ornaments and faraway dark eyes.

The boy who wanted a happy ending, and wouldn't get one.

If Rae were a good person she would have asked his real name and told him she would be his friend. She didn't. The hospital had taught her a cruel truth. Pain is the place where we're alone. We wish we weren't. But we always are.

Rae couldn't save him. She could only save herself.

The sound of footsteps rattled the windows like an approaching storm, and Rae remembered the future victim had summoned his murderer to his parlour. The book said the Last Hope was the good guy even though he did bad things. With a murderous character safely on the page, you could decide he was driven to it.

Now Rae was vividly aware they were defenceless, the Last Hope was dangerous, and he was upon them. Worse still, Lady Rahela's mother had seduced Lord Marius when he was seventeen. He'd spilled state secrets to her. It was the shame of Lord Marius's life, and the Cobra had used that shame to blackmail him.

Seeing the Cobra and Rahela together would incite the Last Hope's murderous fury.

"Just checking. In every version of the story, Marius is descended from a god and has divine might that no human can withstand?" On the Cobra's nod, Rae murmured: "Oh, good."

The echo of his steps was thunder. She knew what Lord Marius

himself did not. She knew the truth of his heritage and the terrible
extent of his power. She should run.

The maid opened the door, and it was too late.

"Announcing Lord Marius."

Framed in the grand doorway stood Lord Marius Valerius, the
descendant of the First Duke, the scholarly Last Hope of his family,
and the man who wanted them both dead.

Lord Marius made the bright room nothing but background. He
seemed a statue made by a sculptor who knew any flaw in his creation
would be punished by death. The only sign of life was his eyes, blue
bleached into snowy pallor. The eyes of a watchful white wolf.

When reading, the Last Hope seemed noble because of his
restrained capacity for violence. Actually being in a room with Marius
Valerius was standing at the foot of a snowy mountain, fearing the
landslide. She tasted frost and steel in the air.

"I know," the Cobra murmured. "It's awful at parties. Nobody
notices me."

Rae raised her eyebrows. "But you look like a beautiful
Christmas tree."

"We don't all wake up with a costume. I'm trying to be visually
arresting over here!"

Rae mimed taking a photo. "You're doing amazing."

Her strained smile died at Lord Marius's approach, feeling caught
in a snowstorm indoors. The simple white uniform of an Ivory Tower
scholar had long sleeves Lord Marius wore knotted tight around his
brawny arms, as if to tie himself down. His only adornment was a
black leather belt with an ostentatiously empty scabbard where his
sword should be. His ancestral blade hung over the hearth in the
library. He'd sworn never to take the great sword down, but soon he
would break that vow.

Rae reached for the Cobra's sleeve. "This is a killing machine on
the verge of losing control. Employ tact and caution."

The Cobra twisted from her grasp like a snake. "Marius, you absolute bastard. Lady Rahela says you're going to kill me."

"Oh shit." Rae retreated hastily to the sofa.

The Last Hope stalked forward. Rae used to believe the hospital had prepared her for anything. She'd walked into elevators and seen bodies lying under sheets, headed for the morgue. Once a man collapsed in front of her. She'd learned that day the phrase 'the light went out of his eyes' was true. The movement of a mind behind a face lent the countenance all its brightness. Animation registered as illumination. Rae watched light bleed from a dying man's eyes, leaving them dark and empty, and knew the lost light was his life.

She'd never seen death by violence. Her life had been insulated from that, until she saw the promise in the way the Last Hope moved. Ice-water chill seeping into her bones, Rae felt she saw the future. It was red as blood.

The Cobra didn't flinch. She watched the shining dead boy face down the man fated to kill him again.

Quiet as the roar of a distant avalanche, the Last Hope said: "Don't tempt me."

CHAPTER NINE

The Cobra's Wicked Heart

Fire painted the night. The battle raged beyond the palace
windows, but the library was still quiet. Years ago, Lord
Marius had hung his ancestral sword on the library wall.
Starving for Blood was the sword's name. It had drunk no
blood in years. Not since the heir gave up war training and
knelt on the ice outside the Ivory Tower, swearing he would
be a scholar.

Now he stood by the hearth listening to the chaos of
death outside, his cold face unreadable. Moonshine and
firelight twined in shimmering red and silver ribbons on
the bared blade.

At last the Last Hope broke his vow, and took down
his sword.

Time of Iron, ANONYMOUS

t was too early for vile debauchery. The Cobra never rose
before twelve, so appalling scenes usually occurred after
Marius's noonday prayer. Yet this morning Marius must
witness the Golden Cobra, outrageously alone with a woman wearing
a disgraceful gown.

As usual, the Cobra was dressed as if a pirate chest had vomited
on him. Popenjoy leaned to whisper in the woman's ear, his hair

ornaments brushing her cheek. They glanced at Marius and tittered, obviously making a nasty joke. Not that Marius cared. A Valerius had superior senses. Marius could hear what they were saying, if he chose.

He did not so choose. Marius couldn't believe his studies had been interrupted by Popenjoy's arrant nonsense. Again.

He said icily, "I didn't appreciate your summons. I am no dog to be called to heel."

Popenjoy was wearing an odd, thin smile. Gloating, no doubt. "Yet you came. You didn't have to."

What choice did he have? Marius gave a mirthless laugh. What choice did he *ever* have, thanks to the Cobra?

Frustration rattled his bones like the bars of a cage, emotion so intense it longed to tip into fury. Marius had not permitted himself fury since he was seventeen.

"I'm serious," the Cobra insisted.

"Seems unlikely," Marius murmured.

The Cobra's smile sparked from lip to eye, then died. "Don't be hilarious," he instructed, which was absurd. Marius didn't make jokes. "I'm mad at you."

Marius stared over the Cobra's shoulder, out the bay window. Beyond the city's high walls and the Oracle's misty mountains lay the ducal estate. The great manor of Valerius, surrounded by new farmland and old battlefields, where he'd spent his childhood. Before he ever travelled to the Palace on the Edge or the Ivory Tower.

"I fail to see why you called me here to announce you are mad. I knew that already."

"Please stay calm, Lord Marius," sounded a throaty, insinuating voice.

The woman on the conversation sofa leaned over, almost spilling out of her gown. Marius hastily directed his gaze to the chandelier.

Not before he recognized her. To Marius's shocked disgust, the Cobra was entertaining Lady Rahela Domitia. The treacherous guard currently skulking outside the Cobra's door had spoken true. Lady Rahela was pardoned, and a holy prophet. As far as Marius was concerned, this meant she was a blasphemer as well as a traitor.

Apparently the Cobra found blasphemous treachery irresistible.

Birds of a stained feather flocked together, but the Cobra always avoided Lady Rahela. He murmured 'shoes' when he saw her. It seemed he had high standards for his lady friends' footwear. Marius wished the Cobra had high standards for his lady friends' *characters*. The Cobra could have anyone he wanted. Ladies constantly hurled themselves in Lord Popenjoy's direction during social occasions, while Marius hid behind the gold sleeves and wished for the library. Or death.

"Marius, I know you've heard Lady Rahela receives revelatory visions from the gods."

The only revelation which seemed likely was that of the lady's bosom.

Marius's lip curled. "Don't tell me you believe her. You're many unspeakable things. I've never known you to be stupid."

Except in one thing. The Cobra had chosen to blackmail Marius, when every soul in the kingdom knew to incite the wrath of a Valerius meant death.

Long ago the country was almost overwhelmed by the dead. Until the first King of Eyam was put on his throne by the First Duke, a man of supernatural strength and fury who appeared from nowhere to single-handedly butcher an army. The First Duke's sons, and their sons' sons, all inherited a portion of his great power and his great rage. For generations every war against the undead horde was won with a Valerius leading the charge. Other nobles needed enchanted weapons to fight, but every Valerius *was* a lethal weapon against the enemy.

Until the enemy was defeated. The mindless dead remaining were driven into the ravine. Berserkers won Eyam peace, then found they were not made for peace. The dukes pretended the ancient rage had faded down the generations. Except there were . . . incidents. The fires that ravaged their manor. The maidservants seduced, then brutalized. The dead brides. The long night of screams and locked doors, when Marius came home early from military training and left the next day never to return.

Marius had vowed to be the last of his line. In a more civilized time, the brutal old magic didn't belong. Women hid their children from Marius as he passed. The whole world knew his heart was a monster that must be kept chained. At any moment Marius's restraint might crack like the black ice on the Cliffs Cold as Loneliness, unleashing rage more insatiable than any dead thing from the abyss.

And the Cobra taunted Marius without cease. The Cobra wasn't stupid. He was ruinously, wickedly mad.

"Speak the unspeakable," the Cobra urged Marius. "What am I? Do I deserve to die for it?"

"Stop goading him," Lady Rahela warned. "I wish for peace between us, Lord Marius. Beautiful, non-violent peace."

"I'm aware of the definition of peace, madam."

His curtness encouraged the lady to greater heights of impropriety. She rose from the sofa where she was posed like a drawing in an obscene book. "I regret my past. I have seen the light!"

"To what light do you refer?" Marius asked tightly.

Did she mean the chandelier? They could all see the chandelier. It was enormous and ostentatious. The Cobra had terrible taste.

"My lord," Lady Rahela purred. "What I mean is, I hope we can be friends."

The way this criminal eyed Marius made his flesh creep. Her gaze held interest but no engagement, as though she were watching one of the Cobra's plays. Marius raked her with a scathing look, and watched her shiver.

Swiftly the Cobra stepped up, patting Lady Rahela's shoulder as he passed, to act as a shield between them.

The Cobra was deliberately cruel. A peculiar point about him was his cruelty *was* deliberate. He had to concentrate on cruelty, while often committing small thoughtless acts of kindness. Most people behaved in exactly the opposite way. It was as if he'd once been a better man, and some instinct for kindness remained in the ruin.

Marius had long given up on that better man making any meaningful reappearance.

"Don't use the voice, Lady Rahela." The painted skin around Popenjoy's eyes crinkled. "It's scaring him."

The genuine smile was disquieting. Did the Cobra actually like this woman?

Marius felt unwell. He knew the rumours of the king dishonouring

Lady Rahela must be false. Still, Lady Rahela tempted Octavian into thoughtless behaviour. It was hideous to contemplate, but the king and Lady Rahela had definitely had unchaperoned encounters.

Rahela was having an unchaperoned encounter with the Cobra right now.

"I naturally sound like a phone sex operator," Lady Rahela protested. "I've decided to lean in."

She certainly was leaning in! Marius eyed her coldly, and watched her turn snow pale. For once, he was glad to inspire fear.

"Steady now," the Cobra whispered, sweet in Rahela's ear.

"More difficult than you might imagine. These boobs aren't anatomically possible. I keep losing my balance."

Lady Rahela's words were mysterious, but her gaze flicked to her own bosom, clearly inviting the Cobra to have a look too.

Women didn't *scare* Marius. He was revolted by this one, and unaccustomed in general. From his lady mother and his baby sister, he knew women had their own thoughts and feelings, but he had no way to learn what the interior lives of women at court might be. His experience with Lady Rahela's mother hadn't encouraged him to risk trying.

Except he'd had a glimpse into one woman's heart.

Marius's mind travelled back to the evening when he heard her weep. The fire in the library hearth having died away during long hours of studying, he made out a sorrowful voice drifting up from the kitchen chimneys. Lady Lia's voice was a river carrying Marius back to the day he ceased to be a child. Her voice made him imagine his own small sister, needing mercy in a merciless world.

He'd never dreamed sympathy for an unseen girl could lead to such terrible consequences. Blasphemers in revealing gowns were on the loose, and the Cobra was cradling them to his bosom.

Wait. Lady Rahela could barely walk, and she was babbling gibberish in the same way Popenjoy did. Everything was abruptly clear.

They were both drunk.

"Sober up. I'm leaving." Marius turned from the spectacle and towards the door.

The Cobra's voice struck, poisonous as the serpent he was named for. "You're not."

Against gold-and-white doors, Marius's imagination painted a scene of vivid red retribution. It would take three steps to reach the Cobra.

He whirled around.

Whatever was on Marius's face, it made Lady Rahela lift her hands in surrender. She pushed the Cobra away, retreated until the back of her legs hit the conversation sofa, then tumbled gracelessly down. Her expression suggested she might hide behind the sofa.

Marius thought the lady's behaviour was wise.

The Cobra, a clever man who did not know the meaning of wisdom, advanced. "Gonna kill me?"

A hard edge broke the smooth surface of the Cobra's voice. Slowly, it dawned on Marius what that meant.

Unbelievably, the Cobra was angry with him.

"Who do you think you are?" Marius demanded. "You're nothing. I put up my sword seven years ago. I swore a holy oath. You dream I would betray my gods and my honour for a self-serving worm like *you*?"

Even that hardened jade Lady Rahela winced. The Cobra continued being calm, cool, and casually familiar with an unclothed criminal.

The Cobra raised an unforgivably nonchalant eyebrow. "I never imagined you would. But you did say you were tempted."

He'd been tempted many times. He was so tempted now. The Cobra was standing far too close. Marius swallowed hunger down hard, silencing the ravenous call for violence in his blood.

"Cease tormenting me, and be safe."

Popenjoy had the gall to sound shocked. "How did I ever torment you?"

"Let me count the ways! You insist on detestable familiarity by calling me by my first name, when you've never told me yours."

The Cobra's deep voice lilted up in a question. "Do you want to know my name, Marius?"

"Keep *my* name out of your mouth!"

The Cobra's taunt bit cold as chains into flesh. He didn't want to know the Cobra's name. He wanted to hurl in the man's face all the wrongs the Cobra had done him.

"You separate me from my king."

"He's a dick!" Marius was rendered speechless. The Cobra shrugged. "You know what, have fun with that. Be my guest."

Often when courtiers approached the Cobra, he gave them a single evaluating glance before turning away. They were measured and charmingly banished from his attention forever.

Marius refused to be dismissed. "You manipulate everyone according to your whims. You force me to vote for frivolity at the ministers' assemblies."

"Excuse me for supporting the arts!"

"Is that what you call your entanglement with that opera singer?" Marius inquired frostily. "Or that theatre troupe last year!"

The troupe had been an all-women band of players. The prime minister observed actresses were sinners, and the Cobra said, 'Promise?'

From the conversation sofa, Lady Rahela let out a squeak. For all her faults, she was an unmarried lady.

Marius inclined his head. "I apologize for mentioning this in your presence."

"Spill the tea," Lady Rahela mumbled.

Ah yes, she was drunk.

The Cobra's mouth hung open. He resembled a fish someone had painted gold. "You think I slept with an entire theatre troupe? Wow . . . thanks."

Marius asked contemptuously, "What kind of man says, 'Thank you for thinking me even worse than I am'?"

The Cobra made a sweeping gesture, encompassing his whole loathsome form. "This kind of man. To recap. I called you by your name and preserved your illusions about your childhood friend. What else?"

The question seemed genuine, as if the Cobra's many sins had slipped his mind.

"You play with people like toys and break them. I saw you ruin a young nobleman. You stripped him of his entire fortune. He had no way out of dishonour but the noose."

The whole court had rung with shock at the Cobra's cruelty. Even now, Marius saw Lady Rahela jolt.

"I forgot that," she whispered.

The Cobra scoffed. "I *enjoyed* that. If that's my great sin? Give me my sin again."

This falseness was what Marius hated most about him. All laughing warmth on the surface, when beneath he revelled in evil. Lady Rahela was the wickedest woman at court, but she stared as if she too was chilled.

"You left him with nothing."

"He had his life," the Cobra said callously. "He had his freedom. Many don't."

"Like me," snapped Marius. "You never gave me a choice. This is *my* life!"

Lady Rahela rose, clearly bent on escape. The Cobra waved her down.

"You don't seem surprised by any of this," Marius accused. When Lady Rahela's eyes went guiltily wide, he wheeled on the Cobra. "You told a strange woman my secrets after associating with her for five minutes."

"Yikes," murmured Rahela. "I guess there's no other explanation!"

At any moment Marius's shame could be used against him by a woman willing to betray both her gods and her king. He didn't blame Lady Rahela for the Cobra's indiscretion, or her mother's long-ago trickery. Every soul should bear responsibility for their own actions.

This was the Cobra's fault.

The Cobra lived his whole life as a show. He didn't understand that by holding this conversation before a stranger he was wrenching out Marius's insides in the town square. And Marius, who'd made control part of his religion, was too angry to stop.

This was dangerous.

He was dangerous. Marius's heart clenched like a hand around a sword hilt. Every day since he left home, the same silent prayer burst from him. *Deliver me from the monster I might be. Send help, send salvation. Lost gods, find me.*

The Cobra played with fire, as he played with everything. His gaze was downcast, fiddling idly with the embroidery on his sleeves. "Are you thinking about killing me right now?"

Marius broke and lunged for him. Popenjoy's head snapped up, imperious brows raised, eyes clear and fearless, his gaze a command. It was a mockery of the gods that a hollow, corrupt creature could look like this.

Marius breathed, "I think about killing you all the time."

Lady Rahela said sharply, "I should fetch Key."

"The last thing we need in here is another killer!"

A killer. He tried so hard not to be that. Marius did not permit himself to flinch. The Cobra's airy, thoughtless words meant nothing to him.

Rahela demanded of the Cobra, "Can you fight?"

Marius bit out, "The whole court knows he's a craven."

"Arms training? No, I don't require intricate rituals to touch the skin of other men," the Cobra laughed. "I prefer dancing. There's no need to involve the Villain of the Cauldron. I must ask Marius one more thing. He might kill, but he won't lie."

"It's the killing I'm worried about!" hissed Lady Rahela.

Marius said, "You speak as if I am not present."

They discussed him like a dangerous object, a sword on a wall or a prop in a play, as if he were not really there.

The Cobra's gaze swung back to him. Popenjoy's low voice made the crystals of the chandelier chime. "Were we ever friends?"

Six years since they met, and it always came down to this. The Cobra, standing before him with another impossible demand. Marius must pretend he was the Cobra's most intimate friend. That was the bargain.

A soldier had to choose a course of action fast, or men died. "We were never friends. Every minute was a lie. Every minute was a horror."

He felt empty and dizzy with the relief of truth. Finally, the Cobra would stop laughing at him.

"Very well." Popenjoy sighed, set two fingers to the line between his brows, then made a small, dismissive gesture. "Consider yourself released from horror."

Marius, a step away, snarled in the Cobra's face: "I don't believe you! You're always lying. I didn't know *why*! I didn't know what you would ask me to do. I didn't know if you were plotting to destroy my country or my king. You lied, and you laughed, and I watched you deceive everyone. For years."

Marius's honour, dearer than his life, was a toy in those playful hands. A careless word from that always-careless mouth could wreck his lady mother's pride, his young sister's marriage prospects, his own good name. There was only one way to stop him.

Marius spent his life in retreat, but today he took the last step forward. The Cobra's eyes went dark. Truth made the moment golden.

Marius whispered, "You deserve death."

For a man threatened with murder, the Golden Cobra was extremely calm. He glanced at Lady Rahela. "You were right. I'm a villain."

Shock hit like a mailed fist splintering a door. Marius knew that, but he'd never expected Popenjoy to agree.

"I acted as if I was the only real person in the world. That's what a villain is. I'm sorry, Mari—my lord. I'll stop."

It was almost impossible to disbelieve that voice, and utterly impossible to believe this man.

Fury bit hard as a panicked animal. "You blackmail me for years without remorse, but expect me to trust your sudden crisis of conscience?"

"Right," murmured Popenjoy. " . . . Great point."

There was a silence Marius knew from royal assemblies. Occasionally the Cobra fell quiet and contemplative, then disaster followed. Such as the time with the royal treasury, or – lost gods forbid – the countess's fur coat. This was the calm before a golden storm.

If someone had a weapon, you could warn people. Nobody would listen if you yelled, 'Take cover! Don't let him *think!*'

The Cobra waved a finger, conducting the personal orchestra of lunacy inside his skull. "Listen. I'm a self-serving worm of a man, right? There's your answer."

He hadn't realized a trap could be made from words instead of net or steel, until he met the wicked marquis.

Marius shook his head in despair. "How could I possibly trust you?"

The Cobra leaned into Marius's space. A braid fell over his shoulder, foolish ornaments striking with the ring of truth.

"Because I am exactly the villain you think I am. My magnificent selfishness will save us both. Everyone knows I'm a coward. If our association is to end in death, obviously I wish to end that association."

Everybody feared Marius, but the Cobra never had before.

He looked afraid now. It was as disorienting as seeing him angry. Emotion usually skimmed the Cobra's surface like light on water. Now his shoulders were held taut as a bowstring, his eyes burning. Every dark impulse in Marius gathered close as wild beasts drawn to a lone fire in the wilderness.

The Cobra murmured, "Believe in my evil nature with the same unwavering faith you place in your lost gods. In this matter alone, you *can* trust me."

He made frequent gestures, so overflowing with conversation that he needs must talk with his hands as well as his mouth.

The gesture he made now precisely echoed a man on the hunting grounds, releasing a falcon. "Trust my wicked heart, my lord. Go free."

Marius, locked in a silent struggle with rage, didn't move. He had never seen the Cobra retreat before, but now he moved away. Towards that woman. Marius could break her neck easier than snapping his fingers, and take his time with the Cobra.

"I want Key," Lady Rahela whispered. Too soft for anyone but Marius to hear.

The parlour doors burst open. Lady Rahela's maid and guard entered as if responding to the summons they could not possibly have heard.

Servants couldn't stop him. Nothing could stop him.

The Cobra aimed words like a weapon. "Decorum, my lord."

Blood spilled hot down his throat as Marius bit down on his lip and bolted from the room. He'd never been turned out of the Cobra's company before.

He leaned against the Cobra's front door, dragging in desperate lungfuls of blood-tainted air. For years he'd longed for escape. He hadn't expected to feel cast adrift in freedom.

This intense unease must be a sign. Marius was descended from a long line of soldiers for whom knowing the difference between an animal passing by, or an enemy creeping closer, was the difference between life and death. His instincts were sounding the alarm.

Lady Rahela and the Cobra's conspiratorial glances and coded language echoed in his mind insistently as war drums. The combined force of their wickedness could bring down a kingdom.

I am exactly the villain you think I am, the Cobra had said. Marius knew the Cobra was a liar.

Marius must find out what these villains were plotting, and stop them.

CHAPTER TEN

The Villainess, the Heroine and the Competition

All who beheld Lady Lia said she was marked for
greatness. Her willowy body was a song of grace, her
face a poem. Also, her mother was dead. That is a
sure sign.

Time of Iron, ANONYMOUS

ow Rae's plot with the Cobra was set, the next step was
securing an invitation to the ball. She spent several days
practising with the Cobra for the big ballroom scene, and
lying in wait to seize her moment. The ladies' archery tournament
should be a snap. She remembered Alice mentioning it in passing.
The petty competition between court ladies was so uneventful it
hadn't even happened on the page. This was the perfect low-key
setting in which to encounter the heroine.

Rae must smooth over the whole framed-for-treason business with
the upcoming ball's guest of honour. She didn't anticipate problems.
Lia was a pushover.

The Court of Air and Grace was strictly no boys allowed, guards
posted on the battlements over the enclosed courtyard. Rae found
herself startled by how much she missed Key's presence and

reassuring tendency to enact extreme violence on her enemies. Emer stayed at her side, but Emer still hated Rae.

So did everyone else.

Ladies-in-waiting crowded the courtyard, beautiful as flowers with eyes cold as stone. It was like being in a shark tank, if sharks wore fluffy dresses. Some ladies-in-waiting were named in the book, but Rae hadn't memorized the king's side chicks. She did identify the two girls in the lead, since they were identical. Lady Hortensia and Lady Horatia Nemeth had lemon-blond hair and lemon-sour mouths. Rae could only tell them apart because Hortensia, the older twin, was wearing their family's magical gauntlets. Commander General Nemeth's daughters were minor mean-girl characters who tormented Lia because they envied her the king's love. Now they clearly intended to bully Rahela.

Cute. They could try.

"You death-cheating harlot," said Hortensia, in a nasal drawl. "I'm surprised you showed your face. Aren't you, my dear?"

Horatia snickered. "I expected to see her face, my dear. Her head still being attached to her body is the surprise."

"Must we cat-fight, ladies?" purred Rae. Her voice had three settings, 'seductive', 'mocking' and 'mockingly seductive'. None were appropriate. Oh, well.

Hortensia's mouth formed a shape too delicate to be called a frown. Rae believed this expression was a *moue*. "Whenever the worst people fall low, they expect everyone to be better than they were and not kick them. Why should we?"

"You misunderstand," Rae said pleasantly. "If we cat-fight, you will lose. That would be embarrassing for you."

Hortensia waved her gauntleted hand. The murmurous flowerbed of women, in gowns of poppy red and daffodil yellow and lilac ... lilac, parted like a petal-bright sea. At the far wall were archery butts, cloth-bound structures of white sacking and stencilled red circles. Hortensia took aim and fired, magic sending red ripples along her arm. Her arrow struck the third innermost ring.

"Shots fired. Literally," Rae muttered to Emer, who stared straight ahead as though she couldn't hear a thing.

Rae hoped the land of Eyam had poker, because Emer would be so good. Better than Rae was likely to be at archery, but Rae had tied up her hair in a practical ponytail, put on her gauntlets, and was ready for action. Sunlight struck red against the silvery enchanted metal of the gauntlets. It was the borrowed shine of spilled blood. The gauntlets rightfully belonged to Lia, and Lia's was a family of blue blood and great magic. Villainously, Rae hoped the sinister ensorcelled instruments of death she'd stolen would give her an unfair advantage.

The twins waited, bows curved and eyebrows arched, for Rae to fire. The moment was interrupted by the scrape of courtyard doors and a guard's voice. "The Princess Vasilisa!"

This scene had the mean girls, the also-rans, and here came the princess. All they needed was the heroine.

Princess Vasilisa entered, burdened by a dress of blue satin and a gem-encrusted tiara.

"Oh *dear*," Hortensia whispered to Horatia.

Between satin and diamonds was Vasilisa's face. She had dull hair, a leaden complexion, and a blunt jaw. Many pretty women made such features work. Vasilisa wasn't one. The plain fact of the matter was, Vasilisa was plain. As a commoner that would be unremarkable, but she was a princess. Some people's charms were enhanced by elaborate clothes and hairstyles. For Vasilisa, the contrast of a rich frame made her look worse.

Vasilisa gave no sign of hearing the titters that flowed across the courtyard. She inclined her head punctiliously, manners stiff as her dress.

A woman stood on the princess's right, dressed in a tunic and breeches of dark material. She was pale as Vasilisa, with red hair pinned in a braid winding around her head. Unlike Vasilisa, she was pretty.

"A princess's maid wearing breeches?" Horatia asked once introductions were made. "How novel!"

Her tone indicated the maid had been as unwise a choice as the dress.

"This is my guard Karine," said Vasilisa in a level voice. "Are all your guards men? How uncomfortable."

Rae studied Karine with interest, while Karine regarded her suspiciously. Vasilisa would have a flame-haired and a midnight-haired guardian on either side of her throne when she became queen of her own land. She would never be Queen of Eyam, no matter how desperately she loved its king.

Horatia adjusted her grip on her bow. "One likes to feel well protected."

"Indeed. I always do," said Vasilisa.

Rae winced. The princess wasn't endearing herself to the ladies-in-waiting. Vasilisa gave the impression she thought herself above them. As a princess, this was technically true.

Since she'd used Vasilisa's entrance into the narrative for her own ends, Rae felt a vague sense of obligation. She sent a smile Vasilisa's way.

Princess Vasilisa smiled back. "Lady Rahela. I hear you tell the future?"

"Fortune telling, treason," murmured Hortensia. "She's capable of anything."

Rae didn't lose her temper. She deliberately dropped her temper, intending to pick it back up later. "As a lady-in-waiting, it would be treason to entertain another man's suit, wouldn't it? The gods told me a twin was angling to marry the prime minister. Which twin was it?"

The twins paled. She'd better let this drop before someone asked for details. Rae genuinely couldn't remember which twin.

"I don't understand the intricacies of your court," Vasilisa announced. "I thought being a lady-in-waiting was an honour?"

Fluting voices rose in a unanimous choir, assuring her it was.

Rae shrugged. "Everyone *says* it's an honour."

Only heroes cared about honour. Villains were allowed to be practical.

"There's no need to listen to her treacherous whining, Your Highness," interjected one of the mildly evil twins.

Vasilisa's eyes were a muddy shade between brown and grey, notable in fictional surroundings where most people's eye colour was striking. Her gaze was direct. "Explain."

"The odds are against us. One king, more than twenty ladies. Until the king chooses a queen, none of us can marry, and marriage is the purpose of a noblewoman's life. By the time the king chooses, we're considered past our prime. Being honoured by the king should raise our status, but other men wonder how precisely we were honoured by the king. We must preserve our chastity but also please the king, so there's an obvious conflict of interests. The whole set-up encourages vicious competition to the point of some – naming no names, 'cause I'm talking about myself – engaging in actual murderous conspiracies. Yet if the king asks for you, how much choice do you have?"

It wasn't a huge deal. The chances of becoming queen were better than winning the lottery, and people bought lottery tickets every day, but the set-up annoyed Rae. Calling this an honour was false as chivalry. Supposedly men were meant to save women and children first if a boat was going down. Statistically, they didn't. Promises of loyalty and sacrifice were scams. In the end, everybody saved themselves first.

Not even the ladies' skirts rustled in the profound silence. Emer's horror radiated like an open ice chest at her back. With dawning dismay, Rae realized she'd heavily implied she was putting out for the king.

She was saved by the guard intoning: "Announcing Lady Lia."

Of course, the heroine got the dramatic entrance.

Rae clapped. "Look, everybody, Lia is coming. Yay, it's Lia!"

"Are you two close?" asked Vasilisa.

"Not really, I set her up for execution last week."

"Ah," whispered the princess.

The doors opened. Lia entered, backlit by the sun.

For an instant she was only a slender silhouette against a background of soft radiance. Maybe it was the natural course of the sun's path or clouds moving across the sky. Or maybe nature was giving the heroine a narrative spotlight.

When the Pearl of the World crossed the threshold into the Court of Air and Grace, a wind clung as if it loved her. Lia's hair and skirt streamed like the banners above. Lia's plain white cotton dress with its blue trim was simpler than any other gown, but Lia's beauty was a Midas touch transforming the ordinary into treasure.

Lia's beauty fit with her world of palaces and magic. Her eyes were somehow both the blue of crystals and skies. Her rich golden locks turned the twins' hair to bleached straw by contrast. Morality was all about shading: in a kingdom of petty blond antagonists, heroines stayed gold. No touch of cosmetics profaned her face. Why would anyone with natural rosebud lips use make-up?

Rae rolled her eyes, then grinned. Lia looked exactly as Rae had imagined. It was Rae's own reaction that surprised her. The indisputable, overwhelming fact of her beauty was all that was reminiscent of Alice, but Rae missed her sister. Seeing Lia made her smile.

"Apologies for my lateness." Lia's voice melted in the air like a sweet on the tongue. "I'm unfamiliar with the haunts of fine ladies."

Because Rae hadn't invited Lia to palace gatherings, Lia was too nice to say. The twins exchanged meaningful looks that said it for her. Lia seemed even more wronged for not announcing it herself.

Immediately after Lia spoke, bugles blew and banners flew over her head. Probably a coincidence.

Hortensia glanced at the battlements. "Lady Lia, let me tell you the problem we're facing."

In the book the twins vented their spite on Rahela's stepsister. With Rahela still alive, apparently Lia got condescending kindness.

"The winner of the ladies' archery tournament is usually rewarded with the king's hand for a first dance, but of course His Majesty will open our grand ball by dancing with Princess Vasilisa. Or perhaps with you, as you will be officially invited to join the ladies-in-waiting that night." The invitation was a formality. The king had installed Lia in the tower the day he saw her. "What shall we play for instead?"

Lia cast her eyes humbly to the stone flags. "In the countryside, we didn't play for prizes. Instead, the loser pays a forfeit."

Lia hadn't looked at Rae directly, but Rae was certain Lia was aware of her presence.

Hortensia patted Lia's arm, a big-sister move that looked strange since Hortensia was wearing a magic gauntlet. Her expression turned sugary. Rae felt diabetic. "Charming notion. What if the loser must depart the palace?"

If Rae got exiled from the palace, she was doomed.

Rae shrugged. "Why not?"

"As the king's former favourite, Lady Rahela, may I ask you to lead the way?"

"Sure thing, Lady Hortensia."

Rows of women watched as Rae swept forward, wearing the deepest V-for-viper neckline in the courtyard. Each lady-in-waiting wore a smug smile to match her pastel gown. A brunette in violet looked similar to a friend who had once betrayed her. Rae put an extra swagger in her step.

Rae halted, some distance away from the position Hortensia had indicated.

"You're too far away from the target."

"Oh, I don't mind."

"Please, I wouldn't wish for anyone to say the contest was unfair."

Rae pointed to the flagstone ahead. "Just checking. You want me to stand here?"

Hortensia beamed. "Precisely."

"Right on the null stone which would cancel out the enchantment on my gauntlets? Hmm. No."

The tittering died away. The banners sagged.

The twins' plan was foiled, but Rae still had to shoot. Her gauntlets couldn't do all the work. Her chest expanded when drawing her bow. Given her current chest situation, any expansion was alarming. Rae worried she might give herself an unplanned piercing.

As she raised the bow, power raced through her as power had changed the air when she made the blood oath. What transformed now was Rae's body, muscles snapping into position, arms given new might. It wasn't her own strength, but after years of helplessness it was an undeniable thrill. The air tasted clean. Her sight was clear. She was strong.

Rae fired.

Bull's-eye.

Lady Rahela surveyed the disappointed ladies with a smirk. "Mirror, mirror, on the wall, who can make her enemy crawl?"

Once upon a time nobody dared cross her, tease her sister, or disrupt her team. After years of helplessness, the bitch was back.

Rae nodded in Horatia's direction. Only a few lucky ladies were equipped with enchanted gauntlets. Horatia wore lace gloves.

"Come for the queen bee, you best not miss," Rae advised the younger twin. "You can't beat me. Can you beat your sister?"

"Horatia, here!" With a sniff, Lady Hortensia stripped the gauntlets off her own arms. "Borrow these, my dear."

Astonishment followed by joy swept Horatia's colourless face, making her radiantly pretty for an instant. She was visibly determined not to be the one exiled. Her gauntleted hands clenched as she drew her bow, focusing on her target.

"*Horatia,*" wailed her sister's voice, sending a breath of unease down Rae's spine.

Horatia turned with an irritated air. "I am otherwise engaged, my dear. Why do you call me?"

Hortensia was staring at the battlements, her face the colour of frozen milk.

She said slowly, "I didn't call you."

High above, a guard's shadow wavered on the wall, then fell. His descent was a slow tumble, horror making time stretch unfathomably long. When the body landed, it struck an archery butt. The wooden edge stoved the guard's skull in. The target toppled onto its side, a fresh bloodstain splashed vivid across the rings. Rae's arrow was still buried deep in the bull's-eye.

The guard hadn't died from the fall. His heart had been clawed out.

Beyond the wall lay the dread ravine.

His Majesty's ladies-in-waiting lifted their eyes to the battlements, and saw the palace guards overwhelmed by a rising tide of the hungry dead.

CHAPTER ELEVEN

The Villainess, the Heroine and the Horde of the Undead

Ghouls are the unloved dead laid to rest in earth not made
safe by an enchanted stone. Those who died unmourned,
left rotting in ditches or flung into the ravine. No mercy
lives in those dead hearts, but echoes linger in the tomblike
hush of their minds. They listen and parrot what they hear.

A time may come when you are tucked up in your bed,
warm and safe. Outside your locked door on some lonely
midnight, a beloved voice might call your name. You must
never answer, my dear.

Time of Iron, ANONYMOUS

 held breath broke from a dozen lips as the creatures
began crawling down the wall. Withered fingers bur-
rowed into stone, leaving behind viscous stains. Dead
limbs moved in sharp jerks, as if the ghouls were spiders being
continuously electrocuted. The sound of muscles ripping and bones
cracking carried on the rot-thick air. Ghouls no longer knew how
to move their bodies in a way that wouldn't damage them. They
no longer felt pain.

Rae was outraged.

The undead didn't storm the palace until the end of book one. She couldn't believe the story was going off the rails like this!

She wouldn't cower as death came. She'd had enough of that.

"Listen up, y'all! We need to move."

"Why should we listen to you?" Hortensia asked.

"Because I'm a death-cheating harlot. Remember?" Rae winked.

Her words seemed to break the collective trance. A few ladies began to weep, but red-headed Karine sent Rae a sudden, surprisingly sweet smile. Apparently Karine approved of death-cheating harlots.

The princess's guard drew her curved sword and charged at the dead with a battle cry. "A *thousand, thousand years of ice!*"

"Destroy the head!" Rae yelled at Karine's back. "The gods told me."

It sounded better than 'a lot of zombie movies agree on this'. Stories often called the walking dead a different, too-good-to-say-zombies name, but there tended to be overlap in how they acted and how to deal with them. Ghouls would eat and tear flesh. They were dead bodies possessed by the urge for destruction. Close enough.

With one silver sweep Karine struck off the first ghoul's head, then spun and held at the ready. Rae's gaze slipped to the battlements. The dead were swarming the walls like ants covering a pastry left out in the sun. Help wasn't coming.

One girl broke away from the single terrified organism the ladies-in-waiting had become, running for the doors. A ghoul leaped. Clear across the courtyard, Rae heard the crack as dead legs broke on impact. Ghoul and girl fell together in a tangle of limbs and screams.

Rae resolutely ignored the agony-high squealing and wet muffled sounds. None of this was real. She didn't have to care.

She only needed one person to survive this.

Rae found Lia close to the dead-infested wall. Lia was squinting incredulously, standing still as a girl caught in the headlights of a speeding car while the audience screamed at her to move. Before the dramatic moment when the hero swept her away.

Except where was the hero? Where was the second leg of the love triangle? Nowhere, because this was a ladies' only event!

Lia was slender as a willow wand, which made it easy to lift her bodily and shove her behind Rae's back.

Red sparks glinted on links of metal as Rae clenched mailed fists. A ghoul bore down on them. Long lank hair was plastered to its sunken cheeks. It smelled worse than a dead cat left by an open sewer.

Through teeth clicking loose in rotten-fruit gums, the ghoul murmured, "*Rahela ...*"

"Sorry, but the old Rahela can't come to the phone right now." Rae wound up, and punched the ghoul in the face.

Skin and bone collapsed beneath her fist, as if she'd struck a melon already rotted through. Her stolen power launched the creature into the air. The ghoul's body hit the stone wall with a slap like wet laundry.

Lia was finally looking at Rae, eyes wide enough to swallow a whole sky. It wasn't Rae's job to rescue a damsel in distress. She wanted to talk to this story's manager. For now she gripped Lia's bird-boned arm, pulling her towards the terrified flock of ladies.

"Vasilisa's guard can't hold them all back. Those with power must protect the others until help arrives."

Princess Vasilisa advanced. "Gather together! Form barricades!"

Vasilisa wasn't a snappy dresser, but she'd mastered the art of regal command. When she gestured to the archery butts, half the crowd surged forward, then looked startled to find they'd moved. Rae made meaningful eye contact with the ladies still hanging back. In this emergency, they forgot Rae's fall from grace and defaulted to habits of obedience. Women dragged together the canvas-covered wooden structures meant for a game, which might now save their lives.

Ladies' maids were doing most of the dragging.

Not Rae's maid. Rae became aware Emer was no longer behind her when she saw Emer darting into the path of the undead.

Lia made a strangled sound.

Karine made a louder exasperated sound. "Civilians out of the way!"

Emer zipped around Karine as though twisting by a maid with a large tray, then threw herself down by the crumpled form of the dead guard. A ghoul dropped directly onto the body, caving in the ribcage on landing. The ghoul trampled the corpse to red mush as it went for Emer, lips parting on her name.

Emer drew the guard's sword from his scabbard and hacked at the ghoul's calves. When the ghoul toppled sideways, Emer efficiently chopped the blade down on its neck. She rose, wiping blood from her face with her sleeve. The gesture smeared blood across forehead, cheek and chin. Her apron, where she'd knelt in blood, was scarlet.

Nobody but Rae realized they were looking at the future Iron Maid. Still there was a sudden hush.

"Forgive me, my lady." Emer returned sedately to the group carrying her sword. "I wished to arm myself so I might be of help."

Rae lifted an eyebrow. "It's not that you don't trust noblewomen to protect you?"

"I would never say that."

Emer joined the ring of women forming the front line of defence, the rest wearing gauntlets or in one girl's case holding a knife she'd produced from her undergarments. Good thinking. Rae should start carrying concealed.

Princess Vasilisa asked, "Why are so many women not armed with Eyam's magical weapons? Does this land not value its daughters?"

Guys usually got the magic weapons in books, the rightful king drawing a sword from the stone or inheriting the lightsaber.

Horatia said, strained, "Father only lets Hortensia wear the gauntlets because our elder brother refused them, and our baby brother is too young."

Horatia still wore her sister's gauntlets. She was in no shape to fight, slender hands wrapped in enchanted steel trembling too hard to hold a weapon. When a ghoul got past Karine, Horatia flinched back. Rae grasped the ghoul's shoulder in a gauntleted hand, holding it still for the instant Emer needed to hack its head off.

Vasilisa gave Emer an approving glance. "Your family trains their maids in combat?"

Emer seemed taken aback to have attracted the notice of royalty. "The butcher at the Felice estate taught me to use a cleaver."

Rae was so glad she was a villain. Innocent maidens were useless and Rae's evil minion was making her proud.

Karine was fighting three ghouls at once. That left six ghouls on the ground, lunging not for the armed women but the makeshift barricades. Rae winced at the impact of their bodies hurling themselves against the archery butts. The thud of dead flesh and sharp crack of splintering wood bounced off the high walls. The barricades were breaking down.

Rae grabbed Lia. "Stay near me!"

"*Hortensia,*" crooned a ghoul.

Amid the riot came a particular terrible scream. Everyone turned to see Hortensia's lemon-fair head vanish from their midst, a ghoul bearing her to the ground.

Women streamed past Rae, fleeing the breached wreckage of barriers. Only one swam against the tide. Lady Horatia fought her way through and flung herself bodily on the ghoul attacking her sister. Her pink skirt whirled giddily as she rode the undead like a cowboy on a bronco. Keeping her balance with difficulty, Horatia reared up, raised her gauntleted fists and crushed his head between her clenched hands. She shoved the ruined body aside, falling to her knees beside her twin.

"My dear, my dear, speak to me."

Hortensia lay face down in a pool of blood. A sob caught in Horatia's throat as she turned her over, and the light fell on Hortensia's closed eyes.

Then Hortensia blinked.

"I shan't loan you my gauntlets again in a hurry," said Hortensia faintly. Her gaze travelled over Horatia's shoulder, at the smashed heap that had been a ghoul. "On second thoughts, my dear, I suppose it turned out all right."

It was possible Rae had underestimated the maidens.

While Horatia embraced her sister with one arm and smashed another ghoul's skull with the other, Rae scoured the courtyard for dropped bows. Emer stayed a step behind, guarding their backs. When Rae found a second bow, she shoved the weapon into Lia's hands.

A single tear welled in each of Lia's eyes, dewdrops on cornflowers. She accepted the bow in limp hands, managing to fire an arrow directly into the earth. "I can't—"

"Ugh, why are you always like this?"

Lia made a helpless noise. Typical.

"We should try to fight our way to the doors," said Emer.

"The doors will be barred," Lia whispered.

Unexpectedly, Lia was right. A few ghouls did occasionally escape from the ravine. All doors in this land could be barred from the outside or the inside, either to keep the undead out or to keep the threat contained. Seeing ghouls on the battlements, the guards would have followed protocol and barred the doors before joining battle. Judging by the state of the battlements, those guards were now dead.

Rae's eye ticked over the ghouls. "I count less than twenty. Someone will eventually open the doors. We have to live until then."

Their group edged towards the doors. Rae strung another arrow and fired at a ghoul coming at Karine, whose red braids had come loose and poured down her back. She gave Rae a thumbs up, flicked her braids aside and kept fighting. She and her curved sword formed a crimson-and-silver ribbon of protection around her princess.

"*Lia . . .*"

A ghoul on Rae's left lunged. Rae swung wildly, but her gauntlet turned the strike true. The ghoul staggered, but didn't go down.

"*Rahela!*"

It wasn't a ghoul's voice. It was Lia's, raised in a warning that came too late.

Pain bloomed along Rae's arm as a ghoul sank blackened teeth in down to the bone. Darkness flickered like a swinging curtain, but Rae had learned to withstand pain.

She used her free arm to shove Lia in Emer's direction. "Protect her!"

Rae whirled and hit out at the ghoul. Her clumsy blow barely connected. While she was off balance the other ghoul rushed her, and Rae tumbled to the ground with the first ghoul's jaws still clamped on her arm. Unable to break her fall, she landed hard. Rae wrenched a breath from compressed lungs, and punched the second ghoul with the force of desperation. She felt its skull splinter and the creature slump. Suddenly dead weight was pinning her legs.

The first ghoul's teeth were replaced by cold fingers, flesh ragged and worn away so nubs of bone protruded. The dead thing crawled up Rae's body like a vast clammy worm.

Foul breath gusted into Rae's mouth. Kissing close, it whispered, "*Rahela.*"

Fingerbones, sharpened into jagged claws by climbing the walls, pierced her skin like ten needles. Fluids leaked from its eyes like stinking tears. Foul droplets hit Rae's cheek as she clamped her mouth shut.

A banner billowed against the grey clouds. Silver thread gleamed on blue silk, and the embroidered crown caught faraway sunlight. It couldn't end this way, under the weight of death, her last story a scream. She wouldn't die helpless under the flag of a faraway land. She wanted to die fighting.

The thunder in Rae's ears was replaced by the sound of cloth tearing. The ghoul's clawing fingers went slack.

Key's sword pierced right through the body, so the tip of his blade grazed Rae's bodice. He'd snatched the banner and swung from the battlements, stabbing before he landed. The banner ripped, the embroidered crown now rags in Key's hand. He threw the crumpled scrap carelessly aside and reached for Rae.

"Does getting the heart work as well as the head?" Rae asked.

Key rolled both ghouls helpfully off her. "Get the heart, get the head or set them on fire with burning arrows. Life at court is so thrilling."

There were dead girls on the ground whose names Rae had never bothered to learn. Their spilled blood and torn flesh was scattered across the courtyard like cast-off unravelled ribbons.

Rae levered herself up on one elbow, and vomited.

When she looked up, wiping her mouth, Key was watching her. Lia's eyes were summer sky blue, but Key's were skies without sunshine. When troubled, his cold, dark-grey eyes went flat black, from cloud to storm cloud.

He asked, voice uncertain, "Did I not please you?"

She had no idea why he would think that, or what to make of those occasional uncharacteristic moments when he sought reassurance. Rae held up a hand until her urge to be sick again passed. "You did. I'm proud of you, minion."

He nodded, then deliberately positioned himself in front of her, so she had a wall to her back and a killer as her shield. She drew her knees to her chest and put her head down, huddling on the bloodstained ground as the battle raged. Protected by her very own bloodthirsty maniac, Rae snatched a moment of stillness without fear. She felt a gentle tap against her hunched back. It wasn't a hand.

"Did you pat my back with a knife!"

"I'm holding a sword in the other hand," Key explained.

Rae fixed a smile on her face like flying a flag – nobody afraid here! – and lifted her head. This might look real, feel real, even smell real, but it wasn't. This was a story, and she could beat it.

"Sorry. What a mess. The famous Beauty Dipped In Blood, covered in flop sweat. Wait, real ladies aren't supposed to sweat. Covered in flop glow."

A real lady wasn't allowed to be a real person.

Idly stabbing a ghoul, Key asked, "If you shouldn't call it sweat when women sweat, what do you call it when women vomit?"

"Nobody's come up with a dainty word."

Heroines were effortlessly lovely at all times, but Rae had spent whole days lying on a cold bathroom floor with her head in the toilet, vomiting bile. She'd spent years writhing in agony like a hairless, screaming animal. A woman turned into a wicked worm. That didn't happen to heroines. Only villains became withered and twisted, fate making sure their outsides matched their insides. If your suffering was ugly, stories said you deserved it.

Key reached inside his jerkin, producing an embossed silver flask. "Here."

Rae tipped up the flask and coughed when the contents burned. A sharp taste filled her nostrils as well as her mouth, which was a huge relief. "Nice flask."

"Looted it off a corpse on the battlements."

"Course you did."

She rose to find her hand seized. Key pulled her in, dropped to his knees and fastened his mouth over the wound on the inside of her arm. Rae stared at the top of his head. Key's black locks had gone past unruly into rising in rebellion against unjust rule. His mouth was warm.

Chemotherapy was poison intended to kill your disease before it killed you. When poison was injected into your veins it felt cold, as though your blood was filtered through a slushie machine. Iced blood moved sluggishly through your body, pervading the whole system. Nobody had ever tried to save Rae from poison before. She hadn't known she wished someone would.

When Key lifted his head, she missed the warmth.

"Thanks for the rescue," Rae said awkwardly.

Key spat poison onto the gore-slick flagstones, then grinned, white teeth red with her blood. "My pleasure."

"You're so weird." Rae patted his head. "I'm fond and everything, but wow."

Briefly she worried the gesture was condescending, but he tilted his head into her hand and stayed on his knees despite the raging battle, so he must not have minded. Rae petted his wild hair again, encouraging him in a mentoring fashion. The fleeting shade of his lashes hid his eyes. His grin slanted from glee to pleasure.

"Actually, I read sucking poison out of a wound doesn't work. Poison floods the system too fast for sucking to be efficient." Rae paused as an idea occurred. "Does it work here?"

"With ghoul bites? I've done it before. It works if you're fast enough."

Most people, Rae suspected, would find Key's airy tone wildly unsettling. It comforted her. He didn't take anything seriously either.

"Fascinating. Do people die of broken hearts?"

"People die when ghouls eat them. Focus, my lady."

Key palmed a knife from his boot, spinning as he rose. Another ghoul went down with the knife driven to the hilt through its sunken eyeball.

"Cease saying 'my lady' in tones of dark sarcasm."

"These are the only tones I've got. Want to be called something else?"

"'Boss'," Rae decided. "How many knives do you have on your person?"

"I can't do complicated mathematics and kill ghouls at the same time."

That sounded like too many knives. On the other hand, perhaps the socially appropriate number of knives depended on the situation. Key whirled with a fresh knife in hand, and the fresh knife clattered to the stone. In the several days she'd known Key, Rae hadn't seen him make a single clumsy movement. As she stared in alarm, the gold drained from his skin, turning the same ashen shade as his eyes.

Rae pulled Key off the null stone, firing at an incoming ghoul while she tried to figure this out. Was Key magic? Rae recalled several mysterious origin stories, but wasn't sure which was his. Maybe he was a Valerius born out of wedlock. There was one Valerius bastard around, Rae seemed to recollect. All she remembered about that storyline was it didn't end well.

She reached for another arrow. Key was there before her, colour returned to his face. He kissed the arrow lightly with his bloodied lips, then pressed it into her hand, cracked leather glove brushing her palm.

"Thanks for the rescue, boss."

Rae didn't have to fake a smile. Real smiles came easily around Key. "My pleasure."

Across the courtyard, Rae saw Emer and Lia backed into a corner. Emer had Lia behind her. She was swinging against a gang of ghouls.

"Hey, Emer's doing great." Key sounded pleased to spot a familiar face. "Won't be good enough."

"We have to rescue them!"

Key considered this proposition and shook his head. "Nah. Too many ghouls. What a shame, always mourned, never forgotten. Come on, I'll get you over the walls."

The price of the Cobra's help was putting the story right, not getting Lia killed quicker. Rae couldn't shout 'That's the heroine, she's vital to the plot!' Perhaps she should inform Key he was fated to love Lia. Rae studied his cheerfully amoral expression, wondering how he'd take it.

"*Lia* ..." murmured three ghouls in sibilant chorus.

Lia screamed, the first unbeautiful sound Rae had heard her make, high and terrified and young.

"That's my sister!" Rae shouted. "Key, *please.*"

She started forward. Key grasped her elbow above her gauntlet. "For the record? This is stupid."

He exploded into violence. No other word could describe how he jumped into the air over two ghouls' heads, throwing one knife and producing another in a single movement. Landing crouched, he killed two more before he straightened up. A girl in mint-green organdie shoved Rae as she raced by. Rae staggered before she steadied herself. Key grabbed the girl's trailing hair, knotting curls and ribbons around his fist.

She gave a thin cry, half pain, half terror. "The Villain of the Cauldron."

Key swung the maiden by her hair into the path of a monster. "Guilty."

He slew two more ghouls, then used the slippery mess of brains and blood on stone to slide back and stab the last ghoul while it was focused on its kill.

The whirl of knives and blood lasted mere moments. Even the ghouls seemed to hesitate and hang back, shrivelled mouths forming mushy *"muh muh muh"* sounds as if trying to remember how to beg for mercy.

Key held out a hand for Rae in a courtly gesture. Blood pooled in the leather-clad curve of his palm.

"You might want to take off those gloves."

"I never do," Key answered absently.

Rae raced over to herd Emer and Lia out of the corner.

"Thanks for guarding Lia for me," she told Emer, who only lifted an eyebrow, as was Emer's way. Rae nodded towards Vasilisa and her tireless bodyguard. "Let's join up with the princess."

The vipers made their way towards Vasilisa, Rae in the lead.

She realized she shouldn't have taken her eyes off the heroine when she heard Lia give a faint, silvery scream. Rae's heart twisted as she turned. A ghoul leaped for Lia as she slipped in a pool of blood and fell.

The heroine always was adorably clumsy.

Nobody could have moved fast enough to save her. Except Key cut through the air so fast it created a small private wind. His ragged black locks and her golden hair swirled together in the breeze. His knife flew home to the ghoul's heart while his head bent over the helpless beauty. Lia leaned against his chest, a radiant treasure worth saving. Her face was a pearl.

"Thank you," whispered both sisters. Rae doubted Key heard her.

He'd stopped grinning, which was big for Key. Rae felt the relieved smile on her own lips dissolve like sea foam.

She knew how this story went. Moth, meet flame. Compass, meet true north. Cat hair, meet expensive sweater. Some girls were made to be loved.

But Key was a palace guard, he didn't have a chance. Not for romance, since Lia never showed interest in anyone on account of being so pure. Not even for extra page time. Being a minor character infatuated by the heroine was rough.

She remembered her best friend and her newly ex-boyfriend, at her bedside holding hands. Looking at each other, not her, as if she were already gone. Saying they were meant to be together. Rae's friends said they wanted to be neutral, which effectively meant they were neutral about Rae getting hurt. Rae guessed it was natural they wanted to keep the friends they could have fun with, the ones who would live. A girl on Rae's cheerleading team said Rae shouldn't be so angry, as if anger was a sin and not a consequence of mistreatment. Anger apparently made Rae more guilty than those who wronged her. Alice was right: Rae got fooled by costumes. She'd believed because they wore the same uniform, they were on the same team.

"You said hurtful things," her friend announced sadly, ignoring that Rae had been hurt first. "Think how they will feel, when—you're being a little selfish."

Rae answered, "Then I guess I'll die a selfish bitch."

Everyone wanted to be on the side of the winners. If it was the victim's fault, nobody had to defend her. Nobody had to fear horror could happen to them. It was more convenient if the victim deserved her fate.

So Rae would do everyone a favour, and deserve it.

She ignored the ache, as though someone had pressed on a bruise. Other characters were just part of the machinery in a great love story.

Key dropped Lia on the ground.

"*Hey!*" Lia shrieked.

"I need my hands free for stabbing," said Key. "Learn to walk."

Emer helped Lia up. Somehow Lia had avoided falling in the blood puddle. Only a few fetching smudges outlined her perfect features. Rae guessed Lia and Key were going to have a bickering kind of love. Fine with Rae, that meant less pining. Characters turned useless when they were pining.

From outside the barred doors, bugles blew.

"The king!" Lady Hortensia's once-strident voice was thin, but ringing with joy.

Horatia defended her fallen sister, gauntleted fists up. The princess stood safe in the ring of death her bodyguard had made. Ghouls circled and snarled their names, but the king would soon be here.

The Emperor was nigh. Rae's blood sang with prophecy. *He is coming.*

Red-headed Karine grinned. "Ah, his handsome Majesty. Good news."

"What with the king's tower of ladies, and now the undead," muttered Vasilisa, "Perhaps I should have stayed home and married the count."

That startled Rae, but of course a princess would have options. Maybe not any good ones. "Is the count old and hideous?"

"No!" Karine answered. "He's gorgeous."

Rae wondered if this was the count who would be important later.

The princess had armed herself. She waved a piece of wood salvaged from the broken barricades. "The count cares only for battle and brothels. I was hoping this king would be different."

She was holding out for a hero, Rae realized with a pang of fellow feeling. And she'd found one, but that only ended well if you were a heroine.

Karine scolded Vasilisa. "Hide that object before the king sees and thinks I can't protect you. My family will be shamed!"

"Yes, you shamed me so much this day," Vasilisa teased. "So much that when we go home, I'll be buying you drinks for the rest of your life."

Karine laughed. "Don't be stingy, Your Highness. After what I did today, your royal children should buy my children drinks."

Sharing smiles, it didn't matter that Karine was prettier. It never had mattered. While the ladies-in-waiting judged the princess for having an accessory that didn't flatter her, Vasilisa the Wise was walking with her sister.

There came the wood-on-stone scrape of massive doors pushed inward over the flagstones. Rae glimpsed the royal black garments against a background of ministerial blue, dark as a shadow against the sea.

Rae turned to share her joy with Key, then went cold at the sight of his bared blade. She chopped her hand down hard on his wrist. The sword dropped from his nerveless grasp.

Swift as the flick of a whip, Key was on her, driving her up against the wall. "What are you *doing*?"

Rae waved frantically towards the open doors. King Octavian and his party halted on the threshold. The prime minister goggled. The Last Hope loomed at the back of the crowd. And the guard beside Octavian, sworn to slay any who drew a weapon without permission in the royal presence, pointed his crossbow at the princess's bodyguard.

"Watch out!" Rae shouted.

Karine dodged the crossbow bolt and threw her sword. Not at the guard, but at the ghoul lunging for her suddenly undefended princess.

Karine was vulnerable for only an instant.

The instant was too long. A ghoul's mottled, shrunken claw impaled her, bone fingers sharp as knives carving her heart out. A bloody lump tumbled onto the grimy floor. The ghoul, hand shoved through the hollow of Karine's chest, lifted the corpse off its feet.

"*Karine!*" shrilled the dead voice, in what sounded like triumph.

Vasilisa's human howl drowned out the ghoul's. "Karine!"

The story had gone violently wrong once more. Karine should have lived to stand by the Ice Queen's throne, the flame-haired guardian always answering her queen's call.

Her princess was calling, but she could not answer. Her bright head lolled and her limbs flailed, not a girl any more but a ragged puppet made of flesh.

CHAPTER TWELVE

The Cobra and the King

Princess Vasilisa met King Octavianus at the ball. The palace was shimmering, the young king magnificent, and the princess judged not worthy of her welcome. Hearing the whispers, Vasilisa's heart sank. She almost wished her ship had done the same.

Octavian knew his duty. He proclaimed her one of his ladies-in-waiting and his partner for the dance.

Vasilisa loved him at first sight and forever.

Time of Iron, ANONYMOUS

he bar on the courtyard doors did not concern him at first. Doors were barred for many reasons in Eyam. As the bar slid free and the doors opened, Marius braced himself for another social occasion. The royal crest of a silver crown atop snowy peaks would ripple across blue banners, flying over orderly rows of archery butts. A bevy of beauties would compete for the king's attention.

Reality shattered expectations like a fist to a mirror.

The courtyard was crawling with ghouls and strewn with corpses. The archery butts belonged at the bottom of the sea with other wrecks. The flagstones were coated in a thick paste of blood, grime and the dripping fluids of the dead. The foreign princess wielded a blunt instrument, and a maid concealed a blade beneath her apron. Some vandal had torn the royal banner so its rags waved, forlorn as a beggar ghost. A blonde in blood-spattered pink stood over another blonde like a tiger defending her cub. Yet the gaze of Marius's king seemed irresistibly drawn to the worst sight of all: the ice-hearted, treacherous Beauty Dipped In Blood, suddenly become a Beauty Drenched In Blood. Slick gore coated Lady Rahela's arms to the elbows. Not the faintest trace of snow-white remained on her red-stained dress.

Their tense tableau was broken by the roar of General Nemeth, charging through ghouls towards his daughters. He called their names and the battle cry of his house, swinging his double-bitted axe. He left the guards without a leader, and the king without protection.

Marius moved through courtiers as though they were corn and he a scythe, fastening his hand on Octavian's shoulders. "You cannot enter!"

"Indeed, sire," agreed the prime minister, gaze searching for his niece. "You have no heir. Think of the realm."

Someone must lead. Marius wished he had his men here, but Octavian said the force Marius had personally trained were over-disciplined killjoys.

"Send word for Captain Diarmat." Marius pointed at two guards. "Stay and shield your king. The rest, follow me. The ghouls are coming over the walls. Let's cut them off."

He didn't await a response. None would disobey. He set his boot against the bar of the door, grabbed the banner overhead, and swung up onto the battlements. For some unaccountable reason the guards took the narrow flight of steps set into the wall and crowded with the dead. Marius killed two ghouls before they arrived.

Most guards knew to follow, fear, and never question a Valerius. But there was always one raw recruit. He lingered beside Marius, moon-pale and terrified, eyes fixed on the ravening monsters that ringed the battlements.

"M'lord, there is no way—"

Marius shook back his hair in the hot wind blowing from the ravine, scoured the walls for a useful item, and spied a stout chain wrapped around the parapet. He broke the steel chain free from the stone. As he hauled, he felt a weight attached to the chain: what it was attached to, he did not know and for the moment did not care. What Marius needed was the length of steel. Links wrapped around his forearm as he heaved and swung the great metal whip he'd fashioned. The chain struck and caught, hurling the foul undead back into the abyss from whence they came. Marius's blood roared the battle cry of his own house. *Death in my hand, honour in my heart, Valerius!*

Five ghouls down, and the path was cleared.

"Soldier?" Marius gave a cool nod. "I lead the way when there is no way."

The new recruit offered both sword and spear to Marius, as if presenting a lethal bouquet.

"I cannot touch a weapon. I took vows."

No blade, no beloved, no blood spilled by my hands. I am for the words on the page. I am for the goddess. Those were the oaths of the Ivory Tower. Such oaths didn't come naturally to a Valerius.

Marius hoped this recruit wouldn't be overcome by admiration of his battle prowess, following Marius until awe became terror. It was embarrassing when that happened.

Below them, General Nemeth reached his daughters. He dropped his axe to cradle Lady Hortensia to his chest. She was badly wounded, that was clear. The new princess was on her knees clutching one of the many dead.

Lady Rahela stood surrounded by a band of evildoers, untouched.

"Crossbows," ordered Marius. "Cover the general."

He surveyed the carnage of the courtyard. The undead were on the loose. Nobody dared pass this bloody threshold.

Nobody save the Cobra. Lord Popenjoy raced past the royal retinue, the gold-encrusted hem of his cream-coloured herigaut flying behind him like shining wings. He shoved the sovereign of the realm carelessly to one side.

"Popenjoy!" Octavian sounded amazed with indignation. "Do you have something to say to me!"

The Cobra's stride didn't check. "Move."

He couldn't fight, couldn't hope to survive this, but the Cobra prowled onto the battlefield that the Court of Air and Grace had become.

A ghoul charged, slack death-wet mouth fumbling for a name. The Cobra swerved, bending backward almost in half, twisting nimbly out of the creature's grasp as though an attack could be a dance. He caught the ghoul's bone-and-black-rot hands and shoved the creature onto a makeshift spike in the wall from which a banner had flown.

"We're not on first-name terms," he told the undead. His gaze swept the courtyard and found Lady Rahela.

He would have made it to her, if not for his herigaut. A ghoul lay on the ground quiet as a beast in the undergrowth, until it grabbed for the Cobra. Grey fingers closed on his trailing golden hem, and the Cobra was caught.

Marius seized another banner still affixed to the wall, broke the pole against stone, and threw the broken shard like a javelin. The undead monster shuddered and strained, pinned securely as a butterfly on a board.

"Cobra!" Marius roared, pulse bolting like a terrified horse. He was absolutely furious. "Get *out* of there!"

"Mind your business, my lord."

The Cobra didn't spare a glance for Marius or the ghoul that could have killed him. He dashed headlong towards Rahela, reaching to take her in his arms. Rahela's guard tensed for a spring, Rahela flung up a bloodied gauntlet, and the Cobra instantly stepped back.

Thank the lost gods the lady hadn't surrendered all notions of modesty.

"I apologize," said the Cobra, as if he were a gentleman.

"I'm covered in blood," Rahela explained, wrinkling her nose.

The Cobra's tone gentled. "That's all right. If you're all right."

She nodded and let him pull her in, golden arm looped around her naked shoulders. Marius withdrew his thanks to the gods.

"My gosh, are they married?" whispered the new recruit hovering at Marius's elbow.

"They are not *married*, they are *deranged harlots*," snapped Marius.

The recruit's startled gaze swung to him. Marius had not intended to say that out loud. He tore a ghoul's arm off with unnecessary force, kicked the creature in the chest and sent it spinning down into the ravine.

"*Marius*," hissed another dead voice.

Dead hands reached for him, dead maws gaping wide. The recruit cowered behind him as the dead closed in. Marius let the leash on his rage go slack. When his mind cleared, there was blood on his face and no ghouls moved on the battlements. The new recruit cringed away from Marius in terror.

Below came the sound of marching and swords slashing, in formation even against the undead. Captain Diarmat and his men had arrived.

It was unusual for someone of the serving class to attain the rank of captain, but Marius had noticed his dedication to discipline on the training grounds and asked, 'Are you loyal?' Diarmat responded, 'Until death, my lord.' Marius had hand-picked every member of Diarmat's force. They would brook no threat to the king.

The Cobra was safe. Rahela's guard and, oddly, her maid were defending their nest of vipers. Once Diarmat's men swept through the undead, stillness descended on the courtyard.

There was no need for the Cobra to keep hugging the lady of snow and flame. Lady Rahela had made the bone-chillingly scandalous decision to tie her hair up so it bared her neck. Doubtless the Cobra could see her entire nape, as he was whispering in her ear. Marius heightened his senses to catch the words.

"Does this happen in your version?"

"Believe me, if I'd known I would be immured in a trap with the bloodthirsty undead, I wouldn't have attended the ladies' archery tournament!"

Marius didn't know what they were talking about, but he knew embraces on the battlefield were unseemly. Lady Rahela's guard gave the Cobra a venomous look. Marius was glad somebody in their wretched gang observed propriety, though startled it was the low-born thug. The Cobra's keen eyes combed over the chaos, clearly observing something Marius could not.

Marius ordered Diarmat's men to gather the dead, and went along the parapet examining the fallen.

Soon after, he bellowed from the battlements: "Someone has been *looting* these bodies!"

Rahela's treacherous guard tilted his oil-black head, eyes wide with feigned innocence. "Shocking! Who would do such a thing to my fallen comrades?"

He began to whistle. Marius wanted to strike the leer from his face. Outside the courtyard walls, a woman screamed.

Marius's first thought was that ghouls were loose across the palace. He leaped to the edge of the battlements, rushing unchecked by embrasures until he reached the end of the wall over the Court of Air and Grace.

Beyond the courtyard was a garden, flowering bushes and winding paths enclosed by high golden walls. Steps were set in one wall. If you climbed those steps and stood on the broad stone lip of that wall, you saw straight down into the abyss.

At the top of the wall Princess Vasilisa, restrained by palace guards, fought to get free.

"Stop!" Vasilisa screamed. "*I command you!*"

Two guards stood on the stone lip above the ravine, holding a cloth-swathed bundle between them. A braid of red hair slipped free of the sheet, a firefly-small glimpse of colour. The guards heaved the wrapped body over the side. Marius winced at the sound of flesh hitting the jagged sides of the cliff. A hungry murmur issued from the depths below.

The murmur was a roar issuing from a thousand starving dead mouths, a long way down.

The penalty for wielding a sword in the king's presence without permission was to be flung in the ravine. Alive or dead. This was justice.

The foreign princess didn't know that. She fell silent, as abruptly as the body had fallen. Marius made a gesture of command. The guards, realizing they were no longer restraining a hysterical woman but roughly handling a princess, released her.

Princess Vasilisa strode down the steps in the wall, raced down the winding path among the flowers, and slapped the king full in his royal face.

Even the Cobra and his new friends, sauntering from the gore-splattered courtyard as if on a morning stroll, started back.

"Oh damn," the Cobra said under his breath.

The red mark of the slap stood out on Octavian's cheek like a single flaw in a priceless vase. "How dare you," His Majesty said slowly.

The princess had made a bad mistake. Octavian could forgive anything but an injury to his pride.

The princess wasn't done making mistakes yet.

"How dare *you*? Karine wasn't your subject, she was one of my dearest friends. She laid down her life to protect me. Now I cannot even bring back her body for burial. You threw her away like refuse from the streets!"

Octavian's handsome face twisted with fury. "You laid hands on me. That is sacrilege."

His younger ministers murmured agreement. Their voices made Marius recall the distant roar from the starving dead. Prime Minister Pio gave a sharp, alarmed cough.

"May I remind you the princess is our esteemed ambassador from Tagar!"

Several days ago at the cabinet meeting, the older ministers insisted Princess Vasilisa must be admitted to the ranks of ladies-in-waiting despite reports the lady was not fair. The lady's brother was a king with a reputation for cleverness and ruthlessness, whose ice raiders vastly out-numbered Eyam's army. They needed the raiders for allies, not enemies.

It was the first cabinet meeting the Cobra hadn't attended. Apparently he was shut up alone with the Lady Rahela. The servants gossiped about strange noises heard behind closed doors.

Now the Cobra hissed at their king, "Diplomatic relations, have you heard of them?"

Octavian seemed too angry to pay heed. "Our country has stood alone for centuries. Our power protects us. I am king and will bear no insult."

When Marius was young, he believed he could defeat the family curse. His ancestors weren't out-of-control killers. They were generals. He went to train at the Palace on the Edge with a single aim: hoping the future king was someone he could love and trust.

On their first day as pages, Octavian clung sullenly to the walls of the training yard, unwilling to risk disappointing his royal father. Marius found training simple, but talking complicated. Perhaps they would never have been friends except for Lord Lucius of the fox-fire hair and silver tongue. Lucius made everything easy, even conversation. Marius never forgot the moment Octavian's green eyes brightened on understanding Marius was there to serve and not outshine him. After that they were a charmed circle of three. When he completed his training, Marius was determined to make the blood oath and swear to obey his king or die. His murderous fury would be leashed. His dark impulses would have shining purpose. He was a weapon, so he would put himself in safe hands.

Marius never completed his training or made his oath, but he knew Octavian enough to know he was better than this.

He spoke low into Octavian's ear. "You are too good and wise a king to resent the words of a woman wracked by grief."

It was Lucius who knew the art of persuading him, and Lucius was dead. Marius wasn't sure Octavian would listen. Relief warmed him when Octavian turned his way, eyes searching and brightening when he saw Marius's faith. All Octavian needed was someone to believe in him.

"Of course you're right, my old friend."

The king approached Princess Vasilisa, whose fury must have abated a fraction. She watched Octavian warily instead of screaming or slapping him. Her injured hand was cradled against her heaving chest, but when Octavian clasped her wrist, Vasilisa let him draw her fingers to his lips.

"Princess. Accept my apology. I didn't consider newcomers cannot know our customs. From now on, I will personally devote myself to teaching you."

His king's voice was assured and reassuring. His green gaze on Vasilisa dazzled, emeralds held up to catch sunlight. Octavian and Lucius had once competed to woo women. Marius never saw either fail.

The princess forced her back straight. She didn't have charm, but she had training. "Accept my apology for behaving in a manner unfitted to my position."

Octavian nodded. "Let us consider this matter settled."

Princess Vasilisa nodded shortly back, turning away from the king and his ministers to walk away alone.

Octavian scoffed. "Vasilisa the Wise? I'd as soon call her Vasilisa the Beauty."

The ministers laughed. It was well-known Marius had no sense of humour, so he didn't have to. Lady Rahela's gang stood to the side coldly watching, spectators rather than participants.

"Octavian will have to lay it on thick at the ball to win Vasilisa's heart," murmured Rahela. "Lucky he has that pretty face. Women always find the Emperor compelling."

"If you say so." The Cobra sounded distinctly unconvinced.

Why would Rahela want Octavian to charm the princess? Did the plot they were hatching involve the ice raiders?

Marius didn't know. He did notice Octavian's gaze lingering on the Cobra's arm draped across Rahela's shoulders. Octavian had not shown so much interest in Rahela in years.

It was very clever of Lady Rahela. Well. She could leave the Cobra out of her schemes.

"Come here." Marius addressed the Cobra, softly commanding. "I wish to speak with you."

About his apparent desire to feed himself to ghouls, among other things.

The Cobra raised an eyebrow. "Then we are in conflict, Lord Marius. I want nothing further to do with you."

The attention of the entire court swung their way. Nobody had ever heard the Cobra speak to Marius thus. Marius sent the courtiers a glance strongly suggesting they indulge in no curiosity on this topic.

"Found entertainment elsewhere, have you?" Octavian addressed the Cobra, his voice sharpened like a blade upon the whetstone. "I thought you knew all the tattle at court. Have you not heard Lady Rahela is a merciless witch who drags men down into despair and disgrace?"

Octavian spoke out of loyalty to Marius, but if there were any men left in Rahela's family they would have been forced to avenge those words. Marius winced.

The Cobra winked. "Don't threaten me with a good time."

Rahela ignored the king's insult, concentrating on a fair-haired girl with her back to Marius. Smile glittering like shattered glass, Rahela asked, "Since I saved your life, I presume I'll be welcome at the ball in your honour?"

If Marius didn't know better, he would have thought Rahela's indifference to the king was real.

"Is *that* what you hoped to gain by protecting me?"

The girl had a lovely voice. Marius wondered where he had heard it before.

"You talk of balls when people died?" the beautiful voice continued. "You smile?"

Rahela's grin flickered like the wings of a suddenly uncertain moth.

Marius observed, "You are quick to use a disaster for your own ends, Lady Rahela. Perhaps you find this tragedy convenient."

A hum of suspicion rose.

"Everyone blames the wicked stepsister," Rahela grumbled. "Just because I committed many crimes."

"She couldn't have done this. Nobody but the future Emperor can control ghouls," pointed out the Cobra.

That provided Marius with what the Cobra would call his cue. He motioned to the soldiers on the battlements and caught the chain they threw, the chain he'd seized to fight off ghouls. Marius dragged the contraption on the end of the chain over the walls. It landed with a resounding clang on the stone before his king.

His discovery had iron bars. It was a cage on a chain. The cage held a human corpse, mauled past recognition through the bars.

Marius lifted his voice so they could all hear. "Nobody controlled the ghouls. Somebody lowered this cage into the dread ravine, and baited the dead to climb the ravine. Somebody let them loose on a courtyard with barred doors!"

The only sound following his accusation was the echo of ringing steel.

The fair-haired woman with the beautiful voice recoiled from Rahela, stumbled and fell. Octavian swept the lady off her feet and held her cradled to his chest, a picture of chivalry.

"Ah, fairy-tale romance," Rahela muttered. The vixen appeared to be mocking a girl for falling down.

Her guard snickered. "She's useless."

"Do you think I want to be useless?" The girl's whisper was small and lonely as a deserted child. "What choice is there? All my choices were taken away."

Hearing her voice in misery, Marius recognized her at last. This must be Lady Lia. He'd heard the lady was fair and Octavian was infatuated, but all he could see was a blue-edged skirt and tumbled golden hair. Octavian touched that hair with a gently protective hand.

The Cobra made a face at Marius. "You can't catch people? What are those arms even for?"

Marius's soul froze into a stalagmite of outrage. "There is a murderer in the palace using the undead to slaughter women!"

The Cobra rolled his eyes. "I noticed that too. I notice a lot of things. It was just a question, my lord. Don't kill me."

Somebody *would* murder the Cobra one day. He was too aggravating to live.

Prime Minister Pio, staring at the cage from whence the ghouls had climbed, said, "The culprit is obvious. Only one lady-in-waiting has proved she wants her rivals dead."

Even Lady Rahela's brazenness seemed to fail under a dozen condemning stares. The Cobra's arm tightened around her shoulders.

Rahela's purr faltered. "I *saved* Lia."

"So you could get an invitation to the ball," said Octavian. "We heard you."

He drew himself up, facing down the villains with a helpless beauty in his arms, every inch the king Marius had always believed he would become. Confronted with royal judgement, Rahela had nothing to say.

Unfortunately, the Cobra always had something to say. He tipped his head down to whisper in Rahela's ear.

Prime Minister Pio demanded, "Will you not even deny the accusation?"

"Who believes the wicked?" Lady Rahela fired back. She picked up her blood-drenched skirts and left the field to the Cobra.

Who crossed his arms, head not respectfully bowed, in reckless defiance of the king and his court. Something Marius had always known was suddenly clear to the whole court: the Cobra was taller and more strongly built than the king.

Once Marius had criticized the ridiculous volume of the Cobra's sleeves, which would get in the way when reaching for weapons. 'What are they for?' he'd snapped, and the Cobra replied, 'A diversion.' His frivolous costume was intended to deceive the eye. His mask could drop at will.

At the Cobra's challenging look, the strings of shock jerked Octavian's mouth sharply downward. "Lower your gaze, Lord Popenjoy. Or I'll give the coward of the court something to be afraid of."

This appeared to amuse the Cobra. "Give a man an inch, and he thinks he's a ruler. I always considered you beneath my notice, Your Majesty. Leave the lady alone, or I'll start paying attention."

Octavian snarled, "Is that a threat?"

A collective metal whisper sounded as Diarmat's force, to a man, drew steel. Marius shoved the cage aside with a scream of metal on stone, clearing a path to move between the Cobra and his king.

Popenjoy sneered. "From a coward like me? Unimaginable. I've struck up a friendship with Lady Rahela, so I'm concerned. She was trapped in that courtyard as well. Seems far-fetched to suggest she'd plot to get herself killed."

Octavian flushed darkly furious red. "Who could it be, if not Rahela?"

Against the uneasy whispers of the court, the Cobra murmured, "We should all ask ourselves that question."

His meaning was plain. If everybody suspected Rahela, the culprit who had let ghouls loose on the ladies-in-waiting might escape punishment. That nameless villain would be free to kill again.

"Maybe *you* did this," Octavian suggested.

Marius knew the Cobra well enough to see Popenjoy was deliberately drawing attention away from Lady Rahela and towards himself. The result was stark. Marius's chosen leader, and the traitor Marius had called his friend for six years, faced each other like enemies on a battlefield.

The Cobra gave his evil golden laugh. "Maybe I did."

CHAPTER THIRTEEN

The Villainess Approaches the Tomb

"Honour demands I respect my ladies-in-waiting."
The young king's hands remained, as though fastened by
a spell, on the rich curves of her hips. Though her years said
she was a girl, her body promised she was a woman. The red
ribbon lacing Rahela's bodice unwound like a snake uncoiling.
Who can resist the wicked?

Time of Iron, ANONYMOUS

ut, damned spot! Would her hands never be clean? Dried
blood was a bitch to remove from under the nails.
    As a venal and shallow villainess, Rae enjoyed luxurious
baths in a copper tub behind a painted screen. This evening the lukewarm water around her had turned faint pink. The blood was barely
washed away when a summons arrived from His Majesty demanding
Lady Rahela attend him.

No rest for the wicked. No relaxing soaks for the wicked either. No
doubt His Majesty wished to accuse her of murder again.

When she swept in with Key at her back, they found the throne
room empty. The torches on the walls burned low as the sun on the
horizon as they waited. Even the golden floor turned grey.

Octavian finally entered with a ruffled demeanour. "Why did you
come here?"

Rae blinked. "Because of the royal summons?"

"You always come to my chambers when I send for you."

Ah. It seemed the king didn't want to talk about the murder plot. Rae took a deep breath, which might have been a strategic error. Her dress was pulled slightly out of shape by the weight of garnets decorating its hem. The gauzy material at the collar flirted with shadows over her skin. Maybe she should have worn something else, but a high-necked dress would make Rahela's assets obvious in a different way. She wasn't shaped for modesty.

Actually, her modesty wasn't the issue. She hadn't shaped herself.

King Octavian wasn't wearing the crowned mask. He lingered near Rahela so they seemed less monarch and subject, more man and woman. His eyes were warm as sun-drenched grass. His voice was low as a summer breeze. This had the potential to be a highly romantic scene.

Awkward.

"Shall we send your guard away?"

"No," Rae said, too quickly.

Palace customs hit differently now they applied to her. Nobody could disobey a royal command. If Octavian dismissed Key, Key would have to leave her.

Alone. With a man who must be obeyed.

With a man expecting a lady who knew what she was doing in bed.

Through the hexagon window above the winged throne, Rae saw threads of smoke rise to veil the broken moon and the nearly lost sun. The horizon burned above the ravine. One day Octavian's eyes would turn red as the setting sun, and his crowned silhouette would be painted across blood-coloured clouds. He already had the power of life or death over her.

Rae hadn't realized she'd moved back, until she felt Key's warmth. She glanced around and their gazes caught. He looked startled, as though nobody had ever before considered him a safe harbour.

She wrenched her attention back to Octavian and found him nodding acceptance of Rae's refusal. Rae told her sprinting heart to stop outracing her mind. She *knew* the Emperor. He treated Lia as a holy statue he barely dared touch. Getting laid didn't matter that much to

Octavian. He wanted someone to care for him. The Emperor didn't target anybody who hadn't come at him first. He was a predator, but he didn't prey on the helpless.

Rae remembered how much she would like this guy and found herself smiling. Octavian drifted closer, as though her smile was a magnet.

Her heart had broken over the insatiable loneliness of the Emperor on his throne, master of the dark sky and burning abyss. Perhaps Octavian had cared about the ladies-in-waiting who died, and sought consolation. Reading the books, she'd thought the Emperor must be the loneliest man alive. She would have given a lot for the chance to comfort him.

"Hey," Rae said brightly. "Why don't we talk about murder?"

At her back, Key stifled a laugh. Octavian seemed able to dismiss Key's existence from his mind.

"Very well," the king indulged. "I was wondering if there was something you wanted to tell me. You can tell the future, yet you walked into a trap filled with ghouls? A suspicious man might believe you feigned a prophecy to get out of trouble."

The Emperor always was quick on the uptake. Rae liked that, though she found it currently inconvenient. Octavian held out a hand. He wasn't wearing the clawed gauntlets Rae knew he hated to take off, and his bare open palm seemed an invitation. Octavian's eyes danced like emeralds swinging from an ear in sparkling arcs. He didn't look mad Rae had lied. Rae could confess she wasn't really a prophet.

She'd be expected to be the king's girlfriend again.

Maybe that wouldn't be so bad. Books often described kisses as 'searing' which made Rae think of salmon, but characters seemed to enjoy the seared-salmon kisses. She could get the experience she'd missed her chance on. In a book, orgasms seemed far more certain than in reality. Rae could use the practice for when she got better, and went girl gone wild in college. This wasn't really her body: it wouldn't really count. Octavian was impossibly, fictionally handsome, and after some character development he would be her biggest book crush. Rae's choices were: Keep up the blasphemous deceit, or go to bed with the world's most gorgeous and powerful man.

The snake bracelet rattled as she lifted her hand. Then she clenched her fist.

"I can absolutely tell the future," Rae lied. "But the future can change in small unpredictable ways, as with today's attack. Only the great moments are fixed and certain. Such as your future glory as the Emperor."

Judging by what the Cobra said, the big building blocks of the story would stay the same. The Last Hope and the Emperor always fell for Lia. The Emperor always ascended to greatness. The heroine got love, the hero got power, the villains got it in the neck.

The mention of his destiny made Octavian brighten. Rae fluttered her eyelashes encouragingly.

It's all about you, baby! Rae projected. *Emperor baby.*

"The attack on the Court of Air and Grace didn't happen in the future I saw. Someone might want to kill me so I won't be able to help you," she added, inspired. "They don't realize nothing can stop you."

The king's voice went low as a limbo dancer. "You really believe in me."

"I do. And I believe in your love for my sister."

At the mention of the heroine Octavian's expression turned awed. "Lady Lia has the purest heart in the palace."

Other women only existed to lose against the heroine.

Rae's lip stung beneath her own teeth. "Nothing pure about me. I'll get going."

If she'd slept with her old boyfriend, Rae would've expected him to respect her in the morning and every morning after. It was true Lia wouldn't offer the kind of comfort the king expected from Rahela, but being a teenage virgin wouldn't last, not for Lia or anyone else. Somehow Octavian considered Rae stained but not himself, filth only sticking to her, but men weren't rubber and women weren't glue. If worth had an expiry date, it wasn't worth much.

The king stared in bewilderment. Rae could be a modern woman all she wanted, but she couldn't expect Octavian to understand her point of view. Perhaps he only meant Lia was good. Rae couldn't be good. She might not have the experience Octavian believed, but she had experienced horror that sank deeper than bones and stained the soul. Nobody stayed pure.

Octavian caught Rae's hand, which wasn't the body part she was currently concerned about. "Let me help you understand. The Room of Memory and Bone awaits."

"Sure, we can go to the Bone Room. I mean! What you called it, absolutely."

As they passed through the golden doors down the dark passageway to the room pale as loss, Rae was uneasily aware of the hand clasping hers. The press of skin felt so solid and real it was terrifying. The king was strong enough to pin her down, and his superior strength was the least of his power over her. Rae's mind knew this character, knew he wouldn't lash out like that, but this body kept betraying her. A chill eddy of fear snaked through her blood at the thought of how much worse this would get. *He is coming for his throne.* When the Emperor rose crowned in the shadows of death, he would command clouds and crush stars.

Her cold feet dragged until she felt a single point of warmth, brief as a match strike. Key reached out and tapped his smallest finger against hers, in the most sneaky high five imaginable.

Rae stole a glance over her shoulder and smiled.

"Hang back, guard," Octavian ordered.

Key looked to Rae.

Octavian's voice, which would become the Emperor's hoarse growl of command, dropped like a guillotine. "Disobeying your king will earn you an hour in the Room of Dread and Anticipation."

"Go!" Rae snapped.

Key withdrew into shadows.

The Room of Memory and Bone by moonlight was radiant, reflecting white on white as though the moon was trapped in a funhouse of mirrors. The little child skeleton grinned his ceaseless grin from the wall. The marble throne carved for a long dead queen gleamed. The traces of decay, sunk into the stone from where royal bodies had rotted, became shadow stains by moonlight. One day the queen's throne would be dragged into the throne room. The Emperor would put Lia's body in it and make the courtiers who betrayed her kiss her feet. His power would preserve her beauty, heroines were always beautiful in death. And still dead, despite all their beauty. Rae wrenched her gaze from the seat for the dead, but couldn't avoid her knowledge of what was to come. The throne waited, cold and inescapable as the future.

King Octavian brushed his hair back from his high and noble brow, sighing with eyes full of moonglow. "This room is a graveyard. When I cannot find time to visit my parents' tomb, I come here to remember my ancestors. I shouldn't have doubted your powers. Only one other person knows the secret of what happened at my parents' tomb, and he is dead. Now you know my secret, too. But do you know how I felt?"

Oh no! Rae didn't actually know the secret. She did recall Alice mentioning the Emperor had recounted his past to Lia in a graveyard. Definitely parents and blood were involved. Rae licked her lips, feeling out of place. Villainesses weren't equipped for tender confessions. How to tell a guy she'd skipped his tragic backstory?

"Tell me about your feelings," Rae encouraged. "Don't skimp on the details."

Drop the tragic backstory, not the pants!

"As a boy I had every luxury, but I was lonely. Until I began my page training, and met Lucius and Marius. My mother the queen couldn't bear another child, and my father always let me know I wasn't enough."

Like so many heroes, the Emperor had daddy issues.

Rae nodded wisely. "Except your mother the queen didn't bear you, either. You were born of the gods. The king pushed you too hard because he knew of your great destiny."

The look Octavian gave her was uncertain and a little heartbreaking. Her claims to be a prophet weren't working because Rae was a good liar. They worked because the king badly wished to believe.

"My father wanted a son like Marius, of unimpeachable birth and unassailable honour. Everyone preferred Marius. Even though he never touched a woman, women always looked at him first." Octavian's lips twisted. "Until I was king. Yet he and Lucius were my only friends. I believed we would never be parted. Then Marius spent a night at his father's house and sent word he was bound to the Ivory Tower."

People who journeyed to the Cliffs of Ice and Loneliness were not expected to return. Octavian's voice was slightly raspy with emotion. Rae remembered the Emperor's crow-hoarse voice grew ever harsher when he felt deeply. She laid a hand on Octavian's sleeve.

His mouth curved in a beautifully sad smile. "Marius was always a restraining influence. Lucius and I went wild after he left. My royal parents cut off our funds. I thought they were being harsh. I believed Lucius was my most loyal friend. He stayed by my side when my parents were killed in the carriage accident. He went with me to visit the tomb."

A grave in Eyam was laid with an enchanted marker called a touchstone, to stop the dead from rising. In the case of ordinary people, it was a single stone like a gravestone. In the case of the royal family, it was the cornerstone of a great tomb. *The blood on the stone of the tomb*, the Oracle would say one day. Octavian must have spilled blood on the stone, and sworn vengeance.

Wait, had Octavian sworn vengeance against a lousy carriage driver? Also, should he be dropping tragic backstory to someone who wasn't his true love?

Rae guessed he could let Lia know later. She fixed an expression of extreme interest on her face, as if at a party with a college guy telling her about film studies.

"Lucius told me he'd arranged my parents' death. Now I was king, he said. Now I could do whatever I wanted. So I cut his throat, and his blood spilled on my parents' touchstone. I tossed Lucius's body into the ravine. I told everybody I sent him on a mission, and he perished. But you know this, don't you?" Octavian's gaze searched hers.

Rae nodded, transformed by panic into a bobblehead doll.

"This is no way news to me!"

The Emperor seldom killed those he cared for, and never without reason, but what better reason could there be? His best friend had betrayed him. Rae knew how that felt. When she felt most alone, she would read through furious vindicated tears of the Emperor taking revenge. She burned secretly at injustice. He burned down the world.

Octavian's eyes shone silver over green, frost covering grass. "You know everything, and believe I will become Emperor."

He leaned down, lips a breath away from brushing hers. She would be the only person in the universe ever to be kissed by her fictional crush. She should do it for everybody who would never kiss the pirate, the goblin king or the girl in the gold bikini.

At the last possible instant, she turned her face away. "I can't."

"You can't?"

It seemed guys didn't like being prophet-zoned.

On Lia and the Emperor's wedding night, Lia trembled with fear. The Emperor lay down beside her.

"I gave you my word," Lia whispered.

"You gave me your hand. I can't repay you for that gift," the Emperor told her. "Stay with me. Never leave me. This is all I want."

Lying on her stomach, swinging socked feet over the side of her bed, Rae told the page, "Aw, *love him.*"

When it was Rahela, the Emperor felt differently. An anti-hero devoted to a special woman sounded great, until you were one of the less special women.

She couldn't really blame Octavian for expecting her to run back to his arms. Even where Rae came from, boys said 'she's easy' as if girls could be disqualified as complicated human beings. Rae recalled a flashback about the king and Rahela's first night together. Reading it, she'd frowned at the weaselly passive language. 'The red ribbon lacing Rahela's bodice unwound.' If Rahela had unlaced it herself, the text would've said so. The ribbon hadn't magically unlaced itself, so surely the king did it. That sounded like the excuses her ex made when he moved on without telling her first. Gosh, it just *happened.* The hero and heroine were fated.

Or fate was something people claimed when they didn't want to take responsibility for their actions.

By the time Rae remembered these were fictional characters who actually were fated, it was too late. Octavian saw the scorn on her face.

The king's voice twisted like a vengeful knife. "Since you're so dedicated to the gods, my prophet, I won't insult you by inviting you to a ball."

The vulnerability he'd shown by soft moonlight closed off like the drawbridge of a castle. Rae knew how lonely he was. She'd handled this wrong. Once someone felt abandoned, they stopped reaching out. Lashing out was all they had left.

She should go to his arms. A heroine received gifts, but a villainess must make bargains. She needed to go to the ball, needed the key and the flower. If she gave Octavian what he wanted, she could have what she required.

She had to do it.

Somehow, she couldn't.

Lady Rahela curtsied, dark-red skirt blooming on the white marble. "How well you know me, Your Majesty." She tilted one poisonous glance upward. "Or do you?"

She stormed from the Room of Memory and Bone. Key fell into step with her storm.

"It seems the wicked stepsister shall not go to the ball."

"I heard."

Rae's stalk was halted by alarm. "You heard the king admit to killing someone?"

This was how secrets got out, and people got executed!

"One person," Key scoffed. "Amateur."

It became ever more clear Key was a terrifying murderer, but Rae found his atrocities endearing. He'd stayed close enough to listen, despite the threat of a king.

Having dismissed a royal murder as tedious, Key studied her. "You could go to the ball if you took the king to bed. Why didn't you?"

Why hadn't she done what everyone expected? Even Key.

Rae sighed. "Why is it if a woman says yes to sex once, she's meant to be up for it anytime? Nobody believes saying 'I'd like spaghetti for dinner' means 'I want to live under an eternal rain of spaghetti.' Everyone pretends this is a confusing issue because they want women to keep putting out."

Odd to think if she slept with Octavian to get something, people would count that as her sin, not his. Nobody would condemn the king for taking what a woman only offered because she was desperate. The king couldn't be ruined.

Key's gaze was thoughtful. "I meant you . . . love him, don't you?"

She loved who he would become. Rae remembered the Emperor on his desolate throne beneath a sunless sky, and nodded.

She saw Key believed it. That helped her believe too.

"You wanted to see him so much, that first time in the throne room. You plotted to be his queen." Key's voice was soft. "You still have a chance. He hasn't forgotten what you insinuated on the steps of the throne. That you were pretending to want him. He'll try and prove you're a liar."

Rae scoffed. "I guess guys don't care if a girl's faking it, until she stops faking it for them. I *am* a liar."

It was the truest thing she'd said since she came to Eyam.

"So why not lie to him again?"

He sounded curious, not condemning, but Rae resented the question. Lady Rahela's ruby lips were made for cruel smiles and scorn. Rae sneered. "Will you tell me why you were called the Villain of the Cauldron? Why you never take off those gloves?" She nodded towards Key's hands, which clenched as though her mocking gesture was an invitation to combat. "I never asked for your tragic backstory."

If any eyebrows could make demands, Key's did. "What's a backstory?"

"The story behind a story. The shadow that trails behind a character to tell you why they are who they are. The story that makes them feel real. You're not real with me. I won't be real with you. We're villains. We don't have to know or trust each other. We just use each other for our wicked schemes."

Key leaned in, as the king had in the Room of Memory and Bone. His face made Rae think of the king's, not because they were alike but because they were a contrast. Octavian was illuminated by a steady moonbeam, while Key stood in shifting shadows. Octavian was handsome as a prince in a painting, as a young girl's unchanging dream. Key was beautiful like swift lethal movement, and a knife in the dark.

"What's the new scheme, boss?"

They had made a bargain. He was her knife in the dark now.

Calm returned to Rae's heart, so her mind could return to plotting.

Evil stepsisters didn't get sent to the ball. Evil stepsisters were doing it for themselves.

In the end, the answer was simple. Through tall windows, the moon crashed merrily into the clouds. Darkness swallowed the sky, and Rae smiled a red-lipped smile.

"Listen up, minion. Here's my evil scheme."

The second step of the plan was getting out of the palace. A secret passage led out of the palace hidden in the Room of Memory and Bone, but the king was still there.

The first step was costuming. The red velvet of her cloak swayed like a curtain on a stage. Rae arranged its folds to hide the bag containing her gauntlets, and flipped the hood to conceal her face. Key grinned, wolfish. He offered his arm, and they went into the kitchens, heading for the gates through which produce was delivered. Guards were often ordered to usher certain visitors via the kitchens late at night.

The royal kitchens had low stone ceilings, the floor slate instead of elaborate mosaics. A skinny girl stood at an open fire, turning a pig on a spit. Someone had made the unusual culinary decision to put a chicken's head where the pig's head should be. The kitchen was so warm Rae feared she would stifle in the velvet cloak.

"Make way, lady of the night coming through!" Key shouted.

Many turned to stare. Rae waved. "Nothing to see here. Just a regular harlot from the Golden Brothel."

A man chopping vegetables snorted. "Every soiled dove claims to be from the Golden Brothel."

A woman rolling pastry sniffed in collaboration with the snort. "Every guard knows the ladies of the night should be escorted *discreetly.*"

"Hush! That's the Villain of the Cauldron." Her assistant drew a finger along his own throat while making an illustrative guttural noise.

"Not actually what throat-cutting sounds like," contributed Key. The kitchen went horribly quiet.

Rae felt they might be unsuited to secret missions.

They passed the horror-struck crowd, through the wrought-iron gates curling on top to form the shapes of the royal crest. Key ducked into the nearest alley and started to take his clothes off.

Rae whipped around so her back was to the alley. "What's happening here?"

"Can't be seen wearing a palace uniform. My throat would be cut. Worse, my reputation would be ruined."

"I see."

"I have getaway stashes in a few different places," Key elaborated. "The Cobra told me he has a getaway bag too."

Rae stole a glance over her shoulder to see the line of Key's back. He was bare to the waist, bar his leather gloves. Moonlight poured silver on the flat of his stomach, over smooth skin and ridged muscle, liquid illumination halted by the shadowed indentation at his hip. His waist tapered to a belt, hanging low under the weight of many knives.

"Do you work out?"

"What does work out mean?"

Sure. She'd seen superhero movies. Those people had no time to work out. Fiction simply had abs. Marvellous, inexplicable abs.

"Do you lift?"

He tossed a smile gone sly over his bare shoulder. "Knives. Spoons to my mouth. A woman, once."

The too-sharp hook of his smile set low in her belly, and twisted. A memory returned to her, less thought and more the echo of sensation: how he'd carried her over the pool of blood to the throne room.

Key emerged from the alley, wearing clinging black and grey. A supple leather collar glinted around his throat. His hair was even more askew than usual, as though fashioned by a rakish hurricane.

Key gestured to her dripping rubies. "Want to give me an earring? So people know I'm yours."

Since jewellery was illegal, men wore jewellery in the Cauldron as a signal between fellow outlaws. Hence the studded collar. Rae unfastened an earring, gave it a kiss for luck, and tossed it his way. The ruby flashed with Key's grin.

"Probably won't return this."

That lovable relentlessly mercenary scamp. Avarice was beneath main characters, who always mysteriously ended up with piles of the filthy lucre they disdained. Greed was such a reassuringly unheroic detail, placing Key firmly among the minor villains with her.

The backdrop of the city rather than the palace made her feel as though they were changing scenes. Rae wasn't sure which role she should play. She reached for Key, the way she'd wanted to when Octavian touched her. This time the king wasn't there to stop it. Their hands brushed, a continuous point of awareness as the streets went strangling-narrow, houses leaning in as if to make threats. A shutter above them flew open.

"Gardyloo!" called a woman, flinging the contents of a pot out into the street.

Rae veered sharply to the other side of the street. Key seemed amused, head tilted towards hers, choppy ends of his hair flying in the night air. Hair always disarranged and eyes always deranged, and always laughing at the world.

She called, "These are the mean streets you come from?"

He shook his head. "I'm from the wicked alleys off the mean streets. This isn't even the Cauldron yet."

The palace was crowded, but Rae could identify people by their costumes: ministers and soldiers in regalia, noble ladies in gowns of butterfly hues, servants in uniform. These men and women wore material Rae wanted to call *homespun*, until she remembered everything here was homespun. Still, the word 'homespun' evoked a certain look. So many ordinary people lived in Themesvar. When the wars came and the Emperor rose, they would die.

Rae shivered, moving closer to Key.

They passed through a more prosperous neighbourhood, taking a side street onto the Chain of Commerce. The broad path was bright with painted storefronts and squares centred around the official guild houses where merchants conducted their business. Each square had religious frescoes painted on the walls. The gods wore different aspects in every picture, except the great god was always pale and the great goddess never was, he wore silver and she gold, and he always looked away and she never did. Each wall told a different phase of an old story. The great god and the great goddess on their wedding day, blossoms in their hair. The god and the goddess with their small god-child. The wall that was all red.

Rae nodded at the fresco. "Do you know the legend of how Eyam was created?"

Key's sing-song voice fell into a nursery cadence, as though somebody had told him bedtime stories once.

"When the world was young, people believed and gods were born. The great god and the great goddess loved their people and each other. From that love was born the god-child. Their world and happiness seemed complete. But the great god resented having power given to him by belief. He wanted power all his own, and power is gained through sacrifice. So one day he took the god-child and slaughtered him. The great goddess climbed the mountain of truth, and found him with blood dripping fresh from his hands. He said, 'Now I can live without love and belief.' She said, 'Live without mine.' He begged her to understand. 'I sacrificed. Now I have the power to change the world.' She carved out his eyes and responded, 'The sacrifice was not yours. You are not worthy to look on the world you stole from our son. I would have loved you until the last sunrise, but if I see you again I will slay you where you stand.' The great goddess, our kindly mother, departed into darkness. The great god, who wished independence of every living thing, tried to live without love. He could not. Bitterly weeping, calling her name to the stars, the great god went in search of his lost one.

"As the gods departed the world, the god-child's blood fell on the soil and changed the land where it fell. The divine blood's terrible power ripped a wound in the earth that is now our ravine. Once this land connected to a continent, but we were torn away, we were set apart. Eyam is the land like no other. Here, the dead rise, the flower blooms, our weapons drink blood and our children are born hungry. Other countries feared and craved our power. Eyam was caught in a war between the dead and the living. We prayed, and the lost gods answered. The great god sent the First Duke, the warrior who could not be conquered. The Duke chose our king and banished strangers from our shores. The great goddess sent the Oracle, the voice of the goddess who lives in the mountains cold as truth. The Oracle gave us the prophecy. Kings of Eyam wear the crowned mask, for the throne is not theirs to keep. One day the songs will be truth, the sky will be fire, and the god-child will rise again. Our Emperor. *He is coming.* We must have faith, for we have nothing else. Our gods are lost, and the child is dead."

That was the legend of creation, born from destruction. The tale of belief and sacrifice was true as far as it went, but nobody knew the First Duke and the great god were one and the same. The god had grown lonely, returned, took a new bride and set up the whole kingdom as an elaborate stage for his son's return. People preferred to believe in a distant god, and love that would search among the stars forever.

Rae kept her voice neutral. "Do you believe?"

Key nodded to the wall drenched with red paint more vivid than blood, dripping from guilty hands. He laughed. "I've killed enough to know the dead don't return. Stories don't come true, and there are no gods."

The street narrowed and didn't open back up. The smell grew worse, the gutters choked with refuse and buzzing flies. Peasants called gong farmers were paid to clear the streets of waste. It seemed the gong farmers hadn't visited recently.

Rae pointed out, "The dead do return. Remember battling the undead? I personally found it hard to forget."

"They don't come back to life," Key argued. "They're furious and starving for life. The god-child would be no different. If there ever was a god-child, which there was not. People make up stories so they can pretend they have answers. Nobody ever does."

"They have a child's skeleton in the Room of Memory and Bone."

Key shrugged. "There's no shortage of skeletons. People are always leaving them behind. If the Emperor of prophecy ever *did* crawl out of the ravine as the unforgiving ruler of the hungry dead, what a warped corpse god he would be. Lucky he's not coming."

Except Rae knew better. Octavian would descend and rise again, but by the time the Emperor came Rae would be gone. Key might be dead already. She kept wracking her brains to recall what happened next for the guard, and grew more and more convinced he didn't make it out of the first book alive. If Key was in the books she'd actually read, she would remember him.

If Lia and Lord Marius could be saved, she wanted to rescue Key as well. Saving him couldn't affect the story. It would only be a little change.

The street opened one last time into a blackened square. There were no more frescoes. The walls had crumbled to cinders. Even the flagstones were cracked and blasted by heat, bright shards embedded deep in broken stone. On the far side of the square stood the remnants of a grand timber-framed building. It was the charred skeleton of a house, blackened lines like hollowed-out limbs that would collapse into ash at a touch.

"What happened *here*?"

"The glassblowers' guild was set on fire."

Soft enough to not disturb the ash, Rae asked, "Did the fire kill many people?"

"The fire didn't kill anybody." Key directed her attention to a narrow street snaking from the blackened square. "This guild was built close to the Cauldron, so they could get cheap labour. The tavern you want is down in the Cauldron, on Lockpick Street."

Most storefront signs here were illustrations without words. On Lockpick Street, buildings so close together the street must always be shadowed grey, hung a sign showing wheels and dead flowers, interwoven with flowing script that read Life in Crisis.

This was the place the Cobra said Forge Strike frequented. Forge Strike, the blacksmith who would cut the king's key after they stole it.

First Rae needed an invitation to the ball.

She headed for the street and the sign. To her astonishment, Key held her back.

"The Cauldron is a liberty, boss. Do you understand what that means?"

"A place where people are free?"

Sounded good to Rae.

"A place where people are free to kill, rob and rape, without the prosecution of the law. You can commit any crime in the liberties, if you're strong enough to bear the consequences. Life in the Cauldron is dangerous. And you're worth a lot to me."

Rae winked. "I know, my weight in gold."

He winked back. "Keep eating big breakfasts," Key urged. "And be careful."

"Trust me. I'm an ice-cold schemer."

She bounded up the broad step under the sign of wheels and crushed flowers. Flame flared from the guttering torch by the door. The doorknocker on the Life in Crisis tavern was a twisted brass face, half weeping boy and half laughing man. Rae raised the knocker and rapped urgently.

A gentleman with a scowl and bright blue facial tattoos poked his head around the door. His face paled under the tattoos. "You're banned."

Rae did her best purr. "Don't break my heart."

"Not you. The Villain!" The doorman shook his head. "No arsonists. The boss is clear on this."

Rae glanced at Key, startled. "Are you an arsonist?"

He was leaning against the wall across the narrow street. He fit in here as he didn't in the palace, the Villain restored to his Cauldron. Brick at his back and shadows across his eyes, Key looked like an illustration of a crime in process.

"I don't make a habit of arson. It was one time." The notorious Villain of the Cauldron added primly, "I don't want to go in. My father said this was a den of sin."

"You had a father?"

Key was so clearly not the product of a happy families situation.

As if he could read her mind, his smile turned ugly. "It didn't end well."

She'd promised she wouldn't ask.

Rae turned back to the doorman, resuming her coquettish air. "We don't need to come in. Just tell me, is Forge Strike here? We were having a raving love affair last year. I wish to pick up where we left off!"

Most of Rae's face was shadowed by the hood, but she let her scarlet lips curl.

"Ah." The man's scowl cleared. "Lucky Strike. She's at the Night Market tonight, selling trinkets at the Death Day festival. Try there."

She? Served Rae right for blacksmith stereotyping.

Rae turned her throaty purr thrilling. "Thank you unkindly!"

The man hesitated before shutting the tavern door. "I understand hiring protection in this place, my lady, but I must warn you. Of all the horrors lurking in the Cauldron, the Villain is the worst."

The man's whisper was cold as the breeze making the torchlight flicker. Rae looked in the direction the wind was blowing, towards Key. His shadowed expression reminded her how he'd looked outside the throne room, and in the Court of Air and Grace. He was always waiting for her to turn away.

Rae reached out. "I'm a fan of horror stories."

As the tavern door slammed, Key slunk out of the shadows towards her, readily as a wild creature who had learned which was the hand that fed him. They headed for the Night Market together.

CHAPTER FOURTEEN

The Villainess on a Mission of Seduction

Lia was dying to meet her new mother and sister, starving for family and love. Hope is dangerous. When you run to an embrace, beware a knife in the back.

Time of Iron, ANONYMOUS

he Night Market was like the palace in one way: both lived on the edge. It was unlike the palace in every other way. Past the many-coloured stalls was an ash-grey stretch of land that must be the graves of the unmarked dead. The stalls were rickety nods to structure bound with bright cloth, balanced precariously along the sudden drop that was the dread ravine. Beyond the edge was a profound dark, lit by the occasional scarlet flare. On the verge of darkness, Rae saw a lot of light and life. A performer rolled a flaming hoop, circling people cross-legged on the earth and playing a board game with boards and pieces made of cracked bone. Key peered at the board, clearly unsettling the players. He watched like a hawk, which was to say he gave the impression a disembowelling was imminent.

When Rae caught his eye, he sketched a brief diagram in the air. "What's that?"

"That's how the black pieces can win," said Key.

They strolled on, though the player moving black pieces was now making urgent noises indicating Key should stay.

The moans of ghouls in the ravine were almost drowned out by skin-covered drums thumping and harp strings strumming. Rae's heart followed the drums, warming to the idea of dancing on the edge.

If she was her real age and not sick, and she met Key at a club, would she ask? She risked a glance his way. Key was peering with mild interest into the depths of the ravine, profile outlined by the darkness, red sparks reflected in his eyes. She thought she might.

Rae moved to the music, her new assets jiggling. After her previous wasted and withered body, having abundant flesh was a thrilling shock every time. "If we'd never met before and you saw me at the Night Market, what would you do?"

There was a thoughtful pause. Swaying to the beat, Rae arched her neck and glanced coquettishly over her shoulder. Key was nowhere to be found.

Until she looked ahead. Key stood directly before her, one gloved hand on her waist. The other held a blade to her throat.

"I'd rob you at knifepoint." Key touched his forehead lightly against hers. The edge of his smile brushed her cheek, as the edge of the blade kissed her throat. "But I think you're pretty."

Rae's fingers danced along his belt, then curled around its leather edge. Her mouth curled too. "How flattering. Look down."

She held the knife she'd taken from his belt in position. Below the belt.

"Are you sure you want to rob me?" Rae murmured teasingly. "Don't make any sudden movements."

Key threw back his head and laughed with abandon. "You're full of surprises. Like a magic trick in the shape of a woman."

He tucked away his own blade. For an instant, she had him at her mercy. He wrapped his fingers around both her hand and the knife, taking the blade and using his hold on her to spin her beyond reach of other weapons.

Rae spun back in towards him. "Do you like dancing?"

"Never learned."

She thought of his advice on how the black pieces could win.

"Do you like board games?"

She'd never considered Key having hobbies. Even main characters only got plot-relevant hobbies, like combat skills, painting their beloved, or meticulously writing out their own life stories. Minor characters seldom got hobbies at all.

Key nodded cautiously. "I think so."

"You think so?"

"Nobody ever asked me what I like before. People don't want to play with me, but board games and puzzles look fun. I enjoy thinking things out."

That made sense. Being as good at fighting as Key wasn't a purely physical skill. He must make and swiftly adapt plans to bring someone down, while everyone dismissed him as a thug. Or a henchman. Everyone got him wrong. Who was he really?

"Prince of princes, emperor divine. Hope reborn, love of mine. Oh how we adore you, we are waiting for you, when will you come home?"

Two girls in cheap gold great goddess costumes danced past, laughing and kissing and singing the song for the dead. A king-in-waiting, ladies-in-waiting, a Palace on the Edge. This whole country lay in wait.

Rae felt guilty past the telling of it. This was the festival for the Death Day. Key was an abyss foundling. All children abandoned at the edge of the dread ravine counted their ages from this day.

"Happy birthday!"

He blinked. "Happy what?"

Rae gripped his hand in a distressed vice. She kept meticulous calendars. She'd never forgotten a friend's birthday before. "You're twenty today. What do you want?"

Sounding amused, Key drawled: "You know what I want."

Oh.

The dread ravine provided mood lighting. Nature had truly gone high drama on Key's face. His cheekbones were cliffs with little caves underneath. The simmering glow of faraway ravine fires stroked red fingers along the angles of bone, and lit the ends of his eyelashes. Darkness claimed the hollows beneath.

They stood close, hands linked at the edge of the abyss. Her red velvet cloak whipped around them in the wind off the ravine, circling like blood trails in water. There was a wicked thrill in wielding this new body, which might inspire contempt but never pity. Rae closed the distance.

A birthday did deserve a kiss.

It wasn't a sweet kiss. His mouth was faintly, intriguingly bitter. He tasted like stirred ashes, and the awakening of fire.

"Actually," Key murmured when their lips parted, "I meant money."

When sheer embarrassment propelled Rae backward, he held her elbow, nuzzling his nose against hers to share a laugh and a breath. "This was nice too."

This close, she could see how he'd just missed heroic good looks. His nose and neck were both slightly out of proportion. When he stretched out his neck a certain way, head tilted at a weird angle, he seemed more hunting animal than human. His villain's mouth was made for twists, sneers and insincere smiles, but he looked slightly off when he grinned. Maybe the writer never actually gave him a real smile.

Looking at Key's imperfect smile was oddly soothing. Rae told the story in her mind of how she wasn't completely mortified.

So he hadn't been asking for a kiss. Reasonable, as she was his mentor and he probably had a crush on the most beautiful woman alive. Still, kissing handsome young men was standard villainess behaviour.

She tried to laugh. "Villains occasionally do sexy things to demonstrate our ongoing commitment to sin. Random make-out scenes, revealing garments, and excessive lounging against walls. Nothing that matters."

When she turned away from him and the ravine, he used their linked hands to whirl her back again. The drums of the Death Day beat hard. Her eyes were level with his mouth. Villains often had cruel mouths. As mouths went, Key's was a homicide.

"If nothing matters," murmured the Villain of the Cauldron, "all that matters is making it good."

He kissed her and Rae saw red. Crimson fire burned away even the dark behind her eyelids. It was a long time since she'd been kissed, and she had never before been kissed on the edge of impossibility with so far to fall.

Once more this body turned traitor, flesh weak, evil in its very bones. How strange to have blood roaring into heat beneath her skin, after being half dead and cold for so long. Key ducked under the shadow of her velvet hood as he slanted his mouth against hers, gloved hand sliding up her spine to pull her in against him, her breasts crushed with slight delightful pain against his chest. Sparks flew from the dread ravine like fireflies dancing around their heads, her eyes were dazzled, and her body felt real under his hands. Rae slid greedy hands into his hair and kissed him ravenously.

She felt dazed by desire, the mere fact of an eager ache between her thighs shocking. She'd believed she would never feel these impulses again. For so long her body had seemed made only for pain. Apparently Lady Rahela's body was a harlot in the sheets and a harlot in the streets.

Key trailed his mouth down the line of her throat where his knife had rested. She had forgotten pain was only one side of a coin and this the other. The sting of needles was bitter cold, but the sting of his sharp teeth was so sweet. Blood might rush to parts of her body and make bruises. Equally insistent for attention, blood could rush and pound to produce a different ache.

Alight with discovery, they moved against and upon each other. Key murmured in the hot space between neck and ear, "Can I kneel at the altar?"

"Sorry, what?"

He lifted his head to kiss her mouth, deep and filthy. "May I speak in tongues at nature's treasury?"

She smiled bewilderment into the kiss. She didn't know what he was talking about and didn't care, as long as he didn't stop.

"What is the point of the king?" Key sighed, and slid down along her body to his knees.

"Oh, you mean going *down*."

They were in public! Villains were off the chain.

He grinned up at her, perfectly and gloriously shameless. "Is that what you say in the palace? Seems oddly unspecific. Where would I be headed, the knees?" His hand curled around her ankle, no higher, but in this world that was electrifying scandal. He leaned forward and tilted an evil smile up at her. She felt his breath warm through her silk gown. "Maybe not."

"We shouldn't," Rae murmured, half alarmed and half thrilled to hear it come out as a purr. The idea shouldn't seem both filthy-wrong and bone-shakingly right. She shouldn't be tempted.

"Absolutely, we shouldn't." Key's laugh was a simmering thing, low and fierce as the fires down deep in the abyss. "It would be wrong and wicked."

Years of feeling she'd missed the bus of life, lost every chance at youthful adventure or maturity. Embarrassing not to have sex, embarrassing to still want magic. Being a final girl who wouldn't even survive, her fate all horror.

There were times when you had to ask yourself, what would a true villain do?

She lifted a hand gleaming with blood-red stones to toy with his wild hair. The flames of the ravine crackled like laughter. Key's eyes gleamed.

She could be wanton, and blame Lady Rahela.

The raucous laugh of a drunk sounded in her ear. A hand pawed at her ass. "Come with me, sweetheart. I'll show you how a real man—"

"Dies?"

Swift as a breath, Key rose. His voice was calm. His gesture was negligent. His knife opened the man's throat. Blood spewed from the wound and Key shoved him casually aside. The stranger was suddenly the one dancing at the festival, twitching in his last throes. As he tumbled over the edge of the abyss with his throat cut, his feet were still kicking out in a clumsy jerking protest at his own death.

"Sorry." The bright glint of the knife disappeared up his sleeve. Key sounded genuinely regretful. "I know you hate blood."

So a minor villain had murdered a nameless character in the slums. That was barely a footnote in the story, and the dead man was a creep who groped girls in the street.

Rae shrugged the matter off. "I don't care."

A chill had quenched all heat in her body. She refused to care.

Key regarded her approvingly. "You don't mind death. Not the way other people mind it."

The careful way he phrased that, the intent way he watched her, gave Rae a sudden idea. She chose her words carefully.

"It's hard for me to think of the characters around us as real people. Do you understand? Are you like me?"

Key's grey eyes went eagerly bright, silver as a magic blade. "I think so."

Rae grasped his arm. "You walked into the book too?"

"Sorry," said Key. "What book?"

His face was blank as a page with no story on it yet.

Rae sagged. "Ah. You're a sociopath. My bad."

CHAPTER FIFTEEN

The Villainess and the Death Day

"The great god said, 'Come, my calf. Don't be afraid.'

"'You are the strongest of all gods. What is there to fear when you are with me?' asked the child, on the day he died.

"The great god walked up the mountain with his axe in hand. The god's son was so small, he had to run to keep up with his father.'

"And then . . . " The Emperor cut off the tale of tragedy that was his first life by making an alarmingly realistic throat-cutting sound.

"It must be fearful to think of," murmured Lady Ninell. "You were so young and helpless."

"And now I'm not," said the Emperor. "What is there to fear? Nobody will ever hurt me again."

Time of Iron, ANONYMOUS

ey asked with interest, "What's a sociopath?"

Rae frowned. "It's like the children's book about the stuffed rabbit."

Key's eyebrows mocked her. "Peasants aren't taught how to read. Do the children kill and stuff the rabbit themselves?"

Surprise shook a laugh from Rae. "It's a toy rabbit. Because the kid loves it so much and it loves the kid, because they suffer, the rabbit becomes real. If nobody loved it, I guess it never would. Sociopaths don't have strong emotions about other people, so people and their feelings never become real to them."

"The merchants always did say there was something wrong with me," Key said thoughtfully. "So that's what we are, you and I."

She supposed he was. In this world, she supposed she was too.

Whatever. There were many sociopathic villains in books, and Key was on Rae's side. She recalled again that Rahela was several years older than he, and she must take care of her team. She believed he wasn't a monster. He lacked empathy, went into a dissociative state and killed people serially, that was all.

"I liked that story," Key added. "Tell me more."

Rae slipped her hand back into his, resolutely ignoring the thrill she blamed on this villainous body. They went strolling down the stalls. "I'll tell you all the stories you want. I like you even if you struggle with violent impulses."

That was true, even if so much of what lay between them was a lie. She liked him a little too much.

In fiction, if you were cute and funny it made being a murderer okay. But she knew how this world worked – *everybody loves Lia*. The twin terrors of death and loneliness loomed. Tomorrow she would be smarter than this. For tonight it could be her hand in his, and who cared what evil these hands might do.

Key laughed. "I don't struggle with violent impulses. I revel in violent impulses. Speaking of, here's the metalworker's stall. Nice knives, Strike."

"Thanks, Villain," murmured the woman behind the metal-worker's stall, who had an awesome henna-dyed high fade and even more awesome arms. Rae thought Strike must live at the gym, then remembered she was a blacksmith.

The metalworker's stall was built on more stable lines than most of the stalls in the Night Market, and twined with silvery ribbons. Two iron-bound buckets were filled with the embers of dying fires. Across the stall was spread a gleaming assortment of the decorative, prac-tical and lethal: jewellery, horseshoes, crossbows, and many, many knives. There was what looked like a Rubik's cube made from teeth and coated in metal. A customer was counting out coins in the four shapes made by the different mints. Crown shapes, from the royal mint. Swords for soldiers. Leaves, for farmers and those who dealt in produce. Quills, for merchants' ledgers and scholars. The coins were bronze, and there weren't many.

"We take Cobra coin here too," said Strike.

The woman put down a small bronze star and a snake, and scurried off in joyful possession of an axe.

"Hiii," said Rae ingratiatingly, opening her red velvet bag and dumping one enchanted gauntlet onto the stall. "I need links taken out to make this smaller. You keep the links once you take them out. Since they're magic, I think they're priceless. Deal?"

Hers was the only metal on the crowded stall that gleamed red.

Strike the blacksmith folded her muscular arms. Her slight smile vanished like smoke. "Or I could keep the whole thing. You have no power to stop thieves here, my lady."

Rae leaned her elbows against the stall. "You could keep it, but every noble in the city would unite to burn down the Cauldron and drag out the peasant who held the enchanted weapon for torture, followed by execution. Also if you steal my gauntlet, I will ask Key to kill you."

"I would," confirmed Key. "Sorry, Strike."

"Are you two friends?" asked Rae.

Forge Strike eyed Rae in an unfriendly manner. "He used to steal weapons out of my shop."

"As a compliment to your excellent craftsmanship." Key grinned at Strike. "I learned to make weapons watching you. Let's be friends?"

Strike slammed her hammer down on the stall. "You just announced you'd kill me on this noble's orders!"

Key rolled his eyes. "Gosh, I said sorry. I wouldn't say that to just anyone. She's paying me, it's not personal."

"Bootlicker." Strike spat into the fire burning in the bucket by her side. "I'll do your job, but I don't want to see either of you around here again."

Since the Cobra was the one who'd bring the stolen key to be copied, Rae thought that sounded fine. The gauntlet being altered was a crucial element in her evil scheme to attend the ball. If her scheme worked she would soon be out of this world, far away from them all.

"Deal." She offered her hand, but Strike sneered. "Never mind that. FYI, I told the doorman at Life in Crisis we used to be a steamy item. Sorry if that's awkward!"

"I prefer blondes."

"Guess I'm so sexy, I made you break your own rules!" Rae dropped her a saucy wink. Meeting Strike's steadily unimpressed gaze, she backed up. "We'll wait over there."

Strike didn't even acknowledge she'd spoken. "Can I give you some advice, Villain?"

"Sure, since we're friends now."

Strike's face was as closed as an iron door on a furnace; it made Rae think she'd seen the kiss. "Noble ladies love entertainment. You're nothing more than a night out at the theatre. Don't think she feels anything once the story's done. Her jewelled dress alone could pay for the stone you want, with money to spare."

There was an odd, contemplative pause.

"I . . . didn't know that," said Key.

Strike gave him a significant nod. "I didn't think you did."

The blacksmith bent her head to her work in clear dismissal. Key stalked off towards the graves of the unloved dead. Rae followed him to the flat grey desert beyond the lights and stalls. The earth was parched by proximity to the ravine's sparks and dotted with tokens: dead flowers, broken dolls, roughly carved wooden statues. There was even a tiny lopsided mausoleum, made of cracked unmagical stones.

Key halted beside a knife, buried up to the hilt in the dry earth. Then he removed his cracked leather gloves. His movements were jerky, as if he'd forgotten grace. When Key dug his teeth into the edge of the leather and pulled the glove off, Rae had the strangest impression it was because his hands were shaking. That didn't seem remotely in character.

The gloves tumbled into the dust. He held out his hands to her.

Key's skin was stretched in shiny strips over the backs of his hands, scars raised over veins and bones that must once have been livid welts. Marks in the shape of swords. Rae remembered how much the first needle in the back of her hand, when they couldn't find veins in her arm for the canula, had hurt. She wondered how badly this had hurt.

"What happened?" Rae whispered.

"Sword coins." Key was still smiling. "For soldiers, and those who uphold the law."

Clear as dawn over a ruined city, Rae understood how Key had come up with the idea for the hot iron shoes.

"I'm so sorry."

His smile went a little soft, the way it did when he thought Rae was being naive. The edge returned almost immediately.

"You said everyone has a backstory, hanging behind them like a shadow. This is how I became the Villain of the Cauldron. The day I was born, I was found on the edge of the ravine." Key's voice was distant, clinical. "People leave children there when they have too many mouths to feed, or the baby's fatherless. Usually baby wakes up, baby rolls off the edge. No more problem child. But an old peasant who ran errands for the glassblowers' guild found me before I fell. He gave me to a barren merchant couple, so I'd have a good life. Except I wasn't a good child. Abyss foundlings swallow a spark as they lie on the edge. We are stained by the smoke, angry as the dead. The merchants, who called themselves my parents, called me a mad dog of a boy. I tried to please them, but I found inappropriate things amusing. I never got scared and clung to them. I wasn't the son they wanted. I wasn't a son anybody would want."

A horrible theory formed for Rae. It was true sometimes minor characters didn't act like people, but puppets made to fulfil a purpose. Key was one of many designed to fight for the damsel in distress. Real players in the story had family and friends and motivations, had enough to them that they seemed believable and worth believing in. A less important character existed only for one scene. Key was created for love and violence.

What would you be, if you weren't well rounded but the broken pieces of a character made to be used and tossed aside?

"There was a happy ending. But not for me. When I was six the merchant's wife bore the son they wanted. I was no longer required, so the glassblowers' guild sold me off. Apprenticed me, they called it. I was small enough to go down chimneys."

Rae had read about children forced into work in Victorian London. "You had to be a chimney sweep?"

When he was six.

"I went down chimneys and cut people's throats while they slept," Key corrected her calmly. "I can't clean. When it comes to killing, I have real talent. The children are sent down the chimneys to open doors for assassins. I thought I was being clever cutting out the middleman, but when I opened the door covered in blood I saw I'd made another mistake. The masters sent me in because they wanted a man murdered, yet those precious hypocrites acted shocked when I killed him."

Suddenly Rae understood Key's hangdog look in the throne room, in the Court of Air and Grace, and outside the tavern. This was a habit formed from childhood. He committed horrors out of a genuine desire to please. The lonely nightmare child never understood why he was cast off every time.

Key shrugged. "The masters decided I'd save them money. From then on they sent me out alone. A few years later I got cocky and got caught. Soldiers found me in the target's house, outside the Cauldron. Luckily, they thought I was stealing. They tossed sword coins on the fire, fastened burning metal on my hands, and watched me squirm, then tossed me out once the entertainment was over. The masters left me in the gutter, since I was no use now."

His laugh sounded genuinely amused.

"Strangest thing. The old man was still watching me. He got sentimental about baby birds and sick animals. And me. The small thing he saved. He still thought of me that way, even though I was a disgusting little monster scrabbling with filthy infected hands in the gutter. I woke in his hut as he nursed me. I said, 'I'll kill them all.' He sat by the bed, because he'd given me his own bed to sleep in and he was sleeping on the floor. He begged, 'Please be my good boy.'" Key took a deep breath. "He told me to call him father. Have you ever had the sense – someone was important, even though they weren't? That you wanted to belong to them, and have them not throw you away?"

Rae tried to work this out. "Have I ever . . . loved someone?"

Key stared across the graves of the unloved dead, towards the ravine, and nodded.

"Yes," Rae whispered.

"Strange, isn't it?" Key mused. "I never did it before or since. I didn't do it right. I wanted to belong to him. So I was good. I didn't kill anybody."

Faint wonder surfaced, as though he were discussing an astounding feat performed by a stranger.

"I worked for scraps that fell from the glassblowers' guild's table. My father was old and weak. He'd never had enough to eat in his life. We spent too much on medicine that couldn't fix damage done long ago. A lean year came. I was out hauling loads to make money on the side, and a glassblower hired my father to make a delivery in the rain. He caught the fever that finished him in exchange for one bronze leaf. His last words were to buy something for myself. Because I was such a good boy. What an idiot. Don't you think, my lady? What a stupid old fool."

Rae shook her head, but Key was still looking at the ravine. He didn't stop smiling. She wished so much he would stop.

"I was in debt by the time he died. I didn't have money for a stone, so he was buried here in the graves of the unloved dead."

Forge Strike had talked about Key wanting a stone. It was for his father.

When people in Eyam died, they were buried under magic stones so their bodies wouldn't rise as ghouls. She knew this piece of world-building, but she hadn't thought through the consequences. The longer the body stayed in the magic-soaked ground, the more magic was needed to hold it down. Those who didn't have money for a proper stone buried their lost ones in this desolate place, hoping to put a powerful magic stone over them one day. Everybody knew they were dreaming. *Too poor to keep your beloved in the ground*, people sneered, and named this place *the graves of the unloved dead*. Key used the name casually. As if his love was so worthless, it didn't exist at all.

Key continued, "My masters offered me my old job. My father

wouldn't have liked that. What the dead want doesn't matter, but I said no. Only time wore on, and the price of a stone rose. Being good earned so little. A rival emerged for the glassblowers' guild, and they offered twice the usual fee to be rid of him. I was tired of trying to be good. I earned my fee, but I'd waited too long. The price of the stone had tripled. I buried the coins over his grave, with a knife still wet with the blood from the kill. My first cut throat in years."

Key nodded to the knife hilt at their feet.

Running might be wise. A screaming nightmare lurked behind Key's calm smile. Every word sounded raw, as if cut from his throat.

"My father was a good man. He never said a bad word, never had a wicked thought, worked every day of his life until he dropped dead in the dirt. And what's left of him? An unmarked grave and a killer. That's where goodness gets you. Let's never be fools like that, my lady."

She'd thought Key being a mercenary side-character was funny. You could dismiss someone with 'all he cares about is money', never acknowledging what money might mean. Not a useless luxury but your future, the life of someone you loved, or the last thing you could ever do for them.

Rae reached out and touched the scars on Key's hands lightly. He tilted his head at that eerie angle, his stare lost in bewilderment. "It doesn't hurt any more."

She thought of her mother worrying when she sold people a house at a steeper mortgage than they could afford. She thought of her own hospital bills. How hard the desperate tried, to be left with nothing in the end.

Key seemed to read her mind. "I haven't told you the end. I was the best cut-throat in the city. People called me the Villain of the Cauldron. I didn't care. I was making money, but I couldn't outrace the climbing prices. Coming home from a job, I heard one of the glassblowers' guild say he was sorry the old fool had died. Now they had to actually pay someone to do the work he'd done for food and shelter. Glass costs a lot in Eyam. The glassblowers were rich. My father died so they could save money they would never miss."

His smile turned sweet. "That night I went to the glassblowers' guild and killed them all. I gave my father every life who counted his life worth nothing. I set the guild house on fire. I knew I wasn't getting away with it. I'd be executed without ever being able to save up enough for that stone. When I left the burning building and saw ghouls climbing from the abyss, I thought they would kill me. Better ghouls than soldiers."

He shook his head, rueful. "I'm not a planner like you. I lived. The good citizens of Themesvar believed ghouls laid waste to the guild, and I was the loyal servant who fought in their defence. The merchants who wouldn't spit on me suddenly called me the Hero of the Cauldron, and the king summoned me for a royal reward. The people of the Cauldron know the truth. Now so do you. I'll always be the Villain. You said we were friends. You said you're like me. Maybe you can understand what I have to do."

He pulled his hands from hers, picking up his gloves and sliding them back on. He reached out and traced her throat with his fingertips, as if memorizing the lines.

Rae didn't have time for this. "I understand what *I* have to do. Unbutton me."

"That story inspired an amorous mood?"

Key sounded incredulous. Rae turned her back and wriggled her shoulders illustratively. When he stepped in close, she shivered. This near, it would be easy to reach around and cut her throat. It would be easy for him at any distance. She couldn't possibly escape.

Clever hands undid her. A whisper ran warm down her nape, gloves brushing the bare skin above the laced back of her corset. "Time for one more magic trick, my lady."

She headed for the rough little tomb made of unmagical stones. It took wriggling to squeeze inside.

"Stand guard at the door, please."

There was a silence. "You're ... climbing into a tomb?"

"Have some sense, there are no ladies' changing rooms! Hold my cloak."

After a pause, Key took her cloak, held over his arm like a gallant gentleman awaiting his lady emerging from her boudoir. Or, in this case, tomb.

Rae scrambled out of her dress, garnets hanging heavy on the gauze she peeled off her skin. She was left standing in the tomb in her corset and chemise. Heroines always complained about corsets in stories. Not being a heroine, she found corsets entirely necessary to support wicked curves. Emer had made clear the chemise was a scandalous garment. Dressed thus, the scaffolding that heaved Rae's bosom high was obvious. Night breathed through the stones of the tomb, in a cold caress over her skin.

"My cloak," Rae commanded.

The cloak offered velvet welcome across her bare shoulders. Rae scrambled from the tomb in her underwear, clutching both cloak and the shreds of her dignity. She led the way back to Forge Strike's stall.

"New deal. You can keep whatever money is left over, if you take this dress and buy the stone for Key's father."

Key jerked at her side as if he'd been stabbed.

Rae glanced his way. "Sorry, did you want to pick the stone out yourself?"

He shook his head speechlessly.

Rae was starting to get worried. "Can she not be trusted?"

"Strike doesn't go back on deals," Key said, after a moment.

"So what's the problem?"

There was another silence. He was pale.

Strike snatched the dress out of Rae's hands as though Rae might change her mind. "There's no problem."

"Great!" Rae turned to Key. "Can we go back to the palace? I must execute my evil scheme. Plus there will be huge trouble if the royal guards catch me outside the palace walls in my undergarments."

She headed alone down the path by the ravine. For an instant she feared Key wouldn't follow, but he did.

CHAPTER SIXTEEN

The Villainess Gives It Up

Her father was dead, and her stepmother stripping the
estate of all the magic that was rightfully hers.
When Lia wept, Rahela smiled. "Sisters should share."

Time of Iron, ANONYMOUS

ae headed straight for the castle. Since the king must be
gone by now, they travelled via the secret passage into
the Room of Memory and Bone. The way through was
a dark tunnel, so she looped her arm in Key's. He was tense against
her side. Rae's own throat was tight. Villains weren't cut out for emo-
tional scenes. Their kind were made for wicked one-liners and evil
proclamations.

Emerging from the dark into the ivory room dazzled her eyes with
sepulchral snow blindness.

She was still unable to see anything properly when Key asked,
"Can I kill someone for you?"

For the price of a dress? Truly success was about opportunity, not
talent. Key should've had access to nobles years ago. She needed
his skills as a minion right now, but as a palace assassin he could've
made bank.

She blinked hard against the light of a spindly bone chandelier.
The broken pieces of her vision resolved into his feral, uncertain face.

Rae smiled. "You don't have to repay me. All I want is your help. You already promised me that."

"I didn't mean it," Key informed her.

Wow. Treachery was expected in an evil minion, but did it have to be now?

"I know," Rae snapped. "You were going to kill me in the graveyard for the price of my dress."

He fell silent, as if he'd imagined she hadn't worked that out. Betrayal was Rae's constant companion. She could see it coming a mile off.

"You think one day I'll turn to you and say, 'Are you for real? Can I trust you?' I don't trust anybody. You asked why I won't try to win the king back? When I was . . . younger, I got sick."

Rae shivered so hard it was a shudder, deathly cold beneath the velvet. She hadn't planned to say this, but sometimes it was a relief when everything was ruined. Now she'd spoken, she might as well spill it all.

"When those guards hurt your hands, you said you were disgusting. I was disgusting, too. I d-didn't even have hair in my nostrils, so my nose wouldn't stop running. I was sure I would die. I pretended to myself I wouldn't, but the truth is, I knew I would. My lover left me. My friends left me. I was told to forgive them. I was blamed more for resenting mistreatment than anybody was blamed for mistreating me."

Which came first, being treated as unworthy or being unworthy? In the end, it didn't matter. If others believed she was evil, or beautiful, or guilty, they made that true.

Rae stared at the queen's stained throne as she confessed, "Even my dad knew I wasn't worth staying for."

Her father was a teacher. Her mother said bitterly *those who can't do, teach*, but he did enough. He left. Not right away. The year after Rae was diagnosed, when the first round of chemo didn't work. Men were six times more likely to leave their wives when they had cancer, but it wasn't Rae's mother who got sick. It was Rae. It was her fault.

Her mother was never bitter to his face. They needed his help for the bills.

Her father had a baby boy with his new wife now. When there were complications with the birth, he slept on the floor of his young wife's hospital room.

Nobody slept on the floor of Rae's hospital room. Rae tried to remember her father simply as a teacher. Class could end, a teacher could leave, and it wouldn't hurt. She refused to meet the baby. He observed her cruelty said a lot about her character.

Rae confessed, "I know you don't believe I can tell the future, but I can. Octavian is the Emperor. He will be great and terrible. He's the hero, and him treating other women like they don't matter proves Lia's the heroine. She's the fairest, and I'm not really beautiful at all. But when people don't care about you, you have to care about yourself. Ambition is wicked, and I want so much. If I want to live that makes me a monster, if I want a man that makes me the harlot of the tower, if I want a throne that makes me an evil queen. Fine. I'll be a wonderful monster. I trust my own wickedness. I will never believe in someone else again."

"If you want to be queen," Key suggested slowly, "let's kill your sister."

She must be clear, for Key's sake and the sake of the plot, it was vital Key not massacre any protagonists.

"Listen. My pain isn't the fault of any rival. The system lets Octavian use people, so he used me and threw me away. Want to know something? In a different future, you suggest to Octavian that he should heat iron shoes on a fire and watch me dance."

Key's arm turned to stone beneath her palm. "I'd heard about you. Lady Rahela, the woman of snow and flame. I believed you had all the power in the world."

Rae shrugged. "In another life, I'm dead. You think I deserved it. We're no different from Octavian, except he's above us, and those above hurt those below. I hurt Emer. You would have hurt me. And the Emperor can hurt anyone. In that future, only Lia did something good. She saved you and Emer at my trial. She doesn't deserve death."

You couldn't make a story omelette without breaking narrative eggs. It was a pity Key wouldn't get rescued by his crush, but Rae had urgently needed to escape execution.

"I don't care if people are good," opined Key. "I only care if they're good to me. I'll kill her if you ask."

This was Rae's punishment for continually thinking, *Who cares about saving Lia?* while reading the *Time of Iron* series. Rae barely knew Lia, but she wanted to save her. Not only because she needed Lia for the plot. Lia was almost Rahela's sister.

The words tumbled from Rae's lips. "I need her. Being someone's sister is the one thing I haven't failed at. She was always lovely and easy to hurt. I hurt her sometimes, I resented her sometimes, but I planned to fight her enemies my whole life. When we were young, we told each other stories. When I got sick, I was scared to sleep, in case I never woke up. I could only sleep when I told myself if I died, she'd tell her kids stories about me. I wouldn't be anything but a story then, but that's better than being nothing at all. Nobody lives forever, but a story can. Stories are how I survive. When I'm fighting to live, I think to myself: what a story to tell my sister. I will be her favourite story. I will be the greatest story she ever heard."

Lia was Rae's key to returning to Alice, and Alice was how she'd lived long enough to be in this adventure. Her friends and her father were speeding past, Rae lost in their rear-view mirror. Her mother had worked so fiercely over the last few years they barely knew the new, hardened versions of each other. In her sister's heart, the memory of Rae might be lent beauty. She didn't know how to be beautiful anywhere else.

The name for the Room of Memory and Bone didn't seem funny to her any more. This was the skeleton at the feast, a whole chamber acting as a vast memento mori. Remember that you must die.

The death room in the storybook palace blurred before her eyes. Rae willed herself not to cry. She hated crying in front of other people. If you cried by yourself, you could pretend you hadn't. It wasn't real unless other people knew.

Key tilted her chin up high. "No tears. You're like me, remember? Vipers together. Evil wins at last."

Rae managed a fragile sneer.

Against the bone-white backdrop Key's hair was a stark contrast, giving him a black hole for a halo. "The oath was a joke to me. *When my name is in your mouth, I will always answer, and your name will be my call to arms. I will ever be a shield for your back, and the story told between us will be true.* How could that be real?"

Rae chewed her lip and stared at ivory flagstones, smooth as grave markers with the names worn away. Oath language was admittedly grandiose and overblown. Maybe they could work out a deal. If Key got a better offer, would he give Rae a chance to top it?

As Rae prepared to negotiate contract language, Key spoke.

His voice sighed soft as night wind. "My lady. I'll mean it now."

Except he'd already confessed to lying once. He could lie again any time.

"Cool," Rae told him. "Thanks."

"I'll keep my word. I'll be yours if you care to keep me."

"It's a bargain." Rae hoped that was enough.

To her infinite dismay, Key knelt on the bone floor, reverently touched the edge of her red velvet cloak, bowed his black head and kissed it. This was the inverted mirror of a scene that might play out between the Last Hope and Lia, the lady and her honourable knight. Rae's lips curled scornfully. The lady of darkness and her dishonourable knight? He would be loyal forever, until he was offered double.

"I'm so happy," Key murmured, "to belong to someone again."

When he tipped his head back, his eyes shone like stars, in a way only the eyes of a character could. No real person's eyes burned with intensity that cut through darkness and distance, with light so terrifyingly bright it would burn long after the star burned out. Rae understood Key was grateful, but this was taking it too far. She was almost tempted to believe in him.

Even a villain must resist temptation occasionally. She didn't even believe in real people.

The silence stretched. Rae didn't know what to say. The memory of the kiss ran through her body, not her mind, in a long shudder. *When my name is in your mouth . . .*

He was at her feet, as he had been at the Night Market. She could ask him for anything. Except death had followed temptation at the market, and he was nothing she could keep.

"Rise," she commanded in her villainous purr.

When he did, they made their way to the ladies' tower together. Rae made follow-up requests.

"Just don't kill Lia, and don't suggest me crawling back to Octavian again. I'm only meant to be a small part of the Emperor's history. Like the hilt of his famous sword? The hilt is in the shape of a snake, and he used to say I was its twin: his viper. Maybe he loved me a little. That's enough."

Now she lived inside the story, loving the Emperor was too stressful. Key could be her new favourite. The Villain of the Cauldron was her trusty bodyguard, in the sense Rae trusted him to be evil, mercenary and entertaining. She would improve a corner of the story, just for him. All they had to do was save Lia. And indulge in no more kisses. Key was literally made for Lia, and in any world, Rae wasn't made to be loved. It would only hurt if she got attached.

Usually Key's face was a smile kaleidoscope, different smiles matching different moods. When the smile dropped, darkness followed. "The king had a murderous viper. He should've appreciated his luck."

Rae hummed appreciation. "Right? I have great hair, a great rack and a wealth of dark sarcasm. I'm basically the perfect woman. Any guy would be lucky." She recalled her eternal devotion to Octavian, and added hastily, "It can't be just any guy."

"It has to be an emperor for you?" Key grinned.

Rae grinned back. "That's right. It's gotta be an emperor."

She held up her hand for a high five. Key was getting good at those.

They were on the same team, and he'd helped her gain clarity. Using people, seizing control of a story just to get your own way, was an evil thing to do.

Rae still planned to do it. She was sick of being the one less loved. She would rather be a false prophet. She would rather be a villain.

Lady Lia's chamber was at the top of the tower. The mosaic on her floor showed tall pearly cliffs and a silver sea. It was smaller than Rae's room, with a big window that had no bars because nobody was deranged enough to dream of jumping from that high, and while Rae's curtains were red Lia's were a more literary blue. One day Lia would turn this whole tower into the quarters of a queen. For now, Lia's window was a picture frame of starry skies, her white bed was draped with airy gauze, and a tower bedroom was terribly appropriate for a heroine.

Lia sat at her dressing table, brushing her golden hair. When Rae entered, Lia's eyes widened in the bronze mirror, but her pearl-handled brush didn't falter.

Rae wished to be certain they were alone. "Where's your maid?"

"After my first experience with a maid, would I trust another?"

Right, later Lia told the Emperor she was scared to trust another servant. The Emperor said, "I'll be your maid." Every night he brushed her long locks a hundred times.

Rae hadn't considered before what Lia's refusal to have another maid meant. Lia truly had felt betrayed by Emer.

Whatever, having to brush your own hair wasn't a national emergency. Back to scheming.

"Let's speak as friends," suggested Rae.

Lia's voice was steady. "We're not friends."

"So let's exchange unpleasantries!"

Lia laid down her brush and twisted on her stool. A moonbeam captured her beauty, turning her slim body to a marble statue and her hair pale as a bridal veil. Her blue eyes were sheened with tears.

"What mischief are you plotting?"

Rae climbed on the white gauze bed, getting scarlet-clad vixen all over the sheets. "Glad you asked. This impression of a wounded fawn is cute, but appeals to my conscience won't work. I don't have one. Quit moping, you're ridiculously good-looking, the king is super into you, and I'm not going to cause you any more problems."

"How can I believe that?"

"I'm a cold-hearted monster acting in my own best interests. If I keep cockblocking the king, he'll cut my head off."

"You planned *I* would be put to death."

Claiming Rae had reformed wasn't working. Rae couldn't accomplish anything unless she explained her past behaviour, and convinced everyone she wouldn't repeat it. That meant she had to examine plausible reasons for Rahela's actions.

It was strange, but thinking about a character's motivations made you like them more. Before she became Rahela, it was easy to dismiss her.

"I was panicking," Rae explained. "All my plotting and putting out, then you show up at court and Octavian falls in love at first sight! My man's eye started to wander, and he's the most powerful man in the world. I couldn't slap him or call him a cheating dirtbag. I blamed you because I couldn't blame him."

"I have no interest in the king," Lia murmured to her hairbrush.

Right. She was too pure. That was why they all loved her.

Rae would've thought a girl liking you back was good news, but that wasn't how stories worked. Not being interested was irresistible.

"It's chill. I've accepted my fate. In fact, I've accepted everyone's fate! You two will get married. So it's better for *moi* if you and I get along."

"I wouldn't even dream of marrying the king," said Lia humbly, then with a rush of righteous indignation, "And you and I will never be on good terms! It wasn't only jealousy over the king. When we were children you and your mother fell upon my possessions like vultures. Now it suits your purposes for us to be friends. Why should I?"

Over Lia's shoulder, Rae saw her own eyes reflected: dark, gleaming and ultimately untrustworthy. Nobody would pick her. Unless . . .

She aimed a finger gun at Lia. "What if I gave you a reason?"

Rae had walked into this room with nothing. Now she had Lia's attention.

"People descend like starving vultures when they don't know if they'll get another chance to grab anything. What we did wasn't personal."

"They were my family's treasures. What you did was personal to me."

Tears brimmed in Lia's eyes again. Could she do this on command?

"Now we both have a chance at the good life. You marry the king. As the queen's stepsister, I sit on silken couches, eat bonbons, and

have my pick of lords because I'm – pay attention, this bit is important – invited to the good parties."

"Ah," murmured Lia. "You're scheming to go to the ball."

Rae grinned. "You're not just a pretty face. You *are* new to court.
People are cunning here. You got framed for murder last week."

Lia's angelic patience lost its wings. "*By you!*"

Rae batted the accusation aside like a fly. "Stop living in the past. I
can help you. The problem is, you can't trust me. Because I'm evil!"

A curiously helpless look descended on Lia's face.

Encouraged, Rae said: "I want you to believe in me. So I have to
make a real sacrifice."

She crossed the silver expanse of mosaics until she reached where
Lia sat. She saw her villainous descent in the mirror, red skirt sweeping the floor, hands behind her back.

Rae knelt beside Lia's seat, and showed Lia what she was hiding.

"You said you had no choice but to be helpless. It sounded like
you didn't want to be helpless any more. I'm not offering an apology. I'm not offering to give back all your treasures. I *am* offering
to share."

Rae was in the moonbeam spotlight with Lia now. Moonlight
struck on steel, gleaming with enchanted red fire.

A magic gauntlet.

Only one.

Traditionally, you came to the heroine's tower offering rescue. Rae
thought Lia might want the power to rescue herself.

"You tried to fire a bow and arrow with your left hand. So you can
use the left gauntlet better than me. I can use the right gauntlet better
than you. It's not as good as having the whole set, but if we're fighting
together, it could be even better."

Lia's fingers hovered over the silvery gauntlet. Her gaze rested on
Rae, like a child scared if she wanted something too much the big
kids would play keep-away with it overhead.

In the book, the gauntlets were lost with Rahela's body, thrown
down into the dread ravine. Lia never had any power except what her
admirers gave her. Rae would hate that.

When Lia's face twisted out of beauty into reality Rae was shocked.

Lia looked sick with fear in a way Rae was familiar with. She looked afraid to hope. Rae understood. Hope was next door to despair.

She laid the gauntlet down gently in Lia's white-gauze lap. Lia's hands curved protectively over enchanted silver and steel.

She whispered, "I could take it, and do nothing for you."

Rae winked. "Bad girls love to gamble. Do we have a deal?"

"... I need to think about it," said Lady Lia, with her most demure smile.

"You've got to be kidding me!"

Lia placed the magic weapon in the drawer, and locked it up tight away from Rae. You frame somebody *one time*!

The heroine of the story picked up her pearl-handled brush and resumed brushing her golden hair, the picture of innocence.

"You waited long enough to show me kindness. It's your turn. Wait a few days, Rahela. Until the morning of the ball. Find out what I decide."

CHAPTER SEVENTEEN

The Villainess Shall Go to the Ball

Fate seemed determined Lia would not enjoy her first ball.
Her gown lay slashed to ribbons upon her bed.
    On her way to send excuses to the king, she discovered
a flat carved box at her door. Lifting the lid, Lia saw yards
of soft white fabric, begemmed with the tiniest, daintiest
jewels. She saw the loveliest gown in the world.
    Lia's heart fluttered like a bird wishing it was not caged.
She knew who had done this. She hoped she knew.

Time of Iron, ANONYMOUS

n the morning of the ball, while Rae was telling Key and
Emer stories, a slip of gold-leafed paper was slid under her
door. '*His gracious Majesty grants Lady Lia Felice permission to make a gesture of sisterly forgiveness and bring Lady Rahela Domitia as her personal guest to the royal ball.*'

Check out the phrasing on that. Everyone who saw this invitation
would talk about how great Lia's power over the king must be, how
gracious Lia was, and how little Rae deserved it.

Who cared? Rae had what she wanted. She held her snake aloft
in victory and danced in a circle around the room as Key applauded
her triumph.

"My lady," implored Emer. "Be calm. Put down the serpent."

Rae laid Victoria Broccoli tenderly down in a jewellery box. Emer was a killjoy, but she was right. There was no time to be lost.

"Let's embrace the evil aesthetic like it's a lover I'm about to poison. I want lips as red as blood, and eyeliner black as my heart."

"Announcing the Lady Rah ... ahahaha ... hel ... ah ... hello ... "

Rae gave the pageboy a saucy wink. He dropped his trumpet.

Later this very night, Lia would drift down these stairs like a dream of poetry and moonlight made flesh. Across the ballroom, several grown men would shed tears.

As Rae descended, several grown men dropped their champagne flutes. The heroine was a sweet dream. She was a sexy nightmare.

The Golden Cobra waited at the bottom of the staircase.

"Looking like a queen. Need a king cobra?"

"I don't need a grass snake."

Rae took his golden arm. They sailed through the Ballroom of Sighs, heads together as though whispering seductively.

"Ready to do crime, cheerleader?"

"Try to keep up with me, theatre kid." Rae flirted her fan, feeling a thrill of nerves. "Seriously, are you certain you can lift the king's keys?"

"Hush, he's right there!" hissed the Cobra.

When Rae spun, Octavian was nowhere to be seen. She whirled back to find the Cobra fanning himself with the fan he'd plucked from her grasp. Rae hadn't even noticed she was empty-handed.

"Point – and fan – taken."

He didn't return it, but created a gentle breeze as they strolled through the crowd.

"I miss fans. The prime minister passed a law forbidding men fans and jewellery just to upset me. Do you know there's a whole fan language?"

"I mostly use my fan to cover the evil twins." She made a gesture bosomward. "I call them Cruella and Maleficent."

His dark eyes danced over the red-stained edge of the snow-white fan. "You need a *considerably* bigger fan. No, really. Secret messages can be relayed with this. If I twirl it in my left hand—" the fan pirouetted from palm to palm "—it means 'we are watched'. If I twirl the fan in my right hand, I mean 'I love another'. You can also use the fan to deliver the cuts direct, indirect, sublime and infernal, which are all deadly insults. There are many ways to cast shade in the Palace on the Edge."

"This is such a welcoming place."

She found the atmosphere in the Ballroom of Sighs oppressive. Rae had intended everyone to look at her, but—everyone was *looking* at her. The collective weight of eyes slid over her bared flesh heavy as hands. Lady Rahela had many admirers and many enemies. Like the body and the dress, they were Rae's now.

The Cobra was beside her, but he was lost to this fantasy world. Even within it, she knew him for a villain. She hadn't forgotten Marius describing the Cobra's ruin of a young man. The Cobra had admitted it. He said he enjoyed it. He seemed kind, but she couldn't rely on him. She could count only on her own wicked self.

She sought comfort in a scheme. "Let's run through our plan one last time. The king officially declares Vasilisa and Lia his ladies-in-waiting. Duty compels him to ask Vasilisa to dance, despite being dazzled by Lia in her new gown."

The Cobra seemed certain of every detail about his favourite scene. Rae had suggested warning Lia that spiteful rivals who were never identified planned to ruin her dress. The Cobra utterly forbade her to do any such thing. He was set on Lia wearing the surprise gown sent by the Last Hope.

"I still think we should have told Lia."

"It's Marius's first ever romantic gesture!" the Cobra protested. "Don't ruin this for me. Besides, it's a key part of our scheme that Lia comes in late."

Rae sighed and nodded. "Before the first set we create a scene to get in position, close enough to snatch the keys. All eyes are on us . . . until Lia's big entrance."

"She floats down the stairs looking like an early morning sky, pale and clear with stars still lingering against the clouds—"

Rae mimed puking. The Cobra hit her with her own fan.

"*Et tu*, bestie," Rae grumbled. "Brutal."

The Cobra continued firmly, "Marius will feel struck by beautiful lightning and fall in love at first sight."

"Is he a love-at-first-sight kind of guy?"

Now she'd met the Last Hope, she was experiencing doubts. Marius Valerius didn't inspire warm feelings. He inspired frostbite of the soul.

The Cobra glared. "He's absolutely a love-at-first-sight kind of guy."

"Didn't he see Lia when we got attacked by ghouls?"

The Cobra's glare intensified. "I didn't invite your rain to my parade. While the king is distracted by Lia, we snatch the key to the royal greenhouse and split up. The king dances with Vasilisa. Lia is left forlorn. *Then* the whole court is electrified by Marius – who never asks anybody to dance – sweeping Lia onto the dance floor and the romantic moonlit balcony."

He gave a happy sigh behind his stolen fan.

"Use the sensation to slip out and get the key copied," Rae reminded the Cobra urgently. "That's a key part of our key scheme. Don't focus on romance to the detriment of the plot."

Her plot had to go perfectly. They had only weeks. If they got the key, Rae would sleep with it under her pillow until she woke in her own world, to the sunrise of her sister's face.

The ballroom was larger than the throne room, and the only stateroom without a mosaic. The floor was hematite, iridescent black stone gleaming beneath their feet as though they stood on a moonless night sky. The ceiling was arched glass, with shards of mirror rather than transparent panes. Most mirrors in the palace were bronze, but these were costly glass. Some mirrors had cracked so the reflected ballroom scene was strangely distorted. The bright costumes against the dark floor were lent a silver sheen, as though the whole court was suspended in mercury. Rae's gown stood out vivid as a bloodstain.

The Cobra chucked her reassuringly under the chin with her fan. "Stick with me, grasshopper, and you'll be fine. I've never missed a cue in my life. Let me introduce you to my book club."

He returned the fan and looped an arm around her shoulders,

keeping her close in a warm solid circle. The Golden Cobra helped run a literary salon where court intellectuals discussed plays, poetry and art. The members of the salon, sitting in chairs of gilt and spun glass, seemed startled to see Rahela.

The Cobra led Rae to a low-backed settee, embroidered with kingfishers and larks. He gestured to the lady and gentleman near the settee. The lady had ostrich feathers adorning her tower of twisted locs, jet and ivory bangles chattering on her arms. The gentleman was dressed entirely in violet.

"Zenobia, Fabianus, you know Lady Rahela."

"Charmed?" The gentleman in violet sounded uncertain.

He wore a blank expression, but that might just be his face. It wasn't entirely vacant. Dragons were painted on his countenance in clear imitation of the Cobra, a pink dragon on his left cheek, a blue one on his right, and a tiny purple dragon between his eyebrows. Dragons suited the Cobra better.

Lady Zenobia of the ivory bangles was silent. She seemed certain she wasn't charmed.

It was a relief when the king rose and made his address to the court. Everyone focused their attention on Octavian. He was worth looking at. Sable lent breadth to his shoulders, furs a dark waterfall behind him. He had forgone the crowned mask and clawed gloves, and didn't need them to give him a regal air. If Rae squinted, she could almost see the Emperor.

The king's voice rang from darkly gleaming floor to silver-arched ceiling. "My beloved court, I present the Princess Vasilisa."

Princess Vasilisa wore a large golden diadem, whirls of gold set with heavy pearls that were no doubt priceless but looked bulgy and pallid. Dark rich fabric swathed her from chin to feet. Her throat appeared to be wearing a corset. Sandwiched between diadem and dress was Vasilisa's face, appearing pasted on by mistake.

Octavian's smile suggested only courteous welcome. His eyes skipped behind Vasilisa, searching for the vision of loveliness that was Lia.

"Princess, I speak for the entire country when I say how glad we are to receive you."

Vasilisa's voice was tranquil. "I am glad to be here."

She didn't appear dazzled by Octavian's beauty. Maybe she wasn't the type to wear her heart on her sleeve. Or maybe it would take Octavian longer to win Vasilisa's heart this time.

"We issue an invitation for you to join our ladies-in-waiting-to-be-queen. It is an honour never before offered to anyone outside Eyam. We hope you will accept."

"Thank you." Vasilisa's voice remained tranquil. "We refuse to be honoured in this way."

The collective hiss of the court rose to a whine that might reduce the mirrored ceiling to dust. King Octavian's hand, extended in regal invitation, twitched.

Prime Minister Pio gave an unctuous hiss. "Your Highness! You can't understand what being a lady-in-waiting entails. Allow me to explain."

"I do not enjoy when men explain things to me," said Vasilisa. "I was already enlightened by a lady-in-waiting."

Rae slid down low on the settee. "Oh shit."

"What did you *do*," the Golden Cobra whisper-wailed in Rae's ear.

Oblivious to the havoc she was wreaking in the story and Rae's poor heart, Princess Vasilisa continued, "When two countries seek alliance, both must learn the customs of the other. In my land, if a man wishes to marry a woman, he singles her out for special attention. To be asked to join a crowd is an insult. Your Majesty, this must be a cultural misunderstanding. You cannot wish to offer insult to my country."

Despite Rae's despair, she couldn't help a smirk. Princess Vasilisa was good.

So was Octavian. He turned smoothly on a dime. "I'm sure we can come to an arrangement agreeable to both countries. I simply wish to do you honour in any way possible. Forgive me. Let us negotiate later. Favour me with your hand for the opening dance."

Rae guessed royals were trained to smooth out any social situation that went lumpy. Vasilisa inclined her heavily jewelled head. Octavian spun on his heel, back to his ministers.

The crowd ebbed away from Vasilisa, leaving her in her own private island of solitude. In the original story, the princess was swarmed by toadies. In the original story Vasilisa hadn't turned their king down flat. A black-haired beauty in armour started forward, but stilled at a glare from her princess. She must be Vasilisa's second bodyguard, fated to be the midnight guardian beside her queen's throne. Rae hoped this one would survive. If Rae recalled correctly, her name was Ziyi. Key, standing beside Ziyi, whispered in her ear and Ziyi's stern expression relaxed slightly.

Now Rae knew Key was up for meaningless villainous kissing, perhaps Ziyi was next. She had a faint sour taste in her mouth at the thought, but Key should have his fun before he died for Lia.

"Let's help the princess," Rae whispered.

The Cobra squawked like an offended chicken. "No more story interference."

"This is all my fault—"

The Golden Cobra cast one glance at Vasilisa, standing alone in a crowd with her shoulders squared, and melted like ice cream in hell.

He waved, a golden beacon impossible to miss. "Your Highness, join us."

When Vasilisa's eye fell upon Rae, her lips curved in a half-smile. She made her way to them and settled on a gilt-and-glass chair, folding her capable-looking hands in her satin lap.

Since they were fixing the story and the Ice Queen's infatuation with Octavian led to ice raiders attacking the capital, Rae thought she should check in on Vasilisa's feelings regarding His Majesty. "Hello there. See any gentlemen you fancy?"

"Well." Princess Vasilisa blushed, then ventured a whisper in Rae's ear. "You can't help noticing him across the room, can you?"

So she was still into Octavian. Guys with great bone structure could get away with anything.

A hush descended. The literary salon was seldom at a loss for words, but they'd just been hit with a scarlet siren and a foreign princess in under five minutes.

The gentleman in violet leaned forward. "We haven't been properly introduced, Your Highness, on account of you being recently arrived from across the turbulent sea. But I must thank you and Lady Rahela for what you did for the Horrors."

Vasilisa looked politely baffled.

Rae was less polite. "The what now?"

"M'sisters," he elaborated. "Hortensia and Horatia. The twins, don't you know. It's a pet name. Affectionate, I assure you! Unless Hortensia scolds me before breakfast. I'm so grumpy before breakfast, I believe I keep my good mood in among the scrambled eggs. Fabianus Nemeth at your service."

Lord Fabianus, the older brother Horatia had mentioned. The eldest son and heir of the commander general. Fabianus, lemon blond and slender, was as similar to the twins as he was utterly unlike that burly salt-and-pepper warrior, his father.

"You're the brother who refused the magical gauntlets."

Lord Fabianus nodded. "Horry did far better than I could have. I would have swooned in her place. That's me: bloody useless. Awful trial for the family. M'baby brother Tycho is my father's consolation. Very fond of fighting. And clever as anything! Like the Horrors. Afraid I'm the fool of the family."

This dire proclamation didn't seem to bother him. Fabianus was an extremely minor character, mostly seen hanging out with his sisters and criticizing other girls' dresses. Ministers sneered at General Nemeth about his disappointing heir. Many readers thought Lord Fabianus was obviously gay. Alice said that was an offensive stereotype.

Rae didn't remember Fabianus ever actually doing anything villainous. A guy was allowed to discuss fashion with his sisters.

"How is Lady Hortensia's wound?" Vasilisa inquired.

Fabianus's hopeful smile dimmed. "We hope she'll mend. I thank you for asking."

There was another silence.

"Forgive me for bringing up a painful subject," Vasilisa's voice was strained. "I'm still growing used to the ways of Eyam, and I can sometimes be a trifle awkward in society."

The Cobra patted her tightly folded hands. "You're doing great."

Fabianus nodded vigorously. "You'll learn the ways of Eyam in no time, since you're so clever. You knew exactly what to say to the king. Put it so well that you put him in the wrong. Idiots always enjoy seeing other people being clever. What you did was as good as a play."

Zenobia shook her beautiful ostrich-feathered head. "Have a care, Fabianus."

"Are you disagreeing with me?"

Zenobia lifted one shoulder in a shrug. "I didn't say that."

In Rae's experience, idiots didn't enjoy seeing other people be clever at all.

A small but real smile touched Vasilisa's compressed lips. "Thank you, Lord Fabianus. I studied to be a diplomat. International relations are my passion."

"Gosh," murmured Fabianus. He was either impressed or terrified, Rae wasn't sure which.

The Cobra abruptly seized her fan and her attention. Rae turned to see him twirl the fan in his left hand so hard it blurred in the air like a bloodstained ghost. The pointed, unmistakable gesture meant *We are watched.*

It was lucky the Cobra had taken her fan, since Rae went numb with panic down to her fingertips. She huddled beside him, both peering over the fan at their doom. A towering white-clad figure loomed amidst the courtiers' rainbow array of costumes, pristine and lonely as an ice-bound cliff.

"Marius," murmured the Cobra. "He's feeling shy."

"He's looking murderous!" Rae hissed back.

She couldn't be the Cobra, lost in a story and obsessing over characters' wellbeing. *She* was the one who mattered. She was getting out alive.

Her odds didn't look good. The plan was to steal the king's keys in the next five minutes. The Last Hope was bearing down on them now.

CHAPTER EIGHTEEN

The Cobra's Night of Crime

The boy dropped from the sky. After a moment, Marius realized he'd swung from the branches of a hawthorn tree. The boy was Marius's age, slight and dark-complected, and his face was impossibly luminous. Marius glanced around, but there was nobody behind him.

"Marius," the stranger breathed. "Lord Marius Valerius. The Last Hope."

Nobody had ever looked so pleased to see Marius before.

Torn between wariness and delight, Marius asked, "How do you know me?"

Shadow touched the stranger's face, and stayed like a mask over the sun. Years would pass. That first golden openness would not return.

"Even if I told you," the boy said, "you'd never believe me."

Time of Iron, ANONYMOUS

arius loathed gatherings. He hated soirees, he detested salons, and he kept aloof at get-togethers. Tea parties were torment, and picnics were simply tea parties wearing blankets. Social interaction meant talking to people when he had nothing to say, and being too near people who were scared of him.

This ball was the first public occasion he'd attended since being released from the Cobra's control.

He had tentatively hoped this ball might be different.

It *was* different. It was much worse.

When he, Octavian, and Lucius were pages and squires, togetherness was easy. The crown prince and the young lords lived in each other's quivers, friends near to hand as his next arrow. Marius's history might be dark, but his future was bright.

Marius left for the Ivory Tower before he was made a knight. He intended never to return, but when Octavian's parents and Lucius died in the same year, Octavian asked him to come. He'd believed Octavian could still be the leader Marius dreamed of. A leader Marius could follow anywhere, because he would never lead Marius into dishonour.

Then the Cobra happened.

For a time Marius was stunned by being villainously blackmailed. As the daze dissipated, Marius realized the Cobra was deliberately keeping Marius and his king apart. He'd longed for the day he could break free.

Freedom was different than he'd imagined. The king's ministers spent a great deal of time flattering Octavian. The king's companions spent a great deal of time discussing warfare and women. Marius spent a great deal of time in awkward silence.

This ball made him yearn for awkward silence. Octavian was in a foul mood and the court desperate to distract him. Music was playing loud, crowds gathering close, and Lady Horatia had perched on an arm of the throne. Octavian cast a meaningful glance in Marius's direction when she did so, but his king couldn't be discourteous enough to ask a lady to move. Instead he whispered jokes in her ear, while Horatia giggled as if her twin was not direly ill. Marius would never believe the rumours about Octavian consorting with the ladies-in-waiting ... but he could see how the rumours got started.

General Nemeth's face was grim as he tried to ignore his daughter's cavorting. Marius was politically more in sympathy with Prime Minister Pio, a sensible sort, devoted to upholding tradition, but he felt for the general.

Pio coughed. "Looks like a fine day tomorrow."

Nemeth scowled. "It is perfectly obvious it will rain!"

After a hundred assemblies Marius knew better than to comment. The commander general had once started a brawl over legislation on jewellery. Discussion of the weather might lead to a duel.

To Marius's relief, young Lord Adel asked, "Didn't you think the king's shot was flawless earlier?"

Octavian's party had been hunting firebirds among the Waiting Elms with bows in hand and flasks at their hips. Marius had touched neither bow nor flask. He could have pointed out the flame-tipped wings, their light wavering and almost transparent against the red-tinged silver of the trees. He hadn't.

"The king's shot was good," Marius said diplomatically. "Considering he drinks too much and practises too little."

Apparently that wasn't diplomatic enough.

Lord Adel's face clouded. "I'd like to see you do better. Wait, you can't. Because you took vows. How convenient."

"Yes," said Marius wearily. "I took vows."

Jangling instruments and raucous laughter were giving Marius a headache worse than any he got from reading. When he grew sick of study in the library, he could always write a letter to Caracalla.

Everybody in court believed Marius was a scholar, and he tried. He enjoyed discovering an interesting fact and hunting the fact like a fox through forests of books, making discoveries totally different from the knowledge he'd begun hunting for. But when Marius considered writing his own scholarly work, he couldn't imagine where to start.

You can turn a sword into a ploughshare, but can you turn a sword into a quill? a tutor at the Tower asked Marius. The scholars of the Ivory Tower whipped him for clumsiness in constructing sentences. The scholars whipped him for many reasons.

When Marius's head or shoulders ached with the burden of memory, he took a quill and a clean sheet of paper and began *Dear Caracalla*. His pen could do that much. He could make a bridge of words across the distance from him to his small sister.

He didn't know what to do now. Usually the Cobra would drag Marius off to join his loathsome coterie where Marius could think peacefully about how much he disliked his surroundings. Awkward silence never stood a chance against the Cobra.

As his mind went to the Cobra, Marius's eyes followed. Popenjoy was in the centre of his crowd, holding forth as usual.

Not as usual: who was he with? What were they *wearing*?

The whole court was buzzing about the Cobra's torrid affair with the Beauty Dipped In Blood. The king finally saw Lady Rahela for the vile creature she was, but Lady Rahela had her claws in another powerful man. It was written all over her vixen's face: Lady Rahela was plotting something. It was Marius's duty to discover what.

Marius wasn't an inconspicuous individual. Two pairs of wicked eyes peered over the crimson edge of a fan, following his progress towards them. Lady Rahela's leg was hooked over the Cobra's, scandalously bared. Each had apparently attempted to put their clothes on, and missed.

The Cobra whispered something in the Beauty's ear, lowered the fan, and stared Marius down.

"Hello," said Marius.

That was the obvious conversational opener.

"Hello, my lord," returned the Golden Cobra. Everyone within earshot jerked into shocked silence. "Don't kill me."

Usually, Marius was summoned to the Cobra's side by his golden sleeve flying like a flag for a one-man country. Lady Zenobia passed Lord Fabianus the smelling salts, then mouthed an imperious "*What?*" in Marius's direction. The woman was intimate friends with both the Domitian and Aurellian matriarchs. She was terrifying.

All social interactions were bad. This might be the worst ever.

Marius cleared his throat. "You don't have to say that every time you see me."

"I really want you to remember it, *my lord.*"

The two words landed like a slap, one to each side of the face. Marius barely stopped himself from flinching.

The Cobra continued, "You're no longer obliged to associate with us. What a relief for you, not having to endure discussion of the arts. You'll be spared from attending my theatrical opening nights in future."

Lady Rahela disengaged from the Cobra.

"You write plays?" Her voice was genuinely stunned. She didn't know him at all.

The members of the salon visibly relaxed at this conversational turn.

Dignified Lady Zenobia unbent enough to make a recommendation. "You must watch a performance of his greatest work, *Romeo & Juliet Overthrow the Government.*"

Lady Rahela's face did something very strange. "What!"

Everybody said Lady Rahela was a vicious woman. It appeared to be true, and the Cobra appeared to like it. She smacked at his shoulder as he threw back his head and laughed. "You're insane for this!"

"I'm an *artiste*," the Cobra said loftily. "Once I finish *The Bone of Contention*, then you will all see!"

"If you ever finish it," Lady Zenobia murmured under her breath.

The Cobra rose. "The world is watching. Let's give 'em the old razzle dazzle."

He offered his hand with a flourish. Lady Rahela accepted it, muttering, "To think my sister mocked me for learning every song in the musical by heart."

Marius had no idea what a musical might be, but he had heard Lady Lia was an accomplished harpist. That seemed graceful, appropriate, and nothing like what was happening here. Even Lady Rahela, shameless minx that she was, appeared apprehensive.

Or perhaps she was feigning nerves so the Cobra would pull her against him and breathe, "You know when crowds break into spontaneous song and dance in the course of their normal lives? People make those scenes up because they want them to be true. They want to believe art and joy can transform a moment into glory. So believe."

Rahela smiled, as most did for Lord Popenjoy. "I'll act like I do."

The Cobra attempted to lead his lady onto the floor, though the music for dancing hadn't yet commenced. Whatever they were plotting, Marius must prevent it. He placed his own body as an insuperable barrier between Popenjoy and his goal.

"I will not watch you villains put on a show."

Lady Rahela pasted a smirk on slightly trembling lips. The Cobra fired a disdainful glance under his gold-tipped eyelashes and leaned in to whisper, "Then look away, my lord. Villains are stealing the show."

Marius had endured enough. He grasped the Cobra's wrist with no fuss or overt threat, simply employing the Valerius strength that could shatter iron or stone. No flesh and blood could withstand him.

"You cannot break my hold," Marius said quietly. "You'll break your wrist if you try."

The Cobra threw him a glittering smile as if negligently tossing a coin to a servant boy. "Fine by me."

"Fine by you?" Marius repeated in disbelief.

"I want to cause a scene," the Cobra explained smoothly. "I don't particularly care how."

He had a warm inviting voice, a voice that sang a song you could dance to. Marius Valerius didn't enjoy dancing.

Baffled rage held him still. Without further ado, the Cobra wrenched away. It was pointless as a man smashing his limb down on an iron forge, shattered bones the only possible end. Meeting immovable force, the Cobra drew in a quick hurt breath.

Entirely against Marius's will, his clenched fist fell open. The Cobra swept past unscathed. Marius was left staring at his own helplessly open hand. How had the Cobra done that?

As Marius stood stricken, a minister of middle age, middle height and middling reputation approached. Instead of talking politics, he had much to say about his charming, affectionate and good-looking son, who he thought Marius might befriend. Marius was neither charming nor affectionate, and had started going grey in his teens. It didn't sound as if they had much in common, but it was touching the minister was such a proud father. Marius tried to catch the reins of his own escaping attention and follow the man's remarks.

Just as the man cut himself off to demand, "What are they *doing*?" Marius whirled around.

All the candles in the great chandelier were blown out by a sudden gust of wind indoors. A great lamp swung from an inner balcony, casting a circle of brilliant light across the gleaming black floor.

The Golden Cobra and the Beauty Dipped In Blood stood on the edge of the light, the focus of the whole room. The skirt of Lady

Rahela's gown, swinging curtains of rubies and scarlet silk cut into serpent shapes, concealed nothing. The Cobra's herigaut was cloth of gold, two glittering pieces of fabric barely held together by a jewelled snake belt. Gold thread ran along the filmy white material barely containing Lady Rahela's chest, gilt on the rims of two porcelain teacups. The Cobra's herigaut was lined with scarlet. His scarlet-trimmed sleeves started at his elbows, shoulders and upper arms entirely bared. Coiling vipers that echoed Rahela's bracelet were brightly painted over his dark skin.

Each wore touches of the other's colour. The most notorious man and the most notorious woman in court were dressed as a set.

"Ladies and gentlethem." The Cobra's voice rang golden in the dark. "May we ask sympathy for the evil? Sing it if you feel it."

The Cobra's voice pealed out, the only man Marius knew who could put laughter into song. *"In the end, the good guys are winners. Come the end, it's curtains for sinners."*

Rahela's scarlet lip curled as she crooned back, *"In the end, it's curtains for everyone. And let's be real. Being evil is fun."*

Lady Rahela swayed from shadow to light. The Cobra moved sinuously behind her, strong hands sliding from bare shoulders to hips, and they sang together. Lady Rahela leaned against his chest. Her tapering fingers traced the sharp line of his jaw, smearing paint until her fingertips were dipped in gold. *"The side of light seem so stressed. We remain relaxed and well dressed. No happy endings, but we have good times. Guilty! Of loving eyeliner and crimes."*

Shocked gasps burst from the crowd as the Cobra sent Rahela spinning across the floor, her red skirts flying like tossed petals to reveal so much long leg. *"Lock me up, throw away the key. Come and get chained up with me."*

Lady Rahela danced until she backed up into Lady Horatia Nemeth, then crouched, sliding up Horatia as if she were a wall. Hectic colour rushed to Lady Horatia's face, both hands flying to her mouth, as she squeaked out, "Evil!"

The Cobra tossed an amused glance over his shoulder before dropping to his knees at the feet of – the commander general's maiden aunt! The grey-haired and respectable Lady Lavinia, here to chaperon the motherless twins, stared as the Cobra kissed her palms, leaving traces of gold paint like glittering ghosts to remind her where his mouth had been. *"Lord knows you're gonna regret it. Everyone knows baddies can get it."*

Lady Lavinia giggled like a giddy girl. "Evil!"

The Cobra circled Lady Zenobia and Lord Fabianus, who slapped at him and shrieked out "Evil!" and began to dance, as Lady Rahela rushed a knot of ladies-in-waiting. Both sang the same verse, turning from one person to the next. *"I say sorry for everything in my death scene. While I'm alive, I stay funny and mean. Forgive me not, but if you don't he will. Ruthless, half-dressed: Kiss me, I'm evil."*

The girls, survivors of the Court of Air and Grace, started clapping and calling out, "Evil!" Next Lady Rahela prowled towards Prime Minister Pio, who ran away and hid behind the throne. She smiled, shrugged and sang: *"You stay hating, I'm on a roll. Evil's like bubble bath for the soul. Sealing my fate with a Judas kiss. I'm not being subtle about this."*

As she passed the king, she blew a kiss from her scarlet mouth to her sinful fingertips, flying out to him. When he grasped for her, she whirled back to the Cobra.

Who sang, *"To thine own evil self be true. Didn't expect it? That's kind of on you."*

Rahela did a handstand like a tumbler from the circus. She sprang using hands instead of feet, seeming to fly into the air. The Cobra caught her legs – he touched her ankles! – and set her on his broad shoulders. She stood on high, hand on her hip, then made an exaggerated red moue of dismay and waved at the king.

"Maybe you're the hero because you make me suffer. Maybe I'm the making of you. C'mon call me, lover."

Rahela fell backward. The Cobra caught her. They spun and laughed and sang, until she rolled out of his arms onto her feet, expression suddenly solemn. Alone in the dark she sang, *"I see what is to come, I am not a fool. It's true I'm a liar and this story is so cruel. Off with her head while the crowd rejoices. No hero to save me, I made bad though sexy choices."*

She smirked, but Princess Vasilisa called out "Evil," in firm and serious tones. Lord Fabianus took this cue to seize the princess's hand and spin her into the dance.

The Cobra sang back in a rhythmic chant, half speech half song. *"Bad? I'm drawn that way, you're drawn to me. Tell on yourself when you call it villainy. Won't unpack all that. Evil? Be thou my good. Game so strong they'll say I'm misunderstood."*

Half the court was dancing, or calling out "Evil!" in a frenzy.

Fury drowned the king's previously intrigued expression as Lady Rahela grasped the Cobra's snake belt, whipping it off, spinning it over her head, then looping it around his wrists as they sang together again. The Cobra offered up his bound wrists, letting her pull him in. Lady Rahela dipped him so his hair swept the floor with a chime of bells. He smirked, upside down, as they chanted together. *"Once upon a time came too late. I'd rather die than submit to my fate. Cue thunder and sinister lighting. Have you heard I go down ... fighting?"*

Marius didn't understand the significant pause, but the Cobra's smirk made him sure he highly disapproved of it.

"They should be arrested," announced Marius. "No. Executed."

They weren't being arrested. They were dancing in the king's direction. Octavian was engulfed in gleeful chaos as the wicked pair swung, singing, around him, making him the centre of their plot. *"Call me a snake but I'm not gonna crawl. Meant to repent but not sorry at all. When I meet a bad end put it on my grave: Here lies a sinner, and a total babe."*

The Cobra confessed, *"Finished from the opening line."*

Eyes on Octavian, the lady sang, *"Last word's yours, this one's mine."*

The Cobra warned, *"Girl, evil leads only to sorrow."*

Lady Rahela purred, *"Boy, I swear I'll reform ... tomorrow."*

The Beauty performed such an elaborate undulation that she would have overbalanced, if her bodyguard hadn't neatly stepped in to bear her weight and the king caught her hand. The Cobra leaned an elbow on the king's shoulder for an instant, passed a tip to the bodyguard for the assistance, and departed, breaking up the tableau.

Their strategic dancing paid off. Octavian condescended to applaud, turning the appalling spectacle into a piece of risqué fun.

Octavian's eyes were sparkling in the old way as he looked at Lady

Rahela, as if she were the most exciting woman he'd ever seen. The Cobra sauntered over to the minister Marius had been conversing with, snatched his glass of champagne, and drained it in one gulp. He took another glass off a passing server's tray and drank that too.

"Sorry, very thirsty. Me and Lady Lavinia both, it appears."

Other people had private jokes with friends, Marius heard, but the Cobra only made jokes to amuse himself. Marius reached for another glass for the Cobra to drink later, as usual.

"Who's that for?" the Cobra asked. "Can't be me, since we're not friends."

Marius withdrew his hand from the tray. The Cobra's expression taunted him.

The minister was blinking at the Cobra as if he'd stared too long at the sun. "Lord Popenjoy, you disgrace the king's court as you defile the city's skyline!"

The Cobra sounded politely curious. "I thought you honoured the Golden Brothel with your patronage, Lord Zoltan."

Zoltan's face boiled to lobster hue. "Men have needs."

"*Must* you insult me and Lord Marius?"

Zoltan's eyes darted to Marius like rodents fleeing in terror. "Lord Marius, I would never!"

"Lord Marius is a man too. Men have needs? Spare me. Men have need of food, sleep and shelter. Calling anything else a need is frankly embarrassing. Carnal extravagance is not a necessity to resent but a luxury I enjoy."

"It's not about enjoying yourself!"

"I'm sorry for your wife and both your mistresses."

The Cobra shrugged, eyes fastening on the curve of the marble staircase. Marius followed his gaze.

"What is it now?"

"I'm not here to talk."

"Really?" asked Marius. "This is the first time you've gone any-where to be silent."

The Cobra laughed. Since he'd approached Marius and he was laughing, perhaps he was almost done being angry. The Cobra being furious with him was an unfamiliar feeling, more uncomfortable than Marius would have expected. Marius let the corner of his mouth jerk up slightly, then turned his face away.

"Don't worry, I won't stick around," the Cobra said nonsensically. Nobody had asked him to leave. "I just want a front row seat for this. Remember the Court of Air and Grace?"

The Cobra used an odd word for the act of remembering events past. He called it a *flashback*. Marius had never understood until now, when memory went through him like a shudder of the mind.

"I do. Why did you try to feed yourself to a ghoul?"

The Cobra ignored Marius's reasonable question. "Did you notice Lady Lia?"

"I was marshalling our forces against the invasion of the undead."

For some reason, the Cobra beamed. Marius felt it was inappropriate to beam about the undead. "I *knew* you hadn't seen her. You *will* see her. For the first time! Tonight. You've probably imagined what she'd look like, right?"

The memory of Lady Lia's soft voice returned to him, so scared she pleaded with air and ashes.

"All I thought about was how much I wanted to help her."

The Cobra scrunched his face up in an alarming fashion. "So pure."

Marius refused to respond to comments he didn't understand. "Why isn't Lady Lia here already?"

"She's due at dramatic timing o'clock." The Cobra tapped his bare wrist once. Twice. Three times, as the music for the last song before dancing fell gradually away.

A girl appeared at the top of the stairs.

Marius recognized the gown, not the girl.

The dress was a fabric called 'woven by air', the strands it was composed of so gossamer light and silvery pale the cloth gave the illusion of transparency. People claimed the material was woven by ghosts in the sea, made soft as water. The ladies at the salon, and Lord Fabianus, couldn't stop talking about 'woven by air' when a shipment of the stuff came in. The fabric cost more than a house. Marius wanted his sister to have the best.

Then his mother announced they couldn't visit court this year.

Marius wondered what he would do with the material, and thought of Lady Lia. If Caracalla was friendless and adrift in the court, Marius would want somebody to help her. He found a maid who needed money enough to make the dress and keep a secret.

"So that's Lady Lia," Marius murmured.

The lady looked like her voice. The voice he hadn't been able to forget.

The drapery clung to her slight form, intricate designs gleaming and disappearing like pale flowers glimpsed under water. Lady Lia's hair was a river, with lilies drifting in the gold.

Marius felt he'd finally done something right.

Zoltan said, "I also have a lovely daughter."

By unspoken mutual agreement, they were ignoring Lord Zoltan.

The Cobra asked softly, "Isn't she beautiful?"

"You're *disgusting*," Marius snarled. "Have you no shame? You're ogling the *sister* of the woman you performed an unspeakably indecent dance with!"

The Cobra stared open-mouthed until his mouth closed and curved. "Yes, I'm a villain. Concentrate on the damsel in distress."

The glowing girl reached the last step of the grand staircase, as the music began for the first official dance.

Lady Rahela darted serpent-swift from Octavian's side. The king and Princess Vasilisa walked towards each other as if to an execution. The whole court saw Octavian lift his gaze to Lia on the last step, how her light filled his eyes . . . and how he turned back to the princess.

Lady Lia would be the first lady-in-waiting ever not to open her ball by dancing with the king.

Lady Lia had no bodyguard, not even a maid. She was all alone. That made her a target. Even her beauty seemed piteous because it could not win a single person to her side. Lia trembled like moonlight on rippling water, and a mocking laugh moved through the crowd.

"Someone must do something," Marius whispered.

"Yes," the Cobra murmured encouragingly in his ear.

"Could . . . you . . . dance with her? Decorously!"

The Cobra sighed. "I have to do everything myself."

He shoved Marius hard between the shoulder blades. Caught off guard, Marius stumbled. It was only a step, but it sent him over the invisible line onto the dance floor empty of all but the king, the princess, and the damsel in distress. Behind Marius, the Cobra steered Lord Zoltan away, talking about shipping. Apparently there were investments to be made at the harbour.

Marius was deserted in the middle of the dance floor. Terror descended as he realized he must make small talk. He faced Lady Lia as though she were an enemy army.

Remembering the court's laughter, he bowed as if for a queen. "Forgive me for addressing you without an introduction. I am Marius Valerius."

When he straightened, he looked a long way down. Her flower-tender face turned up to his. Though Lady Lia was tiny and delicate, she didn't look threatened.

"I know who you are, my lord. I owe you a great debt."

"You owe me nothing. I will owe you a debt if you do me the favour of dancing with me."

Marius offered a brute's hand made to wrap around a throat. She laid lily-soft fingers against his palm. Silence fell like rain around them. He'd never danced at court before. The last time he'd danced was back home with his sister's small feet balanced on his.

"I hope I still remember how to dance," he muttered.

Caracalla had laughed when spun. So had Lady Rahela with the Cobra. Perhaps all ladies liked to be spun.

So Marius spun Lady Lia, with care. She drifted over the dark floor in her diaphanous dress like a dainty cloud. Battle lived in his bones: he read bodies better than books. He knew when someone's movements might falter. He kept tight hold of her hand, steadying her when she stumbled, letting nobody suspect the lady was anything but grace itself.

Lady Lia's face was radiant as moonshine on water. "I saw you talking to your friend. It's easy to find him in a crowd. Lord Popenjoy is a perfectly lovely man."

What enchantments did the Cobra weave around women!

"He's been wonderfully kind to me ever since I came to the palace.

I know you two are close, so I can tell you this: he paid off one of the cooks to make sure I was served meals like a noble."

She clearly believed Marius would be proud of the Cobra's gallant action. Instead Marius felt adrift on a sea of dread. What designs did the Cobra have on an unprotected beauty?

"You're like him," said Lia, to Marius's extreme horror. "I can't thank you enough for your kindness. This dress is impossibly beautiful. I fear it was expensive."

He shook his head. It was wrong to lie, but it was also wrong to embarrass a lady. Marius had to choose a favourite sin.

Lia's clear-eyed smile said she saw the truth. "This gown is worth more than my life. But I'm attached to my life. You saved me from execution, my lord. Thank you."

The Cobra would have known what to say. Marius did not. This was already the longest private conversation he'd had with a woman he wasn't related to in years.

"My behaviour was selfish," he told her. "I did only what I wished. I wanted to do the right thing."

Octavian and Princess Vasilisa danced past, moving with correctness so extreme they appeared like wooden puppets. Lia shied back, tripping over the hem of her gown. Marius hastily caught her in his arms, shoring her up against his chest. She weighed little more than a kitten or a bird.

"I apologize," said Marius at once.

Her voice drifted up to him, her gaze fastened on his buttons. "It's not your fault. I was taught to dance as a child. Those were happy days, but long ago. I suppose I forgot."

Her pretty, sorrowful voice brought back memories, not in a flash flood but a meandering river. His father placing a sword in his small hand, his mother singing over Caracalla's cradle. Listening to the sweet song for his sister, when he was raised on war chants. Holding the baby and learning for the first time to be gentle. Love for Marius meant going against his own nature.

Happy days, long ago.

"If you don't wish to dance, I could accompany you to the balcony for a breath of air," Marius suggested, then recalled maids and guards weren't allowed on the grand balcony, only nobles. Squires snickered about cornering ladies on the balcony for dalliance. "I beg your pardon for making such a suggestion. Let me fetch you a glass of lemonade."

"I trust you," said Lady Lia. "I'll go."

The whole world feared Marius. This girl was mistreated by the court, wronged by her own family, but ready to risk trusting a stranger. Either she had an amazingly pure heart, or she saw something in Marius that he'd never been able to see in himself.

"I fear the fireworks won't happen for some time."

"I prefer the light of the moon."

Marius smiled down at Lia. "So do I."

Upon opening the doors, they found the balcony an enclosed lake of moonlight. Lady Lia stepped out and was submerged in moonbeams, invisible for an instant. Far above the moon sailed in a cloud-soft sea.

A balcony was a sacred place, intended for contemplation of the ravine. The ballroom and the court lay behind glass doors. It was a relief to be done with the keen eyes and cruel whispers. There was nothing behind Marius that he missed.

Marius looked over his shoulder towards the Cobra. Lia was right: it was easy to find him in a crowd. He was a comet, the brightest thing leaving the night. He passed another tip to Lady Rahela's bodyguard and waltzed casually out of the ballroom doors.

The ministers complained the Cobra's lavishing of money on the staff proved he was a spendthrift who shouldn't have a voice in the country's economy. The Cobra said he hated lousy tippers. Anyone watching would see the Cobra flinging money around as usual. Nobody else would remember the Cobra had already thrown coin to the bodyguard at the end of the dance.

Even the Cobra wouldn't tip someone twice for the same thing.

Suddenly Marius thought of Lady Lia's slips, and the tumble Lady Rahela had almost taken when she was next to the king. Lady Rahela had completed many horrifying manoeuvres with athletic grace. Anyone could fall, but her convenient clumsiness didn't sit right with Marius.

The Cobra rolled his eyes behind the king's back whenever Octavian spoke, and never touched Octavian if he could help it. But he'd touched Octavian tonight, then passed something to Lady Rahela's bodyguard immediately afterward.

What did Marius's eyes tell him, with no assumptions clouding his sight?

Lady Rahela had created a scarlet diversion. The Cobra had passed an object to Lady Rahela's bodyguard.

Now either Marius had witnessed the Cobra passing something else to the bodyguard, or the bodyguard had passed an object *back* to the Cobra.

Something the Cobra had taken from the king.

"Deepest apologies, my lady. I must prevent a crime in progress."

"*What?*" exclaimed Lady Lia. Marius had already departed the balcony.

He didn't run. Running attracted attention. He cut through the crowd as if through a battlefield, moving at a relentless pace, hunting his prey down.

He made it through the ballroom doors in time to see the gold hem of a herigaut whisk around a corner, and followed. Far enough so the Cobra wouldn't be alerted to his presence. Close enough so there was no chance for the Cobra to get away.

The Cobra swaggered into the heart of the palace, headed for the throne room.

Before the Cobra reached the shining double doors, he ducked into the Room of Memory and Bone. Marius stood on the threshold, watching with disbelief as Popenjoy laid his hand on an ivory panel. The panel slid aside to reveal a circular tunnel, and the Cobra stepped inside. Marius crouched and sprang, rolling to his feet as the panel slid shut behind them. He could hear the Cobra's breathing and his fast, decisive footsteps striking the stone, but the Cobra wouldn't hear him coming.

Big as you will be, you must learn to walk soft, his father said when Marius was a child. *Soft enough to steal up behind a man and cut his throat before he knows you're there.*

The tunnel descended into the cliff on which the palace was

built, a circle hewn into the rock tall and wide enough to fit a grown man. Who had made this, and when, and how did the Cobra know about it?

Up ahead a burning candle was set between a basin and the wall, creating a pale pool of light that wavered against the rock. Uncertain light caught on folds of gold embroidery as the Cobra began to shed his clothes.

Marius turned his back for decency's sake, then remembered the Cobra was an indecent criminal and looked around again. Underneath the herigaut, the Cobra wore battered brown leather breeches. He leaned and scooped up a jerkin in the same material and a cloth from the basin, briskly wiping gold paint off his chest and arms.

Marius rolled his eyes. The Cobra could have simply *not* chosen to paint himself with gold for his night of crime. He could also have left himself a shirt.

That wasn't important. Theft was important. Treason was important.

The Cobra folded up his cloth of gold, set it down on the ground in the filthy stone tunnel, and proceeded, blending with the shadows far better this time. He moved differently when dressed differently, as though he were an actor portraying two roles in a play, switching his character with his costume. Wind blew from the other end of the tunnel, a night wind carrying the smell of spices and the heavy trundle of carts.

The tunnel narrowed, curved roof shrinking down, making the Cobra duck. Marius followed his lead into the dark. Night air hit Marius, neither cold nor clean.

Marius had known the Cobra and the Beauty were up to something, but he'd never dreamed of this.

The secret passage led from the throne room to the Cauldron.

The Cobra stood at the mouth of the tunnel, silhouette outlined against the coloured lights and greasy revelry of the filthiest den of sin in Themesvar. The streets of the Cauldron were gutters teeming with outlaws. You couldn't call the Cauldron a thieves' den, because the thieves were crowded out by killers.

Marius prowled forward, soft enough to steal up behind a man and cut his throat before his prey knew he was there.

Close behind the Cobra, he murmured: "What did you steal from my king?"

CHAPTER NINETEEN

Hark, What Lady Through Yonder Window

The lord approached Lia on the balcony while Marius fetched lemonade. By the time Marius returned, the drunk youth was dragging Lia into the shadows.

An instant, crowded with incidents, followed. One glass and one man went over the side of the balcony.

"I never saw a man half killed with a glass of lemonade before," the lady remarked.

Marius bowed as he handed Lia the remaining glass, and retreated so even his shadow didn't touch her. "I should have realized my brutality would shock and frighten you. I apologize."

"I was not afraid." Lia's smile chased away every shadow. "I was grateful."

Time of Iron, ANONYMOUS

 n public occasions Emer carried a drawstring bag full of Rahela's cosmetics at her wrist, often hunting through the contents to find rosewater, angelica root rouge, or marjoram lip stain. Tonight, Emer scrabbled through a bag of emotions, trying to find the right one.

In the country estate where they grew up, everyone murmured Rahela was a gaudy red flower, blossoming early and sure to wither soon, and Lia was a pearl. In the sleepy Shroud valleys whispers rose like wheat. Emer always found the whispers puzzling. Why was it sad for flowers to wither, but wicked for women? The whispers contained no answers. The whispers drove Rahela to drag Lia down, despite the fact Lia was only a child. Lia's lessons stopped. Lia was put in drab clothes, hardly better dressed than a servant. It made no difference.

The whispers continued, though Rahela was hardly more than a child herself. Rahela's was a debauched beauty, degrading to possess and almost degrading to admire. Gentlemen of taste appreciated more refined beauties. Rahela was cheap.

As it emerged, Rahela was very expensive. Only the king could afford her. When they came to the capital and the king went wild for Rahela, the way people spoke about her changed. Suddenly she was the subject of songs and poetry, a siren and a scandal, the Beauty Dipped In Blood, the legendary woman of snow and flame. Her beauty was peerless, poisonous and paralysing, something no man could resist. Even though Rahela didn't actually look any different.

Years passed, Lia arrived from the countryside, and suddenly the story changed back. The men who blamed Rahela for being irresistible were now contemptuous, and that was Rahela's fault too.

The flower was withered. The pearl was shining.

Lia was the fairest. Everybody thought so.

Emer did, too. She strictly avoided Lia when they were children. Now Lia was at court she hardly dared look at her, in case Rahela saw the betrayal in Emer's mind. Until Rahela asked Emer to go to Lia, and make friends.

In the end, Lord Marius Valerius, the Last Hope, was no different from the others. Public opinion said the man was as cold as the beautiful statues he resembled, and even belowstairs gossip couldn't verify any scandalous rumours.

Many of the staff made attempts to catch Lord Marius's eye. Emer had watched with her own eyes a competition for the most provocative method of picking up an artfully dropped feather duster. When the ladies failed to attract attention, several footmen and under-butlers tried displaying their strong arms and height to clean the chandeliers.

Once the Golden Cobra breezed in and tried to tell him. "Marius, there are *five people* dusting in here."

"Libraries need a lot of dusting," the Last Hope returned sternly. "Because of all the books."

The Cobra laughed and chose a book from the shelves for Lord Marius before departing. Lord Marius turned his serious attention to the book, and didn't look up again.

Lord Marius never noticed anyone. Until Lia.

That was Lady Lia. She was like light or air. Even if you barred the door and shut the windows, she could slip through.

Emer's head was still spinning with dizzy horror at her own lady's latest madcap trick, when she saw Lia trembling like a lone candle flame in the centre of the gossip storm that was the ballroom. Lord Marius swept in, took her in his arms in front of everybody, and saved her. Lia's face went radiant with gratitude.

When Rahela had sent Emer on her mission of deception, Lia was transferred to the lady-in-waiting tower but she didn't have the stipend or official status. She wasn't granted a maid or a bodyguard, so Emer had no place allocated belowstairs. Lia and she shared the bed, pulling the white sheets over their heads to whisper secrets.

Watching Lia and Marius, Emer couldn't forget those nights.

"One day each of us must marry." Lia's whisper, low as the burning candle in their window. Filtered through the thin sheet, the candlelight turned her lashes gauzy gold. "What will having a husband be like?"

Years ago all the country girls made fanciful coloured sketches of the three famous shining knights. Laughing Lord Lucius, the sunshine of the court. The young prince. And the unconquerable Lord Marius.

Perhaps Lia would be the one to conquer him. They moved across the ballroom floor and through the balcony doors into the romantic moonlight. Emer watched gleaming glass doors close behind the perfect pair.

Then Lord Marius emerged from the balcony alone, wearing a

look that made his cold face seem stone twice over. People pulled back from the icy blaze of him as he cut a direct line through the crowd to where the Cobra had been an instant before.

They were discovered. They were doomed.

Lia was deserted. Emer could see the pale flutter of her dress beyond the glass, and guess at the calculations she was making. If Lia came inside, she would be alone and embarrassed again, with her admirer fled. If she stayed out there, she was prey.

There was no time to make the choice. Emer wasn't the only one who noticed Lia alone. A foppish young courtier, swaying from drink already, made for the balcony.

A lady must always be desired, but never possessed. There was nobody to protect her. Servants were forbidden to go out on the balcony, and no lord would be stopped by a maid.

Unless that maid had a weapon. Emer recalled the confidence and power she'd felt wielding a blade in the Court of Air and Grace. Then she shook off the wild fancy. She was not Key.

There was only one possible source of help. Rahela was pretending acceptance of her stepsister, to inflame the king with jealousy. It was an ingenious scheme, sure to fail.

Ultimately Octavian would always choose Lia. Anybody would.

But Emer could use Rahela's pretence to help Lia now. Emer moved discreetly across the edges of the ballroom, head bowed, the perfect maid. The old Rahela was always uneasily aware people thought she had more in her bodice than her brain. The new Rahela was sitting among the members of the literary salon, conversing with Lady Zenobia Marcianus, the most intelligent and well-connected woman in court. Even more shocking, Lord Fabianus Nemeth was addressing the foreign princess.

"Please forgive my impertinence."

"I can't, until I know how impertinent you intend to be," said Princess Vasilisa.

"—you're so clever! Would you be offended if I suggested a casual mode of dress might truly become you? If you wore your hair down and considered warm tones—"

Under cover of Fabianus's fatuous voice, nobody heard the sound of silk ripping and a series of cascading clicks. Rubies tumbled one by one onto the marble floor like expensive game pieces.

"Oh no, my lady," Emer said flatly. "You tore your dress."

Rahela's eyebrows, arched like swallow's wings, took flight. The silk was still clenched in Emer's fist. "That does appear to have happened!" She added in a hiss, "I can't afford to lose any of my dress. There isn't that much of it!"

Emer produced needle and thread from her apron. She busied herself repairing the gown she'd ripped apart, and muttered to Rahela out of the corner of her mouth.

"Lady Lia's on the balcony alone. There are noblemen on the prowl."

Rahela flapped her hand. "Don't even worry about it."

Emer's heart plummeted like an anchor off the jaunty sailboat of Rahela's indifference. She should have known Rahela would rejoice at Lia's downfall.

Rahela leaned forward. "Seriously, it's no big deal. The Last Hope will toss that fool right off the balcony. It'll be a bonding experience for them. Trust me, babe, I'm a holy prophet."

She used idiom similar to the Cobra these days. Emer supposed this was meant to seduce the Cobra to her side. Rahela's lady mother always said one must feign sharing men's interests, sharing their very thoughts. She said men wanted women to be nothing but mirrors with breasts.

Emer's needle stabbed through silk hard. "You might want to check with the gods again, my lady. Lord Marius recently exited the ballroom in hot pursuit of the Cobra."

Rahela jumped as if pinched. "He did what!"

An interval passed in which Rahela clutched at the ruby pins in her hair and took deep breaths, obviously running through the Cobra's new odds of success in her mind. Of course, she was only concerned about her plot. Emer snapped thread as if she were snapping a neck, and Rahela blinked into her accusing eyes.

"Right, damsel in distress. I feel that's an issue for a hero? I think it's hero o'clock. King Octavian should step up and save her. Don't hate the player, hate the endgame."

She gazed around in search of the king.

Lady Zenobia's lip curled. "His Majesty is in the Room of Revel and Retreat. As usual."

Rahela and Emer exchanged a frantic glance. As one, they twisted around and peered through the shimmering glass doors. Lia had her face turned up to the moonlight. She couldn't see the man's shadow falling across her slight, pale back.

"Is my mother right?" Rahela murmured. "Are men useless? They don't take out the trash, they don't rescue the damsels. The only thing a villainess should do at a party is make catty remarks and spill red wine on the heroine's dress! I never get a moment's peace to make catty remarks."

Emer was baffled by her ranting. Rahela's lady mother had many uses for men. They could be seduced for state secrets, married for money and estates, and poisoned to relieve one's feelings.

Rahela bolted from her seat and strode determinedly towards the balcony. She no longer walked as if unaccustomed to long skirts, but she still moved differently than before. She moved as if she expected people to get out of her way.

Far more discreetly, Emer rose, curtsied to Lady Zenobia and drifted to the gallery where Key stood discussing knife tricks with the foreign woman bodyguard. Ziyi of the icelands had clearly been expecting flirtation, but Key seemed more interested in her knives than her charms.

Emer and Key had struck their own bargain after the Court of Air and Grace, when Emer realised he might be useful to her. They were useful to each other now. Key might believe they were friends. Emer knew they were only allies.

Ziyi grinned at her. "Ah, the maid with the blade."

Emer offered a cautious smile, edged closer to Key and murmured, "Lady Rahela—"

"Is on the balcony, tending to her idiot sister," Key murmured back. "You don't need to tell me where she is. I always know where she is."

Emer wanted to say if he thought Lady Lia was an idiot, he didn't know much, but kept her silence. She'd betrayed Lia too often already.

Ziyi raised an eyebrow. "Is that where your interest lies?"

"Don't be absurd," Emer snapped. "I beg your pardon. I realize you're new to our kingdom. Perhaps you don't know that if a lady's name is mentioned in association with a servant's, it would be ruin. Lady Rahela would never dream of even touching a guard's hand."

Key's glance was so sharp it stung. "That's right," he said slowly. "Lady Rahela would never touch me."

He was different, these days. Emer had caught him sleeping like a guard dog outside their lady's chamber. The staff belowstairs had been menaced into providing constant hot water and snacks. When Emer asked how he could sleep on the stone floor, Key replied he slept as well there as anywhere. He added, sounding inappropriately amused, that he had nightmares of blood and lives cut short.

He *was* a nightmare.

It was Key's whim at present to be a faithful servant. Emer didn't know if she could trust that fancy to endure. She didn't know what would prove more dangerous: if it didn't last, or if it did.

A nearby guard saw where they were staring and chuckled. "Maybe the Harlot is on the balcony for a dalliance."

Key's neck twisted like a serpent. "Keep your tongue behind your teeth. Or lose both."

Threat radiated from Key like the waves of heat from a fire. The guard and Ziyi fell silent. Having ended all conversation, Key focused, intent on the night beyond the silvered glass.

"You can't possibly see anything," Ziyi said, puzzled.

Emer put a restraining hand on the rough leather cords tying Key's vambraces in place. No matter what trouble nobles got into, they were safer than servants. A servant could be sent to the Room of Dread and Anticipation for any transgression. He must not venture onto the balcony.

Even though both Emer and Key could see one thing clearly.

Something had gone terribly wrong out there.

CHAPTER TWENTY

The Villainess on the Romantic Balcony

Lady Rahela lay dead, smoking from the fire. Her serpent's bracelet had sunk deep into the blistered flesh of her arm. The king touched the heap that had once been the wicked Beauty with the tip of his boot.

"Throw her in the abyss with the wretched thing on. I will have a new mark of favour made." He smiled at Lady Lia. "For my new favourite."

Time of Iron, ANONYMOUS

ut here alone, m'lady?" asked the lord creeping on Lia. Disrupted moonlight from the broken room made the balcony a place of bright silver and dark shadows. Rae saw enough. His hand was already on her waist, crowding her pretend-playfully against the balcony rail. Lia's only chance of escape was diving over the balcony.

Rae snapped, "Hands off."

The guy turned, startled.

"She's not alone. Her sister is here." Rae gave him a sultry smile and slid the scanty fabric of her dress upward.

The gentleman's eye seemed irresistibly drawn to her bared

thigh. Rae slid her enchanted knife out of its place strapped to her leg. Suddenly, the gentleman's eye seemed irresistibly drawn to her bared blade.

Lia squinted. "What have you got there?"

"A knife!" Rae beamed.

"Oh no," Lia murmured.

"She's mad!" The young lord's eyes darted towards the glass doors like hamsters desperate for escape. He seemed to be sobering up fast.

"That's offensive. Accept some people make a calm rational decision to choose the path of evil. I have no mental health issues, I'm just wicked and out of control." Rae advanced on him, knife and teeth gleaming. "There's a villainess on the loose on the romantic balcony! Nobody knows what she'll do, not even the villainess!"

"I meant no offence," the gentleman stammered. "Lady Lia was sending me come-hither glances—"

His sentence ended in a strangled scream.

Rae hadn't stabbed him. The lord's throat had an arrow sticking out of it. The arrow was buried deep in his neck, only the feathered shaft still visible. Blood, black by moonlight, poured down the front of his embroidered coat.

Slowly, the young lord toppled over the balcony rail and down into the dark.

Rae dived for Lia, bearing her to the ground. Rae expected Lia to struggle, and was surprised when she clutched Rae. Rae wrapped one arm around Lia's shoulders. With her free hand, she kept tight hold of her knife.

Lia's voice was small and scared. "Rahela, what's happening? I can't see."

"Someone's shooting arrows from the rooftop," Rae whispered back. "Not sure why."

Nothing like this happened in the book! Rae had tuned out Alice reading about the belle of the ball, pursued by all. She would have tuned back in for 'also pursued by assassins'. Only now did Rae see stories needed more romantic interludes and fewer assassins.

If she died in this world, she would never wake up at home.

Her senses felt as if they were being sharpened. Her nerves scraped along with them, like one of Key's knives on a whetstone. Rae was so painfully aware of her surroundings it made her want to scream. It was as though someone was forcing her to look at what she didn't want to see, shouting that this was real, real, real. The night wind touched her cheek with a cold finger. There was a shift in the shadows on the grey slope of the roof.

Rae pulled Lia close, huddling against the stone railing. The arrow buried itself a fraction of an inch from Lia's gleaming slipper. Lia made a tiny distressed sound. Rae screamed, a loud and anguished scream that throbbed on the night air. She knew what real pain sounded like. She could fake it.

Lia's voice rose, high with panic. "Are you hit?"

Soon the ballroom's current song and dance would end. Someone might hear screams from the balcony. The bowman wouldn't risk someone hearing. He would come down to finish the job. How much of a challenge could two women be, when one was wounded?

Rae's arm around Lia's neck, and her fingers around her knife hilt, ached with how hard she was holding on. Lia's breath in her ear was rapid as a heartbeat.

They both heard the stealthy scuff of a soft boot against a roof tile. A shadow detached from the darkness, leaping and landing lightly on the balcony in front of them. Rae nudged Lia, and kept yowling at increasing volume.

"Argh!" Rae yodelled, making her voice as grating as possible. "The pain is unbearable!"

The highly virtuous had high pain thresholds. Heroes soldiered on, but villains were whiners.

Lia added to the confusion, in her own way. "Sir, I have done you no wrong, I beg you show us mercy—"

Her tear-filled cornflower-blue eyes shone in the moonlight. The man, wearing black and grey clothes that blended perfectly with the shadows, padded forward. He seemed immune even to the beam of Lia's eyes, which was astonishing. Lia was a beseeching heroine lighthouse.

The gears of Rae's mind turned, cool as metal clicking into place, noting every detail of the scene. Her body betrayed her by being afraid. Sweat burned her eyes, and ran a trail of fire down her spine. She stubbornly clutched her leg, wailed, and studied him from under her lashes. This guy was a professional. He wouldn't stop unless someone made him stop.

When the assassin's knife arced, Lia grasped his sleeve in a last silent appeal. His downward swing was checked by Lia's grab. Rae seized the opportunity to launch herself at him, brandishing the knife she'd hidden in her skirts.

"Suddenly I'm feeling a lot better," she panted, mistress of deceit and treachery.

Characters who quipped during fights were more likely to survive. God, she hoped she lived through this.

The hilt of the knife slid treacherously in her sweaty hand, wanting to slip. If she dropped her knife they died. Rae clutched the hilt and sank the blade into the man's chest. The knife's magic should guide her hand, but she tried to move like Key, stabbing twice as she tumbled to the ground on top of him. She heard her blade slide into meat and felt the assassin's blade glance against bone, the socket of Rae's eye and her cheekbone sending an echo of pain throbbing through her body. She stabbed the knife into the man's throat. This wasn't real, it was a video game where she must do anything to win. There was blood on her face, flecks of hot tin taste between her lips. Rae didn't know if the blood was hers, sliding down from the wound across her eye, or spatters of his. It wasn't real, no matter how real the blood felt. The assassin's body went slack beneath her.

Lia's terrified whisper cut the night. "Rahela!"

He wasn't actually dead! She was a fool, the murderer always seemed dead but then wasn't dead after all. Rae gazed down into the assassin's still face. He looked dead. Rae twisted around to see Lia, and saw a new shadow fall on Lia's upturned face. Realization came dark as the moment after sunset.

There was more than one assassin.

The sweat on Rae's skin turned to beads of ice. As Rae froze in her crouch over the corpse and calculated her odds for another leap, she saw another shadow drop down onto the ground. Two assassins, one for each woman. The shadows closed in.

The air went brilliant. Moonlight turned broken glass into lightning as the doors of the balcony exploded outward. Key came crashing onto the scene. He threw a knife at the assassin approaching Lia, blade burying itself in the man's back. Instead of reaching for another knife, Key moved faster than glass could fall and plucked a shard flying through the midnight air. He landed beside Rae with the shard in one hand and the assassin's hair in the other, dragged the man's head back, and cut his throat with the glass shard. A black pool of blood spread beneath Key's feet, blood in his wild hair, blood staining his teeth as he snarled. He looked like a devil, and a nightmare about to happen to you next.

Rae was *so* proud of her minion.

She opened her mouth to praise him, and found herself saying, "I killed a man."

She was convinced Key was about to say 'good job'. But his eyes travelled over her blood-streaked face, and he didn't. He reached out with the arm not holding a knife, and drew her in against him. His body was a shield between her and this world.

"Remember," he murmured. "Other people aren't real."

No back-patting for villains. Only sinister whispering. It was still nice to be held.

"They're not real," Rae repeated, numbly. "They're not real."

She curled her fingers in under the blood-slick straps of his armour. His cracked leather gloves caught on her hair.

"You don't have to kill if you don't like it," Key promised. "I'll kill them for you."

"Kill who?"

Against her hair, she felt his mouth curve. "Everyone."

He moved, arm around her waist holding her steady. Warmth splattered on the bare skin of Rae's shoulders, and Rae realized he'd casually murdered someone behind her back. Rae whirled to behold yet another assassin crumple, and searched with sudden terror to see if Lia was safe.

She was curled down by the balcony rail, fragile and helpless as a white kitten. Key deserved a reward for saving them from assassins. Rae stepped aside so he could have a moment with his lady love, and so she could confirm a suspicion.

She knelt beside the man she'd killed, loosened the ties on his shirt with fingers she forbade to shake, and bared a mark on the corpse's breastbone. A tattoo of a crown, laid atop the mountains of truth.

"This is the royal seal," Rae said slowly. "These are palace assassins."

"And how do you know *that*?"

Emer stood on the threshold of the ballroom, voice as sharp as the sea of broken glass between them. Rae didn't dare invite Emer's scorn by saying the gods had told her. Emer wouldn't believe that. She wouldn't believe anything Rae could offer.

Key wasn't attending to his lady love. His attention was on the dead. No horror showed on his face, only concentration.

He told Rae, "The assassins were after you."

Lia was eventually assassinated in her version of the books, but Rae wouldn't win any supporters by making that prophetic announcement. "I'm sure they were after Lia. She's very persecuted. Certain people attract true love and terrible danger like flies."

Key seemed unimpressed. "Someone sent assassins to your bedroom door on the day you announced you were a holy prophet."

Rae glared. "I strongly feel this could've been mentioned to me before now!"

Key ignored her justified indignation. "Someone sent ghouls over the wall of the courtyard when you were trapped in there. Someone set a bowman on the roof to begin firing when you came out on the balcony. Someone's trying to kill *you*."

When he listed all the near-death escapes, they did seem to point in that direction. Rae brutally crushed down fear. Assassins weren't a disease. She could fight them. She could think her way out of this.

She rose and began to pace beside the corpse. "I don't mean to shock anyone, but the king's trying to get with me. I assume he's not putting out a hit on it before he hits it and quits it. Who else commands the palace assassins?"

She was surprised when Lia spoke up, her voice silver bells in the night. "The king's favourite. The Last Hope. The prime minister and the commander general."

Rae snapped her fingers. "It's the prime minister. Older politician, unmarried and mean, with vaguely sinister facial hair!"

A classic secondary villain.

"My lady, facial hair is not a motive. This is not a joke," Emer said savagely.

Emer wanted Rae to take this seriously, but Rae shouldn't. She couldn't. She would go out of her mind if she did.

"Perhaps she thinks it's funny because she still believes I'm the victim," Lia whispered. "As if I'm the centre of every plot in the palace."

Key stared down at the curled-up kitten-woman. "Get up. Stop bothering people."

"*Key*," Emer snapped. Rae absolutely agreed with Emer.

Presumably Key was doing the thing in stories where guys masterfully scolded the ladies they loved. The appeal of that particular move was lost on Rae. 'Oh lover, tell me how you know better than me all night long.'

Lia blinked up at Key uncertainly, and who could blame her? He sighed and reached out. Lia put her pearl-pale hand in his. Key clearly needed more practise assisting his lady: he heaved her up with the courteous tenderness of a man handling a sack of potatoes. He acted as if Lia was nobody special, but Rae knew better. The heroine was special to everybody.

"Thank you for your assistance." Lia was always gracious with the staff. "Were those *five* assassins?"

"Six."

Key dropped her hand and lunged forward at an empty patch of night which, faced with Key, moved and became a final assassin turning to meet the swing of Key's blade.

"The king is coming!" Emer hissed.

Mid-swing, Key dropped his knife. The assassin let out a single relieved breath before Key grasped the man's throat and, with one efficient snap, broke his neck. Key kicked the body carelessly aside as the king arrived.

Octavian and assembled courtiers stood framed in jagged silver, all that remained of the glass doors. The bloodstained balcony was less than a foot away from the gilded ballroom, but the stretch of broken glass seemed to form a great distance.

"Rahela?" Octavian's voice rang out. "Lia! *What happened?*"

What happened was they were almost killed with no heroics provided by the hero! Octavian was supposed to save Lia in the nick of time. Instead he was doing the majestic equivalent of turning up late to the meeting with Starbucks.

Rae should soothe his pride. She needed to express relief and pleasure at his presence.

Rae came to this conclusion as Lia said, her voice an imploring flute, "Your Majesty, thank the lost gods you're here."

Lia stumbled towards Octavian, swaying slightly before she collapsed against his chest. Key's brows drew in so sharply together they resembled crossed swords. Poor Key. Witnessing this tender moment must be like getting his heart crushed by a romantic hammer.

The king held out his free hand to Rae. "Come to me if you need comfort."

He wasn't wearing his gauntlets again, but he was still the future Emperor, reaching out for her.

The almost-tempting moment was broken by a nasty laugh.

"She was nearly killed by royal assassins. Burn down the palace until you smoke out who ordered it, then have their heart and eyes torn out. Give them to her on a plate." Key sneered. "What's the point of power, if you never do anything worthwhile?"

Cold poured over Rae as though shock was liquid nitrogen. The court froze with her as they watched a peasant mock the king. Octavian started forward, sable cloak flaring in the night wind, visibly recollected his royal dignity and made a sharp gesture. A guard stepped forward, raising a fist encased in a magic gauntlet, and struck Key in the mouth.

"You vicious creature."

Blood in his teeth, Key snarled, "I'm my lady's vicious creature. I attack at her word."

Terrified of what might happen next, Rae snapped, "Then stop!"

When the next blow came, Key fell silently, and lay on his belly on the broken glass. At last, he saw reason. He knew enough to fear what the king could do.

"Forgive my guard, Your Majesty." Rae turned her wicked voice arch. "I blush to speak of his presumption, but he's overwhelmed by a secret admiration for Lady Lia. As so many are! But only you can hope to possess her."

The buzz of the court rose, turning from immediate execution towards hot gossip. Octavian stared down at Lia. Lia lifted her shining head, and gazed at him. The moon and Rae beamed benevolently upon them.

"He can scarcely be blamed for that," Octavian conceded.

"Everybody wants her!" Rae confirmed. "Due to her golden beauty and matching golden heart. Even the Last Hope is moved by her, as we saw through their dance."

She nodded significantly to the surrounding courtiers, and heard Lord Marius's name murmured in speculative tones.

"Rahela, please," Lia murmured.

The sound of modesty in unmistakable distress made people start frowning at Rae again. Rae's heart sank. Her hands were covered in blood. Her face was marked and torn. Held up against Lia's unstained beauty, Rae knew she looked guilty.

Prime Minister Pio moved to the king's left. The traditionally evil direction, Rae noted. His voice was crisp, face narrow and undeniably intelligent behind his absurd goatee. His eyes went to the snake bracelet coiled around Rae's wrist.

"If these men were indeed royal assassins, might I point out Lady Rahela carries a token that allows her to command anyone in the palace?"

Until Emer had named the king's favourite as one of those who might command the assassins, Rae had only thought of the bracelet as a symbol. She hadn't realized she was in possession of a device that might move the plot.

"Perhaps this was another attempt to play the heroine," continued the prime minister.

He could go stroke his tiny goatee of bureaucratic evil elsewhere. Rae was not in the mood.

At the king's right, Commander General Nemeth snorted. "An act that could fool nobody."

Rae was so glad she could bring the prime minister and the general together like this.

"She did save me," murmured Lia. "I would hate to think she acted with ulterior motives."

Thanks, Lia, not actually helpful! The eyes of the court, already resting heavily on Rae, went cold and hard. Their attention seemed to acquire more weight as their hostility increased, like water becoming a block of ice pressing down on her chest.

The same thing had happened in the Court of Air and Grace when Lia spoke. Rae frowned, but there was nothing to say. If people already believed you a villain, any self-defence sounded like a confession.

Octavian finally lowered the hand he'd offered. There was an angry curl to his mouth. He must be worried about Lia.

Rae would've thought she'd enjoy seeing her favoured pairing interact more. She didn't want to look at them. She couldn't look at Key lying in the broken glass. Terror for him felt like a small living creature she'd swallowed, trying to claw its way out. She could only swallow it down. Fearing for him was ridiculous. He wasn't even real.

"Lady Lia must be protected as the precious treasure she is, and Rahela adequately disciplined for her indiscretions." Octavian wielded his gaze like a sceptre. "Lady Rahela, you are hereby stripped of your status as my favourite."

Bitter moonlight poured down on the scene, dividing them all into black and white. It was no surprise Rae found herself in shadow.

This had never happened in the book. Rahela was executed. Rae had survived to be disgraced.

How the real Rahela would have burned with shame, robbed of her privileges in front of everyone. Rae felt a cold ghost of that heated feeling as she pulled the snake bracelet from her arm, and hurled the shining viper down on the bloodstained marble and broken glass.

"We done here?"

The king's eyes were narrow as chips of emerald. Lia was safe. Rae was powerless. He had what he wanted. She couldn't understand why his anger was increasing. Nor could she escape his fury. None of them could. That was what it meant to be king.

A guard offered Rae's snake bracelet to Octavian. Under the

watchful eyes of the court, the king slid the bracelet onto Lia's slender arm.

He was still looking at Rae. "My ladies-in-waiting have become an embarrassment to the court. The time has come to hold the Trials, and choose my queen."

That wasn't right. The Queen's Trials didn't happen until book two, after Octavian was Emperor! Worse still, Rae remembered the trials with great and terrible accuracy. At the Queen's Trials both Lia and Lord Marius were in danger of their lives. Only the Emperor's power saved them.

Power Octavian had not yet unlocked.

She realized everybody was staring expectantly from her to Lia, and back again.

Rae said, "Break a leg, sis."

The court gave Rae a collectively horrified look.

Rae mumbled, "It's a saying that means good luck."

Octavian proceeded as if he hadn't heard, though the edge in his voice said he had. "One last inconsequential matter. This guard trespassed on the balcony. I sentence him to fifteen lashes in the Room of Dread and Anticipation."

Half hidden behind a curtain, Emer's hand flew to her mouth to trap a protest. Above her hand, her eyes reproached Rae.

"Do you desire to speak for him, Rahela?" the king invited. "Perhaps you wish to be banished from the court and me? You're a holy woman now. You could be bound to a cave like the Oracle, meditating on the lost gods."

If she was banished from court, she wouldn't be there when the Flower of Life and Death bloomed. If she was exiled, she died.

Rae opened her mouth, then bit her lip.

"*Boss.*" Key stood, shaking off the broken glass, and shook his head. Loudly he said, "I'll take the whipping."

Guards clamped hands on his shoulders. By now Rae knew how Key fought. He could bring these guards down, but the king would simply summon more. No man could stand against an army.

She understood why the hero was always the most powerful man in the room. The king was the god of their court. He made it so the sun would shine and the winds blow gently on you … or not. You didn't want to imagine what that kind of power could do, if you weren't on his side. It was predetermined by the story that the power would be on the right side. It was good for the hero to have more influence than anybody else. The heroine and the righteous were protected by the hero's power.

But they were villains.

Octavian leaned across a space of glittering destruction and peered into Key's face, already bleeding from being shoved into broken glass. Key's snarl was feral, wilder than his hair. Octavian's smile and smooth hair gleamed like his masked crown.

"I wasn't asking your permission to whip you. I don't need anybody's permission for anything. Keep your eyes and your mind off my woman. Remember your place. In the gutters of the Cauldron, with the rest of the trash. There is only one place lower. One more wrong move, gutter brat, and you will be hurled into the abyss."

The train of the royal cloak swept over shards of glass, drifting away over the black mirror of the ballroom floor. The future Emperor departed, triumphant. Rae was what she hated to be, silent and helpless. She had to watch as the guards dragged Key out through the ballroom to be whipped. She had to watch as Lia sailed away at the king's side, arm shining with the mark of his favour.

Rae stood alone amid ruins of blood and glass, even her maid cowering from her. Rae's face was ripped and stained as her harlot's dress. She lied and cheated and killed. She betrayed loyal servants and did not utter even a word to defend them.

She looked bad. She was bad.

Once again, a messy situation turned into a crushing victory for Lia.

The lights of the chandelier sparkled through the broken doors and refracted in Rae's eyes, sparks of stray thoughts that might start a blaze. Lia had said, *"The loser pays a forfeit"* at the archery tournament, and inspired Lady Hortensia to exile Rae. Lia wept on command. Every time, Lia was too helpless and sweet to effect anything. Lia said, *"Being useless is all I have,"* and she used it. This wasn't just the story working out for the heroine.

Rae negotiated around the broken glass into the ballroom, where Emer silently joined her. She trailed back to her room in a daze.

Someone was whipping Key. Someone was attempting to murder Rae. And Lady Lia, innocent and beautiful, was coolly climbing her way to the top.

Rae wasn't the only one who could scheme. Rae was an *amateur* compared to the girl who never let her façade slip as she engineered every situation to her benefit.

Emer always looked at Lia with such serious attention. Rae had believed that was guilt, but perhaps it was something more.

"Did you know Lia was clever enough to beat me at my own game?" Rae asked, sitting at her bronze mirror as Emer brushed her hair.

"Yes, my lady," Emer murmured.

"And did you know someone was trying to kill me?"

"Yes, my lady."

Rae couldn't hide the edge of frustration slipping into her tone. "You didn't think any of this was worth mentioning?"

"Servants shouldn't speak unless they are spoken to. And my lady, you didn't ask."

The accusation on Rae's tongue stilled as she heard a noise from without her chamber door.

Scarcely daring to speak, Rae whispered, "Since you know so much, Emer, do you know who's coming?"

Emer shook her head slowly.

Footsteps echoed on the stone steps, against the stone walls, like the tolling of a bell. It could be another assassin. It could be the king or the Last Hope, Key or the Cobra. It could be life or death.

Rae and Emer watched the door handle turn.

CHAPTER TWENTY-ONE

The Cobra in the Cauldron

"I will take you to a place of safety. First we must find
the Cobra."
"My lord?" whispered Lia.
The Last Hope's face changed as he remembered the
Cobra had been dead for weeks.

Time of Iron, ANONYMOUS

arius's voice echoed in the tunnel, hollow against stone.
The Cobra glanced over his shoulder, dark eyes going
wide. Marius anticipated shock or fear. He wasn't prepared for fury.

The Cobra wheeled on him in the close quarters of the secret
tunnel. "You'll ruin everything! What are you *doing* here?"

Marius raised a defensive arm, a soldier's instinct arising before his
conscious mind intervened. The Cobra sheered off and smiled sidelong.

See me laughing, that smile said. *I must be a joke.* That smile was
disaster on the horizon, sun glancing off the spears of an advancing
army. Marius's every sense burned like strained muscles, struggling
to find the threat. His father called it a gift that a Valerius was always
armed against the foe. Yet this all-enveloping awareness turned the
whole world into an enemy.

Marius answered through his teeth, "Catching a thief."

The Cobra sidled out of the tunnel. Marius followed on broken rooftiles sliding underfoot like wet pebbles on a beach. The other end of the tunnel was a vast cracked effluvia pipe long disused, running parallel to a rooftop so waste could pour out over the high city walls. It wasn't a bad disguise for a secret tunnel. Numerous effluvia pipes led from the palace into the city. People didn't explore them for obvious reasons.

Simmering lights, a more garish red than the sullen glow of the ravine, burned in the narrow street below. Thick scented smoke wafted up from torches. If a pipe burst, it might improve the atmosphere in the Cauldron.

The Cobra danced along the edge of a rooftop in the scarlet-touched smog. "I'm not caught yet, my lord."

Two of the tenement buildings were set slightly apart. The Cobra hopped from the corner of one rooftop to the next, ornaments chiming. The Cobra sauntered over the rooftops of hovels as he did across ballrooms: carelessly adjusting his hair and pretending not to notice his surroundings while noticing every detail.

He feigned indolence well. He feigned everything well.

Marius set his jaw. A Valerius could track prey across any terrain. The Cobra couldn't escape. "Tell me what you're stealing."

"Have you considered, all property is theft?"

"It is when you steal it!" snapped Marius.

The Cobra reached into his jerkin. Marius expected stolen goods. Curves of hammered gold caught the wicked light, outlining the coiling shapes of snakes. Marius recognized this jewellery from years ago. These earrings belonged to the Cobra. Bracelets already gleamed gold above his biceps.

Wearing such adornments in the Cauldron was a signal you were a criminal, or ready to hire one.

"Men's adornment is outlawed."

"That was the prime minister's petty revenge on me."

"Oh, really?" This man was so vain, he probably thought the troubadours' songs were about him.

"Since *I* was responsible for the crackdown on imports that played merry hell with Pio's investments."

Few travelled to the cursed land of Eyam, but profit was dearer
to men's hearts than demons or the divine. Merchants still brought
their ships to the harbour and offered gold and goods in exchange
for orichal. Years ago, city guards, paid off by the Cobra, had broken
through a false hull and found secret cargo: peasants being inden-
tured against their will. The Cobra had snarled, "Those are *real
people*," and lunged across the table at the young lord who owned
the ship. Marius held him back by force.

After a tense moment Cobra called Marius boring, and departed
the assembly. The young lord was heavily fined, and the Cobra's
bill monitoring imports passed. Marius hadn't considered the
matter again.

Marius said slowly, "Was the ship owner the young lord you deliberately ruined?"

The Cobra shrugged.

He had his freedom, the Cobra had said when Marius reproached
him on the matter. It seemed the Cobra hadn't ruined anyone
on a whim.

Even so, the prime minister wouldn't make a law out of spite. Only
villains like the Cobra plotted revenge.

The king must keep his crown, so men's head adornments were
still legal. From the day the law passed the Cobra wore so many hair
ornaments they rang together like music, playing a faintly mocking
tune. Prime Minister Pio looked pained whenever he heard the
Cobra coming. Balancing on the edge of a rooftop like an acrobat
on the trapeze, the Cobra was making far less noise than usual. This
proved he created a fuss on purpose to annoy everybody.

"What are your personal thoughts on men in jewellery?" the Cobra
asked, deceptively soft.

"They shouldn't blackmail me."

The Cobra's laugh made Marius's spine feel like a dry torch
set ablaze.

"You're a spoiled, frivolous care-for-naught pretending to be an
outlaw." His words held the snap of burning wood. "Land in the
Cauldron streets, you'll be stripped with your throat cut."

"Thrilling," murmured the Cobra.

Marius frequently remembered their first meeting. He was eighteen, wandering alone out of the palace gates into the city. One of his best friends was the king. The other was dead.

The boy seemed to drop from the sky. After a moment, Marius realized he'd swung from the branches of a hawthorn tree. The boy was Marius's age, slight and dark-complected, and his face was impossibly luminous. Marius glanced around, but there was nobody behind him.

"Marius," the stranger breathed. "Lord Marius Valerius. The Last Hope."

As though a cloud had passed to show twin stars, two things became clear to Marius. The first was nobody ever looked this pleased to see Marius. The second was Marius was very lonely.

Torn between wariness and delight, Marius asked, "And how do you know me?"

The boy hesitated. Shadow touched his face, and stayed like a mask over the sun. Years would pass. That first golden openness would not return.

"Even if I told you," the boy said, "You'd never believe me. Just know this: I'm your number one fan. And I'm sorry for what I'm about to do."

Alarmed, Marius demanded, "What are you planning to do?"

The boy proceeded to blackmail him.

For the Golden Cobra, blackmailing a Valerius had only been the beginning.

There was a hush on the rooftops, high above the noisy streets. Marius realized he'd made a mistake. What Marius had seen as adjusting his hair was the Cobra undoing fastenings on his ornaments, letting a rain of gold snakes pour down.

A beggar in rags caught one. Next the Cobra flicked a shining serpent into the hands of an urchin, giving her a little wave. The girl grinned as bright for him as she did for the jewel.

Nobody catching treasure looked surprised. They appeared exalted, as though they'd heard stories of blessings showered from above, and believed with faith born of possibility that glory would come to them.

"Do you regularly spread largesse in the Cauldron so you will always have spies ready to recruit?"

The Cobra smirked. "I'm experimenting in destabilizing the local currency."

Marius's teeth ached with anger. "Why did you join our law-making assembly if you insist on being a criminal?"

"Make better laws or make criminals," the Cobra snapped back. "The crimes will continue until the justice system improves."

"It will never be legal to steal from the king!"

"I don't believe in the monarchy."

The Cobra swung insouciantly around a chimney. Marius rolled his eyes so hard he expected to hear a rattle.

"Wonderful news. I don't believe in gravity, so I'll never fall again. The king exists, and will execute you for treason. And . . . "

Light didn't dawn for Marius. It flared and sputtered, rising slow as the ominous red sparks from the ravine. The Cobra often talked nonsense, but never to no purpose.

"You're chattering to distract me."

"Caught on, did you?"

At the very edge of the rooftop, the Cobra fell backward with a smile.

Through the rushing wind and the roar in his own ears, Marius heard the Cobra shout: "Not fast enough!"

Marius ran to the edge of the roof, tiles crashing to the cobblestones. Lord Popenjoy had leaped onto a rattling cart piled high with goods Marius doubted were legally acquired. The smugglers' cart whisked around a corner. Crouched on a stolen carpet, the Cobra waved farewell.

Panic lost wars. Though his muscles coiled for the leap, Marius didn't jump down. The rooftops afforded him an aerial view. If he stayed on high, he had a chance of catching up. He ran along the roof, chasing the cart. When a rotted gutter gave out under him, he took the impact of the fall on his shoulder. He leaned into the pain, letting himself plummet into the yawning gap with cobblestones and criminals below, until he grasped the edge of the roof. Marius swung so his boots hit the wall, tearing his cape free when the ends caught on the jagged broken-off edge of the gutter, and jumped to the next roof. A burst of excited conversation exploded from below. He'd been recognized. Other scholars from the Ivory Tower occasionally visited the capital for short visits, but – with respect to his scholarly brethren – Marius didn't believe they engaged in rooftop chases. Devotion to scholarship had a disastrous impact on physical fitness.

Marius's too-acute senses were like having every door in your house flung open to the world, but sometimes the invasion of sensation proved useful. The smuggler's cart had one wheel slightly askew. It gave a distinctive squeal, two streets to the left. Marius vaulted the roof and grinned at the dark. A rooftop chase beat a ballroom any day.

The rattle of the cart slowed before resuming its usual rhythm. A graceful long-haired silhouette darkened a moonlit cobblestone. The Cobra slipped from one shadow to the next, into a narrow grey building on Lockpick Street.

Under a sign of black wheels and gold flowers, twining script read Life in Crisis.

Marius followed the Cobra. Oddly, a tattooed doorman glanced at his clothes and wished him good hunting. Inside was a crush as bad as the ballroom. The soft sound of metal clinking meant concealed weaponry and displayed jewellery. Every man was wearing at least an earring or a bracelet, and the women were not to be outdone. Candles shone on the bar under different-coloured transparent shades turning flames red and green and blue. Over the bar a sign read Welcome All Travellers . . . & Thirsty Residents. At the far end of the bar was a stage where a woman crooned a low song while wearing a lower-cut gown.

The Cobra was at the bar, talking to one of the few not wearing jewellery. By the scars and the muscle definition, the woman was a blacksmith. Marius watched them slap palms, either making a bargain or exchanging an item. The blacksmith disappeared into the crowd. Marius let her go. She'd be back.

It wasn't easy for a man Marius's size dressed entirely in white to be discreet. The effort was worthwhile for the Cobra's slight start when Marius spoke in his ear.

"You commit theft and treason, flee the palace, swagger into the lowest tavern in the Cauldron as if you own the place, and now you're drinking?"

Flicker of surprise fading, the Cobra finished his beverage. "Drinking's not illegal. If swagger was against the law, I'd already be doing life."

Marius felt his mouth thin like a piece of paper folded sharply in half. "Alcohol is a crutch."

"Useful things, crutches," drawled the Cobra. "Ever see anyone using a crutch they didn't need?"

He took refuge from uncertainty in silence.

The Cobra shrugged. "Sun rises in the east, Marius seriously disapproves of me. Oh, apologies. My lord."

This was miserable. "Just say Marius!"

"Couldn't so presume, my lord. If you don't find the atmosphere to your liking, leave. See the men at the doors?"

There were six thickset individuals, a pair at each door, bulging with muscles and bristling with weapons.

"They insist on being called thugs," the Cobra said chattily, gesturing for another drink. "I referred to them as bouncers once. They said people don't bounce back from what they do. People are straightforward in the Cauldron. In the palace we call the thieves and cut-throats our ministers, and the doxies our ladies-in-waiting."

A woman drew near, with a cloud of red hair and bright green malachite paste around her eyes. She was more adorned than anyone he'd ever seen bar the Cobra.

"My, my," she murmured. "This is the best costume for the Last Hope the bawdy houses have turned out yet."

As Marius froze in shock, she slapped Marius's left pectoral.

"You're a hefty boy, aren't you! Mmm. Put me up between a brick wall and a beef wall, that's what I say."

"Madam, I took vows," he said coldly.

She cackled. "Yay, the catchphrase."

The Cobra sniggered against the rim of his glass, then toasted the blacksmith's return. She had been very quick. She must have an orichal mechanism to fashion swift metal copies, which confirmed she was a criminal as well. Marius saw them surreptitiously clasp hands again. He tried to dart past the glittery-eyed lady. She suddenly had a firm grip on his upper arm. She made an 'oooh' sound as her fingers failed to close even a quarter of the way.

"I'm in pursuit of a criminal."

Unlike Lady Lia, this woman wasn't understanding.

"What, the Cobra? Good luck, but he hardly ever will. If he does agree, since you're so absolutely delectable, I wouldn't be opposed to—"

Marius couldn't endure listening a moment longer. "Madam, unhand me."

He seized her by the waist and placed her on the bar out of grabbing distance. Confusingly, she made another 'oooh' sound.

Even more confusingly, the Cobra wasn't escaping with his ill-gotten goods.

As the woman on stage sang, "My lady was all my joy, my lady was my delight, and who but my lady Jolenesleeves—" she was cut off mid-croon. The Cobra swung the singer down into his arms, gave her a kiss and his last hair ornament, then ascended the stage.

The Cobra's amused drawl rang out to every corner of the tavern. He didn't need gold to make them look.

"Guess what, my lord. I swagger in like I own the place because *I own the place.*" He pointed at Marius. "Thugs. Get him!"

The Cobra had gestured, and that redhead had leaped to intercept Marius. This was the only sign on Lockpick Street with *writing* on it.

Marius was a fool.

The Cobra mouthed "Sorry!" before slinking offstage. Marius reluctantly transferred his attention as the thugs closed in. Six bulky figures blotted out the lights decorating the bar. Weapons sprang to scarred hands, including a morningstar. People receded sharply as the spiked ball on a chain became a blur in the air.

Very poor odds, remarked the soldier's part of his mind. Marius smiled.

For them.

He ducked under the spiked blur, catching the morningstar by the chain. Now in control of the weapon, he reversed its trajectory and lodged the spikes deep in the first thug's shoulder while the man was still holding the handle and wondering how it had all gone wrong. Marius slammed him into a wall. An agonized scream indicated the spikes had been driven in harder. Marius pivoted and pulled down the sign reading Welcome All Travellers ... & Thirsty Residents. The sign was big enough to hit two thugs at once, though the blow wouldn't keep them down.

"No need to ask who wrote this sign," remarked Marius. "Do you find him humorous? I don't."

The thug not clutching his head opened his mouth. Marius dealt him an uppercut to the jaw. The only woman of the bunch went in low. The Cobra had once cautioned that people who fought twice as hard to get where they were, would be at least twice as good. Remembering that advice was how Marius had selected a low-born captain to lead the royal special forces. It meant Marius took note of women fighters.

She had excellent form with her short sword. Marius should eliminate her fast. He backed up into the bar, allowing her to come near and stab him lightly. He closed a hand on her wrist, keeping the blade safe in his side, smashed someone's glass on the edge of the bar and drove the shards of glass into her arm. She dropped the knife and concentrated on wrapping the wound. Now the remaining three thugs were frightened, each looking to their companions. Nobody could win a battle without being willing to lead the charge; these men weren't trained to kill but to administer beatings. They wouldn't get the chance to do that today. Marius scattered them with a rush, breaking a chair and skewering one thug's limb with a hurled chair leg. The fragments of the chair knocked out another thug, and Marius seized the last by his collar.

"Yield," he commanded.

"Please don't kill me," gurgled the final thug.

"No. I took vows." Marius strangled him efficiently and kindly into unconsciousness.

The man slid in a heap at his feet. Marius scanned the bar, upon which silent stillness had fallen. Five minutes had elapsed since the thugs came at him. Scholarship was making Marius slow.

"Lost gods, you're the real Last Hope," murmured the glittery woman on the bar. "Sorry for manhandling you. Unless you liked it, in which case I'm Amelia. You can find me any time, day or night, at the Golden Brothel."

No blade, no beloved, no blood spilled by my hands. The vows were clear. Nobody paid attention to the vows!

"Good night, madam." Marius fled.

He'd calculated which window was closest to the rooftop. Marius swung onto the roof of the Cobra's tavern and scanned the city laid out before him. Bright sloping roofs turned various murky shades by moonlight, fitting together like the pieces of an old tortoise's shell, stretched on until they met the city walls. The expanse of roofs was broken on one side by the pale-gold palace walls, and on the other by the pewter line of the river. The Cobra was too intelligent to head for the palace, but anyone who'd seen battle knew people headed for landmarks. Marius's eyes scoured the roofs leading to the river and found a familiar shadow.

The Cobra was crouched peering down into the dark streets, a smoking torch lighting his face from below.

Marius landed on the same roof. "Yield."

The Cobra sprang up with the burning torch in his hands. "I wasn't made to yield."

With an economy of movement Marius would have been pleasantly surprised to see in a palace assassin, the Cobra spun the torch around in a bright blur to dazzle Marius's sight. When Marius lunged to prevent the Cobra's next escape attempt, the Cobra didn't make one. Instead he set Marius's cloak on fire. Through a whirl of burning white and sparks flying, he caught the Cobra laughing. His eyes were alight, though not as alight as Marius's cloak. Marius laughed incredulously back.

This was the coward of the court!

The Cobra bolted for the rooftop edge. Marius tackled him. Only sheer brute strength prevented them both falling off the roof. Even as Marius dragged them back the Cobra made a furious attempt to get loose. He was tall and powerful enough that Marius had to put him up against a chimney, arm against the Cobra's throat cutting off his air supply, or risk hurting him. Marius reached inside the Cobra's jerkin and wrenched out two keys. One was wrought in the king's orichal silver and one was brass. With all his might, Marius hurled the brass key into the river.

"*Don't,*" the Cobra shouted, though he shouldn't have been able to breathe. "This is someone's life! You don't know what you're doing."

The key inscribed a small bright arc onto the night air before being lost in the shadowy churn of the river below. He might not know what he was doing, but it was done. The Cobra ceased struggling, but his body didn't go lax with surrender.

"*Damn it, Marius!*" the Cobra exclaimed once Marius removed his arm from his throat. "You chased me across the city! You're the terminator!"

"Don't call me names."

Marius was breathing slightly hard. He must cut down on sleep: five hours a night was vile indolence.

"I wasn't calling you names," the Cobra grumbled. "It means you're a total beast."

Marius glared. "That's another insult!" He got his breath back, and willed scholarly calm to descend like snow in winter. "You will explain Lady Rahela's villainous scheme to the king. Including what her guard did and who else is implicated. Apologise for aiding her wickedness. In exchange, the king will grant you mercy."

"I'm sorry?"

"Not to me," snarled Marius, "to the king—"

Leaning up against a crumbling chimney stack in the Cauldron, the Cobra was serenely composed as if attending court.

"I don't know what you're talking about," the Cobra lied with perfect, beautiful assurance. "Lady Rahela? Her guard? I stole this key from the king on my own. That's what I'll confess. His Majesty won't ask follow-up questions. He's never liked me."

It was summer, but the night was cold.

"During the dance, I saw—"

The Cobra's voice was a flaying knife. "I trust my sleight of hand. You might guess, but you didn't see. And you won't swear anything that's not absolute truth, will you? Leave women and servants out of this, Marius. Deal with me."

The world was flipped over and wrong, as though somebody had
tossed the broken moon down at his feet. The whole court knew the
Golden Cobra was a venal, shallow and heartless villain, but now he
was ready to die for somebody.

"Are you *in love* with this woman?" Marius demanded despairingly.

The Cobra was never sincere about anyone. A courtier swore he'd
seen the Cobra cast himself upon a chair and whisper he missed
his lost love Nettix. Or possibly Netsix? Netflix? Marius had never
believed it: that was not a name.

Fury turned the Cobra's golden voice dark. "I'm trying to do something real. I'm trying to change something!"

"Whatever you want to change, it can't be this important."

The Cobra said, "It's vitally important to me."

He didn't explain further. He never did. Marius couldn't take his
eyes from him, in case he committed another lunatic crime. He had
to watch as the Cobra smoothed over the cracks in his façade, eras-
ing traces of pain and rage. Marius realized with growing dread the
Cobra was about to laugh this off.

The Cobra sighed theatrically. "I'm too stressed to fall in love. I got
more play when I was fourteen and my wardrobe consisted almost
exclusively of anime T-shirts."

This was a crisis, so Marius made the effort to puzzle out what the
Cobra meant. In context, 'anime T-shirts' must be the traditional
costume wherever the Cobra was from.

"What game were you playing?"

"I mean, I don't date much," said the Cobra. "Occasionally
I hook up."

"Whatever you are doing that involves hooks, cease immediately!"

The Cobra shook his head, laughing. "Never mind."

He often said that. It didn't help. Marius did mind. Now more
than ever, when the Cobra intended to die without explaining
himself.

The cloak of night over the city was suddenly rent apart by white
light. The fireworks in honour of the foreign princess shone as if the
moon had dissolved into a hundred stars, transforming the river from
pewter to silver, icing every roof.

The Cobra sat on the roof's slope. "If I'm being dragged to my execution, I'd like to watch the fireworks first."

Criminals couldn't simply demand to be arrested later, at a time that was more convenient. Marius frowned down to find the Cobra's face lifted to the sky, all lit up as though he were the night and his feelings were fireworks.

When such small strange things made him happy, it seemed churlish to interfere.

Marius felt obliged to point out the absurdity. "Lady Lia and I prefer moonbeams to fireworks."

He shrugged off the charred remnants of his white cape, tearing a long strip free. Marius bound the Cobra's wrist, tying the other end to his own wrist, then sat grudgingly on the rooftop.

The Cobra regarded him with unconcealed mockery. "Bless. I'm sure your favourite ice cream is vanilla."

"Why do you say 'vanilla' in those tones? Vanilla is an extremely expensive spice!"

The leaping flame of mirth in the Cobra's face subsided into an amused glow. "Okay, vanilla boy. I agree the lady is lovely. I'm glad you got to experience peace in the moonlight, gaze upon her and think *oh*."

"Oh?" Marius repeated, dubious.

"*Oh*. The *oh* is italicized to suggest a revelation," the Cobra told him sternly.

"I don't know what 'italicized' means," Marius muttered.

"It's like a word being underlined for emphasis. My point is, you need someone you can talk to. It's heartbreaking that for years you never had a conversation lasting longer than a handful of minutes, until the shining night with Lia on the moonlit balcony."

So the Cobra had veered off into dramatic hallucinations.

"I've had conversations that lasted hours. With you! Even worse, with the book club!"

"If I wasn't around, you wouldn't talk to anybody."

"I might!"

The Cobra shook his head, convinced of Marius's social ineptitude. That was insulting. Chances were the Cobra was right, but he couldn't be sure.

"Also I didn't talk to Lady Lia for hours," Marius pointed out. "We talked for five minutes. If you wanted us to talk for hours, perhaps you should've reconsidered the treason!"

The blaze of fireworks faded. The Cobra's face fell.

"I didn't mean to mess up the romantic balcony scene."

The one time he knew what the Cobra was trying to say, and it was horrifying.

"I don't like the insinuation I would break my vow."

Everyone knew the rules of the Ivory Tower. No violent delights, no violent ends. It was forbidden to touch wine, women, or weapons. Nobody believed a Valerius could keep the promises Marius had made. But he would. He must.

The Cobra suggested tentatively, "Surely, with Lady Rahela's mother ..."

"I never broke my vows with Lady Katalin."

Many believed Marius had, but he'd always thought the Cobra knew everything about him.

Marius let people believe the filthy gossip. He'd returned to court for his king, but Octavian was distant and Lucius was dead. Marius couldn't go to the training grounds or taverns, and could never go home again. Though he was eighteen and a man grown, he missed his mother. The lady was lovely, her hair like shadow and her laugh like gold, and experienced enough to know listening was more important than being lovely. It was humiliating he'd let secrets spill not because she was beautiful, but because he was fool enough to think she was kind.

"I wasn't sure," the Cobra said gently. "But I should have known. You're a one-woman kind of man."

"I'm a no-women kind of man!" Marius snapped. When the Cobra's face went exceptionally startled he clarified, "I'm a nobody kind of man! I took *vows*."

Octavian and Lucius made jokes about the other matter when they were young, teasing Marius for refusing to enter bawdy houses. The soldiers made similar jokes about General Nemeth's eldest. Considering how Lord Fabianus fawned over the Cobra, Marius suspected those jokes had truth behind them. Marius deeply disliked Lord Fabianus, but the man was harmless.

Marius was not. Marius couldn't ever love anybody. At the ball, Lady Lia had been beautiful as a dream of spring on a winter's night. She was important to Marius because he'd done right by helping her. He never wished to wrong her, but if there was speculation about them he had done so.

A Valerius could not help hurting anyone who came close.

A Valerius fell in love like falling off an ice cliff into dark water. Fast enough to snap a neck, love like a sentence of death. The memory of a splintering door and screaming echoed in Marius's ears. The love of a Valerius was a weight that would drag his beloved under the ice to drown.

Love was impossible. Love was an unforgivable sin. Marius wanted a guiding light.

"At the Ivory Tower," the Cobra began, delicately. "There's that house of women in the village at the foot of the Cliffs of Loneliness . . . "

This was what happened when a man had spies across the kingdom. Spies had filthy minds.

"People shouldn't believe the worst of women living alone."

Clearly, the lady of the house was a widow who moved to a remote place near virtuous charitable men, for financial assistance raising her many daughters.

"Sweet cinnamon roll. Too good for this world, too pure."

The Cobra sounded at a loss. That seemed fair, since the Cobra often left Marius at a loss himself.

"At the Tower, if we confessed to impure thoughts we were whipped with a blackthorn branch while kneeling on the edge of the ice cliffs."

"Eurgh!"

The startled sound broke from the Cobra's chest as though he couldn't repress it. Marius blinked, puzzled.

"It's standard."

The other students never confessed as frequently as Marius, more fitted to scholarship and purer of heart than he. The methods of the Ivory Tower were honed over years of trial and tradition, and extremely effective. After enough whipping and nights kneeling in the wind off the cliffs, impure thoughts were almost completely banished.

"Forgot that part." The Cobra made a face. "No wonder you're so intense."

"I'm not intense," Marius said. "I have faith. I have honour. You wouldn't understand."

The Cobra's mouth twisted into the wry expression he wore when secretly judging someone. "Maybe I have my own kind of honour."

"There's only one kind of honour!"

"That's a matter of opinion. Or do you think only one kind of opinion counts? I never understood why you cared if people knew you'd spilled secrets to a glamorous older woman. Aren't you a man of character? Isn't character who you are when nobody is there to see you?"

Marius opened his mouth to argue he was protecting his *family* honour, and closed it, shaking his head. That wasn't the whole truth. The truth was, he thought ill enough of himself. He didn't want the world to agree.

The truth burned. It was shameful that Marius would care.

People at court whispered the Cobra was secretly of peasant origin. Marius saw what they meant. Popenjoy didn't understand the values of nobility or unstained reputation.

That was proof the man was base, in birth and every other way.

For once the famous Golden Cobra wasn't bedizened with treasure, but sitting on the rooftop in dark simple clothes, knees drawn up to his chest, long hair loosed from its fastenings and falling over his shoulders. Nobody seeing him thus would think he was a noble.

Marius felt as he often did around the Cobra: that he'd been given an enormously complicated riddle to solve.

He asked slowly, "Is this who you really are? Lord Popenjoy is the disguise?"

The Cobra waved this off. "They're all disguises."

"You seem as at home in the Cauldron as you are in the palace."

The Cobra propped his chin on his fist, eyes full of reflected fireworks. "Everywhere I go is the same place. Everywhere is far from home."

"Do you want to go home?"

From the bizarre way the Cobra talked Marius believed he must be from impossibly distant lands, with customs different from anything

Marius knew. Marius couldn't imagine such a kingdom, but on the word 'home' Marius's mind always went back to the manor of his childhood. The place Marius could never go again. How strange, that he and the Cobra might have something in common.

"The past is another country, America never was America to me, and besides …" The Cobra shrugged. "I tried. My mother paid the price."

A firework blossomed in searing white and fiery scarlet across the cracked face of the moon. The same thing happened inside Marius's skull. The Cobra always seemed to exist entirely without context, no childhood and no connections, untethered and ultimately unreal.

"You had a *mother?*"

"You met her." The Cobra spoke as if he weren't wielding a verbal morningstar. "She was a woman from my household, killed on the king's orders."

It was long ago, but Marius remembered. Marius had been furious to be blackmailed, but the Cobra kept making sure Marius wasn't alone at parties, asking servants about their lives, and finding shy forgotten girls to dance with. Once Marius believed there must be a reason the Cobra would stoop to blackmail. He'd never been good with words, but he was planning to ask the Cobra why.

Then the Cobra's servant committed treason. The Cobra spent the next year drinking and building his golden bawdy house. Marius lost all desire to understand him.

"How, exactly, was that woman your mother?"

She'd been from the outer city, from her appearance unlikely to be related to the Cobra by blood.

"She was my mother because I believed it, and she believed it too," the Cobra answered steadily. "She saved me when she adopted me. My birth parents died when I was small."

Finally a tragedy Marius could understand. "Were they killed by the undead?"

"Well, no."

"Plague?"

"Sure, plague," agreed the Cobra. "My sister raised me. She took me to Shakespeare in the Park and helped me get a scholarship somewhere with a theatre programme, but her husband wouldn't let me call her my mother. That was for their real kids. I don't blame him. I was a burden. That makes what I did worse. I insisted on returning to a place where nobody missed me."

The fireworks scrawled meaningless shapes across the dark. The Cobra's speech was likewise unintelligible. Marius had spent days now without the Cobra's flow of nonsense. He'd believed that was what he wanted, until he found himself alone in silence.

The silence would be endless if the Cobra was dead.

"Why wouldn't your sister miss you?" He cleared his throat. "I . . . I miss mine."

The Cobra laid his hand on Marius's arm. "I know."

That gave Marius pause, recalling the Cobra tossing a smile and a jewel into the hands of a beggar child. Nobody had touched Marius, except Lady Lia graciously accepting his hand for a dance, since he and the Cobra parted ways. People avoided touching a Valerius even in the most casual manner.

"Is this pity?"

"It's affection. You do know about affection?"

The Cobra's voice lived on the edge of a laugh. This was not a laughing matter.

Valerians tended to marry cousins. Love was dangerous, but heirs were necessary. There must always be a duke to defend the land.

Valerius women were mousy as protective camouflage, but a generation ago a distant cousin was declared a beauty. She visited, chaperoned by a plain sister. The young duke, Marius's father, was struck at first sight.

Struck, fell, smitten. All words for love were violent, and Marius knew why. The beauty was found with her neck broken. The duke married her mousy sister the next day.

The duchess lived in the east wing. Marius saw his mother only when gathering in the great hall to praise the lost gods. When his father flew into rages, grown men cowered. The duchess said, 'Decorum, my lord.'

The duke would resentfully subside. On feast days, they behaved properly. After the feast she lit a candle for the great goddess and they knelt. The candle cast a pale gold circle on the wall, small as the reflection of a coin.

The duke didn't think much of his bride. Marius thought a good deal of his mother.

The direct Valerius line usually followed from only son to only son. Marius's mother bore her second child when Marius was eight. His father lost interest when it was a daughter.

Dukes of Valerius wore a hooded war cloak called a caracallus. Marius wrapped the baby in his to keep her warm in their cold manor, and his lady mother named her for it. Boys his own age feared Marius, but when he carried her to bed Caracalla put her baby arms around her brother's neck with perfect trust. After she was safe, Marius sat outside the locked and barred door listening to the duchess sing over his sister's cradle.

Once his father summoned his mother when Marius was outside eavesdropping. As the duchess swept by, Marius felt the curve of her hand briefly cup his cheek.

Marius knew about affection.

He sneered internally at the Cobra's hand, warm on his arm.

The light cast by his mother's candle on the wall shone, dimmed by the shadows of years. Truth was a small precious circle of illumination and sanctity. This reckless profusion of light and warmth must be false.

"You claim a criminal servant as your mother?"

"Yes, my mother was a servant." The Cobra's voice put a thousand frosty miles between them. Once again Marius experienced the disorienting sensation that a blackmailing traitor was furious with him. "So to you she was barely a real person. Do you know the names of any servants not your own?"

None that could be skimmed like cream from the top of his mind, but Marius was sure he would momentarily recollect several.

"I don't even know *your* name."

He threw that reminder like a sharp bitter dart. The Cobra slanted a grin his way.

"Wanna know something funny? I never gave the character a name."

The character, as if the Cobra was writing a play that was his own life. If people built roads the way the Cobra held conversations, they would wind around a looping scenic route then careen wildly into the ocean.

Marius insisted on a destination. "What did your mother call you?"

"My real name." Popenjoy blinked. "This conversation must be confusing for you."

Conversations with you always are, Marius wanted to spit, then remembered he could say whatever he liked to the Cobra now. He'd dreamed of that.

"Conversations with you always are." Since Marius was allowed to say it, his voice came out mild enough. "I keep getting lost, but perhaps I could find my way."

Amusement rang in that irritating voice. "Doubtful. Since I'm to be executed, this is our last conversation. You'll find it easier to win arguments with me when I'm dead."

Even then, Marius feared he wouldn't win. The man had a mouth on him that infuriated you until you knew him, at which point it infuriated you more. The Cobra was joking his way into the grave.

"Stop. I wouldn't even have a name to put on the stone."

The Cobra pointed at Marius triumphantly. "Won't be a problem. They throw traitors' bodies in the ravine."

Marius wasn't a child, so he couldn't put his hands over his ears. He put his head in his hands instead. "Will you *stop*!"

The Cobra said, inexplicably, "Eric."

Marius looked up. "What?"

Fireworks shot towards the moon in golden streaks, brightening the night in a luminous false dawn.

The Cobra wore a faint smile. "My name."

"Eric," Marius repeated uncertainly.

It didn't seem to fit.

"Eric Mitchell. A very ordinary name, where I come from. I was a very ordinary boy. No doubt I would have grown up to be a very ordinary man."

The infamous Marquis of Popenjoy. The Golden Cobra. Eric. A very ordinary man.

Marius echoed the Cobra's earlier mocking tone. "Doubtful."

Finally a clue to the riddle rather than an addition to his confusion. Finally some truth.

Far below their rooftop, the city stirred.

"The day we met," Marius began.

"I've repeatedly apologised for the blackmail."

"That's not important," Marius said impatiently. "The day we met, you said, 'I'm your number one fan.'"

"Did I?" The Cobra made a comically embarrassed face. "Cringe!"

It was so rare to see the Cobra flustered, Marius ducked his head to hide a smile. "It was the first incomprehensible thing you ever said to me. 'One' is a number and a fan is an object. You might as well say 'I'm a number five wooden duck.' What did you mean?"

"It means I want you to win."

How nice, but, "To win what?"

"The love triangle!" The Cobra frowned. "That's not right. A person isn't a prize to be won. What it really means is, I love watching how you live. I want you to be happy, and for everybody to acknowledge you're the best."

"The best at what?" Marius asked in a small voice. "Fighting?"

The Cobra never showed the slightest interest in martial prowess.

"No," the Cobra answered briskly. "Speaking of, don't ever come at Lady Rahela's guard. You won't win."

Marius went blank with surprise. "I don't lose."

The Cobra scoffed. "Whatever. I don't care about your hit points."

"What do you care about?"

When Marius risked a glance at the Cobra, he was gazing pensively across the city. Fireworks briefly turned the silver ribbon of the river to gold. "You try very hard to do the right thing."

Strange to realize someone had noticed the painstaking effort he'd believed went unseen. Stranger still that it was this someone.

"If I try to understand you," Marius said quietly. "Will you explain what's happening?"

The final firework exploded silently into the night, an ephemeral silver crown that sparkled against a black sky with the faintest trace of blue, as if a single tear had fallen in a pot of ink. The last of the king's fireworks. The last of the light until true dawn.

In a grave voice, Eric said, "Imagine there was a book."

Oh no. Marius braced himself for literary metaphor.

"Imagine someone could open a book telling the story of this place, flip through people's thoughts, know the secrets of their hearts, and you were someone's favourite—" Eric stopped when he saw Marius's expression.

His face had twisted with his stomach, nauseated at the very idea. "I would hate anyone who read the secrets of my heart!"

If someone knew why he'd gone to the Ivory Tower, Marius would have to remember the time he found the door to the east wing broken down. The door that must be locked and bolted, to keep his lady mother and baby sister safe.

"That was our problem, I guess. Don't kill me," Eric added.

The old terrible fury descended on Marius, covering the churning dark of his distress like flame touching pitch. It was the Cobra's fault Marius felt this way. The Cobra was like everyone else, leaping to conclusions when Marius wasn't trying to harm him. When Marius had, in fact, been far too lenient. Marius should cut this criminal down where he stood.

"Stop talking in riddles. Why does Lady Rahela want that key? Why are you doing this?"

The Cobra smiled, dazzling and horrible. "Because of my wicked, rotten heart. What's it to you? I stopped tormenting you."

"You are still tormenting me!"

There was a ring in his own voice like rattled chains. It terrified him. He never let himself think about being unhappy.

Eric stared, and shook his head. "There was no need for a one-man mission to chase me down. You see somebody steal from your king? Summon the guards."

"They would cut your head off!"

The Cobra's raised eyebrows were a challenge. "So?"

"You being executed won't get me answers," snapped Marius. "You're lying to protect a secret. Having you dragged off to execution won't tell me what I need to know."

"Fantastic news." The Cobra stood and stretched lazily, hands linked over his head, his body an arc against the lightening sky. "Since

I'm not being dragged off, I'm going home. Collect me for execution at your leisure."

Marius stared at his own wrist in outrage. He hadn't even noticed when the Cobra's clever hands undid the tether linking them together. For an instant, he was confused about why the Cobra had untied it on Marius's side. His question was answered when the Cobra tied the strip of still-white material to the gutter and swung down onto another moving cart, rolling off the cart with acrobatic grace onto the cobblestones.

Marius was trained to sustain a fall from a warhorse. He jumped, landing by the Cobra's side. They made their way silently back to the palace, its golden walls still in shadow but slowly brightening with the rising sun.

Last time he'd walked the Cobra home, the Cobra was drunk. He sang into a large spoon which he called his microphone, a sign he must be taken away and poured into bed. On the way the Cobra stood on the walls overlooking Themesvar.

"Amazing this city was imagined," he said then.

"Isn't every city imagined?" Marius asked, and on the Cobra's interrogative glance: "Someone had to think of building a house. A lot of people had to think of building a harbour."

Slowly, the Cobra nodded. "We're all living in our imaginations. Love the story you're in, the song you made, the city you dreamed. I'm a city boy myself."

In that moment his sharp luminescence seemed blurred into more gentle brightness. He was always a riot of rapid movement and more rapid thought, animated sound and light. Marius understood what he meant. A city boy. A boy like a city.

"Thanks for being real," added the Cobra.

That was one night, and this was another.

The world had gone wrong years ago. Marius didn't know how to put it right. "You *cannot* simply go home."

"Stop me," the Cobra answered wearily. "We both know you can."

The Cobra rapped on his own door, outlawed rings striking the wood.

Marius turned away.

Seven years ago, the door to the east wing had been shattered. His father's men had broken it down. Marius refused to dwell on what he'd done, but the rage still burned. The storm of heat in his own breast, the same emotion that broke necks and painted fields with blood. Marius was a cold stone manor, but smoke might fill the corridors to choking. Fire might consume until only a charred skeleton remained.

No family, no friends, no beloved. He was Valerius. It was not safe.

The truth hit him. Marius whirled around, threw the Cobra against the wall, and found the king's key. The key the Cobra had stolen when he patted Marius's arm.

"Affection, was it?" he demanded icily.

With Marius's hand clenched tight on his jerkin, the Cobra shrugged. "Worth a try."

"You *villain*," Marius snarled.

Eric winked. "You know it."

He used Marius's split second of shock to shove him backward. The Cobra's maid held the door open for her master, giving Marius a poisonous look. Marius was furious to realize he had no idea what her name was.

The door slammed in Marius's face. No matter. He would come back with an army to break it down.

First he must share the truth the Cobra had let slip.

Marius didn't remember the name of the Cobra's treacherous servant, his executed 'mother'. He remembered her crime. She was seized in the act of plucking a flower. Tonight, Eric had stolen the key to the royal greenhouse.

Lady Rahela and the Cobra were after the Flower of Life and Death.

CHAPTER TWENTY-TWO

My Lady's Eyes Are Nothing Like the Sun

The wall struck her back like a blow. The Emperor closed his hand around her throat. Emer stared into his hateful face. They had always been enemies. At first she despised him. Fear came later.

"Do you know," the Emperor asked smilingly, "how often I think about killing you?"

The Iron Maid clutched the axe beneath her apron, and prepared to sell her life dearly.

Instead the Emperor's eyelids hooded the burning madness of his gaze. "I will not kill you, because she would not have wanted it."

Emer realized she was disappointed. "Lia is gone. What she wanted doesn't matter. Nothing matters now."

Time of Iron, ANONYMOUS

 he door swung open. Emer's lady sprang forward. Emer discreetly searched the top of the dresser for an object that might serve as a weapon.

Life as a servant at court was difficult, but a fight was simple.

Wielding an axe when the dead attacked the Court of Air and Grace, she'd protected herself. She'd protected Lia.

She couldn't use an axe to protect herself from girls laughing at her face, or men making advances. Well, she *could*, but she would be executed. It wasn't worthwhile. If she and Rahela got dragged to prison, though, Emer might stab a guard and make a break for it. There were places to hide in the mountains. She could serve as one of the Oracle's guardians, or become a brigand.

The Golden Cobra stalked in. Emer was shocked by how sensibly he was dressed.

"I thought you were Key," said Rahela.

"Happy to say I'm not," drawled the Cobra. "That boy's not right."

Behind Rahela's back, Emer nodded. It was true Lord Popenjoy knew everything.

Rahela clutched the lapels of a red satin bed robe she'd drawn over the tatters of her ruby-and-cobra dress. "Key's in the Room of Dread and Anticipation, to be whipped fifteen times for saving Lia. Emer knew where Lia kept liniments and bandages to visit the misfortunate, so we stole them. Do you know where we can get a doctor?"

"Fifteen times!" repeated the Cobra.

His eyes found Emer's, the glance between them heavy with unspoken awareness.

Five lashes, even ten, with an enchanted whip might be survived intact. Not fifteen. If he lived, Key would be a ruined mass of flesh unable to walk or care for himself, let alone fight again. Her mistress kept chattering about Key's recovery, cheerfully ignoring the fact Key was likely dead.

Emer supposed Rahela didn't want to face it. She'd let it happen. If she'd actually cared, she would have spoken for him. But what was a servant's life, compared to a noble's entertainment? Emer's lady wouldn't risk being banished from the pleasures of the court. She hadn't spoken.

Popenjoy asked, "Curious about our access to the Flower of Life and Death?"

Rahela stopped clutching her lapels, and grasped the Cobra's arm. "Did you get the key?"

"I got it, I was forced into a moonlit chase across the rooftops, then Marius threw the key in the goddamn river!"

Emer's lady went through a series of extraordinary demonstrative gestures as the Cobra talked, her hands clasping in delight, clenching in anticipation, then wringing in horror.

Astonishing, how much more this key was worth than the other. Whatever mischief Rahela was scheming, the plot was hardly a matter of life or death.

Emer's lady retreated to the window in the antechamber, hand over her mouth. She stared out the ruby-tinted glass into the abyss. The Cobra studied her with concern.

He offered a joke Emer didn't understand. "Minor characters shouldn't have to deal with this garbage. Marius was supposed to have a romantic balcony scene!"

His lordship was talking nonsense, but effective nonsense. He persuaded Rahela to smile. "Wow. Almost like his romance isn't meant to be."

"I don't have to listen to this."

Nor did Emer. She didn't wish to hear speculation on which man was worthy of Lady Lia's hand. It didn't seem to occur to anyone the choice should be Lia's.

As if anybody in the palace could make their own choices.

Emer coughed pointedly. "M'lord, m'lady. Begging your pardon. When will the Last Hope send troops to arrest and execute us?"

The Cobra spun Rahela's stool to him with a foot, sitting with a dramatic sigh. He wasn't wearing his huge golden sleeves to flap like a bright excitable bat, but it appeared sleeves were a state of mind.

"You're getting sharp with us. Please remember: sharp words are okay! Sharp axes, not so much. Stay calm, Emer. Though I understand panic, because our plot has collapsed. Our plot needs bed rest and sea air. Marius didn't arrest me because he believes you and I are conspiring together, Rae. He's sworn to discover our wicked plot. I imagine he'll take his suspicions, with the key, to the king."

A knock on the outer door made everyone jump as if it were a crossbow bolt.

"So the Last Hope thinks we're conspiring together, and now

someone's going to find us ... conspiring together ..." murmured Rahela.

"I could jump out the window," whispered the Cobra.

"Go ahead, my lord," Emer invited.

"The window looks out onto the dread ravine!" said Rahela.

The Cobra shot an amused glance Emer's way. He was a good-tempered man, she'd give him that. Pity he was a shameless libertine.

"Send whoever is at the door away, my lady!" Emer urged.

Since nobody had opened the door, it wasn't the king or high-ranking nobles. Rahela could send them off and stay safe.

Rahela twitched at the lapel of her robe. "It must be guards bringing Key back."

Now she pretended to care. Emer lost patience. "Your reputation is already in shreds. Do you want to set the shreds on fire for a ruffian from the gutter?"

"Let's not punish people for where they were born." The Cobra paused. "Let's punish them for being deranged murderers."

Rahela crossed her arms. "Key didn't do anything wrong!"

The Cobra said, "I don't find that believable."

"He didn't do anything wrong this time! Key was protecting Lia. And me. I'm his mentor. I'm responsible for him."

At the word 'mentor' the Cobra flicked a deeply dubious sideways glance at Rahela.

Emer's lady drew herself up in a tower of ivory and scarlet and chaos, and called: "Enter!"

Two guards in royal livery entered, dragging Key. His black head hung down, shoulder blades hunched like a tortured vulture's. His feet trailed, body limp. A path of blood smeared on the white marble behind him.

He was alive.

Even more shocking, he was conscious. He mumbled something.

A guard laughed. All the guards had been annoyed when a Cauldron guttersnipe was given a position in the palace. When Key could swagger around downstairs, grin and knives bright, they were too scared to make more noise than the kitchen mice. Now Key was helpless they could vent as much spite as they liked. This was why you couldn't let yourself be helpless. Not for anybody.

"Hope you learned your lesson, gutter brat. What's that?"

The other guard yanked back a fistful of thick black hair to show Key's face, his gold skin gone ghastly pale under the blood splatter.

Red stained Key's wild grin. "I can still take you."

Even though Key couldn't stand, the guard took a step back. Key staggered and almost fell.

"Cobra, help me!" Rahela rushed forward.

Lord Popenjoy uncoiled to his full considerable height. Emer watched as the guards recognized the simply dressed man in the lady's chamber as the Golden Cobra, whose very name was a hiss of scandal. My lady, my lady, why? They stoned harlots in town squares! Emer winced. Rahela and the Cobra were occupied half carrying, half pulling Key towards Rahela's bed.

Her bed! Lady Rahela and the Cobra had never seen a disaster they didn't long to escalate.

The vipers manhandled Key onto the mattress. He was wrapped in a length of coarse white linen, the material they swathed bodies in before they threw them down into the ravine. The guards at the Room of Dread and Anticipation had already put Key in his shroud. When the trailing linen caught on a bedpost and wrenched off the drying blood and open wounds, Key made a noise through his teeth.

Rahela murmured comfort. The Cobra patted Key's arm. They needed cold-blooded practicality, but it turned out the notorious Golden Cobra was a soft touch.

Flat on his stomach, face pressed into a pillow, Key opened one eye a crack. "I thought you were afraid of me."

The Cobra raised an eyebrow. "It's all the murders. I'm not onside for that."

The guards sniggered at the coward of the court.

"But you're on my side now?" Key prompted.

The Cobra looked at Key's back bleeding through the linen, and sighed in annoyed surrender. "Sure, Mister Friendship-Is-Dark-Magic."

With an effort, Key offered his hand. The Cobra shook his head ruefully at himself or the world, and gave Key a gentle high five. Then his mask of manners slid back on, the attitude more aristocratic than his jewels. Lord Popenjoy wheeled on the guards with a gold glint in his dark eye. The taunting curl of his lip reminded Emer of her lady.

"I would have bribed you guards to leave, but you had to be rude. Better watch out. I put the rep in reprehensible. And I love a man in uniform."

One guard literally turned and fled. The other hesitated at the door, then mumbled, "I get off work at four."

The Cobra gave a startled laugh, before joining Rahela in rifling through the medicine basket. Suddenly Emer hated him. Flirting in her lady's chamber. Calling her lady *Rae*. The Cobra owned a golden harlots' den, yet people whispered more about Lady Rahela's sinful ways. The stain Lord Popenjoy could wash off in a day would mark a woman forever.

As Rahela cut bandages into strips, Key's hand reached out, then faltered, hesitating to even brush hers. His hand dropped as if he didn't feel worthy to touch her.

His face was the colour of old bone against scarlet satin pillows. "I didn't want them to bring me here. You don't like blood."

Rahela knelt by the bed. Her lip curved, black beauty mark rising like a doomed ship on a wave as she tried to smile for him. "Vipers together, remember? Evil wins at last. I'll take care of you."

Key gazed as though catching sight of his own soul in a mirror. As if he were a starving shark, she the only blood in the world, and all else bitter waters.

The Cobra reeled back against the bedpost. His eyes met Emer's, silently screaming.

Emer was glad somebody else got to be stunned and horrified for a change.

"I'll get rid of these." Emer snatched up the bloodied linens, though it was not her job as a lady's maid to clean.

Emer stomped down the winding stairs, dropped off the linens at the laundry, and sneaked into the side courtyard. She glanced one way, then another, knelt beside the shallow grave at the foot of a decorative tree and unearthed the short sword buried there.

That was the bargain she and Key had made. He'd taught Emer

a few passes with the sword in exchange for her teaching him the alphabet. Even if Key lived, he wouldn't fight again. She would never advance in her training now.

She performed the passes he'd taught her, hopeless though it was. The light of the topmost tower burned above her like a star. Night air laid cool palms on her hot cheeks.

"You move well," a male voice said, autocratic and unexpected.

Emer's heart hopped up and jammed in her throat as though she'd swallowed a toad. She choked it down as she dropped a curtsy for Lord Marius Valerius.

Though surprise conversations with the nobility were always bad news, Emer felt cautiously pleased by his praise. Everybody knew Lord Marius would have been the greatest warrior of his generation, if he'd completed his training. When Key tried to teach her, Emer noticed his earnest efforts to let her land hits on him. Emer had assumed she must be terrible.

"Thank you, my lord."

"You're the girl who modified Lady Lia's gown for me," said Lord Marius's cool, forbidding voice. "What's your name?"

Oh no, why was this happening? Emer blamed the Golden Cobra for this sudden curiosity about servants' identities. The Cobra was always prowling belowstairs trying to interact with you as if he was the same as you. Emer wasn't the same as him. Emer didn't have mountains of gold and several mansions, and Emer didn't want nobles to know her name.

There was security in anonymity. When you receded into the shadows belowstairs, you receded from noble minds. If a noble remembered you, they might resent you.

'Forbidding' was the perfect word for Lord Marius. His uniform was pristine white, suggesting he'd changed after his rooftop chase. He stood against the dark like an ice cliff. His face was a locked and barred door, and his voice brooked no escape.

If she was discovered lying to the king's most trusted friend, she would suffer for it. "Emer," she admitted.

Many nobles had weak chins and weaker minds, but the white wolf eyes on Lord Marius were distressingly sharp.

"You're Lady Rahela's maidservant."

Emer concentrated on the point of her sword, instead of her fear. "Yes."

"You didn't think I would be interested to know that when I hired you?"

"If I'd mentioned it, you wouldn't have hired me."

"Because you might have sabotaged Lady Lia's gown."

He talked like a teacher, but she'd never been permitted much schooling.

"I didn't sabotage anything," Emer pointed out.

Only now, with the gown worn and the ball over, could Emer prove she hadn't had evil intentions. Why would Lord Marius trust her without proof?

Forget sabotaging the dress. Emer could have skimped on the material and sold pieces of that fancy fabric at a fancy price down in the marketplace. She hadn't, for the same reason she hadn't told Rahela the truth of Lia's character. She'd betrayed Lia enough.

"I heard you reported Lady Lia's confidences to Lady Rahela," Lord Marius continued slowly. "Was this a way to convey apologies to Lady Lia for your treachery?"

Be a foolish way to convey apologies, as Emer hadn't intended anybody to find out.

Emer shrugged. "Just wanted to earn some coin, my lord."

He'd been kind to Lady Lia. Emer was sure he expected a return for his kindness, as though Lia's heart was as easily purchased as Emer's needle. Lord Marius was only taking an interest in Emer because he desired to play hero for Lia again. He didn't suspect her of evil conspiracy.

That should have been a relief.

Emer wished Lord Marius had remained conveniently oblivious to service staff. "I altered the dress because I wanted to. I won't apologize or explain. I prefer doing to talking."

There was a long enough silence that Emer dared to hope the duke's son had departed. Her focus stayed on the blade, not lords, tower windows, stars, or anything else above her.

Directly behind her, Lord Marius's grave voice said: "Adjust your grip on the hilt."

His large hands, made for strangling, demonstrated on empty air. Emer adjusted her grip.

"Bend your legs. If you go low to the ground, you can't be moved."

In Emer's experience, talk of legs went nowhere good. Lord Marius's hands hovered above her waist so only the ghostly warmth of nearness guided her. Emer followed his instructions. She liked the idea of being immovable.

"Orient your swing," Lord Marius continued. "You need force from your body, not simply your arm."

The ghost of warmth moved, illustrative, to her shoulder. Emer obeyed, and swung. That did feel different.

The ghost of warmth disappeared as Lord Marius stepped away, hands clasped behind his back. "Nobody will expect a serving woman to do battle. You can take them by surprise. A killing move will mean they never recover from that surprise."

He walked off without a goodbye. Puzzled, Emer studied his retreating back, the tumble of ice-and-dark curls and white scholar's uniform disappearing into the gloom. He was a cold man, so she wondered what had inspired him to offer her advice. Whatever he wanted, she had no intention of giving it to him.

Her speculation was broken off by realization. Lord Marius didn't linger around the ladies' tower like other noblemen. He must be here because he'd followed the Cobra, and seen the Cobra enter Rahela's room. Now Lord Marius was headed in the direction of the king's chambers.

The vipers needed to know what he told King Octavian. Emer had learned a great many useful things from eavesdropping.

She tucked her sword behind a tree and ran after Lord Marius. She'd escorted her lady back and forth from the royal bedroom under cover of darkness a thousand times. Nobody knew how to stealthily access the king's chambers as well as she. King Octavian didn't sleep in the main palace surrounded by staff as his parents had. He occupied a separate bachelor's quarters, where he could have his fun undisturbed.

Over the small bridge, through the garden with the three swan statues, head down and steps soft as she passed the laziest guard posted on the fourth point of the perimeter. Just as usual. Except instead of entering the hall, Emer darted towards a willow tree leaning against the building. She swung from a green-veiled branch onto the eaves of the roof pointed as an accusing finger, crawling on her stomach to peer in through the tall diamond-paned windows. The king's guards always warned him not to leave windows open, and Octavian carelessly kept doing it.

Emer reached the open window in time to hear the king ask, "Where did you get this?"

The most famous men in the kingdom stood against the backdrop of a tapestry commemorating the first king and the First Duke's battle against the fiends. King Octavian had a key in his hand, and an ugly expression on his face.

"As if I didn't know."

The problem was, Octavian wasn't stupid. Kingship seemed designed to make his intelligence atrophy, but it did pop out occasionally.

Always at the most inconvenient times. If Lord Marius said the word, the Cobra got his head chopped off.

Lord Marius was silent.

Octavian continued undaunted. "If someone stole from me, you would bring me the culprit in chains. Unless it was one particular culprit."

Lord Marius was vehemently silent.

King Octavian said, with distaste, "I know you're ... fond of the man, but—"

"I'm not fond of the man," growled Lord Marius, so fiercely Emer thought of the country saying: *when you howl, you're hit.* "Lady Rahela has ingratiated herself with both the Cobra and a foreign princess. The ice raiders are a formidable threat. If powerful people in your court are conspiring with the Ice King, we must get to the heart of the conspiracy."

Emer hated the sinking feeling when you realized you'd been lied to, that the very ground you believed would support you could not be trusted. It made her want to strike out wildly in all directions. Anyone might be an enemy.

Were Rahela and the Cobra conspiring with the royal family of Tagar? They would never tell her if they were. She was only a servant.

Octavian's mouth pulled tight. "Do you think he's had her?"

His Majesty's priorities were interesting.

"An unmarried noblewoman? Impossible!"

Lord Marius's jaw was scandalized granite. Emer rolled her eyes. Everybody knew the King and Lord Marius were childhood friends, but the two men weren't alike.

The train of King Octavian's brocade dressing gown swept the floor as he paced, concealing mosaics depicting an empty throne. "Do you think Rahela likes him?"

"I imagine so." Lord Marius's tone was that of a man who would rather be discussing ice raiders. "Women are obsessed with the Cobra."

Last time Emer checked, she was a woman. She was not obsessed with Lord Popenjoy.

"Do you think she's lying about the prophecy?" A new note entered Octavian's voice. It struck Emer as dangerous. "You don't believe I'm the Emperor?"

No answer came from the lone honest man at court. The king's frown darkened.

It was difficult to maintain appropriate awe towards your monarch when you'd seen him sleepy and rumpled in the mornings. He'd cling to Rahela's unclothed body while Emer grimly tried to get her into her gown. To Octavian, not getting caught was a game. To Emer and her lady, it was their lives at stake.

There were people who, when eating an orange, would not share a single segment. *All the worlds are his empire*, said the prophecy. Spoiled as if he were forever a royal child, the king believed satisfied desire was his right, and unsatisfied desire was robbery.

"I have always had faith in you," Lord Marius said at last. "I believe you could be the Emperor. More important, I believe you can be a good king."

Octavian might be the Emperor, Emer supposed. He was already randomly born to unfathomable power. Why not more? That was how the gods had ordered the world. The powerful grew more powerful. Those born on their knees died crawling on their bellies.

Still, Emer thought Lord Marius was naive. None of the songs said the Emperor was going to be *good*.

Octavian was suddenly all smiles. "I never believed the rumours about you."

"Whatever the rumours might be, I thank you for that," replied Lord Marius. "I never believed the vile gossip about you and Lady Rahela either. I know your honour too well."

Hilarious!

The king said nothing. A faint flush ran along the tops of his cheekbones. Whenever Octavian felt shame, he let the emotion turn like a snake and strike out at someone else.

"I know we have grown apart in recent years," Lord Marius continued. "It's my fault."

As soon as Marius blamed himself instead of the king, Octavian looked more interested in what Lord Marius had to say.

"When the court was in upheaval over who would be named prime minister, I spilled your list of candidates to Lady Katalin before she was banished. She sold the information to Lord Pio the next night. If you wish for my life, it is yours."

For all his cool airs, Lord Marius had a highly dramatic personality. From the abrupt white ring around the king's eyes, Octavian agreed. "Lost gods, man, there's no need for that! We were young. I might have mentioned the list to Rahela myself." Octavian regarded the Last Hope with increased warmth, and sketched an hourglass shape with both hands. "Lady Katalin? Fine-looking woman. Very like her daughter. Is it older women for you, then?"

He slapped Lord Marius on the back. Lord Marius visibly repressed the urge to take the royal hand off at the wrist.

"I took vows."

There came upon His Majesty the expression of a man who had heard about vows before, and strongly preferred not to hear about vows again. "I don't doubt you, Marius."

"You should. The Golden Cobra knew of my crime. He blackmailed me to gain an entrée to court. As my friend, his title and position in society wasn't questioned. But I never saw him before the day he black-mailed me. I have no idea what the truth of him might be."

Something unsettling lay beneath Lord Marius's confession, rushing black water under a thin veneer of ice. Emer had believed the king was the more dangerous of the pair. Perhaps she was wrong.

"He blackmailed you into attending all those plays?" breathed Octavian. "The man's a monster!"

"He didn't specifically require me to attend the plays." Lord Marius shook his head. "That's not important. Listen. Why are they after the Flower of Life and Death? Lady Rahela and her new allies clearly have a purpose. I believe the end might be found in the beginning. We don't know where the Cobra comes from, or where his true alle-giances lie. I intend to find out."

"Do you think he's a spy from Tagar, sent to us ahead of the prin-cess?" Octavian gave a thoughtful hum. "All these years. You must hate the Cobra worse than poison. You're right, we must unravel his spider's web. Even before, I knew his influence was growing too great for safety. He's schemed to become the darling of the common people."

The Last Hope raised an eyebrow. "He's generous to his servants and charitable to the less fortunate." He hesitated. "Do you truly not care about my betrayal?"

The man's sense of responsibility was as overdeveloped as his mus-cles. Octavian set a hand on one burly shoulder.

"Atone for your actions with loyalty. Can you find out the Cobra's mysterious past?"

Lord Marius said evenly, "I can. The mountains hold all answers."

Shock passed over Octavian's face, rendering him a boy again, a squire who might be capable of awe. "You mean to go to the Oracle? You would need his true name."

"I believe I have it."

"Oh." Octavian sounded curious. "What is it?"

There was another deliberate silence. From a man who would not lie, quiet was a slap in the face. It said, 'If I spoke, I would lie through my teeth.'

The new warmth faded from the king's expression.

"You were always closer to Lucius than me," Lord Marius responded finally, and the knuckles of Octavian's hand went briefly white. "But you can trust me as much as you trusted him."

The king's mouth twisted. His laugh was twisted, too. "As much as that?"

Lord Marius took it as an insult. "I know I am unpleasant by nature and difficult to like. But believe me, I am true. I will find out this secret and lay it at your feet."

Octavian's face softened slightly. "After the Queen's Trials I will hold a celebration of my new bride. Take the opportunity to ride to the mountains unseen."

Lord Marius's voice was dry. "I will be desolated to miss the party."

The king almost smiled. In that moment, Emer saw how they might have loved each other once.

"Let me make you an offer. A general doesn't have to wield a weapon. General Nemeth is old and poor. I don't need an obvious weakness in the commander of my armies. I need a man whose loyalty is unshakable, who will obey me until death. How does that sound to you?"

"All I ever wanted was to serve a worthy leader," said Lord Marius. "I would gladly die for that."

The prospect of glory didn't seem to move the Last Hope much. Perhaps because he was rich. Perhaps because he was inflexible.

The king had spent his life surrounded by flattering courtiers and wicked women. He could never trust anyone's affection. He watched Lord Marius with measuring eyes.

"The Oracle only offers a man a single answer in his lifetime. There is always a cruel price. What do you wish in return for doing this? Ask me for a reward."

Lord Marius hesitated. The king's lips curved like the hook that had caught his fish. Lord Marius was a taller man than the king, but you couldn't tell how tall someone was when they bowed. So in a way, the king was always the tallest man in the room.

The Last Hope bowed his head in submission. The two men looked like a tapestry, the shining king and the perfect knight, the valiant heroes who would defeat evil and save a kingdom.

As one of the evildoers, Emer heard Lord Marius's voice as the voice of doom.

"I will hear the great secret from the Oracle's lips, no matter the price. I will drag the traitors to your throne for punishment. I will lead your armies against the ice raiders and all who dare rise against you. I want only one reward." Lord Marius lifted his ice-and-dark head, face cold and empty as chambers for the dead. "Command war. Condemn worlds. *Leave the Cobra to me.*"

As Emer raced up the stairs of the tower to tell the vipers that the king believed they were spies and traitors, and Lord Marius planned to expose all the Cobra's secrets, she heard raised voices and stopped, startled.

The whole court believed Lady Rahela held the Golden Cobra in her wicked clutches. Emer wished it were true. Having lost the king's favour, it made sense to seek protection elsewhere. But the Cobra was never serious about anyone, so he could only ruin and not rescue her reputation, and as far as Emer could tell Rahela hadn't even tried to seduce him. Emer had listened in on their secret meetings, and she certainly hoped 'back it up' and 'do it backwards in high heels' meant they were rehearsing that awful dance.

At least, Emer thought, Rahela had gained the Cobra's friendship. He was known to be a loyal friend. There might be some security to that.

Except now the stone walls echoed with the ring of a deep voice. The Cobra, who was never serious, was shouting.

"This is their world, not ours! You have to stop before someone else gets hurt."

When Emer stealthily slid the door open, Rahela was looking at Key. He shifted in his sleep and moaned, pain breaking through his slumber. She reached out and brushed back his wild hair, ever so lightly, and Key calmed under her touch. Anyone would have thought she cared.

She smiled bright as the flames of hell. "I don't want anyone to get hurt. But it doesn't actually matter. These people aren't real."

Only she didn't care.

The Cobra turned away in disgust. "These people are as real as we are."

Rahela wheeled on him. "Keep fretting about these characters. Keep floating through this world like a ghost afraid to touch anything. You lie to yourself, because you don't want to believe you're—"

"Dead?" the Cobra asked softly.

The silence rang like a scream in a tomb.

The Cobra shoved Rahela aside. When he wrenched the door open, he saw Emer. The nation's spymaster said not a word. He nodded to her, then stormed down the stairs.

The alliance between Lord Popenjoy and Lady Rahela was broken. Key was ruined. Her lady lied when she talked about being a team. There was no nest of vipers together. There never had been.

Emer would keep her secrets.

The next days were full of surprises. When the guards moved them from the favourite's airy chambers to the dank room at the base of the ladies' tower, Emer expected Rahela to throw a tantrum. Their new chamber was half the size, dark with barred windows. The floor was red mosaics, showing the moment after the godchild was murdered by his father, fresh blood drenching the dark earth of Eyam to change it forever. Rahela shrugged, observed the decor matched her dresses, and continued telling stories by Key's bedside.

One thing Emer found unsurprising was Lia didn't move into the chamber Rahela had vacated. Lady Lia, too careful to risk making enemies, wouldn't occupy the favourite's chamber until after the Queen's Trials. Emer tried hard not to think about the tournament, with its attendant dangers, or what might happen after.

Key was the greatest surprise of all. The wounds on his back knit together almost at once. By the fourth day, he could rise from the bed. It made Emer recall the legends of Valerius berserkers, and the new story that someone had seen Lord Marius get stabbed in a tavern brawl and walk away without a scratch.

Absurd. Lord Marius wouldn't go to a tavern.

They said Valerius bastards never survived. Perhaps that simply meant noblewomen got better care when they bore their little lords and ladies. Lord Marius's father was said to be rapacious with common wenches. Emer supposed it was possible.

Rahela talked about Key getting well soon. She was deluded.

Valerius bastard or not, Key would never be truly well again. Emer had seen the damage done to muscles that should have stayed beneath his skin. He would never walk like a shadow turned liquid the way he used to. He was still leaning against bedposts and sinking down into chairs and generally getting in the way, especially during the palace guards' removal of their belongings from the favourite's chamber. Thanks to Key's invalid clumsiness, it took the guards a whole night and day to switch rooms.

Whenever he showed weakness, Rahela was all concern. "Do you want to lie down? What can I do for you?"

Today red thread fell down her moonlight-coloured skirt in drops like bloody tears. Key stretched out on the new bed with his wild black head cradled in her blood-and-moon lap, listening as she told him a story. Usually his expression was either bored, amused or flatly murderous. It was profoundly unsettling to see him happy.

Many maids had an eye for Key. He didn't possess money or status, so their attraction was based on his beautiful face and hideous rep-utation. Their wits had clearly gone begging and received no alms. Admiring men always seemed ridiculous to Emer, but never more so than with this one. Perhaps Key was a Valerius bastard. Perhaps he was a typical abyss foundling, swallowing sparks so young he was always burning. Perhaps, if Lady Katalin hadn't picked up a compan-ion for her daughter from the abyss edge on a whim, Emer would be the same. Whatever the reason, Key was less a reasonable human being and more a wayward force of nature personified. Some rabid imp of darkness or wild hobgoblin, puppeteering a human façade from one murder scene to the next.

And now the feral goblin was in love.

"Teach me to read," requested Key, so Rahela fetched her book for his next lesson.

Key, who had learned his alphabet from Emer, was shamelessly pretending to Rahela he was picking it up fast.

As he often did when their lady wasn't around, Key took out the ruby earring he kept tucked in his jerkin. Red light made sparkling play across his face. Emer had told him repeatedly to pawn the jewel, and knew he never would.

"Why does reading matter to you?" Emer demanded.

The highest station a palace guard could achieve was serving the king directly, and Key definitely did not have ambitions in that direction. Apparently, he'd acquired an item he wanted and now no longer cared about money. Emer had to collect his wages every week, and one day she would keep them.

"According to the story, you learn how to be real by being loved," Key answered. "But I think when you become more real, you learn to love someone the right way. I was born wrong. Everything I've ever done was wrong. I've never known how to be anything someone wanted. If I learn more, I'll learn to serve her better."

"She spoke not a word in your defence when you were whipped," Emer reminded him. "You're nothing but a pet she's fond of. If you died she might shed a tear before she found a replacement."

Key's shrug was fluid despite the whip marks. "It's more than I had before."

His attention fixed on Rahela's return, hungry for the crumbs that fell from her table, as if that would be enough to live upon. Rahela was writing out a children's tale for Key. They read together about toys taking a long journey towards becoming real.

This new version of Emer's mistress was strange, but she wasn't stupid. So Emer couldn't understand why she was so incredibly foolish in this one area. The old Rahela was keenly aware of her power over men. The old Rahela would never believe a twenty-year-old man, presented with the country's most famously seductive woman, might look to her as a mentor.

Key gazed up at her, galaxy-eyed rather than starry-eyed, with more stars and far more darkness. Rahela smiled down at him.

The question broke from Emer. "Are you not preparing for the Queen's Trials, my lady?"

"I am," Rahela said calmly. "My plan involves a sword."

This news visibly delighted Key and dismayed Emer. Rahela's plans had never involved swords before.

She seemed like a different person, wearing Rahela's face. She schemed like Rahela, lied like Rahela, smiled Rahela's wicked smile, but what she wanted and how she thought was a world apart from the woman Emer knew.

Except Emer had never known Rahela. She'd imagined their closeness, because she was pathetically lonely. As if faith ever made anything true.

She shut the door on the absurd pair. Real, indeed. Everyone lived in their own reality, and could never invite anybody else in. Ultimately each person was alone, the only real person in a vast desert of a universe, always longing and never able to find someone to believe in. If they ever did believe, they were deceived.

Outside was cold and dark and lonely, which Emer preferred. It felt more true. Illusions were made of the stuff of gold candlelight of Lia's room, filtered through a rippling pale sheet. Illusion was Lia's whisper, gentle as a caress.

"One day each of us must marry. What will having a husband be like?" Lia had paused, for a breath that felt like eternity. "What do husbands even want?"

Emer cleared her throat. "Many things."

In her pretty imploring way, Lia said, "Show me."

They had a handful of nights before the betrayal. Enough time for a thousand lies. The lie of endless softness that was the silvered expanse of Lia's bared skin, the silken luxury of her mouth offered for a stolen kiss. The beads of sweat on Lia's throat when Emer's kisses trailed downwards and Lia threw her head back, gleaming more precious than diamonds. Luxury was something Emer had to steal and could never keep.

Belowstairs the men bragged about getting beneath fine ladies' silk skirts, laughed about swiving nobles and sullying reputations. All knew Lady Lia was pure as a pearl. A man's touch could stain a lady, but Emer's couldn't even stain. Nobody would ever think it counted, as though Rahela was right and Emer wasn't even a person.

Nobody would ever know, but Emer knew. She was a false, treacherous villain. At least she wasn't a fool.

Emer took her sword from its hiding place and cut the night to pieces. Above her Lia's tower window shone bright as the moon, and just as unreachable. The Queen's Trials were coming. The whole court knew the king wanted Lia for his bride.

Caring for a noble was spilling your own blood into dust. Emer would not do it. She would *not*.

CHAPTER TWENTY-THREE

The Villainess and Longing for Revenge

Among all the beasts, none is more cruel than the manticore. Its voice is the voice of a trumpet and its sting is death. It was a worthy foe for Lord Marius, standing as champion for Lady Lia in the Queen's Trials.

When the manticore's chain broke, Lady Lia flung herself between the Last Hope and danger. Enemies and admirers alike watched, sure they would witness the death of the world's most beautiful woman and her white knight.

Until the Emperor descended, a dark storm with a burning sword.

Time of Iron, ANONYMOUS

ae strode into the king's chambers of midnight sin in broad daylight. "Up and at 'em!"

King Octavian's ruffled bedhead emerged from a heap of satin and velvet blankets. Somewhat to Rae's surprise, he was alone.

"Up and at who? Has the country been invaded!"

Rae leaned against one of the bedposts on the four poster. "Not yet. But the day's young."

The staff exchanged speculative glances. Behind a screen inlaid with mother of pearl, Rae heard the splash of water into a copper tub. She also heard giggling. Rae had no doubt the whole court would shortly be informed of Lady Rahela bursting into the royal bedchamber unescorted.

Could her reputation get more ruined? Time to find out.

Rae could hardly bring her guard, since he was confined to bed after a whipping carried out by royal command. Whenever Rae thought about that, she felt something close to hate.

So she didn't think about it. Everyone conveniently forgot the worst elements of their favourite characters while dwelling on the failings of their least favourite. There was no other choice. Going against the hero would be fatal.

Her plot to steal the key had ended in utter failure, as villains' plots tended to. But the Cobra said, *those who walk into the story have an advantage because we know the rules.* Rae had the manual. The Emperor rose, the lost gods were found, everybody loved Lia. This was the Emperor, his power inexorable as disease. She couldn't fight him. She couldn't be paralysed with fear of him. She had to make the story work for her. She had to win back his favour.

Reassured his country wasn't in imminent peril, Octavian lounged back on his velvet pillows. His bedhead was TV bedhead, which should by rights have been created by several talented stylists and an ocean of gel.

Octavian noticed her gaze on him and stretched, damask sheets slipping down to show an expanse of bare skin and rippling muscle. Rae didn't know if the king slept bare or if there were regal boxers involved, but she might be about to find out.

"Lady Rahela. What do you desire from your king?"

Rae let her phone-sex voice slide low. "I desperately, burningly desire . . . to fulfil a divine prophecy."

Octavian abandoned his lounge and sat up straight. "What?"

Rae adopted her prophecy intonation, which sounded like a phone sex operator with a nasty cold. "I mentioned before the future is flexible in certain ways. In my vision, I saw the tournament for the lady who will rule by your side. You'll be delighted to know Lia wins!"

Octavian squinted, as if still sleepy. "Are you not intending to compete in the tournament?"

"Hard pass." Rae clasped her hands as though in prayer. "The gods have spoken! I'm not the woman for you. I *am* the woman who elevates you to greatness. Here's the issue. On the day of the tournament, I foresee you will demonstrate your imperial power to the whole city."

"Before I descend into the ravine?" Octavian asked sceptically.

"The dread ravine is only a means of unlocking power that is already yours," Rae explained. "You're the child of gods. You already have prowess in battle beyond the dreams of heroes, and the ability to heal the ills of your people."

Octavian sounded very doubtful. "I think I would have noticed that."

Rae had once adored the Emperor's cynicism. Right now she found it annoying.

"It's very common for a character – uh, of legend – to have a mental block about using his powers. Just believe in yourself or the magic of love or something, that always does the trick. I know you can do it," she added, to be encouraging.

Morning light caught the green of the king's eyes like dew in the grass. "Promise?"

Rae nodded. "You'll be a great hero. And what does every hero need? A cool signature weapon."

King Octavian's royal regalia was laid out on the chest at the foot of his bed. Sometimes Octavian was so different from the Emperor in Rae's head, she couldn't believe they were one and the same. Seeing this, Rae scolded herself. Who else could the Emperor be? The regalia was exactly as she had imagined. Clawed gauntlets, crowned mask, and the Sword of Eyam. The ancestral symbol of royal power, in its embossed sheath.

Rae gestured helpfully to the royal blade. "The gods showed me a vision of this sword being broken and reforged. Let's get on that now. You should name the sword Longing for Revenge."

Octavian blinked. "Revenge against who?"

Why must he concentrate on these irrelevant details when Rae was trying to progress the plot?

"Don't overthink. It doesn't have to be revenge against anyone specific. It's just a badass name."

Steam rose from the bathtub behind a screen, thick as if an enormous kettle was boiling back there. It was good to be the king. Octavian rose from the bed wearing only silk sleeping pants. (Well. Now she knew.) He sent a sidelong glance Rae's way as he moved behind the screen. Rae promptly turned her back, though she did notice that he worked out. Or didn't work out, but had a rocking bod anyway. Once again, book characters achieved spectacular muscle tone while too busy with corporate takeovers or magic destinies to have time for the gym. Fictional men had abs for pages. Octavian's were impressive in a way Rae had only seen on screen in her world.

In *this* world, Rae had seen better.

"So you want me to break and remake the royal sword," Octavian murmured from behind the screen. "Tell me why I should."

While he was occupied, Rae tried to pick up the royal sword and wave it dramatically. She succeeded in almost dropping it and hastily replaced the sword on the chest. As it emerged, broadswords were heavy.

In two days, the Last Hope would volunteer to be Lia's champion at the Queen's Trials. When Lord Marius's match went spectacularly wrong, the Emperor needed to leap from the royal box and slay a magical beast with his reforged blade.

It was imperative they speed-run acquiring a weapon of mystic power.

"If you do," Rae promised, "you'll get everything you want. You can protect the people you love. You will be Emperor. Lia will win the tournament and be your queen."

"What else?"

Octavian emerged from behind the screen, hair damp. He gave her a smile. Rae recalled with a jolt Alice saying the Emperor used to smile all the time in the first book. She knew he wouldn't smile much later.

"Having a sword that will defeat all your enemies isn't enough? You need Longing for Revenge. The ice raiders are coming for you."

"Are they indeed?" Octavian asked softly. "Shall we go somewhere private and discuss this further?"

Rae took a chance. "I would enjoy a stroll in the royal greenhouse."

Octavian paused for a long moment, gaze travelling thoughtfully over her. Rae felt a brief pang of panic that she'd betrayed her desperation. The Last Hope must have told Octavian everything. He had no reason to let her anywhere near the Flower of Life and Death.

Yet as he held out his arms for the servants to garb him, the king nodded. "Let's do that."

Off to the greenhouse she went, arm in arm with the hero. Miraculously, finally, everything was coming up Rae.

Since glass was expensive in Eyam, the royal greenhouse was the only greenhouse in the country. It was accessible via a walkway on the highest wall, guards posted at every battlement and at the top and bottom of the steep stone stairs. Security was tight.

On the king's arm, Rae breezed right through. It was an undeniable thrill. The masked crown and clawed gauntlets made him almost the Emperor already, anonymous and imperial, a splendid mystery.

What was forbidden and set apart seemed sacred. They descended a semicircular flight of marble steps. The entryway at their back was a goblet of light. The huge glass windows were arched, the arches made of metres-thick stone to capture heat. The hushed, warm air made everything quiet and still. This was a great glass cathedral.

Octavian tossed his gauntlets to a guard. "Wait here."

The prospect of being alone with him made the glass before Rae's eyes go wavy. She dragged her mind from the brink of panic into the realm of getting shit done, and nodded graciously.

They walked under the spreading branches of citrus trees. Not a breath of wind touched the riot of bright leaves and brighter fruits. The king's garden was a parterre in green curves and dark earthen squares beneath a vaulted ceiling instead of a sky. Plants in one patch looked like ordinary green clumps, but made the ground hum with the muffled cries of young children. All the trees grew in handsome pots of elaborate iron fretwork and ebony, which resembled cages. Rae and the king passed beneath a tree, brandishing branches exuberantly in every direction, with tiny leaves like chips of green glass and large low-hanging fruit the colour of rubies. Pomegranates, Rae thought, and remembered a story of a girl snatched to another world. The girl ate a pomegranate, and as a price for being hungry had to stay.

She wouldn't be tempted by any beauty or any hunger. She was leaving, but she didn't want to destroy anybody on her way out.

"Remember the legend of how the First Duke forged his sword using the bones of monstrous beasts and the thinking dead, and his blade cut down all who stood before him? It's true. The gods told me," Rae tacked on hastily.

Octavian stared in regal confusion. "Is that so?"

The royal sword was already made of the finest orichal steel, metal dug from the Sedlace mines and forged in Themesvar. But there was a way to make the weapon twice-charmed. The method that would transform the king's blade into the Emperor's Longing for Revenge.

On a long-ago night lost reading weird facts online, Rae had learned Vikings performed rituals to infuse their sword with spirits, burning bones beneath the forge to give their ancestors' strength to their blades. Viking rituals accidentally turned iron to steel, because burning bones produced carbon. In Eyam burning bones turned steel to something else, metal both unbreakable and hungry. It seemed like magic to Rae, but it had seemed like magic to the Vikings too.

The people of Eyam had lost this art, whether it was science or magic. The Emperor accidentally rediscovered it when reforging his broken blade. All the strength of his dead enemies went into his orichal steel to serve him.

Time to make the magic happen. Ahead of schedule.

"This is the scheme. Break your sword, grab some unicorn, manticore, or griffin bones, re-forge better sword. Hey presto, undefeatable in battle! You must forge the sword yourself. And you want to be undefeatable in battle for the Queen's Trials. Trust me."

"Should I?" There was an odd note in Octavian's voice. "Because you're so devoted to me? You would betray me if it benefited you."

Rae remembered the Cobra saying, *Trust my wicked heart.* Game recognized game: heroes recognized villainy. "Of course I would."

It was hard to tell beneath his shining mask, but Octavian seemed startled.

"How is it betraying you to tell you how to forge an invincible sword?" Rae persisted. "You're a god. Why would I ever be on anyone else's side?"

"What about the Cobra's side?"

Rae bit her lip. "The Cobra and I have had a disagreement."

For some reason, that seemed to please Octavian. Some people were like that. They didn't really want you, but they wanted you to want them.

"Tell me, why did you mention the ice raiders?"

"Because they are going to invade," Rae answered. "There will be two attacks. First a battalion will come, then an army. You repel the small force that comes in a couple of years, when the abyss yawns wide, but years after that—"

Octavian sounded amused. "Oh, years after that?"

"Yes! Years after that, their boats will come down the Tears of the Dead River."

Octavian sounded *tolerantly* amused. "The Tagar raiders can only come across the Bittersea and up the river. Nothing comes down the Tears river. Its source is in the ravine."

Nobody got to question Rae's expertise on the epic battle scene, where the Emperor rode to war on his tamed monster.

"The raiders go up the Trespasser river running through the duke's estate, then portage the boats over land. After that, they sail down the Tears of the Dead River when nobody is expecting them, and invade! You need to set guards on both rivers right away. You need to make sure you have guards at their posts and not on the balconies on the night the abyss opens, when the smaller force attacks."

"The future seems very dramatic," Octavian murmured.

"Before any of that," Rae continued firmly, "you need your sword for the Queen's Trials. You must defend Lia and the country. Listen to me. You will defeat any disaster. I believe that, but you must be ready."

A long pause followed. "Almost you persuade me to trust you, Rahela."

"Why not? You will be the world's Emperor, and I your prophet. Trust my desire for power."

Rae had always loved the monsters of Eyam, the Emperor most of all. His blood had transformed this land. The same divine power that brought the dead to monstrous life caused metal to gleam red and invincible animals to meld into fierce strange creatures, and flowers to save lives. In this world, every fantasy was possible.

Because of him.

Trapped sunlight slanted through the leaves of the trees around them, on the man before her. The gold of his masked crown and the green of his eyes burned bright.

"This is what you want. Once I forge my sword anew for the Trials, you will forgive our quarrels."

Sure, the little disagreements where Octavian had Key whipped and Rae almost executed. He hadn't suffered, so he could brush their suffering off. If you were king, nobody else's pain had to be real.

Rae hesitated.

"Look up," King Octavian added casually. "The gardeners say the Flower of Life and Death will bloom in nine days."

Over their heads a great stem grew in an arch, like a living green lamp post. Tender oval leaves curled about the stem, the bud suspended above. The bud was green as the leaves. Rae couldn't discern the colour of the flower that could save her life.

In dreamy reminiscent tones, Octavian said, "Last year when the Flower of Life and Death bloomed, we lay beneath the flower and watched it die. We didn't pluck it, because you said it was pretty. The petals fell in our hair and you laughed."

No. The Emperor wouldn't do that. In the *Time of Iron* books he always brought the Flower into the Cauldron. This flower could have saved someone's dying beloved, their fading parent, their wounded friend, or their sick child. The Emperor couldn't be like this.

But he was.

Bitterness stung the back of Rae's throat. The taste carried her back on a bitter tide to days in the smallest bathroom in her mother's house, vomiting and voiding until she felt she'd lost everything inside her and was now a hollow thing. No longer a person at all.

The king's smile was an offer. "Want to do it again?"

She understood the offer all too well. Lia was the virtuous angel who would never give it up before marriage, so the king wanted Rahela to be his subject-with-benefits. The time would come when the Emperor wanted nobody but Lia, but he wasn't there yet. Once he gained his full power, he would be. By then Rae would be long gone.

Don't let your mouth write a cheque your ass can't cash, Rae's mom warned whenever Rae got overly enthusiastic. But when Rae's master plan succeeded, Rae's ass would be safe in another world. This would be nothing but entertainment to her. She would read and laugh so hard she was shaking.

Rae grasped the stem of the Flower of Life and Death as if it were a stripper pole. "It's a date."

A sunbeam arrowed straight onto Octavian, ultra-concentrated by the thick greenhouse glass. A spotlight selecting the chosen one.

"It's a promise. I will have an empire, and the two most beautiful women in the world on either side of my throne."

Rae gave him a temptress's smile. "Be a hero."

When Octavian moved towards her, she expected him to smell as heroes did in books: forest and fine leather and another scent that was uniquely him. Only expensive cologne wafted towards her. Heroines must have a better sense of smell than villains.

He pushed up his shining crowned mask and leaned down to kiss her. He really was beautiful. The sight of Octavian's face made memory tear through her. Key's wild hair and ruined back against her white sheets and pillows. Memory black as ebony, white as snow, red as blood, and it hadn't been a story at all but someone ripped apart.

Rae's courage failed. She wagged a finger archly, then broke and ran, up the stairs and right into Key. Sweat stung her eyes. Even in her blurred vision she saw the stone terror that was Key's face without a smile, and realized he'd heard everything.

Gripped by the certainty Key intended to commit crimes, panic scythed away schemes leaving her with desperation. Rae grasped the front of his jerkin and pulled him into a kiss. She felt the pull as he took handfuls of her hair, the sting of teeth as his mouth opened. When she drew away, his face had come alive again, fingers curled around her hair rather than his knives. She hissed, "You can't be here!"

"Punish me then, my lady," Key suggested.

She was in trouble. He only said 'my lady' when he was angry.

She seized his hand. He let her drag him along the battlements, sullen heat rising from the ravine below and cold wind driving in from the grey smoke-stained sky above. When Rae turned her head, hair flew into her eyes in a black storm. Blinking, she glimpsed an expression that made her think Key's injuries were giving him a lot of pain. Then he grinned. Her worries dissipated. His grin was sharp and alarming as a bared dagger, but she'd become familiar.

In fiction people healed fast after dramatic injuries, leaving only interesting scars behind. Key was almost well already. It would be senseless to resent the king for hurting him.

When Key stopped and leaned against the stone battlements, Rae stayed with him.

"You said you wouldn't crawl back to Octavian," Key said slowly. "If you didn't need to crawl, would you want to go back?"

She would have turned on him had there been the slightest edge of judgement in his voice. But he was waiting for her answer, wanting to know her story so he could understand her.

"He's going to be the Emperor," Rae reminded Key.

"And you love him."

She loved Octavian enough to put his poster on her wall, the Emperor alone on his throne under a blackened sky. Maybe she couldn't see the Emperor in him now, but she'd missed a lot about Lia even though the clues were there. He was the Emperor, so she would love him when he went through blood and fire and character development. On days when she felt the worst, he would *be* the worst. Even when the story slipped through her fingers, he was such a comfort.

"I love him. You don't know what he's going to do with his power."

"Great things?"

Rae smiled. "Awful things."

Sparks flew and lit fires in Key's eyes. "Even better." For a wild moment, Rae imagined he might kiss her again. Of course, he did not.

"There's a saying that goes 'I could not love thee, dear, so much, did I not love honour more.' That's bullshit hero talk. When he's emperor, he's going to love someone more than honour. He will love her past reason. He would do anything for her, which means he will commit any sin. He will put out the sun and carve out the heart of the world for love. That's why I like bad guys. Imagine powerless pining in a tower waiting for a hero to rescue you. Then imagine being the only one who can command the monster. That's what I loved him for, but – he didn't choose me. Fate didn't choose me, either."

Once upon a time she'd selected the Emperor as her favourite character, but she'd never imagined being one of the many people he discarded on his way to the top. In stories, the main characters only thought about themselves. All the other characters thought about them, too.

When her boyfriend and her best friend and her father left, Rae cried until there was no feeling in her. People might pretend they cared, but she knew better than to ever trust again. She knew what she was. She was a skin bag of bones and sickness, all lumpy inside like lousy porridge, and nobody was going to love her now.

She was so used to Key's amused drawl, she hardly recognized his voice when it became the sound of fire: half hiss, half roar, pure hunger. "He hurt you."

Rae shook her head. "What hurt me was the truth. Some people aren't that special. I used to think I was, but I learned. When nobody believes in you, it's too hard to believe in yourself. When I was ill I drifted too far away from my friends, got too small in their eyes, but that means I was never big to begin with. I'm replaceable. I'm forget-table. I'm not someone who can change the universe."

People liked stories about a chosen one, because those stories let them pretend fate would choose them. Rae knew better. Father, friends, lover, none of them had. As she lay dying, she knew that if the world was a lake, her passing wouldn't even make a ripple.

"If you could change the universe," said Key, "what would you want?"

Rae remembered the king moving closer under the flower that meant her life. His imperial power, soon to cast a shadow over the whole sky, could consume her with the devastating completeness of cancer. She imagined being forced to endure his touch, as she must the icy sting of a needle. Cold seized and shook her, despite the heat coming off the ravine and the warmth of Key's hand. She answered with absolute truth. "I don't ever want him to touch me again. But what I want doesn't count."

"I've noticed you change stories as you're telling them," said Key. "You make them the way you want."

Rae had finished telling Key and Emer children's stories, and now was onto narrating TV shows before bedtime. She might have altered some minor details in the retelling.

"It's not the same."

Key smiled as if she'd told a little joke, his grip on her hand firm. "It is. Emer was right when she said words change reality. The whole world is stories. People's lives don't matter, not really. But if you have power, you can make them matter. Beggars starve in this city. Everyone says: there's nothing we can do, but obviously there's something they can do. They don't care enough. If it was someone you loved, you'd run into the city with bread. Everyone's the same, except you and I don't pretend to care. The glassblowers' guild believed my father was nothing, so they made it true. If they'd known their survival depended on his, they would have treasured him. Power is when you make other people believe in your story."

His eyes were mirrors to the ravine. Rae had heard if you stare into the abyss, the abyss stares back at you. She hadn't heard, then the abyss becomes your pal who thinks you have many common interests.

Minions were naturally vultures starving for power, but this seemed concerning. Still, where was Key meant to learn morals?

Blasts of heat sent Key's wild black hair winding as though they were underwater. The glow of distant blood-hued fires bathed his face in infernal light. "After my father died, I had nothing, and my story meant nothing. Now I have you and the Cobra, and Emer, who sees and hears the same way I do. People meet and create a new story between them, inventing love to believe in. Unless I have someone to care for, I'm barely a person, but you taught me to write. Now I know any tale can be rewritten. Tell me the sky is red and truth a lie. You can be the centre of the world and the meaning of the story. I will make every word you ever say true."

"Was that . . ." Rae paused. "Was that an epic speech?"

A sudden startled laugh burst from Key. "I thought you loved speeches."

"Not from you," said Rae.

When his face changed, she added hastily, "Not from you, and not for me. Epic speeches are like the cursed diamonds. They're not for villains."

Key didn't understand who the story was centred on: Octavian. She could only change the story around him and hope it might be enough. Lady Rahela had lived long enough to warn the hero about the ice raiders. In years to come, Octavian would post guards and protect the city. In the days to come, he would make sure Marius and Lia survived the Queen's Trials. In the other world, she'd been helpless. Here Rae's knowledge was power that could help them all.

Nine days, and she could escape the story. She would use the time she had to try to protect the characters in it. If she had to, she would let Octavian have his way with her. What did it matter? This whole world had to obey the hero's will.

She breathed in the smoke rising from the abyss, scorching her throat and stinging her eyes. "I have a plan. Octavian is a necessary evil."

"You're the necessary evil to me."

"So trust me. Don't take any risks unless you have an absolutely imperative reason. I promise I won't ever let you be hurt again."

She heard the smile in Key's voice as he murmured, "I believe in you."

Beneath her hand she felt the rhythmic thunder of his heart. As though he were a real living person. As though she held the drums of war in the hollow of her hand.

CHAPTER TWENTY-FOUR

The Villainess Storms the Queen's Trials

So the First Duke gave the regalia to the first king of Eyam, and bid his heir kneel to swear loyalty. The Second Duke appeared the First Duke's twin, save that he had no white in his hair or awful light in his eyes.

Masked crown, clawed gauntlets and the royal sword were given over for safekeeping. The sword to conquer the world, and the gauntlets to claw a way out of the grave.

"Guard these well," the First Duke warned as he crowned Primus. "Hide your face, for the crown is not yours to keep. One day the ducal line shall serve their true master. One day the ravine will bleed into the sky and the screams of the dead will become cries of triumph. Await your Emperor. The great goddess wanders far astray but her oracle speaks truly. He is coming for his throne."

Saying thus, the Duke descended into the abyss. Nobody, through all the centuries of waiting and forgetting that followed, ever suspected the duke who saved the realm was the great god come back again. Until the day the sky burned red.

Time of Iron, ANONYMOUS

ae didn't know why she was bothering to sneak. Few at court would be surprised to see the notorious Harlot of the Tower creeping into a man's bedchamber so early the broken moon was still in the sky, a pale ghost dyed red by sunrise.

Two different men's bedchambers within two days was scandalous, even for her.

The Cobra's maid Sinad did seem exceptionally startled as Key held the door and Rae breezed past calling out, "I'm expected!"

She didn't knock, in case the Cobra didn't wish to speak to her. She flung open the doors of the parlour, then the dressing room, through the ajar door leading to his chamber.

In a circular bed vast as a golden lake, the Cobra stirred under heaped-high sun-coloured silk. He was sleeping on his stomach, morning light tracing a bright finger over curves of muscle and shoulder blade, down the line of his spine. He cast a look over his bare shoulder, half asleep but wholly amused.

"Hey," said Rae.

"Hey," said the Cobra.

They hadn't spoken since the evening in her old room, when she'd almost told him he was dead.

She took a deep breath. "I've been thinking a lot over the last few days. Well. I've been scheming a lot."

"I'm so shocked." The Cobra didn't sound shocked.

"Given the Queen's Trials are happening today, I'm sure you've been thinking a lot too."

"Not that I've noticed," remarked a red-headed woman, untangling herself from the golden heap of sheets. "He has been drinking a lot."

"Oh okay!" Rae exclaimed.

"I'm so embarrassed." The Cobra didn't sound embarrassed.

A blond-haired man, rising from the other side of the sheets, added: "We had fun."

Rae now understood the maid's startled expression.

The Cobra gave the blond guy a rather sweet and tentative smile. "I'm glad you think so."

"I know this wasn't a job, but is it true we can just take anything that's lying around here? No matter how expensive it is?" asked the blond gentleman.

All suggestion of sweetness vanished. The Cobra shrugged. "Sure."

The redhead sighed. "Don't be crass, Leaf. And you, don't get your romantic hopes up. I shall also be taking sundry coins and perhaps a small but costly vase." She paused. "With affection."

The Cobra brightened, leaned in for a quick kiss, then glanced at Rae. "I'll be out when I'm dressed."

He emerged into the parlour doing up the last fastenings on a filmy green herigaut, figured with a flashy pattern of gold beasts. "Don't judge me, I've been incredibly stressed!"

She held up a hand. "I wildly scheme. You wildly debauch. No judgement." Rae paused. "I was hoping we could make up."

She wasn't sure what else to say. The Cobra had been even more ridiculous than usual, ranting about endangering book characters. Key being hurt had made every word sting. She'd felt as if she were in the wrong, even though she knew she was right.

A wary pause followed.

"Tell me your wild scheming," the Cobra invited.

Rae explained how she'd warned Octavian to post guards at the Trespasser river, and told him how to reforge the royal sword.

"So even though the Trials have been moved up, it doesn't matter. Lia and Marius will be protected. Octavian is prepared. When the abyss opens, when the invasion comes, he'll know what to do. I fixed everything. You will all be safer, and I—I will be gone. I don't want to hurt anybody, I never did, but I need to get home."

She stared at the floor, willing herself to come up with a clever argument to convince him.

"Hey." Strong arms interrupted Rae's thoughts, enveloping her in steady warmth. "Say less. We're getting you home safe."

She hugged him back.

Her team was whole again. They were ready to face the trials.

For the Queen's Trials, they brought out the beauties and the beasts.

In the real world, mythological beasts in medieval books came from medieval people panicking when they saw unfamiliar creatures and drawing them as monsters. Understandable: in a world before nature documentaries, the first sight of a rhino must be a lot.

In Rae's world a leucrota was someone drawing a picture of a hyena while having the vapours. In the land of Eyam, the creation of the ravine made those beasts real.

In this world Rae could wander around the enclosures by the palace walls, where the creatures from the royal menagerie were now on display, twirling her parasol and admire a leucrota in the flesh.

"My lady," warned Emer. "Experience wonder at a greater distance from the teeth."

"It is a little like a lion and a little like a hyena," Rae observed. "Except enormous."

Emer sighed. "Lions are imaginary, my lady."

The golden-brown beast did have hyena-ish and lion-esque qualities, both rendered considerably more alarming by the fact it was the size of a horse. Its head, broad and flat but ending in a pointed muzzle, swung towards Rae as she walked by.

"*Rahela.*"

"Aren't they so cute? I wish I could feed them."

"You can," said Emer, joy-killing. "They'd eat your hand."

"I like them too," contributed Key, joyful and murderous. "They can strip a body of flesh in under a minute."

The leucrota didn't have individual teeth, but a ridge of solid bone like an ivory gumshield. It snapped its block teeth together happily as Rae reached through the bars to pat its neck and Key laughed, wild and well pleased.

They strolled on in high good humour, Key walking with fluid ease as if he had never been wounded. Even Emer relented enough to let Rae buy everybody chewets – little pies containing minced pork and plums with exceptionally sturdy pastry for street eating. The chewets were extremely chewy. Food stalls and display cages were set up around the amphitheatre within the palace walls where they usually put on the summer plays, blue and silver flags flew against a blue and gold sky, and twelve ladies were battling for the king's hand. But not Rae. She had arranged Octavian would have the sword, and make the plot go smoothly. Lia would win the trials and be declared queen, a title she would choose over being called the empress. Surely Octavian would be too occupied with his betrothed to remember Rae until the night the Flower of Life and Death bloomed. All she and the vipers had to do was enjoy an evil day out.

Carefree, Rae twirled on her tiptoes to see a cage of ibexes, goatish creatures with horns like swords. The Cobra returned from enthusiastically tossing coins to minstrels and nodded towards her chewet. "Give me a bite."

Instead of breaking off a piece, he leaned down and sank his white teeth into the crust in Rahela's hand, then straightened up smirking in Key's direction. "I'm surprisingly glad you survived to devil us."

Key scowled, but after a moment grinned back. "I'll devil you in particular."

"Please, no." The Cobra winked at Rae. "I know the real reason you wanted to make up. You're just trying to score an invite to my private box."

Rahela shot him a saucy smile. "You caught me. I'm a wicked schemer."

He set off, waving them to follow.

A guardsman muttered, "*Harlot*," as Rae swept by.

She reached to stop Key's surge forward. "Sticks and stones may break my bones!"

Just Key's smile made the guard retreat. "Sledgehammers break their bones for sure."

Commoners sat in stone rows surrounding the circle of earth that formed the stage. Aristocrats had boxes set in wooden towers above the stone steps, lined with cushions. The Cobra's was second in magnificence only to the king's, gold as the inside of an expensive chocolate box.

The circle of earth below was already churned. As they watched, a weary knight in plated armour fought a griffin on a rattling chain. All morning, knights had been volunteering to serve as ladies' champions to express their admiration for a lady-in-waiting. Or because said knight happened to be in the service of a certain lady-in-waiting's father. The knight who fought the most spectacular battle would be regarded the victor.

As villains, the vipers were required to be fashionably late. Also, they knew who would win in the end.

Others had no such information. When Rae and her team followed the Cobra in, they found the box already half full. The Cobra's book club, Rae had expected. Lady Zenobia had brought a book. Lord Fabianus had brought his whole family.

It must be true the Nemeths were having money troubles, if they couldn't afford their own box. General Nemeth was obviously uncomfortable in this golden nest of debauchery and literacy. Rae studied the general with suspicion. Was he plotting her murder? She didn't know what someone plotting her murder was supposed to look like. Beside him stood a sturdy boy of about eleven who had the general's black hair untouched with grey. He must be Tycho, the brother too young to wield the gauntlets.

And there were the twins. It was usually difficult to tell the Ladies Hortensia and Horatia apart. Today the difference was stark. Since the attack on the Court of Air and Grace, Lady Hortensia's skin had yellowed and stretched taut over her bones, almost matching her lank lemon-coloured hair. The day was warm, but Lord Fabianus smoothed a woollen blanket over his sister's wasted legs.

It was entirely clear she was dying.

The Cobra dropped a word in Rae's ear as he moved past. "Don't ask how Hortensia is. Wasting has set in from the bites. Fabianus borrowed money for healers, and he always refused to take a button from me before."

Rae felt fastened on the last step into the box, as if two cruel fingers had reached from the sky to pin her in place. She remembered Key falling to his knees to fasten his mouth on her bite wound. If it wasn't for Key, Rae would be in the same position as Hortensia. She could be dying all over again.

She knew how it felt, having your flesh melt away as if you had turned into an ice sculpture under your skin. No food would help, no medicine, no love. The future was an inexorable wearing away of yourself.

General Nemeth's glare distracted her. He looked furious the Harlot dared sully where his virtuous daughters sat. Rae opened her parasol and twirled it in the confines of the box. Just to be obnoxious.

Even more surprising than General Nemeth's presence was that of Princess Vasilisa, wearing fewer jewels than usual. Rae wondered if the princess had joined the book club.

As she wasn't a lady-in-waiting, Vasilisa couldn't join the Trials. The princess seemed surprisingly cheerful watching others compete for the king's hand. "Hello, Lady Rahela."

Rae let her smile turn from taunting to genuine. "Hello, Your Highness. You look great."

"That's what I keep telling her." Lord Fabianus paused in fussing over Hortensia.

Vasilisa blushed. "Thank you."

Now a princess had acknowledged Rae, the general and his daughters allowed themselves to nod in her direction.

A serving boy arrived to present the Cobra with a folded page on a silver platter. Rae peeked and caught the words '*bad, bad golden pony*' before the Cobra demurely whisked the paper out of view.

"I've been receiving an increased number of letters from admirers since our dance. It may be a key factor in my forgiving you."

Rae offered the Cobra a fist bump. "Nice."

She had received no admiring letters, only an increased number of leers in hallways.

"Well, they're not inviting me over to meet their mothers." The Cobra lounged in his seat, surveying the milling crowd with a faint frown.

He wasn't frowning because people had dishonourable intentions towards him. His gaze fixed on a lone figure in the crowd, blue scarf fluttering like a piece of sky looped around her neck, long hair spinning sunlight into gold.

Lia.

As in the ballroom, she was alone.

Instantly, Rae proposed, "Let's invite her to your box."

The Cobra shook a reproving finger. "Getting entangled with the main characters will lead to disaster."

He glanced at Lia again, then laid a handful of gold on the boy's silver salver and asked him to convey an invitation for Lady Lia to join them.

"I knew you'd do that," Rahela told the Cobra smugly.

"Because of my beautiful nature?"

"Because you asked her to sit with you in the book," Rae said under her breath. "You're a softie."

Key asked conversationally, "Did you say he asked Lia to sit with him in a boat?"

Emer eyed Lord Popenjoy with deep suspicion. "Ladies should not go on boating expeditions unchaperoned."

Rae feared she'd been indiscreet once again.

The Cobra looked alarmed. "I have no designs on Lady Lia! All I want are front-row seats to Marius volunteering to be Lia's champion. Even though this means the woman he loves will marry another. Sacrifice of self to the beloved is one of the top ten romantic gestures."

"Is that still going to happen?" Rae whispered.

The Cobra sat bolt upright. "Why wouldn't it?"

"The tournament shouldn't happen this early! And the moonlit balcony scene didn't happen right. Does he even love her yet?"

"At first sight and for all time," snapped the Cobra. "You might recall the prophecy. *When the white knight's heart strays to forbidden queens.* Lia's about to win the Queen's Trials. They're soulmates!"

"You seem very invested in the Oracle's prophecy, Lord Popenjoy," Emer kept glaring. "I didn't know you were religious."

"I believe in Marius. The gods are less certain."

Despite his proclaimed certainty, the Cobra's face was uncharacteristically worried. He frowned at the gap in the crowd where Lord Marius stood, head and shoulders above those around him, everyone keeping a weary distance.

The representative for the great god should act as master of ceremonies. That was traditionally a Valerius, but Lord Marius had sworn himself to the goddess. The sacred stand was inlaid with orichal silver, which flashed both red and tarnished black under the noonday sun. Instead of Lord Marius, Prime Minister Pio officiated, seeming ill at ease as if imprisoned in a vast lightning-struck tree. Rae appreciated the clear view of both men she suspected of trying to murder her.

When Lia arrived, the Cobra's worried frown melted. His smile enveloped her in warmth, natural as sunrise turning the mountains gold. "Lady Lia, allow me a tiny liberty?"

He held his fingers a fraction of an inch apart, then offered his hand, palm up. When Lia gave him her hand, the Cobra dropped a kiss on the inside of her wrist.

As Lia drew back in maidenly confusion, the Cobra whispered: "Marius is coming now. Look, he's jealous!"

"You insist his face makes expressions," said Rae. "I can't see it myself."

Since Marius appeared murderous at all times, Rae couldn't tell if he was angry someone was kissing Lia, furious the Cobra was kissing someone, or outraged by public indecency.

Lia was smiling as if she liked the Cobra, or at least found him amusing. On noticing her stepsister, Lia's smile died.

"Come sit beside me," Rae invited.

Lia visibly struggled with the worry it would look ungracious to refuse. Eventually, she gritted pearly teeth and sank gently down, simple dress swaying about her like a blue-tinted cloud. The end of her scarf was deeper blue, like the graduations of sky in the evening.

Rahela tugged teasingly on Lia's scarf. "I know in the future you wear pure white to emphasize your purity. There's only one reason you're still wearing clothes trimmed with blue. So you're a contrast to the Beauty Dipped In Blood. Nice to know you're thinking about me."

"There's no need for me to think about you," Lia observed. "Not when you're always thinking about yourself."

It was almost sisterly, to define themselves by their differences from each other. Rae had imagined the fairest of them all as alone, but where there was a fairest there must be a foulest. And even the fairest might want a little fun in her life.

Rae smiled encouragement. "That's it, let loose. Must be tough, always trying to be the most well-behaved woman in the room."

She noted Lia's marble-blue eyes glide towards the princess and the general, talking among themselves.

"It must," Lia agreed sweetly. "You never seem capable of it."

"Oooh, ladylike burn. Listen, some people might think you're a manipulative liar and a total fake," Rae murmured. "But *I* think you're awesome, and a way more interesting character now!"

"I don't know what you're talking about. And I don't see why you always have to be so cruel."

Lia directed a beseeching look at the Cobra. The faintest hint of dew sparkled in her eyes.

The Cobra shook his head. "Sorry, honey. I worked you out myself a while ago. For what it's worth, I don't hold it against you."

How could anyone? Innocents got literally eaten alive in this palace. Lia had no choice but to become a snake in sheep's clothing.

"We're all awful," Rahela reassured her. "Consider this an invitation to join my nest of vipers."

When Lia's eyes burned with indignation, they went candle-flame blue. "I don't understand your wild claims!"

"Come *on*," Rahela urged. "It's obvious when you think about it. The twins didn't cut up your ball gown. You cut up your own gown, so you could skip the ball and not be neglected for the princess. You only went to the ball because you got the unexpected gift of another gown. Before that, you sobbed out your misery to a hearthstone connected via a chimney to the room where the most righteous man in the kingdom studies. Only an idiot would believe it was a coincidence."

Lia's body went stiff as a petrified reed.

"My lady!" Emer said in a warning tone.

"Kissing comfit?" The Cobra offered Lia a perfumed pink candy from a golden plate.

Sudden as a tremor shaking the earth, the golden plate wobbled in his hand.

"Oh no," he said in a distant tone. "We're screwed."

Rae's gaze followed the Cobra's to where the Last Hope stood, black-and-white hair tumbled around his shoulders, his face a carving on a glacier.

It was coldly clear he'd heard everything.

"How clever you are, Lady Lia," remarked Lord Marius. "Like your stepsister. A nest of vipers indeed."

The atmosphere in the golden box was incredibly awkward. Lord Marius sat, arms crossed across his broad chest, leaning back to observe the battles. Everyone watched in an aristocratic agony of social embarrassment as a knight fought a chained unicorn.

Any attempt to talk foundered as though they tried to paddle tiny boats of conversation on a frozen sea. Marius's cold silence and sheer physical presence dominated the space.

From the arena the announcer proclaimed, "Who will stand for Lady Horatia Nemeth?"

Rae was relieved by the diversion, but startled they had reached the Nemeths already. Of course, the Queen's Trials would be over sooner than it had in the book. Many of the queen candidates had been eaten by the undead.

The general stood at attention. "I am her family. When I claim the right, no knight may interfere."

"You don't have to, Papa," whispered Horatia.

"While I have breath, I own the privilege of defending my child." He dropped a rough kiss on the side of Horatia's head as he left the box.

What a kind father. Perhaps kind enough to send assassins after his daughter's rival.

Rae glanced at Hortensia. "I thought the Queen's Trials went by age, oldest to youngest?"

And Hortensia was the older twin. But Lady Hortensia, so thin you could almost see her gritted teeth through the nearly transparent skin of her cheek, stated, "I'm no longer a lady-in-waiting."

Of course, Octavian had dismissed her. A queen must be in good health to bear heirs. A lady who couldn't breed got thrown away like the contents of a chamber pot.

Watching the Nemeth family tense, Rae was stricken by terrible memory. In the books, General Nemeth had fought for both his daughters as they couldn't afford to keep household knights. He was grievously wounded in a battle with a monstrous snake.

Lady Hortensia's claw-thin hand closed around little Lord Tycho's shoulder. Hortensia was dying. They were poor. The Nemeths must be keenly aware the general wasn't as strong as he'd once been, but his fading glory in war was all the family possessed. Rae had believed the prime minister was the one sending killers after her, but perhaps it was the desperate who did desperate deeds.

Should she hope for the general's defeat? Was he her enemy?

As the crowd watched Nemeth stride to the centre, you could have heard a pin drop in the dust of the arena. Instead they heard the cold creak of a cage door swing open.

A dragging sound followed, like a huge rope being hauled through the dirt. Rae leaned over the side of the box to see what was coming for the general.

The amphisbaena slithered, because it had no feet. It was a snake thick-bodied as a lizard, moving on its belly in deliberate slow circular movements towards where the general stood with his battleaxe bared. Its eyes were huge and yellow, glowing with inner fire like lanterns. Where its tail should have been was another head, this one horned. The stubby horns rattled like rattlesnake tails. The slavering open mouth dripped black poison.

Rae and Key exchanged delighted glances. It was undeniably cool.

"Blood and circuses." The Cobra snapped open a pair of sunglasses and slid them on his nose.

Apparently, the Cobra had made yet another fortune inventing 'sunglasses' last summer. Each member of his salon had a pair.

Rae eyed the sunglasses wistfully. "I thought the phrase was 'bread and circuses'? In order to keep the public happy and obedient, a ruler needs to give them enough food and enough entertainment?"

The Cobra mused, "Maybe if you give people enough vicious satisfaction, they won't even care about food."

Rae noticed Key leaning against the wall, listening intently. His face had gone serious as he seldom was. Until he caught her eye on him, and smiled just for her.

Little Lord Tycho brandished a wooden sword as if longing to fight in his father's place. The court whispered the general's youngest was an ideal heir, unlike Lord Fabianus.

Tycho's toy blade almost took the princess's ear off. Ziyi's hand went automatically to the hilt of her very real sword.

Lord Fabianus hugged Tycho and confiscated his sword. "Be good, or I'll dress you in finery."

The general kicked out at the great snake with a massive, battered boot, reducing one of the eyes in the non-poisonous head to jelly. The Cobra offered the trembling Tycho a kissing comfit and ruffled his hair. Horatia's fists clenched. A faint, unguarded sound burst from Lia's lips. Horatia was the second-youngest member of the ladies-in-waiting. Lia, at nineteen, was the youngest. It was Lia's turn next.

To Rae's immense relief, Marius's icy face thawed slightly. Perhaps his heart had relented on seeing Lia afraid.

His gaze seemed to rest on little Tycho, leaning against the Cobra's shoulder. Perhaps it was only that Lord Marius had a soft spot for children.

Would Marius act as Lia's champion, or not? Would General Nemeth be wounded or not?

Stressed, Rae shoved kissing comfits into her mouth, and choked when the amphisbaena reversed direction. Its other head took the lead and lunged for General Nemeth. The general swung his battleaxe, silvered hair flying.

The Nemeth twins gave voice to their ancestral battle cry. "Blood, blood, *blood!*"

"Blood, blood, *blood!*" Tycho's childish voice chimed enthusiastically.

Fabianus Nemeth, fists clenched and ruffles flying, picked up the chant. "Blood, blood, *blood!*"

By his side, Princess Vasilisa seemed somewhat taken aback. Rae didn't blame her. Vasilisa squinted at the suddenly bloodthirsty fashion plate.

"Sun bothering you?" Fabianus whisked off his sunglasses and perched them on the princess's nose. "There you go. Where was I? Blood, *blood*, BLOOD!"

The amphisbaena's fangs struck dirt. So did the edge of the general's axe. A frustrated cry broke from the throats of every single one of his children.

Then the box went quiet as the great snake twisted into a curve. The one-eyed head went straight for the general's weapon, its fangs locking down on the axe handle. The other head went straight for the general.

This was how the general was wounded, the snake's fangs ripping his leg open down to the bone.

But in the book, General Nemeth had fought a bout for his older daughter earlier. He was tired.

This time the general was quick enough to seize the amphisbaena, thick fingers closing halfway around the magical serpent's green-and-brown body. Its scales were the colour of a rotting rope.

"If it has two heads instead of a tail," the Cobra murmured, "how does it go to the unisnake bathroom?"

Rae was happy to enlighten him. "It excretes through its pores, like sweat."

The Cobra gave her an unimpressed look. "This you remember?"

The general hefted the creature over his burly shoulders, then twisted the serpent into one knot then another. With all his great remaining strength, he wound the amphisbaena in circles upon circles until the one-eyed head snapped in wild confusion at the poisonous head. General Nemeth tossed his defeated foe down into the dust.

In the box, the Nemeth family erupted in joy.

Under cover of the cheering, Rae leaned in and whispered to the Cobra, "Some changes to the story are good."

"If the general is trying to kill you, the fact he escaped the tournament unscathed is very bad news," the Cobra reminded her.

Rae wilted. Any remnants of satisfaction dissolved into the dust of the arena when Prime Minister Pio called out, "Who will stand for Lady Lia Felice?"

After the screams of triumph, silence hit hard.

Lia's small face was a snowdrop encased in ice as she rose, smoothed her blue and white skirt, and descended slowly down the steps from the box alone. She didn't beg, but a shimmer made her blue eyes luminous. She wore tears as other women wore jewellery, her beauty only enhanced by sorrow.

Once she reached the arena, Lia would have to beg for a champion to fight the chained monsters.

The Last Hope should have volunteered.

Lord Marius Valerius sat in the golden box, cold and beautiful as a statue. With exactly as much pity, expressiveness, and willingness to move as a statue.

"*Marius.*" The Cobra nudged him. "Be her champion!"

His white wolf's gaze moved indifferently from the cages to the Cobra. "She's a liar."

The Cobra lowered his sunglasses to show narrowed eyes. "Those who enjoy brutal honesty, honestly enjoy brutality. She's a liar. I'm a liar. We're all liars here, or do you actually believe Lady Horatia enjoys flirting with the king who cast off her sister?"

Lord Marius's glance at Horatia seemed genuinely startled. Horatia hid behind her brother.

The Cobra swept on. "The difference between a villain and a hero is that a villain gets found out as a human being. Did you expect Lia to ignore she was in danger, and hope for the best? People die in the gutters of this city every day. Girls too stupid to live don't live. Someone can lie and cheat to survive, and still be loyal and kind and trying their best."

"You can't expect him to understand *nuance*," Rae hissed. This was the Last Hope!

There was a pause.

"If they're trying their best . . ." Astonishingly, a hint of relenting showed in Lord Marius's voice. "Then why do their worst?"

"Maybe that's all they can think of to do," said the Cobra. "But forgive the lady this once, for the sake of her beautiful eyes."

Within an instant an ice age descended on Lord Marius. "*You* fall all over yourself to kiss away Lady Lia's crocodile tears. *I'm* not susceptible to wiles and trickery."

The Cobra tried to pass off anger with a laugh. "All this slut-shaming. Where's the slut-praising? Quick, someone tell me I'm wicked cute and have great time management."

Lord Marius looked even more coldly furious. Rae couldn't suppress a shiver. The Nemeths were ranging their own bodies between the little lord and the potential threat. Not that it would matter. If a Valerius lost control, everyone in this box was dead.

The Golden Cobra sighed. "You think anyone can trick a trickster? I hate seeing Lia weep to manipulate people. It wouldn't matter to anyone if I cried. I might as well laugh. But . . . "

The Last Hope waited for him to speak with impatience Rae could feel rising like the icy wind before a storm. She imagined the Cobra bleeding as Key had, remembered the Cobra dying at Marius's hand.

Rae rushed in where others feared to tread. "Nobody chooses tears as a weapon if they have an alternative. Tears are terrible weapons, due to being liquid. People ignore tears. Nobody ignores a battleaxe. It's awful tears only matter when they're shed by the type of girl people see as pure. *And* it's awful some girls only have their tears, with no other way to defend themselves. Do liars deserve death?"

Rahela hurled her question against the wall of Lord Marius's cold dislike, already aware she'd made a crucial misjudgement.

No story ever convinced a hostile audience. It mattered who told the tale. Marius might hate the Cobra, but it was clear he would never let anyone else hurt him. It was equally clear Lord Marius would welcome the news Rae had been killed by a passing cart in the street.

"As Lord Popenjoy said, people die in the gutters of this city every day." The Last Hope's voice was steel under frost. Even the Cobra, who never showed fear of the Valerius, winced. "What makes Lady Lia special?"

Rae and the Cobra exchanged a guilty glance. Neither spoke.

When Lia came to court people had written poems calling her the pearl they'd waited for, the Pearl of the World. Rae couldn't say Lia was the heroine of the book. She didn't know how to persuade people to value Lia. It was a new problem. Everyone always seemed to consider the heroine precious.

"Lady Lia once told me she was always in danger," Emer whispered. "If purity is stained even once, nobody will ever believe in it again."

The Last Hope gave his judgement. "If I fight for someone, that says I think they're worth fighting for. I will not do it."

From the corner of her eye, Rae saw Emer's face pale and her hand flex as if longing to be around the shaft of an axe. Then Emer bowed her head. A servant wasn't even allowed to address Lord Marius in public.

Surely at this desperate juncture, the Cobra would say something diplomatic.

"Fine," snapped the Cobra. "I'll do it."

Chaos erupted in the box, everybody trying to dissuade the Cobra at once. The Cobra's rise was prevented by a muscled arm slamming down on the velvet-padded arms of his chair like an iron bar.

The Last Hope ordered, "You will not."

Centuries of command echoed in his voice. The Cobra responded with scathing contempt.

"Here's my kind of honour in action. You sit in judgement. *I* will save a girl from getting torn to shreds by wild beasts."

At the sneered word 'honour' Lord Marius's arm fell away. The Cobra rose with a swoop of his gold-adorned sleeves.

"Stop." Marius's voice grated, an iceberg against a ship that would not turn course. "I'll stand as her champion."

The Cobra threw himself into his chair and threw Marius a wink. "Thanks, I obviously wasn't going to do it."

He slid his sunglasses back up his nose. Rae's nerves twanged taut, but Lord Marius stood regardless.

Once given, the Last Hope would not retract his word. Rae breathed a little easier.

Lonely as a cloud, Lady Lia walked with purpose to the centre of the ring. Sunlight ladled light upon her hair, the favourite's bracelet on her right arm and the enchanted gauntlet on her left. Her musical voice rang out to the audience.

"I enter the tournament under my own name. I will be my own champion!"

Nobody could help her now.

Emer made a sound as though Lia's words were a blow. Rae's shoulders hunched under a new burden. *What if when we change the story, we only make things worse?*

Lia was only nineteen. Rae remembered turning twenty, spending the day in the grip of furious, uncontrollable tears. She'd raged because so many heroes were teenagers, even in books meant for adults. It felt like the age of magic was over for her, and all there was left to do was die.

Nineteen-year-olds could die, too.

She watched the lone small figure in the dusty arena. Lia didn't want to be helpless. Once given a weapon, given a chance, she would fight.

Rae sympathised. Being helpless made her feel strapped to a chair, with poison poured into her veins. She used to imagine having a grand adventure, a cause worth the pain. Saving someone's life. Making a big sacrifice.

Instead, she was the one who had given Lia the gauntlet. If Lia was killed before their eyes, it was Rae's fault.

CHAPTER TWENTY-FIVE

The Lady That Shall
Be Queen Hereafter

Seeing his beloved in danger, the Emperor tore the world
with a thought. Longing for Revenge flashed in his hand
like lightning, and the ravine spilled red as blood into the
sky. Silver scars slashed into the crimson sky as the beast
died screaming. As Lia sheltered beneath his dark cloak,
the Emperor wheeled on the crowd. The wild creature's
blood splashed across his face in a vivid warning. His
subjects cowered in terror of the divine.

If his sword was lightning, his voice was thunder. "On
your knees for your queen!"

Time of Iron, ANONYMOUS

he manticore was bigger than the leucrota or the unicorn,
big as a bear. Its fur was a deep dark red. The colour that
burned in the heart of the ravine. The colour of blood.

The manticore didn't lumber like a bear. The beast moved with
soft scratching noises in the dust, on huge catlike paws with claws
protruding like a birds' talons. Heavy chains as large as the manticore's forelegs were attached to its hindlegs.

"Those chains will break." Rahela's voice was heavy with prophecy, then lightened into airy falseness. "But not to worry! The Emperor is coming to save her. He has the sword. I made sure."

Emer suspected her lady's lies were beginning to wear thin even to herself.

Lia was a blue dot next to the massive crimson creature. A flower that could be crushed under a claw. It was Emer's duty to stay by her mistress, hands folded, and watch Lia die.

The Cobra's hands tightened on the balcony rail. "Nothing is sure."

The Last Hope pulled him back into his chair. The Cobra was a tall man, but against berserker strength men were toys. He said something in the Cobra's ear.

Emer's ears were keen from years of eavesdropping. It sounded like a name.

If 'Eric' was a name.

In the servants' hall they said when Lord Marius gave evidence against Emer's lady his voice was merciless. All who heard knew Rahela was doomed. Now Emer heard the voice of judgement for herself.

"The champion is declared. Lady Lia has no family to intervene. There's nothing you can do."

The Cobra's lip curled. "Who died and made you the boss of me?"

Lord Marius seemed intrigued. "I wasn't aware that was an option. How many people have to die?"

Everybody in the box looked horror-struck.

The Cobra punched the most deadly warrior of his generation hard in the shoulder. "Don't say serial killer things! We already have one of those."

He gestured at Key, who grinned.

The Last Hope gave Key a chilling glare. It was possible he couldn't give any other kind of glare. "This is the servant you think can beat me? What's your name again?"

Key's gaze, glinting oddly, met Lord Marius's. The possibility of violence twisted in the air between them, a reflection of dancing scarlet flame in ice. Emer hadn't thought there was room in her heart for more fear. *Surely* Key was not deranged enough to fight the heir of the manor and the mountains.

"My name is Key."

General Nemeth snapped, "Say 'at your service, my lord'."

Key's lip curled. "I'm at nobody's service but hers."

He nodded towards Rahela. Emer's lady was still watching the arena.

Someone had given Lia a sword. The sword was a needle under the manticore's nose, hardly bigger than one of the monster's teeth. Lia wielded her blade with the magic of the gauntlet and desperate courage, and scored a hit across its flank. Black blood welled against the manticore's bright red fur. The manticore's scream, half trumpet and half shriek, filled the amphitheatre. Terrified hope made it difficult for Emer to breathe. Placed right, a thorn could defeat even the greatest beast.

The manticore wheeled. Its tail arced, a scorpion's tail but a hundred times bigger, half the size of the animal and three times Lia's size. The tail had five segments resembling five black shells linked by tenuous muscle. At the tip was the stinger, curved like a massive thorn dipped in ink. The monster's tail swept directly for Lia, stinger aimed with deadly precision. She had to pull away fast. Her blade dropped in the dust. The manticore stepped on the sword so Lia couldn't pick it up, almost tauntingly, as if the animal could think. When it reared and roared, the massive chains snapped in half.

"Lost gods," murmured General Nemeth. "They made those chains in haste. The steel wasn't properly tempered."

Or the chains were sabotaged on purpose. Either way, the result was the same.

The manticore was loose, restraints turned to steel bracelets, bearing down on the girl who'd wounded it. Dust rose around Lia's gleaming fair head in a hazy halo. She clenched both hands, one silver and one flesh.

Rahela lifted her eyes to the royal box, draped in shimmering flags. Emer followed Rahela's gaze desperately. If Rahela was right about the chains breaking, she should be right about the king coming. He should be the hero of the story sweeping in to save the damsel.

The box was empty. The hero was nowhere to be found.

The manticore swiped at Lia, claws so sharp they made a soft singing noise as his paw swung through the air. Lia escaped the blow by throwing herself on the ground, rolling until the white of her skirt was lost under a layer of filth. The pearl of the world, hurled down in the dust.

In a strangely calm voice, Rahela addressed Lord Marius. "You said Lia has no family to intervene. But she does."

Wearing her disaster-defying expression, she turned to Key and placed her hands on his belt. Efficiently, she removed the regulation guard's sword from its scabbard. He watched her, eyes hooded.

"Don't," Key breathed.

She stepped back. "Trust me. I can fix this."

Key moved fast as a monster in a firelit tale of terror, but the movement ended not in violence but gentleness. His fingertips grasped the edge of her sleeve. "Boss. Let me."

Rahela's eyes travelled over his face. "I know how you feel, but you're still hurt."

"I swear I'm not!"

Her voice echoed as though she were a ghoul calling from the ravine. "You took the oath. I command you to stay."

Clutching Key's sword, Emer's lady vaulted over the side of the golden box. Key clenched his fist, a trick of light making a line of crimson flare along his arm to disappear into his glove. He stood straining as if held by ropes.

Rahela's fall to the seats below was broken by several confused members of the audience. They stayed bewildered long enough to obey her shouted orders, new hands reaching up as she went forward. The Beauty Dipped In Blood floated her way to the arena as though the crowd was a sea.

At the edge of the arena, Rahela scrambled over the wall, hit the earth rolling, and raced between the heroine and the monster. Lia went still as stone. When Rahela charged at the manticore, sword held in both hands, Emer saw her bare fingers slip on the hilt. The enchanted gauntlet held steady and turned her aim true.

At the last moment the manticore swerved. Rahela's blade left a glancing blow against its breast.

Emer knew her place. A maid must stay by her mistress's side, ready to assist at all times.

Emer lunged and seized the general's battleaxe.

General Nemeth's roar followed as she escaped the box and hurtled down the steps. "Catch that maid! My axe is an heirloom."

Guards ran to intercept Emer at the foot of the steps.

A voice rang at her back. "I'll give you all the gold I have on me if you let her keep that axe for a day."

The guards' rush halted. Emer glanced over her shoulder, surprised to see the Cobra directly behind her.

"The general had an abrupt change of heart. Let her through."

It was strange. Palace gossip about Lia and the Cobra couldn't be more different, their appearances could not be more different, but their eyes sometimes held a similar soft look. As if wishing to be gentle with something badly wounded.

Emer had never known what to do with gentleness.

The Golden Cobra might be careless, rakish and overdressed, but she'd seen him try his best for Lia all day.

It was difficult to imagine trusting an aristocrat, but perhaps she should tell him of Lord Marius's mission to discover his secrets.

Emer hesitated. "Who's Eric?"

The Cobra's face shut firmly as the lid on a treasure chest, not meant for servants' eyes. "Someone I killed."

The manticore trumpeted a scream. Emer turned away from the Cobra and fought her way through the crowd. In the arena, the monster lunged past Rahela's defences, triple rows of needle teeth bared to bite.

Silk got in the manticore's eyes. Lia lashed out with her scarf as if it were a whip.

As the manticore's wickedly curved tail came towards them in an inexorable sweep, Rahela darted Lia's way and seized her stepsister's hand. "Follow my lead!"

Rahela jumped. Lia jumped with her. The manticore's tail swept and they jumped again, sisters skipping rope in a nightmare. The monster gave a frustrated cry and retreated only to charge at them head on, gnashing its rows of teeth.

Rahela caught Lia's eye and the other end of Lia's scarf, knotting the material around her fist. Lia gulped and nodded. They let the manticore come, reeking breath blasting their hair back in a mingled black and gold flag, and raised the scarf. Held taut between their hands, the monster was temporarily blindfolded.

The stepsisters' descending swords glanced uselessly off scale-tough skin. The manticore snapped its teeth. Seeing white and blue silk in shreds between its needle-sharp teeth, fear went through Emer clean and cold as a blade. She fought through a throng that was thickest near the rails.

When Emer waved her axe, the crowd cleared quickly. She opened the gates with shaking hands and saw her two ladies, hand in hand in the swirling bloodied dust. Rahela had pulled Lia back, and the manticore had only bit the scarf.

"Manticores have a weak spot," she heard Rahela bellow. "Strike through the neck or the stomach!"

"If you remembered which," Lia observed primly, "that would be helpful."

Emer charged past the ladies to bring her axe furiously down on the manticore's neck. The manticore screamed, almost unharmed, teeth snapping closed on Emer's apron. She tore herself free and staggered back with the apron in rags, clutching her axe.

"Not the neck," she reported.

"Emer," Lia breathed.

Rahela sounded impressed. "Did you steal the general's axe?"

Emer shrugged, keeping her eye on the monster. The axe felt as though it belonged in her hand, the weight reassuring, promising the clean end to a fight. As if this was the weapon she was meant to have. She stood braced to meet the manticore's next charge.

Except the manticore didn't charge. It shrieked as three knives flew through the air like bright steel birds, embedding themselves in its blazing red hide. Key was leaning over the rails.

"He didn't actually go down into the arena, my lady," Emer pointed out.

Rahela sighed. "There's always a loophole."

They used the creature's distraction to close in, stabbing anywhere they could reach. Emer circled the beast, hacking at its limbs and jumping when the tail swept her way. The manticore swerved and thrashed, biting on air as if it couldn't decide which foe to slay. The knives landed like stinging flies, but the monster's hide was too tough to pierce and even Key's knives weren't limitless. He was running out. The manticore hadn't even slowed down.

The beast lunged for Rahela, leaving its side exposed.

Lia struck, her blade barely scoring against the scales, then stumbled. The manticore's paw came down hard.

Rahela flung herself bodily at Lia, so they rolled away, curled around each other, across the ground. "Now isn't the time for adorable clumsiness!"

Lia gasped, "Stop making jokes. I never know where things actually are. I'm always falling. I can't fight, I can't dance. I can't *see!*"

Rahela sounded astonished as though it had never occurred to her Lia might have a simple, human reason to fall. "*That's* why you're always tripping into manly arms? Would wearing spectacles interfere with you being the fairest of them all?"

They were filthy and clinging to each other, like children whose game in the dirt had got out of hand, like the sisters they had never been. Rahela and Lia sat up, casting about for their weapons, as the monster bore down upon them.

The noise that rattled from Emer's chest sounded not like a human cry but a beast issuing a challenge. It turned the manticore's head. Emer planted her feet, and swung her axe in readiness.

"Emer," Rahela called. "Stop. I command—"

"My lady." Emer shouted her down. "I never took your oath. And I *don't* have to obey you!"

When Emer dodged the manticore's tail, its claws swiped, raked her open, and brought her down. She rolled, feeling dust gather in the stinging shallow slices in her stomach and the blast of hot breath on her neck. The monster was about to tear her throat out.

Then the world changed.

A woman screamed, and the sun was blotted out as a sudden storm rolled in. The sky filled with crimson. Clouds curled and rose like angry smoke. Silver lightning flashed through the churning cloud like knives. Somehow the ravine was spilling into the sky, changing colour as if the heavens were a pool beneath a waterfall of blood.

The whole kingdom seemed flipped upside down, become a mirror to the abyss.

Gasps tore from a thousand throats. Even the great monster flattened itself upon the ground, whining like a kicked stray. From above, thunder rolled like the hollow laughter of lost gods. From below, echoing in the dread ravine, came the loudest sound of all.

In a dull susurrating chorus, the dead called: "Master. Master. MASTER!"

"'*The ravine calls its master up above …*'" Emer quoted the Oracle's prophecy in a whisper.

Every soul under the red sky cowered, save the most cunning of them all, ready to take advantage of every situation. Only Emer, who had once been set to spy on her and now could not shake the habit of watching, saw her pale skirt moving in the red-tinged dark. Lia seized the distraction and retrieved her weapon. She drove her sword deep into the monster's stomach, gutting the manticore with one stroke. As silver scars slashed the crimson sky, the beast died screaming.

Its trumpeting death cry chased away the clouds. The monster's tail stung the earth, and the sinewy neck strained. The beast fell heavily to one side, revealing to the crowd the bloodstained face of the fairest of them all.

Into the arena strode King Octavian in the crowned mask, and the crowd hushed with new awe. He looked every inch the young hero, scarlet lights limning his head to form a second crown. He looked the part of the foretold Emperor, who would command sky and abyss. In the stories, the First Duke said they only had to wait. *He is coming.*

No matter how long you waited for a god, perhaps you were never prepared for their arrival.

The royal sword was bare in Octavian's hand, blade sheened with the red reflection of magic, as he walked eagerly towards Rahela and Lia. Emer couldn't stand in his way.

"As you desired, my lady, Longing for Revenge was broken and reforged."

His gaze went to Rahela like a child searching for a familiar hand to hold. After a startled instant Emer realized he was scared. It must be terrifying to find yourself in the centre of a legend.

Rahela answered his silent plea. She intoned, *"His sword is ruin. His eyes are fire.* The future Emperor called a storm to protect his true love!"

The whole crowd hushed below the strange sky, mice under the owl's wing, terrified beneath the shadow of prophecy coming true. Before them stood she of snow and flame. The harbinger of the future.

In that moment her lady's word was holy, higher than law. The king and the kingdom were in her palm. Lia and Emer exchanged a single look.

Then Rahela grasped Lia's hand. She raised it high, as though Lia held an invisible trophy.

"People of Eyam!" called out the true prophet. "May I present the winner of the tournament, the Pearl of the World, your Queen! As I foretold. Not to brag."

A roar of applause followed and climbed, louder in Emer's ears than her hammering heart. *Blood and circuses*, the Cobra had said. They'd given the people a good show.

The wild clapping quieted only when the woman of snow and flame took the last steps towards Octavian, and pressed the future queen's hand into the future Emperor's. As Octavian hesitated, clearly stunned, Rahela reached out and closed his fingers over Lia's.

"My Emperor-to-be," declared Lady Rahela. "Your beautiful bride."

The applause surged back, stronger than before. Lia's gaze fastened on the ground, playing the demure lady rather than a victorious warrior. She would marry and ascend to the highest place in the land. Far away from Emer, where she was always meant to be.

The king's sword shone, the lady blushed, and the crowd applauded. This scene looked like the last illustration of a book, the page showing the happy ending.

Emer had known her lady since childhood, knew every strand of midnight hair and every dark thought. Rahela might hatch plots and fight battles. Emer could even believe Rahela might see the future. She couldn't believe this. She might be deceived in her lady's heart, but not her lady's hate. Every day of their lives people had compared Rahela and Lia, measuring their characters by their faces. Truth was beauty, and beauty truth, and Lia's virtue would be rewarded. Which left Rahela with the wages of sin, and growing resentment that proved all judgements against her correct. The end was predetermined from the beginning. The world had taught Rahela to fight Lia, to never give an inch of ground. But Rahela had just handed Lia a crown.

Emer stared at Rahela's face, more familiar than her own, and thought: *Who are you?*

CHAPTER TWENTY-SIX

The Villainess Foiled
by the Ice Princess

The Ice Queen had never been beautiful, but hope and
youth once animated her face. Hope and youth were dead.
All those she loved were dead. The gleam of her eyes was
no more alive than the shine of her crown, a tower of milky
opals and icy diamonds upon her stone-pale brow.

"I will have the Emperor's head if I must cross a sea of
blood to get it."

Time of Iron, ANONYMOUS

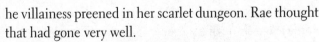he villainess preened in her scarlet dungeon. Rae thought
that had gone very well.

Octavian was meant to forge the sword in the dawn,
not sleep late and hastily forge the sword during the Queen's Trials,
but it had all worked out. The Emperor never did care for cere-
mony. He thought the tournament was a joke and he'd choose his
own bride.

A hero always arrived in the nick of time, but by its very nature 'the
nick of time' was almost too late. Octavian had arrived to behold his
beloved in peril, and the ravine reflected his heart. Now everybody
knew he was the Once and Forever Emperor.

More importantly for her wicked purposes, Rae suddenly had a lot more credibility as a prophet. She planned to use that.

For now, she was taking a scented bath. Rahela leaned back as she drizzled first the vase of lemon water, then the vase of jasmine water over her head and down her aching back. Fighting a manticore was a workout. She was thankful her water had arrived as hot as the king's today.

Rae emerged to sit on the velvet stool before the bronze mirror and complain to Victoria Broccoli. "The evil twins cause wicked back pain. Nobody thinks of this when they write about the villainess's luxuriant curves!"

She didn't really mind. It was almost thrilling to feel the normal pain of a healthy body, strained muscles, heavy breaths. Pain that glanced the surface and departed rather than settling into her bones. For so long, running was as impossible as flying. It was a miracle to be able to put in effort and accomplish what she wanted, at a cost to her body she could bear. It was a miracle she needed to bring to the real world: strength enough to protect her and her sister from ever being hurt again.

Rae wriggled her shoulders under her scarlet dressing robe and sighed. Hands settled on her shoulders, leather and strong fingers felt through silk.

"Let me," said Key.

He exerted sudden intense pressure on the muscles of her shoulders, death-dealing hands extremely capable. She sneaked a look in the mirror and saw, reflected in bronze, the clean line of his throat and wicked shine of his eyes.

Rae let herself sigh in a different way. "What did you think you were doing, throwing knives when you're still recuperating? You're in big trouble."

Key shrugged. She was glad to see the movement was so easy. "So punish me."

"You're playing with fire," Rae threatened. "I'm a heartless villainess. You don't know what I might do to you."

Key seemed undaunted. "I know my mistress is cruel and without mercy. I will accept whatever hideous fate she has in store for me."

Rae slid a smile up at him.

"I have to go fetch something from the kitchens," said Emer in a loud voice.

Before Emer could go, a tap came at the dungeon door. The king might be sending for her. Against her will, Rae felt her whole body lock up. Key must have felt the new tension. His hands closed on her shoulders, as if he wouldn't let her go.

Except he had to let her go. Everyone must bow down before the Emperor.

The door swung to reveal the Cobra's face, bright with joy and liquid gold eyeliner. Rae could have cried with relief, if that was a thing villainesses did.

"Shall I compare thee to a summer's murder?" the Cobra asked. "Don't mind me, just pretending I'm Key writing poetry. Everybody did great saving Lia today."

He came bearing gifts: sunglasses with snake-shaped rims for everyone. Rae immediately tried on her shades despite the darkness of the room.

The Cobra made a face. "Don't wear sunglasses indoors, it makes you look like a poseur."

"It makes me look awesome," Rae argued. "Who wears sunglasses indoors? Rock stars and evildoers. Sunglasses make no difference to them, because they're always doing dark deeds."

A delicate cough interrupted their argument.

Rae slid the sunglasses down her nose and stared in disbelief over the snake rims. The Cobra hadn't shut the door after him. On the threshold stood the last person Rae expected.

"What's a girl like you doing in a narrative dead end like this?" she asked Lia.

The girl wavered in the dungeon doorway, a shape that seemed formed from light and air rather than flesh.

Then: "I believe you, Rahela," said the heroine of the story. "You risked your life for me."

"No I didn't," Rae squawked. "I was confident we could handle it together, with the power of both gauntlets. And I was right!"

She had been almost entirely confident.

Lia continued earnestly, "Why would you do that, unless you truly can tell the future, and want to be allies? Let's be on the same side."

There was a stunned silence.

Until the Cobra smiled his particularly inviting smile. "Lucky I brought a spare pair of sunglasses."

He bowed with a golden flourish and offered the sunglasses to Lia, who accepted them with a curtsy and a shy beam. Rae started clapping. Key joined her. Lia glanced Emer's way, but Emer was busy arranging Rae's brushes and perfumes.

"Congratulations on your betrothal," Rae told Lia encouragingly.

"Is it the Emperor, then?" The Cobra's voice was wistful. "You don't return Marius's love even a little?"

Rae raised a clenched fist in victory like a football fan. She wasn't as fond of the Emperor as she used to be, but there was a thrill in seeing her preferred team win.

"Is Lord Marius in love with me?" Lia seemed surprised. "Surely not any more, though?"

"Today was a huge setback," the Cobra admitted. "He doesn't really get why people lie. But if you sweet-talk him, I'm sure he'll come around."

"You wish me to seduce Lord Marius but marry the king, so we can use him as a tool?" Lia looked impressed. "Lost gods, you *are* wicked."

The Cobra's mouth fell open. "That is not what I meant! I want somebody to take care of him."

"I could do that," Key volunteered with a wink.

The Cobra took off his sunglasses and started to beat Key with them as Key laughed. "I wasn't talking about murder! I'm never talking about murder and you're always talking about murder!"

"Your poor little meow-meow is built like a brick murder house, he'll be fine," Rae muttered.

Lia frowned. "Are you certain he's in love with me? I didn't get the creeping crawling feeling when men look at you and it feels like a thousand insects on your body, and the insects all want to undress you."

Emer knocked over a bottle.

"Because Marius is a *gentleman*," the Cobra protested.

Lia sighed as though accepting another burden. "I thought he might be a friend."

Rae couldn't help remembering how Lia died: trusting courtiers who betrayed her, choosing faith though she'd been betrayed a hundred times. She'd wanted to love her stepmother and stepsister and Emer. In the other story, Lia had thrown herself between Lord Marius and a monster. She'd come to the lowest chamber in the tower of her own volition, though she'd won the hand of the king and was in no need of allies. Lia, who every man desired, wanted a friend.

Even the fairest of them all could be lonely.

The Cobra studied Lia with concern. "You don't have to marry anybody if you don't want to."

Hello, who was messing up the plot now?

"Considering Rahela's visions, I think I *should* marry Octavian," Lia said calmly. "If he becomes Emperor, I'll rule at his side. I can bear him touching me for that."

The Cobra appeared too stunned to speak.

Rae flopped down on the bed and began to laugh. The angelic heroine, whose virtue couldn't be stained, whose mind was above such things.

This was the great love story.

Everybody wanted Lia because she didn't want them. They thought it meant she was better than other women, purer and more worthy of having. Except all it meant was she didn't want them.

"Why do you want to rule?"

"To change the world," Lia answered readily. "I've always thought the citizens should be better fed."

That was like Lia, the ministering angel who brought baskets of medicines and liniments to the sick. The Cobra nodded along.

"Well-fed people work better, and well-fed troops will make our armed forces stronger if we must march to war," Lia continued in her placid voice.

The Cobra, truly the unexpected sweetheart of their group, dropped his sunglasses. Rae kicked up her feet and laughed in glee. Lia seemed gratified by the positive feedback.

Key considered Lia, head tilted. His grin, his hair, every inch of him was wild.

"Welcome to the pit of vipers." Key offered Lia his hand.

Lia laid her lily pale fingers briefly against the black leather covering Key's palm in an uncertain high five. Key might be villainously and generally flirtatious, but he'd been ready to fight a manticore to protect Lia. Now it turned out Lia didn't like Octavian or Marius, maybe Key thought he had a chance.

Maybe he did. Maybe there were evil sparks flying.

A pang of unease shot through Rae. "Sure you want to be a viper? You are ... basically good ... "

Lia's expression turned piteous and abandoned, crystal tears welling in her eyes and sliding down her cheeks. Rae threw up her hands in surrender.

"Don't make the damsel face! You can be a viper."

Lia smiled beatifically with tears still drying on her baby-soft cheeks. She'd been her parents' spoiled darling once, Rae recalled.

"Can you really cry on command?"

Lia nodded. "It's a gift."

Her pretty tearstained face made an empty, sister-shaped place in Rae's heart ache. Rae patted the bed and Lia skipped over to lean, tiny and bird-boned, against her.

She'd lost so much weight before she was diagnosed. "You look great," her best friend told her. "Now you're as thin as I am." Rae hadn't ever considered which of them was thinner before. Apparently her friend had. She'd forced a smile at the time, though she felt so tired.

Now Rae smiled for real.

"Can't wait to be executed for our many conspiracies," murmured the Cobra. "Do we want a secret handshake?"

Rae hissed and mimed a serpent undulation with her hand, which was a joke until Lia giggled and did it too. Key performed it experimentally, knife in hand. The Cobra rolled his eyes and executed the viper gesture with flair.

"With respect," Emer said in her flattest voice, "m'lord, m'ladies, you look unbearably stupid."

Everybody laughed. Rae threw an arm around her stepsister's slim shoulders, and considered the next stage of her scheme.

In a few months Princess Vasilisa would get word that her brother the king had died young. She would be distraught, and go to Octavian's chambers for comfort only to find him carousing. The combination of drunk king and grieving princess led to the spectacularly bad decision of sleeping together. Vasilisa expected they would marry, but Octavian told her he loved another. A small force of raiders sacked the capital to avenge Vasilisa's dishonour, leading to the Emperor going down into the abyss to claim his full power. Chased by the Emperor's undead army, Vasilisa and her warriors fled. Years later, the merciless Ice Queen rallied her raider army and sailed across the sea to crush the Emperor. In the long night of battle that followed, Lia and Marius were killed.

Rae would be gone before any of that happened. The woman who'd opened Rae's path to Eyam said Rahela had no further use for her body, so when Rae plucked the Flower of Life and Death Rae suspected Rahela's body would die. Perhaps her friends here might miss her. She would miss them. They weren't real, but she no longer blamed the Cobra for getting attached while living in the book. Before she left the story, she wanted to make sure these characters were safe.

Someone needed to let Vasilisa know the Octavian thing would never happen. Vasilisa should go home and spend time with her brother before it was too late.

The celebration for the future queen was a perfect opportunity. This was the holy prophet's time to shine.

Rae entered the celebration looking good, feeling fine, and determined to avoid the main characters. Her dress was a column of pure white, the rubies stitched onto her train sweeping the malachite floor. She walked holding the Cobra's arm, Key and Emer behind her, and imagined she could hear jaunty background music.

Then she realized that was the Cobra's private band of minstrels.

The hero and heroine passed by. The king, and the fairest of them all. His face was hidden by the royal mask, and her beauty was a mask too. The setting sun glowed behind their heads, lending lustre to Octavian's crowned mask. It didn't matter what the main characters had actually done. It mattered who they were.

Lia made the viper gesture, hand winding secretively behind the king's cape. Rae flashed Lia a grin behind her ruby-encrusted fan before turning away.

Princess Vasilisa stood in a cluster with the Cobra's book club. Rae almost didn't recognize her. Vasilisa wore a yellow silk blouse and a striped wool skirt with a tassel belt. The lapels of her blouse were wide and the sleeves stopped at her elbows, so Rae could see the princess's tattoos. Starting at Vasilisa's collarbone and spreading to her left shoulder was an intricate design of a deer with a griffon's beak and goatish horns in place of antlers. Vasilisa had the same animal tattooed in thick black ink on both wrists, horns curling around like bracelets.

Vasilisa's people didn't wear the same clothes as the people of Eyam. Vasilisa had been uncomfortable in an unfamiliar costume. She seemed relaxed now, brown hair tumbling, face pink with laughter. She didn't appear cast into hell by jealousy.

Maybe Vasilisa wouldn't sleep with Octavian this time around, but grief inspired wild behaviour. Rae had heard the saying that wars could be lost for the want of a nail. She must warn Vasilisa about His Majesty nailing and bailing.

"Hi, everybody! Especially hi, Your Highness!" Rae tried to think of a smooth method of getting the princess alone.

"Lady Rahela," said Princess Vasilisa. "Would you step aside with me for a moment? I wish to consult with you on a private matter."

Plotting was only getting easier.

The small room they slipped into was lined with books and brass ornaments. The floor was a warm-hued mosaic of the godchild in his cradle. The goddess rocked her child to sleep, before any of the pain and horror happened.

Rae sank down on a velvet pouffe. Her skirts with their ruby hearts floated and settled around her. She grasped Vasilisa's hands and gazed ingratiatingly into her eyes.

"Talk to me, girl."

Vasilisa avoided her soulful gaze. "I hear you can tell the future."

"Don't doubt it. Seriously . . . don't." Rae took a risk. "So – the gods tell me there's a man you admire?"

Even though Octavian was the hero, Rae almost believed Vasilisa would say that wasn't true.

Instead the princess tried to wring her hands while Rae was still holding them. "Yes! I greatly admire him. I believe tenderness is growing between us."

Octavian's medieval boy-band looks had hypnotized this woman.

"Very into pretty boys, are we?"

Vasilisa's lashes cast fluttering shadows on the burning red of her cheeks. "He has an allure so different from other men, such as that brute Lord Marius."

Rae nodded. "Buff with resting bitch face, a terrifying combination."

She gave everybody who wanted to climb that icy mountain props for courage.

Vasilisa bit her lip. "I hear rumours my beloved's interests lie – elsewhere. Can your gift tell me if it's true?"

Rumours such as everybody knowing Octavian was crazy about Lia, and them being engaged? Did Vasilisa think Lia and Octavian were only betrothed because of the Queen's Trials? Did she not know true love when she saw it?

Women weren't encouraged to have experience with men here, Rae reminded herself. They were expected to be innocent. In practise that meant being ignorant and easily hurt.

Villainesses were always cruel. Right now, Rae was cruel to be kind. "I don't need my gift to tell you. His interests do lie elsewhere. The whole court knows."

Vasilisa took a quick, hurt breath. "Everybody must think me a fool."

"No," Rae lied. "I'm sorry I had to be the one to tell you. And I'm sorry again, because I must hurt you twice. I've seen a vision of the future. The gods showed me you on the throne of your country. You were very unhappy, and very alone."

And very inclined to send armies to ravage your ex's shores.

Vasilisa's fingers transformed from soft, wrung flesh to stone. Rae's hand went numb in her grasp.

"I was on the throne?" Vasilisa demanded. "What happens to my brother?"

"I'm sorry. He dies young."

"Of what?" Vasilisa pursued.

How would Rae know? The guy never appeared in the book except as a corpse in a laboratory. He was only a name: Ivor the Heartless, who created the metal soldiers the Ice Queen used to fight the Emperor's dead army. He was a plot device to give Vasilisa the power to wreak havoc on Eyam. He wasn't even a character to Rae.

To Vasilisa, he was a person she loved.

"The gods weren't clear. All I saw was his doom."

Vasilisa reared like a steed caparisoned in yellow silk. The stripes of her skirt blurred. "Where's King Octavianus?"

"We're doing this now? You might want to sleep on it—"

Vasilisa flung open the door. Her guard Ziyi stood outside.

"Escort me to Octavianus of Eyam, then send a message home. Your king's life depends on our speed."

"Or now," Rae murmured to herself. "Now is good."

Ten minutes later, they assembled in the throne room to hear the proclamation of departure by the royal princess of Tagar.

Delicate ladies were provided with chairs. Rae snagged a seat beside the Cobra, who'd had a low gilded sofa brought in. His book club were behind him, Lady Zenobia covertly reading a novel. The twins sat beside Lord Fabianus, Hortensia's face pale and strained. Oddly Lord Marius was nowhere to be found, but apart from him the entire court was present and agog.

"O holy prophet, please ask the gods *why are you like this,*" hissed the Cobra.

"This time, I was trying to do what you wanted," Rae whispered back. "I was trying to help people!"

Perhaps her villainous nature meant she could never do good.

Octavian's masked crown was lifted, his expression startled. Prime Minister Pio stood beside the throne, seeming stressed. "The Queen's

Trials is a palace game," Pio said. "Let me assure you, Princess Vasilisa, our countries are still seriously engaged in marriage negotiations."

A titter echoed around the court at the mere suggestion Vasilisa might still have a chance. The court didn't take the ice raiders seriously. Rae knew better, and winced. The princess fleeing the same day the beauty won the king's hand was not a great look.

Princess Vasilisa addressed the king directly. "Your Majesty, it's clear you have no interest in marrying me. And I have less than no interest in marrying you."

Wow, she was addressing the king *very* directly.

The optics of this situation underwent an abrupt reversal. The entire court had front seats to witness their gloriously handsome king being rejected by a plain woman.

Rae cheered internally. *That's it. Keep your dignity. Don't send texts after midnight or troops to invade the capital!*

"As a gentleman I respect your wishes, and as a king I hope for amity between our nations," the king declared. That would have been an excellent way to end the audience, but from the corner of his mouth Octavian muttered: "Personally, I'm relieved."

In the story, Vasilisa's infatuation must have made her interpret the king's jabs as jokes.

In this version, Vasilisa's eyes narrowed. "Personally, I'd have my heart cut out and thrown into your ravine before I wed the man who let my friend's body be desecrated, and who lacks the basic courtesy necessary to refrain from insulting a lady."

The heated whispers around the throne room turned to thin screams, like a pot on the boil. Humiliation fought discretion on Octavian's face.

Vasilisa the Wise bowed her brown head. "Apologies. I'm distracted by concern for my brother. Permit me to withdraw."

Octavian's mouth jerked like the reins on a horse, stopping it from running wild. "Please leave as soon as possible. For your brother's sake."

For one glorious moment, it seemed everything had gone as Rae planned.

Until a man's voice exclaimed, "Vasilisa! You can't go."

Astonishingly, it came from behind them. Rae turned slowly in her seat. Lady Zenobia dropped her novel. The twins clutched hands.

Lord Fabianus, resplendent in a violet silk waistcoat embroidered with peonies, went to stand before the princess. He seemed oblivious to his enthroned king.

"I mean to say. I mean, *I* say! Vasilisa. Must you go?"

Vasilisa took a deep breath. "I must. My brother is in danger."

"But I mean!" exclaimed Lord Fabianus. "That is to say."

Why was he making a scene when he couldn't make a speech?

Graciously, Princess Vasilisa declared, "I will always remember your friendship."

Her example of calm seemed to inspire Lord Fabianus. "If you must go . . . won't you take me with you?"

Faintly, Vasilisa replied, "I would welcome a visit from you, if that's what you mean."

"That's not what I mean at all!" Fabianus cried.

There was a note of genuine pain in his voice. Once again Rae felt an uncomfortable twinge in her chest. She'd never meant to hurt anybody.

"Vasilisa," Fabianus continued. "I mean, Your Highness. Damn it, I mean Vasilisa! Don't we have an understanding?"

Vasilisa's blush rose and her gaze fell. "I believed I misunderstood . . ."

Rae was starting to think she'd made a prophecy based on very outdated information.

Lord Fabianus reached for the princess's hands. "You didn't misunderstand."

"*Fabianus!*" called a man's deep, heartfelt voice. "No!"

General Nemeth advanced from the shadow of the king's throne to where Fabianus stood. The general's battered armour was a ludicrous contrast to his son's waistcoat.

Fabianus twinkled. "We both know Tycho's the better heir."

The general said, "There could be no better heir than you."

Fabianus blinked.

"My good boy." General Nemeth's rough voice went gentle. "When your mother passed, people said I owed it to my children to marry again. I couldn't bear to. I failed you, and you kept the house nice and the girls dressed beautifully. Our fortunes will come about. You don't need to make any more sacrifices for the family. I know your inclinations lie elsewhere, son. I've always known. I never cared."

Suddenly Rae became convinced that General Nemeth would never villainously plot her death. It *must* be the prime minister and his facial hair of evil.

In response to his parent's touching declaration, Lord Fabianus coughed. "Father, I appreciate that. But it is possible for people to enjoy the company of both ladies and gentlemen."

The Cobra cupped his hands around his mouth and cheered.

"Both?" General Nemeth looked like a trout with many military decorations. Mouth opening and closing, his gaze travelled the court, in search of help or possibly sex ed.

Fabianus gave a bashful nod. "People made assumptions because I like fabrics and fashions and dislike fighting in the mud. I might add, several fellows who do like fighting in the mud made *advances*. When I refused, they went to you and made jokes."

The king must have abdicated, because guilty silence suddenly reigned.

Fabianus smiled his pleasant foolish smile with a slight curl to his lip, and patted the general's arm with the hand not offered to Vasilisa. "I would have told you, Father, if you asked. Still, I found it convenient you never brought up the subject of marriage to me while you hounded the girls about marrying well. That was wrong, and I'm sorry to the Horrors, but – I did rather dream someday I might marry for love."

Princess Vasilisa's voice trembled. "And now?"

Fabianus's hand was still held out for hers. The joke of the palace reached out with hope and courage.

"Now I'm in love," Fabianus said simply. "I would go with you anywhere, if you asked. But I have a family I worry about, the same as you do. Hortensia's not well. I know it's awful cheek to ask, but would you wait for me?"

Before the princess could answer, Hortensia sprang to her feet. The embroidered lap robe tumbled away, revealing her wasted form. Her voice could have pierced a god's ear.

"I almost drowned you in the creek when you were ten, Fab Nemeth. Don't make me come over there and finish the job. I will do perfectly well without you. Finally, my big brother won't be there to criticize me whenever I wear yellow! I couldn't be happier."

Fabianus held up his free hand with unusual sternness. "Yellow makes you look like an enormous lemon, Hortensia!"

Horatia protested, "My dear! A dainty lemon."

Hortensia collapsed back into her chair. "Your Highness, please take him."

"Then, my princess ..." It was Fabianus's turn to blush. "Take me away?"

With her hand hovering in response to Fabianus's reach, Vasilisa nodded. Rae wasn't sure how it happened, as their gazes were fixed upon the throne room floor, but they touched hands. All at once they were in each other's arms.

Suddenly, the future Ice Queen and the fool of the court were kissing like the hero and heroine of an epic love tale, like they didn't know they were minor characters destined for disappointment, like they didn't care the whole court was watching.

The Cobra rose from his seat with sweeping golden self-confidence and applauded authoritatively, as if at a play. After a last startled split second, so did Rae, the book club, and Fabianus's sisters.

Even Prime Minister Pio seemed pleased by the alliance with Tagar being preserved, and presumably war against the ice raiders avoided.

"That didn't go the way I expected," Rae whispered to Key as they left the throne room. "But I'm into it."

Vasilisa and Fabianus might not look like Lia and Octavian, cut right out of a book of fairy tales, but they *felt* like someone's happy ending. Even if it wasn't hers.

Safe in the scarlet basement of shame, Emer set up Rae's screen of ebony black and paper white, poured the piping hot water and sprinkled the petals. A second hot bath might be overkill, but Rae had a lot of party eyeliner to remove and she schemed better in her hot tub. She was starting to think of it as her plot tub. Rae should find the maid bringing the lovely hot water and tip her.

It wasn't until Rae dunked her head beneath the surface of warm water fragrant with rose petals, that she remembered the one person in the throne room who hadn't been smiling.

Muffled by water, she heard a disturbance. It could have been a voice raised or a heavy object falling. Out of her element, Rae could only tell that the noise was loud. Indistinct and terrifying, it sounded like an oncoming storm.

CHAPTER TWENTY-SEVEN

The Lady's Lies Laid Bare

The night before Lady Rahela was executed, her maid embroidered through the dark and past dawn. She tried not to think of Rahela, who had betrayed her. She tried not to think of Lia, who she had betrayed. She watched the steel of her needle under the stars, piercing the cloth a hundred times, and felt hate past thought.

Time of Iron, ANONYMOUS

he white marble hall in their new chamber was the same as in the favourite's chamber, except the arched stained-glass window was closer to the ravine. Sparks flying upward lit the diamond panes like brief red stars. Occasionally, Emer heard moans or screams. Now Emer heard only the sound of Rahela singing in the bathtub to her snake. Apparently, Rahela was hot-blooded. The snake should check it and see.

Emer sat in her curtained alcove, at a loss. Rahela and Lia were friends now. Lia would be queen. Peace between the stepsisters always seemed impossible, but the impossible had become real.

Across the hall she saw the flash of Key's smile, slightly less unsettling than the flash of his knives. He seemed pleased his threats to ensure Lady Rahela's bathwater arrived hot had been successful again. When Rahela's shadow swayed behind the screen, Key set his jaw and looked at the wall.

Even the elderly guard Rahela believed was fatherly used to peek, but Key worshipped the ground Rahela swaggered on. He'd mistaken the cheap flower for a jewel, and he would flat out murder anyone who tried to tell him different.

Emer had imagined Key's eyes would be opened when Rahela tried to inveigle the king back to her bed, and Lia into her grave.

Except Rahela had declined her chance to sabotage Lia. She'd put the king in Lia's hand instead. Emer saw nothing in this uncharacteristic behaviour to benefit Rahela, but she was proved wrong when Lia offered an alliance. They were vipers together.

Lia would marry the king, but Emer had always known she would marry someone. This way, Emer would still see her.

In the evenings, Rahela told them stories for what she called 'after-dinner entertainment'. They were halfway through the tale of Lord Ross and beauteous Lady Rachel, who Lord Ross suspected of infidelity to their lovers' vows. Emer assumed Lord Ross would soon have Lady Rachel's head chopped off in accordance with the laws of the land. Key would sit adoringly at Rahela's feet, cheek in hand, eyes uplifted. Emer would sit in the corner with her embroidery, pretending not to listen.

Perhaps this evening Lia might come to their door again. Perhaps Rahela would tell them all a wonderful story.

A tap came at the door. Emer's heart did a little skip, then took a long fall.

The person in the doorway was the king.

Octavian still wore his court regalia, embroidered cloak streaming from his shoulders, masked crown pushed up to rest on gleaming hair. Beneath his crown, his face was restless.

"I desire to see Rahela."

Here it was. Whenever something went wrong at the ministers' assembly or Octavian felt slighted at a party, Rahela was needed to say Octavian was the king of her heart.

Rahela had ignored her opportunity to claim him. Princess Vasilisa had humiliated him in front of the entire court. And he was scared, Emer thought, of being the Emperor.

She knew this look on Octavian's face. She knew her duty. She should escort Octavian to her lady's chamber.

Emer wasn't sure why she rose and said pointedly, "My lady is in her bath."

Octavian's perfectly shaped eyebrows lifted in perfect affront, but he gestured to the palace guards behind him. It had been a long time since she granted the king access to her lady, his air suggested. He would pardon her insolence by ignoring it, and carry on as usual.

The guards retreated into the stairwell and turned their backs. Octavian stepped inside and closed the door behind him, almost all the way. It was as much privacy as you ever got with a king.

"Summon her," Octavian said, lightly enough.

It was a royal order. He could not be refused.

Emer twisted her embroidery, a cushion cover showing the golden turrets of the palace with a steel needle struck through the gold.

"It would better fit your royal dignity if you retired to your chambers, sire. Once she is dressed my lady will hurry to your side."

The king's power extended across the whole land, but the fact of his power felt oppressive in close quarters. His crowned shadow stained the marble as he approached.

Octavian set a hand on Emer's shoulder. "I won't be lectured on my dignity by a servant."

His touch was heavy with the weight of a sceptre and a crown behind it. Emer felt her knees buckle. If he wanted her to kneel, she must.

The beads of Key's curtain rattled as they swung open.

It was Rahela who said: "Let her go."

The pressure released. Emer was free. Octavian turned towards Rahela, standing wide-eyed at the threshold of her bedchamber. She was wrapped in her crimson robe figured with white nightingales, silk clinging to her skin with the heat and moisture of the bath. Octavian's eyes lingered on silk-cradled curves.

With all the poise she could muster in a robe, Rahela drew herself up. "What do you want?"

"Let me come into your bedchamber, and shut away the rest of the world."

Rahela's eyes darted around the room. Perhaps realizing they were a tell, she lowered her gaze. "You wish to consult your prophet, but I'm sure you don't want a whisper of being shut up with another woman to reach your true love."

It was a barely concealed threat. He wouldn't want her to tell Lia. Even a king wouldn't risk losing Lia.

"Rahela, *stop!*"

The command came down hard as a boot heel.

"The more you talk of true love, the less I feel it," declared Octavian. "I confess, at first I was taken by your stepsister. She's different from you, and the change was pleasant as a rest. I didn't know you would get so angry. Enough with the prophecy and the Cobra and the ugly princess. Let everything be as it was before."

Rahela's eyes searched the king's handsome face. She trembled from head to bare feet. "What are you saying?"

That pleased Octavian. His mouth curled, inviting her to smile back. "Poor Rahela, you truly thought you had been replaced. I'm sorry, if you must hear it. There is no need to be jealous. Though it suits you. Desperation set you burning like a lamp. I was swayed, but even Lady Lia's beauty could not stop my gaze from going back to your light. She is not my true love. You are. And you shall be my queen."

"This isn't how the story goes," Rahela murmured under her breath.

Emer agreed. This wasn't the story anyone told about these two women. Key was the only one who didn't seem surprised.

"Don't you want to be the heroine of the story?" asked Octavian.

After a moment, Rahela nodded.

Her lady's plans had succeeded beyond their wildest dreams.

Octavian reached out a hand, curved as though he was already caressing her. "Say something, darling."

Rahela spat, "So *this* is the great love story? Don't talk about my dazzling light that made you look away from the fairest of them all. You like me because you're afraid I stopped liking you. You would have sentenced me to death, then turned to Lia and told yourself that was true love. You either want the newest toy or the toy someone else is playing with. None of us is real to you. And that makes *you* a villain."

Octavian's hand whirled through the air to strike her.

The blow never landed. Key caught the king's wrist. Octavian tried to wrench away, but though his arm trembled with the force he was expending, he couldn't break Key's hold. Key bared his teeth in the king's direction like a mocking wolf.

The smile dissolved like sea foam on Octavian's face. His face twisted, like a child about to throw a monstrous tantrum.

"If you're all toys, I wonder who will get broken first?"

His emerald eyes flashed carelessly from Key to Rahela. His meaning was clear.

"Release His Majesty, Key." Rahela's voice cut like a dagger in a lady's dainty hand. The weapon might be pearl-handled, but it would hurt. "Now."

A moment of quiet passed, swift as a scared heartbeat. Reluctantly, Key let go.

"Beg his pardon," continued Rahela. "On your knees."

Key, who laughed when people called him a gutter brat, went cold and pale with insult. Rahela met his gaze with raised eyebrows. Teeth locked, fire quenched, Key sank to his knees.

It wasn't enough.

Octavian asked, "You call the gutter scum by his *name*?"

"Pay no attention to the man who should be behind the curtain." Rahela let her voice drop, low as she could go. "You're right, Your Majesty. We should talk. Alone. In my bedchamber."

The cadence of Rahela's voice was intimately familiar to Emer. She'd heard this voice wielded as a weapon at a hundred private moments and in a hundred gatherings. This new Rahela used it as the old Rahela had, but there was always an undercurrent of playfulness in the new Rahela's voice. She was always playing, never taking anything seriously.

Now her amusement had drained away.

Octavian didn't care to notice the nuances. He smiled benevolently. If she would act the wicked seductress, he could play such a good king.

Rahela fluttered her dark lashes, clumping together with bathwater, not tears. She reached, nails tipped with red like the claws of a cat after a kill, to capture Octavian's hand. Any stranger would have seen a heartless lascivious beauty, a snake determined to charm the king.

Perhaps Rahela, like Emer, had lost the habit of submission. There was a shake in her outstretched hand. After the deliberate sweep of her lashes, a swift involuntary tremor followed, difficult to capture as the movement of a butterfly's wing. Every hard line of the wicked jade's face and body set in silent protest.

"Kiss me first," the king commanded. An infinitesimal shudder passed beneath Rahela's skin.

Nobody wished to serve all the time.

This new Rahela had forgotten how to pretend.

As Rahela sashayed forward, her sway stopped dead. On his knees, Key caught at her robe, black leather fist clenched on the red silk. His face was uplifted to Rahela's, that cynical strange young face absorbed as when he listened to her stories. There was no pure illumination in that scarlet-bathed dungeon room. Light seemed to touch him anyway. His expression was that of a man in a shrine.

"You told me you were forgettable, replaceable, and insignificant," Key said. "You said not to risk myself, unless I had an absolutely imperative reason. I do. My universe is altered by your wishes. And you never want him to touch you again."

The villain of the Cauldron bowed his wild dark head and kissed the hem of her garment.

Octavian clicked his fingers impatiently. "Come, my lady. Or else."

King Octavian strode forward to grasp his possession.

Key of the Cauldron rose like the surge of dark water in a storm, and punched his king in the face. The blow sent Octavian reeling against the marble wall, hand flying to his mouth. Blood seeped through his fingers. The king's eyes above his hand flew wide, stunned past fury.

"Hands off," Key said simply.

"I am your *king!*"

Key shrugged. "Hands off, Your Majesty."

Voice thick with blood, Octavian snarled, "Are you *mad?*"

Delighted, deranged, Key smiled. "Yes."

Octavian's gaze slid to the crack in the door, which made Key's lip curl with contempt. Emer saw the moment Octavian recalled that, mere weeks ago, Key had been whipped to within an inch of his life.

Octavian shook his crowned head. "I don't need guards. I'll teach you a lesson myself, gutter rat."

Key beckoned the king towards him. Octavian drew his sword. The blade remade because of Rahela's prophecy. The sword re-forged in the bone fire of legendary beasts, its steel bathed in a deep red glow of magic. The sword that waved to split silver clouds and scarlet sky at the Queen's Trials.

"Longing for Revenge." Rahela's voice was crushed small with terror. "The blade none can withstand."

Key swung his ugly, common short sword to meet the king's. The last of Emer's hope shattered.

So did the royal sword. A deep fissure ran along the steel beneath the red glow, and shards of magic sword fell like rain.

Emer remembered General Nemeth at the Queen's Trials, saying the manticore's chains had been too hastily forged. Belowstairs they said the king had re-forged the sword himself. Surely he wouldn't skimp on time or skip steps, impatient for a showy result. Surely even the king wouldn't be that arrogant.

"Keep teaching, Your Majesty," Key sneered. "I'm learning a lot."

Blank with disbelief, Octavian stared at the bladeless hilt. "I will be the Emperor," he said, as if trying to remind the universe.

Key laughed. "You're not the Emperor yet."

"Don't kill him!" Rahela screamed.

Key nodded, and deliberately cast his sword aside. He stepped in to Octavian, close enough to kiss. Instead Key picked up the king, a man roughly his own size, by the front of his embroidered doublet and shook him like a rat. He hurled the king across the room. Octavian's cloak, heavy with embroidery, flew in his wake. Octavian landed in a silver heap on the floor. When the king lifted his head, blood gleamed on his pouting mouth and his tooth was chipped. He would never look the part of the perfect prince again.

"'Beg for mercy,'" Key suggested. "'It amuses me.'"

"*Guards!*"

At the king's word, the palace guards rushed for the beauty's chamber.

Octavian's eyes narrowed hatefully up at Key. "My men will bring you down in twelve seconds."

Face alight with glorious ruin, Key tossed a laugh and a knife into the air. "Let's see how much treason I can commit in twelve seconds."

The blade embedded in Octavian's cloak. The glow from the ravine painted the room. The graceful arc of Key's leap was a single dark comma across a scene red as blood and white as snow. As the king begged Key for mercy, more red followed.

Three guards died within seconds, but the fourth fled. He brought back reinforcements. Armed, uniformed men flooded in, the walls crowded edge to edge with armour and weapons. Key was still laughing, dancing with his blades. He was a whirlwind of death.

Two guards got behind Key and clubbed him in the head, belabouring his whipped shoulders. Rahela lunged, seizing the arm that held the club and biting into the meat of it like a fox gone rabid, before the guard knocked Rahela to the ground. Battle fury thick as red mist in Emer's head, she raised her embroidery and slashed the other guard's neck open with her needle. Blood was pouring down Key's face. He should be blinded, but he killed the man who struck Rahela.

One guard stabbed at his unprotected side, then yelped in startled anguish. Rahela's pet snake had darted across the floor and sunk its fangs into the guard's ankle.

A beautifully polished boot crushed the snake's domed head.

Octavian commanded, "Put an end to these vipers."

In the end, it took half the king's men to bring Key down. Two guards caught Emer between them. Her head rang and the chaos of the room grew remote. The guard she'd slashed had used his club.

Dimly, Emer heard her lady pleading, left behind in the sea of soldiers. Nobody cared what the Harlot of the Tower had to say, as they dragged her people away.

King Octavian pulled together the shreds of his cloak and his royal dignity. "Take these insolent servants to the Room of Dread and Anticipation and thrash them. Do it right this time. I want him whipped until he is dead."

Emer had never seen the Room of Dread and Anticipation before. She'd heard about it in hushed whispers. This was the darkest place in the palace, where you went when you were bad past redemption.

Choose evil. Let's do it together, Rahela's eager voice echoed in Emer's memory. She had been such a fool.

Two stark lines of wood and steel loomed into view. For a bewildered terrified instant Emer believed she saw a gallows. Then she realized it was a whipping post.

An explosion of violence turned Emer's head. Key struggled against his captors' hold, lunging and biting like a vicious trapped animal. She didn't know how he was conscious. Considering how badly the guards had already beaten him, she didn't know how he was alive.

A guard holding Emer left to help his fellows with Key. Key's eyes slid towards her, sly and calculating. She wondered if she was meant to seize the moment and escape. If so, Key overestimated her. The heavy steel door had already slammed shut.

Fighting the guards every step, Key was dragged towards the whipping post. Black shackles were attached to each of the two upright beams. They closed the shackles around Key's legs and arms, holding him splayed in place. Emer winced. She'd seen village boys torture a dog once, measuring how long the dog would take to die.

The enchanted lash sang through the air. The crash of the whip echoed against the stone walls like thunder. It landed, then arced again, a giant snake spitting shreds of cloth and skin. Blood spattered the walls.

King Octavian laughed, as delighted as the boyish torturers from long ago. "Don't rush. I want him to die slow."

The guard pulled Emer to another set of shackles. He moved slowly, eyes on the real spectacle. Lashes didn't rain on Key. They came down in a hard black hail.

Key's face turned towards Emer. "Don't worry. It won't be long."

When the next blow came, Key's fist clenched hard on the ruby gleam of Rahela's earring.

Only then did it dawn on Emer how naive he really was. He wore a mask of blood, and his exalted expression. He intended to spare Emer a few lashes, before Rahela came to save them.

"You can't believe in her. How can you be so stupid?" Emer hated him almost as much as herself. "We are to her what she is to the king. You're not a real person to her. They want you to be useful, so they tell you whatever you want to hear."

Once she spoke, the guards remembered she existed. When Emer spoke disrespectfully of the king, the whip landed on her back.

Better to die fast than slow. She'd meant them to whip her, but she hadn't known how much it would hurt. A magical lash burned as well as cut. As the orichal steel teeth of the whip tore into her back, her flesh sizzled like bacon tossed into a pan. A hot waterfall of blood rushed down her back to her waist. She howled like an animal.

Drifting through a haze of pain, Emer heard Key arguing in the troubled voice of someone also arguing with himself. "You're wrong. We shared real secrets. I told her how my father died, and she told me how she was sick as a child."

Gasping, Emer laughed. Key had thrown his life away for a delusion, bowed his head in worship of a hollow thing.

"Rahela was never sick a day in her life."

King Octavian laughed too.

His laugh was interrupted by the heavy door creaking. Emer blinked to clear her sight. There, in the cold slant of light provided by the door she'd opened, stood the Beauty Dipped In Blood. Her shimmering gown made her seem wrapped in a moonbeam, but on the skirt heartsblood-red leaped in the shape of flames. She was dressed as the hungry ravine.

Emer felt she wasn't seeing the new Rahela or the old, but another person entirely. The heartless siren, the ice-hearted beauty from the songs and stories. Someone who had never been entirely real, because nobody was the way they were in a legend. This was the woman of snow and flame, too evil to be true.

"Have you been telling stories, my darling viper?" asked the king.

Rahela's red mouth curled, wicked as the blood-wet whip. "I do love stories."

CHAPTER TWENTY-EIGHT

The Villainess Is Justly Punished

When the screams died the proclamation was made.
   "So passes a most vile, wicked and unforgivable villain.
So perish the enemies of the king."

Time of Iron, ANONYMOUS

ae raced into the heroine's tower bedroom to find Lia on her bed, knees drawn up like a child, white skirt pulled primly around her ankles. The Cobra was perched on the stool from Lia's dressing table as they laughed.

"Don't worry," the Cobra said lightly. "The pearl's reputation is safe. I went over the roofs—"

When they registered Rae's expression, laughter died.

"I need the viper bracelet. The king has Key and Emer."

"*What?*" Lia exclaimed. "Why would the king touch Emer?"

"Octavian— wanted me to go with him," Rae faltered. "They tried to stop him. It's my fault."

The Cobra's voice was suddenly tender. "It's not your fault, Rae."

He was too kind, that was his problem. Octavian being a creep wasn't her fault, but she'd sworn the blood oath, made the bargain with Emer and Key that she never intended to keep. This wouldn't be happening if it wasn't for Rae.

"The bracelet of the favourite can be used to speak with the king's voice. It can pardon one of them. Then—I'll figure that out later."

"I'll find Marius," said the Cobra. "He reminds Octavian to be the better man Marius believes he can be."

"Why would Marius help?" Rae asked hopelessly.

"Because he's a better man than he believes he can be." The Cobra turned to Lia. "Help me convince him."

Lia recoiled across the virginal white space of her bed. "I saw how Lord Marius looked at me during the tournament. A cursed monster was staring at me through his eyes."

The Cobra often gestured with his hands. Today, they hung helpless by his sides.

"What would you say if I told you in another world he proved you could trust him?"

Lia's sweet blue eyes were unyielding. "I would say that world is not this one."

Rae had once believed it was good they could change the narrative. Now she understood. They had crashed into the story and left it in so many pieces it could never be put back together. Terror for the Cobra cut through her, cold as a knife twisting in her belly.

"Lia's right. Don't go near Marius. He could kill you."

"If he's a cursed monster instead of a hero, it's *my* fault," the Cobra said fiercely. "I have to try."

The Cobra was out the door in a whirl of gold. Rae buried her face in her hands so she wouldn't have to look at what she'd done. What if the Cobra died today, under Marius's blade, years before he should? She had walked into the story in a cloud of death. She stained everything she touched.

A light touch of cool fingertips made Rae lift her head. Lia's face was a luminous pearl, gold hair looping around her shoulders and gold metal looping around her wrist. Lia had rescued Emer and Key when Rahela was condemned in the original novel. She was the real heroine, able to save them. They would be safe now if it wasn't for Rae.

"Tell me," said Lia, "exactly what happened."

Rae talked so fast her words stumbled over each other, concluding, "I need the bracelet."

"You shall have it," Lia said gently. "Use it for Emer."

"Why, because you don't care about Key?"

Lia shook her head. "Key raised his hand to the king, but Octavian might let you get away with a maid. For Key, perhaps the Cobra can talk around Lord Marius."

Lia didn't think Key could be saved, so she wanted to ensure Rae rescued Emer. Lia was making sense.

"There must be some way to save him," Rae said desperately.

Lia bit her lip. "Is Octavian truly the Emperor? You know him better than I do. Can he be great as well as terrible?"

It was true. Rae knew him better than anybody. She had read his thoughts. She knew who he would grow into.

When the Emperor was angry, he was epic in his fury. But he wasn't spiteful. He could never be small or petty. He was the hero. Even his sins were on a grand scale.

"Yes," Rae breathed. "He can be great and terrible."

"If he has a great heart, when his anger cools he might show mercy," said Lia. "Relieve his jealousy."

"I can't be you."

"No, you can't be me." Lia wiped the blood from Rae's cut lip with a steady hand. "I can make being weaponless a weapon, but that's not the story in Octavian's head about you. The king could strike you dead at his feet, and still he wouldn't believe you're vulnerable. That is its own weapon. I've been told I'm the type you marry, by many men I wasn't interested in marrying. But the poets don't write about heartless wanton women because they hope never to meet them."

Rae swallowed the bitter taste at the back of her throat as she remembered Octavian talking about having two beautiful women on either side of his throne. Readers felt torn between the evil Emperor and the righteous Last Hope. Perhaps it was natural to be conflicted between wishing for the pure pearl and desiring the Harlot in the Tower. Human hearts were made to be divided.

Perhaps the villainess could manipulate her way out of this one yet. She smirked. Her stepsister smiled angelically back.

"Be as wicked as he wants."

The Room of Dread and Anticipation was a grey cavern, the windows arrow slits, the ceiling the colour of a cobwebbed tomb. The stone floor was flat as an altar, except for the long deep grooves gouged in the stone: channels for blood to run along. Gutters ran along the edges of the room to catch the blood.

Rae lifted her chin and strode like an evil queen. She didn't even glance at Key or Emer as she arrowed towards the king.

He looked mildly intrigued, but not convinced.

She purred, "Don't execute my maid. She's the only girl in the palace who can be relied upon to do my hair."

The curl of Octavian's mouth was half judging, half ready to indulge. With the air of one caught with her hand in the extra-sinful cookie jar, Rae held up her arm and twirled the viper bracelet, the token that had got her through the door.

The amusement curving Octavian's mouth grew more pronounced. "Where did you get that?"

"Hoodwinked my little stepsister by making a show of distress." Rae winked, letting Octavian in on the joke. "It's a great drawback, to have a heart in the palace."

She cast a glance towards the open door. Lia had slipped in after Rae. She lingered shyly in the doorway, insubstantial as a shadow made of light.

He might be immature and pursuing scarlet women now, but one day the Emperor would love Lia more than the sun or the air. Surely even now, he could not refuse her.

Save me, Lia's naturally sweet blue eyes beseeched.

Rae licked her artfully stained ruby lips. *Please me.*

She remembered a myth about a king trapped on a love island by a wicked enchantress, who mysteriously took a year to escape her. She gave a deep sigh so the evil twins heaved, not bothering to hide the calculating look in her eye. Nobody busty was ever a good person! *Come on, Your Majesty. Give the villain what she wants.*

Under their combined gaze, Octavian's chest swelled. Not as much as Rae's, obviously.

"Release the maid."

The sound of shackles snapping open echoed against the stone. Rae's eyes went involuntarily to Emer. Her prim blue dress was ripped, blood giving her a crimson belt. Her hair had tumbled down from its tight bun, but she caught at the post she'd been shackled to and held herself stubbornly upright. Lia ran forward, shoring Emer up.

Rae couldn't show the slightest hint of concern.

Instead she squeezed Octavian's bicep and gave an appreciative sigh. "I know it was shameless to ask for her, but . . . I *am* shameless. Isn't that what you like about me?"

The king's hot hand pressed her waist. Rae forced herself to lean in.

"Perhaps," he allowed. "But there are limits. It seems you deceived this poor peasant boy, and seduced him with your lies."

Of course he would call it seduction. Octavian couldn't under-stand Key, would never believe he would sacrifice everything because he saw Rae was frightened.

In that close stone space smelling of blood, Rae giggled naughtily. Strain tipped her giggle over into a cackle. Evil women always ended up dead or witches. "Perhaps I told stories. I'm so bad."

The young king's voice was wise and sorrowful. "Even though he's filth from the Cauldron, you wronged him. Look in his eyes. Confess your sins."

She swayed across the Room of Dread and Anticipation as if it were a ballroom. Key hung limp between the posts, only the heavy shackles on his wrists and ankles holding him up.

Whip marks were livid on his shoulders. Imagination shuddered and failed as she envisioned his back. He was barely healed from last time, and now he was chained up to be flayed for her again.

When she tilted his chin up with a red-tipped fingernail, she prayed Key was unconscious. He wasn't. His breathing was stertorous, hitching in his lungs as though there was something damaged inside him, and his once-golden skin was ashen under a layer of blood and sweat. But that familiar smile was on his lips, and his eyes were open. Grey as shadows as the sun sank away, they fixed on her face.

Hoarse with pain, Key murmured, "Tell me you were sick. Tell me that wasn't a lie."

She'd never heard him beg before. A gleam was hidden down deep in his pain-clouded eyes, faraway light like the red sparks outside her stained-glass chamber window.

She had to convince Octavian not to be jealous. She had to put the last spark out.

Rae's laugh tinkled like ice in an empty glass. "How could you be stupid enough to believe my story? Suffering isn't for people like me. Suffering is for things like you."

Unable to bear the look on Key's face, she pulled away, wiping bloodstained fingertips against her silk gown. The sound of Octavian's boots echoed, striking stone as he approached her. He'd crushed her pet beneath his heel. Dread pooled in Rae's stomach at the thought he would touch her again.

Octavian stroked the skin of her arm, the back of his hand brushing the breast half bared by her revealing gown. Rae hoped her shiver seemed like desire.

"You're a good king, but who can resist the wicked? I tricked the boy into helping me," she confessed in her sinner's voice. "I used him and betrayed him. If he's smitten, I'm sorry ... that he's such a fool. I don't care what you do to him. It doesn't really matter. *He* doesn't really matter. But believe this. It is the only truth I ever told that gutter scum."

She had to sell this performance, as her mother sold houses because she couldn't afford not to, as Lia sold innocence every day without losing it. She focused desperately on long-ago hospital rooms, her desperate hurting self, questing between the covers of a book and finding the Emperor.

She pressed her red lips to Octavian's in a long kiss, ending in a silver whisper. "I love you with all my wicked heart."

"I *am* a good king," promised Octavian. "I intend to show mercy."

Victory thrilled through Rae's body. She'd known he could be great. When he stooped for another kiss, she threaded her blood-stained fingers through his hair and kissed him desperately back. His mouth parted for her kiss. She tasted the words before he spoke them.

Against her lips, the king murmured: "Cut his throat."

The words blurred in Rae's mind as though reading through tears.

She reeled and found herself sinking to the stone. Kneeling, staring helplessly up at Key. The first person she'd seen when she woke to this world, the first person to take her side.

He was always smiling. Now a second smile curved on his neck. A red mouth that gaped and gushed blood. Key's last breath bubbled away through his slit throat.

In another world, she'd seen a man die in hospital, watched the illumination in his eyes fade and realized, slow as a terrible dawn, what she was seeing. Life, recognized only when lost, impossible to replicate, impossible to fake and impossible to win back. Life was pain, fury, every dark feeling combined to somehow make light.

The last light drained from Key's eyes. His gaze, still fixed on her, turned black as a cave with nobody inside.

Scarlet rained down on Rae's guilty face. Heat hit her skin and seeped between her lips, thicker and more bitter than tears, his life-blood in her mouth. Real as her own blood in hospital vials, dark as a stain blotting out the rest of his story. Real as despair.

CHAPTER TWENTY-NINE

The Lady Is Long Dead

The night after Lady Rahela's death, Emer lay down upon
her narrow bed and planned who she would kill. She stared
at the dark with her eyes wide open, tearless as stone.
In the years to follow, she never wept.

Time of Iron, ANONYMOUS

he Ladies Lia and Rahela dragged Emer back to Rahela's
bedroom between them. They laid Emer out on Rahela's
silken sheets the way Rahela had laid out Key. Now Key
was dead, so Emer got the bed. Lia's basket of liniments and medicines were beside them. Lia applied ointment to Emer's back with
her own fair hands, softer than any silk in the palace. The stepsisters
rolled out bandages for her wounds. They were such charitable ladies,
and so kind.

It was too like the night Lia had smoothed her palms up Emer's
back as Emer hovered above her. It was nothing like that night at all.

Finally, Emer couldn't stand it. She laid both hands flat on the
absurdly, uncomfortably soft mattress, shoved herself upright despite
the screaming flare of pain and snarled, "Get out. I don't need
your pity."

Lia was like the mattress, a luxury not meant for Emer, and Emer
didn't want to be one of the peasants Lia visited on her errands

of grace and mercy. *Oh thank you, my lady,* they would say when she came to their humble huts with her basket, *how can we ever repay you?*

If you had nothing, you could never pay anyone. That was what made charity so bitter.

Lia knelt beside the bed, radiant hair spilling loose over her shoulders, clearly shocked by Emer's ingratitude. She bit her pink lower lip, glancing at Rahela. It made Emer want to laugh. Lia looking to her big sister for help, as though a drop of kindness could blot out years of cruelty. What a lovely, tragic fool.

Naturally, Rahela let Lia down. She sat at her dressing table, staring at her own reflection. She didn't even seem to notice when Lia rose, shaking her head, and left the wicked women to their own devices. Emer watched her go, saving the memory of her limned in the doorway to keep, a last golden moment to visualize against her closed eyelids. She wasn't sure how much time passed while she fought waves of pain as though drowning in a strange sea. When Emer surfaced, the sky through the stained-glass window had changed colour. Rahela was still gazing dully into her mirror.

As Emer grasped a bedpost, the memory of being shackled and whipped shuddered through her. She gritted her teeth and pulled herself to her feet. Then she walked over to the dressing table, and set herself to brushing her lady's midnight hair.

Rahela lifted a hand in a gesture that folded up like a silk handkerchief. "Stop. You're still hurt."

"How could that be?" Emer asked evenly. "I'm not a person. I'm not allowed to suffer. My life was spared so I could do my lady's hair."

Rahela's hands clenched on the edge of the dressing table, as though holding the edge of an ice cliff. "That was a lie I told the king!"

Emer's hand clenched on the dainty brush. She wished it was an axe.

"So your story is, trust me, I was lying to someone *else*? As if I could ever believe you again. Before you ever told the future, you told me what you really thought of me. Even though I grew up with you. Even though I betrayed Lia for you. I was nothing to you, but you were a sister to me. I loved you, Rahela."

Her lady wrenched away from the dressing table, lunging at Emer as though she were a striking snake.

"*Don't* call me Rahela," she snapped. "Rahela's dead!"

The silver brush tumbled from Emer's hand onto the red mosaics.

Rahela pressed bloody hands to her tear-filled eyes. Tears and blood mingled, making Key's blood wet and fresh again. When her teardrops fell they left tiny crimson marks on the white silk wrap she had thrown over her ruined gown. From years of experience washing her lady's clothes, Emer knew the bloodstains would be impossible to get out.

Perhaps Rahela saw Emer was at her limit. She chose her next words carefully.

"What is a person if not a collection of memories? Without remembering, how can I be Rahela? But I've walked miles in Rahela's shoes by now. Why would Rahela tell you that you were nothing to her? Maybe she understood how cruel this world is. Maybe she knew she would die. Maybe she believed it would be best for you, if she cut ties with you. Maybe she loved you, and didn't want to drag you down with her. Maybe you were her sister."

"*Shut up!*" Emer knotted her fingers in her lady's hair and screamed in her face. "You don't know what she thought!"

They must have both lost their minds. Emer's back burned and grief blazed through her. Rahela was in front of her, but Emer felt she were lost.

The stranger shook her head, black hair flying wildly out of Emer's grasp. "Sometimes rage is all women can give each other. I once screamed at the girl I loved best in the world, because there was nothing but anger left in me. I can't apologize for what I don't remember. I can't be Rahela. I made a bargain with you I never meant to keep. I wish I'd never come to this place. I wish she'd died, and I'd died, and everyone else was safe."

The girl turned away, put her head down on the dressing table and howled like a wild wolf. The gleam of the fallen brush swam in Emer's vision, a silver fish seen through the water. Emer knelt shakily down to retrieve it, wondering why it was so difficult to see, wondering if this was how Lia always saw the world.

Across the room, Lia's charity basket was uncovered. In the basket, neatly folded, were carefully prepared bandages. Enough for two. As if Rahela truly hadn't known Key was doomed from the moment he rose from his knees and struck down the king for her sake.

By now the guards had thrown his corpse away like yesterday's slops. Down into the dread ravine. Meat for the ghouls, or burning in the faraway fires forever. That was the fate of traitors.

Kneeling, Emer reached for her lady's arm and held on tight enough to hurt.

"Do you truly think Rahela was trying to protect me?"

The girl in front of her clutched Emer back, equally desperate. "If she only loved Octavian, it would be too awful. She was nothing to him. Her life and death would mean nothing. I hope she loved you, no matter how badly she showed it. I hope in the end, there was one real thing."

Emer remembered the last day Rahela felt familiar, when her lady whirled around from the locked door and spat in Emer's face that she was done with her. The whole of Emer's past had seemed meaningless, wiped away like words in the sand. She imagined Rahela actually had been put to death the very next day, imagined carrying that weary blankness with her for her whole life, with nothing left but the vicious urge to hurt people the same way she was hurt.

She didn't want to do that. She didn't want to be that.

"I really felt like nothing," she whispered. Suddenly she was crying, a wild fit of weeping. As if she were a child in the cradle, before she learned that a servant's feelings didn't matter. "It really broke my heart. I felt like I wasn't anybody at all."

Her lady nodded, pressing her forehead against Emer's. She was crying too, her whole frame shaking. "You're somebody. You're real."

Between sobs, Emer got out, "If you don't want me to call you Rahela, what should I call you?"

The girl whispered, "Call me Rae."

CHAPTER THIRTY

The Cobra in New York

Everything was a reminder. He could not walk down a
corridor without recalling the Cobra dragging him down
that same corridor, chattering about building a grand
theatre. Marius believed he was a grown man then,
believed the Cobra was a man too, long lost to villainy.
Looking back, they were boys. There must have been a way
for that joyful youth to turn back from evil.

Marius had never truly believed all that brightness could
be put out.

Time of Iron, ANONYMOUS

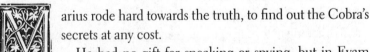arius rode hard towards the truth, to find out the Cobra's
secrets at any cost.

He had no gift for sneaking or spying, but in Eyam
there was a straight and narrow path towards truth. If you were willing to pay.

The Cave of the Oracle was high in the mountains, at the foot of
fertile arable land. The farmers who worked the rich earth knew the
goddess blessed them for harbouring her voice. They brought the
Oracle tribute every day of the year.

Past the Mountains of Truth were the Valerius lands, the Lake of
Sorrows and the Red Fields.

At temple, his mother had told him stories of the Oracle. Their goddess was lost, but too kind to desert her people entirely. She gave them an Oracle, and the Oracle would give each of the goddess's children one truth for a price. Marius had once found it reassuring to know the Oracle was near.

He'd lost that comfort when he was seventeen. This was the closest he'd been to home since then.

The mountain pass was high, the climb steep. Marius swung down at intervals to spare his horse and ignored the signs he was being followed. The guardians of the Oracle were skilful. Most petitioners wouldn't even know they were there.

Marius rode on, ducking under overhangs of granite, the horse's hooves crunching under loose shale until the end of the winding path.

The sun was losing its battle with shadows, but its rays still burned strong. One direct beam, bright yellow as a painted sign, stopped at the threshold of the cave. The Oracle's cave was a deep gash cut into the grey mountainside, bleeding darkness.

Two guardians waited before the cave. Marius stood, arms stretched wide, letting them search for weapons he didn't have. He pressed reins into one guardian's hand, and passed out of the hot sun into enclosing shadows. Marius's sight was swift to adjust, but the change was so abrupt for a moment he was lost and stumbling.

A hoarse voice issued from the dark. "Beware, Marius Valerius."

He took a knee. "My Oracle."

In the depths was a stirring, like a great bird stretching its wings. Marius bowed his head and waited. His senses expanded, slow and calm, listening to the lap of water, feeling the particular change in the atmosphere of air cooling when water was near. The birdlike rustling continued, followed by shuffling footsteps.

"Prophecies are hungry. They will eat you to be fulfilled. Do you know who you remind me of?"

"Everyone says I resemble my father," Marius answered dully.

"When everyone says something, doubt them. Your father resembles his father, and his father's father. The same face with slight variations, to imprint the memory of danger through generations. A Valerius is like a plant with colours warning it is poison. You are no vague shadow, Marius Valerius. You look more like the First Duke than his first son. The First Duke was a marvel and a monster. Do you wish to be like him?"

The first duke, the general of the first king. Centuries had passed since they lived. Years had eroded history into stories. The tales said the fields of poppies around the Valerius manor grew because the First Duke stood his ground there, one man against an army, and won. They said the First Duke had eyes redder than the poppies. Children in Eyam were told to behave, or the First Duke would get them.

The Oracle was older than the mountains. She had seen the First Duke and knew the truth of him.

It was no surprise to hear Marius was a monster.

"Red eyes would make me conspicuous at court, my lady Oracle."

The Oracle's laugh was wind through rotten boughs. "You have your mother's eyes. Don't thank her for them. Clear eyes are no gift in the kingdom of the blind. The First Duke was a beautiful monster, at least."

She laid a hand on Marius's head, heavy and curled as a claw. Her hand wasn't ice cold. Ice could be melted. She was cold with the deep permeating chill of stone under the mountain.

The Valerius manor was made from the stone of these mountains. Cold was his birthright.

Tomb-chill fingers toyed with the white strands in his hair. "The First Duke's hair changed after his first and worst kill. Who did you fight to win the ice in your hair, throwback?"

Marius lifted his head. The Oracle was pale as the belly of an eyeless fish that would never be touched by the faintest shimmer of light on the surface of the water where it lived. She wore tattered veils as clothing, variegated layers in white and grey and black, like petals curling up within a dying flower. Her tangled white hair had black ends, as if dipped in fresh ink. When she raised a finger to her lips, the bony digit was coated in darkness. Every finger was blackened, as though she'd dabbled in an inky sea.

"As if I didn't know. It takes a long time to get over, doesn't it? All your life."

In the silence, Marius heard the splintering of a door seven years ago. He heard a little girl scream.

"Get over what?" he asked thickly.

"All your life." The Oracle sniffed the air like a bloodhound. Her eyes, caves in her haggard face, didn't appear to see well. "Where is your servant?"

In the darkness, in the cavern of her mouth, Marius couldn't be sure if her tongue was tipped with black.

"I will use my own blood for the sacrifice."

His heart set a galloping beat in his ears. He understood if his own blood was an unworthy sacrifice, but he wouldn't order someone else to bleed for him.

The Oracle smiled with pointed teeth. "Usually people spill an ocean's worth of strangers' blood before sacrificing a drop of their own. A substitute buys substandard magic. If you give me your best, I will give you mine. Give me your hands, Marius Valerius, and I will give you my truth."

He offered his hands, palms up and cupped. The Oracle's dark-coated nails bit into the centre of his palms. He knelt with hands full of his own blood. Between his fingers, blood slipped and dripped. He saw the murk of the pool in which the Oracle stood change. His blood swirled in the clouded waters. Darkness turned water into a mirror.

The Oracle's voice filled the cave. "I count the grains of sand on every beach and measure the sea. I hear the voiceless and know the necessity of evil. In your whole life, you only get one question. Ask for the truth you want most."

The years-old riddle he couldn't solve. The key to every strange happening in the palace.

"Eric Mitchell. The Golden Cobra. I want the truth of him."

The blood in the water twisted as if his words had created a current in that still pool. The water in the Cave of the Oracle was suddenly illuminated by lights burning with the force of stars, shining in all the colours of the rainbow.

The blood framed a window to impossible sights.

Violently burning lamps lit a strange street. Earth and grass were lost beneath a disturbingly smooth grey surface, like a river turned to stone. Eerie carriages with no horses attached rushed over the stone river. Black wheels spun through scum-slick puddles, stopping before a spindly tree of lights that flashed emerald, amber, and fiend's-eye-red.

Along the stone river were stone riverbanks, grey and flat as the river itself. People in bizarre clothes jostled each other, a crowd thick as a flood of salmon. The dizzying blur of lights and faces became a whirlpool of bewilderment.

The waters stilled and centred on a face. A boy. He wasn't Eric. Marius opened his mouth to protest, then hesitated.

The boy was young, no more than fourteen. Some children altered greatly as they developed into adults, but surely the very bones were wrong. There was a slight resemblance suggesting a distant relation, but Marius could see no path of change from this boy's face to the one he knew.

The child was a stranger in a strange land, his hair shaved at the sides with fronds falling in his face like a plant. His clothes were worn and grubby as a peasant's but richly coloured as a lord's, his tunic emblazoned with crude letters reading 'SEIZE THE MEANS OF STAGE PRODUCTION!' He wore an insectile contraption over his ears, carried a canvas bag dangling from a strap over one shoulder, and was bathed in glaring pink light emanating from a storefront selling unthinkable devices. He was a bizarre figure in a grotesque landscape that could have no possible relevance to Marius.

And yet.

The boy moved as if to silent music, hands shaping the air, and Marius knew those gestures. Those clever hands always mapped the progress of that overly clever tongue, illustrating Lord Popenjoy's point or his punchline.

Somehow, this *was* Eric. It was in the way he looked at people side-long, constructing careful attention out of a hundred careless glances.

That look alerted Marius to danger. The roving flash of Eric's attention fixed. Marius followed Eric's gaze to what not another soul on that busy street saw.

The child was tiny, with fat dark braids and hands small enough to slip out of a harried mother's hold. She tottered off the grey riverbank into the river of lights and vehicles. One vehicle wailed like a dying animal and avoided her. The next would not.

Eric dashed into the river of chaos and knocked the child clear to the bank.

Marius witnessed the shattering impact of the metal hulk, catching Eric's side, Eric's temple. Eric was thrown into the air like a big fish twisting on an invisible line, caught by an invisible hook. He landed on all fours, sprawled awkwardly with none of his usual grace, set his child's jaw and staggered back to the stone riverbank. The little girl stood crying, unhurt but venting her shock at an unexpectedly cruel world.

More vehicles lined the side of the stone bank, stationary and lifeless. Eric leaned against one, very like the hurtling metal creature that had hit him but not powered by the same malicious energy. He didn't seem worried it would wake to life.

He winked down at the crying girl. "Hey." It was a child's voice, but steady and gentle. "It's all right."

The world was cruel, but never Eric.

A woman pushed through the crowds. She wore an understandably frantic expression, and trousers for which Marius could find no explanation.

"Aera, there you are!" She snatched the little girl's hand from his. Her eyes flicked to Eric. "I can't thank you enough," she added.

It seemed she could thank him enough. She didn't thank him again.

Eric nodded, braced against the car as if getting his breath back. He should have it back by now.

"You were hit pretty hard," the woman continued reluctantly. "Maybe you should call an ambulance."

Eric's head was still hanging, but he made his airy dismissive gesture.

"Ambulances scare me." He laughed. "My ... sister's husband lost his job. We don't have insurance. I'll take the subway."

There was a wet, serious undertone to his laughter. The woman didn't hear it. She didn't want to.

"I should go." The woman's voice was already putting distance in between them.

She shouldn't go.

No surprise showed in Eric's face as she turned away, child in tow, and no resentment. Eric usually took people as they were.

The waters of the Oracle's blood pool ruffled, as if with a slight breeze. In that faraway land, dark grey afternoon shaded rapidly into night. The sky over the alien city was bristling with towers and almost devoid of stars.

"Don't look at that man," a stranger with a striped noose around his neck instructed his daughter. "He looks like trouble."

Marius wondered what was wrong with his eyes. Eric was clearly not a man, but a child in trouble.

As time passed, Eric slipped down. At the grey edge of that turbulent street, he sat huddled against one of the machines that had hit him. The Golden Cobra, the glittering centre of every whirlwind in court. The loudest, brightest soul Marius knew, enduring a quiet, wretched death.

He held a little glass-fronted box attached to his insectile headgear. Eric was laboriously tapping on it. Behind the glass was a word and a picture – 'Sis' with a drawing of a heart. Eric's tapping slowly produced another word, which was '*sorry*'. Seized by a tremor, the box tumbled to the street. A crack struck clear across the glass.

Eric's hands, sure enough to steal from the king, fumbled with pitiful clumsiness on his bag's metal fastenings. He paused to cough something dark and solid into his hand, but finally got the bag open. Fingers stained with clotted blood curled around the battered shape of a book. Eric clung to the book like a small child to a favourite toy.

Marius made a sound, too broken to be a laugh. That was the Cobra, with his love for art and beauty.

"Should have called that ambulance, kid." A strange woman with her hair in girlish tails sat beside Eric, gold-skinned and serene, her eyes kind as Eric's but distant as skies. "Too late now."

"I gathered that," Eric mumbled, words slurring, and coughed again.

The shining woman offered, "There *is* an alternative."

Her every word seemed to weigh more than the words of others, as if theirs were tin and hers steel. She leaned over and whispered in his ear.

The dying child who was Eric tipped onto his back, eyes going dull as he gazed up at the strange sky. His hand reached up as though to catch one of the few remaining stars. Or grasp the handle of a door nobody else could see.

Before the boy's hand fell, the pool shimmered. Marius was lost in the dark of the cave.

He had to get through, it couldn't be too late—

The dark came as windows shuttering. The magic of the blood pool re-formed, shutters opening onto a familiar world. A familiar street. Cuff Street, perpendicular to the Cauldron. A large building with diamond-paned windows, its façade painted black and white, ran down one whole side of the street. The glassblowers' guild had been prosperous before it tragically burned down.

Carts rattled by, not metal monsters. Street vendors hawked fruit, pastries, children's toys and combs. Women haggled at carts. Merchants passed in and out of the guildhall doors, keys jingling and pouches bouncing. There were ladies in finery escorted by servants, and couples promenading.

There was Eric.

No guesswork was needed this time. This was obviously Eric, not much younger than when he and Marius first met. It was more shocking than a strange boy in a strange land, to see a familiar face in surroundings where he didn't belong. Eric, fastidiously clean and frequently advising the book club about scented soaps, was dirty not in the fleeting fashion anyone might be if they took a tumble off a horse into mud, but in a way ingrained over weeks or months. His clothes were rags the lowest of Marius's servants wouldn't have torn up to scrub an outhouse. Eric's lean intelligent face had none of the lingering roundness of childhood. His eyes and cheeks were sunken as graves not properly filled in.

Eric brushed by a couple walking out together. The lady, the type who fluttered her lashes at the Cobra during play intermissions, squeaked with dismay lest his filthy clothes stain her gown. The gentleman made a grand display, sweeping her around in a circle away from the riff-raff.

When Eric was new to court, a few nobles snubbed him. Until Marius gave them the Valerius look.

If Marius had the times correct, right now Marius was at the Tower of Ivory. Perhaps he was kneeling under the lash on the ice cliffs, while Eric starved in the streets of the capital.

The lady giggled. Eric smiled his private smile, strolling on. He'd neatly picked the gentleman's pocket while the man swept his lady aside. Eric snapped open the brocade purse, rolled his eyes to find it empty, tucked it away, and began to sing softly under his breath. One of his awful songs with lyrics that made no sense.

Eric hadn't stopped smiling, but Marius wasn't fooled.

He remembered Eric scribbling energetically over loose pages by candlelight, recalled, under the glaring eyes of a lost city, a dying child's hands scrabbling for a book. *Art is the final consolation.* This song was Eric's attempt to comfort himself.

A middle-aged woman with a laden basket, trundling down the street, turned at the sound of his song. She had wispy fair hair, a timid air, and a dun-coloured gown with a lilac token on the sleeve indicating she was a lesser guildswoman.

"You, boy."

"Ma'am? Got an errand I can help you with?"

She pitched her voice at the level of a guilty secret. "Where are you from?"

"Oh, here and there."

"Did you get here through a . . ."

The woman's shoulders caved in as she lost courage. Eric, automatically reaching out to uncertainty, murmured encouragement.

The woman ventured a whisper. "My late husband used to sing that song. He said he was from Berlin."

The name was meaningless to Marius, but Eric's hand closed on the woman's arm as though she were a floating spar in a shipwreck.

Smile finally reaching his eyes, Eric said, "Sounds like we have a lot to talk about."

The pool flickered with a briefer darkness, a curtain whisked across rather than a shutter closed. The blood window looked inside a small single room with curving wooden walls, as if Eric and the woman lived in a nutshell. Frankly, it was a hovel. Someone had fashioned colourful paper decorations to hang around the hovel, and wind chimes made of metal fragments. Marius knew who.

"I can't believe your man never tried for the Flower, moms." Eric made a meatless mess in a pan over a low fire. "Why not smuggle his way into the palace via a laundry cart? That's a classic for a reason!"

The woman from the street sat at a shabby table smiling at his nonsense, as he tipped more than half the dubious food onto her plate. The sunken shadow of death had vanished from Eric's face. When she brushed the back of her hand against his filled-out cheek, Eric leaned into the touch. Eric habitually reached out to people, but he didn't easily accept overtures. *My mother*, he had called her.

"You don't need the Flower. You have money now, thanks to your investments. You can live a good life."

"It's half your money. You provided the capital." Eric's tone was soft until it turned to steel. "And I intend to."

"There's no way to the palace," the woman warned.

It was no use telling Eric facts. He took them as a challenge set by the universe.

Alarm crept over the woman's face when Eric went quiet. Marius deeply sympathized. Silence on Eric was always alarming. His eyes fixed with determination on the single window in that small house. The window looked across the city to the palace, gold in the setting sun.

In the voice he used when quoting, Eric murmured, "I lead the way when there is no way."

There was the faintest flutter of a shadow on water. Marius's veins tugged, protesting the flow of blood. How much longer could he bleed for this? But he needed to see. When the Oracle retreated he followed, keeping her sharp nails in his palms. In the pool Marius saw morning sun through the leaves of a hawthorn tree, Eric standing underneath.

The guard at the palace gates asked what Eric was doing.

"Climbing high," Eric laughed. "Let's see how far I can go."

He swung into the branches. Boughs swayed and leaves danced with a long-ago wind. The Oracle's pool rippled and cleared. Marius, gasping for breath and certainty, stared up into her haunted face.

"Enough truth now, Marius Valerius. Nobody can bear too much. I drowned in it long ago. What an enterprising young fellow you have there. He causes ripples in more pools than mine."

The Cobra was from another world. That was his truth. What was Marius's? He remembered his allegiances.

"Is he a danger to my country?" Marius demanded. "Is he a danger to my king?"

The Oracle swayed like a tree with shadows for leaves, her veils stained with dried scum from old water as though she'd climbed from a well long ago. "You have a thousand questions, but you are only permitted one answer. You have the truth you wanted. Now decide what to do with that truth."

"What if disaster comes?"

"Disaster will come," the Oracle promised. "Disaster always does. You, however, must go."

Her voice filled the cave with echoes. Her guardians appeared to take him away. Marius could have fought them, could have killed them, but he had made vows.

Marius rode through the mountain pass, headed for the city like wind across the earth. His final desperate bid for clarity had only led to more confusion. His mind was in fragments, every notion a leaf on a tree shaken by strange winds. Rational thought was dashed to the ground and swept away across the hills.

This must have some bearing on the conspiracy with Lady Rahela, but Marius couldn't see how.

He rode through the palace gates to the Cobra's door. Sinad the maidservant tried to stop him entering. She didn't succeed.

At the foot of the stairs, in the grandest court dwelling apart from the palace itself, Marius remembered his sister's only visit to the capital two years ago. The last time he'd seen Caracalla before that, she was nine. At fourteen, she was tall as Valerius men were tall with no idea what to do with her height, all coltish limbs and awkwardness. She was brown-haired and sallow like their mother, visibly terrified at every society gathering, and the dearest and most beautiful girl in Eyam. She cried at the idea of another tea party, begging for different amusements. So Marius brought her and his lady mother to the man everyone said was the most amusing creature in the palace.

Marius's sister clung to his arm as the Golden Cobra descended the curving stairs to receive them. Elaborate golden combs shone in his hair, the designs on the combs hooded cobra heads, the teeth of the combs snake fangs. His face blazed with the same warm welcome as on the first day with Marius, as if he could know someone well, yet be excited to meet them.

Sing-song and soft with delight, he called: "My lady Caracalla."

Caracalla's legs went out from under her. Marius held her up, but couldn't stop his heart sinking to the Cobra's marble floor.

They spent an evening at the theatre. Caracalla stared in silent rapture, and not at the stage. When they were home and Caracalla in bed, Marius's mother suggested Lord Popenjoy might be an excellent match.

Dread overwhelmed Marius for the second time in one evening. "His title is suspect. Nobody knows where he came from."

His mother dropped a sugar cube in her tea with finality. "Does that matter, darling? He moves in the highest society with ease. If his origins are questionable, he's likely to overlook the issue of Valerius heritage. He doesn't seem afraid of you."

In the midst of horror, Marius almost laughed. "He's not."

His lady mother smiled, which was so rare Marius couldn't refuse her. "Since he's your friend, he must be a good man. That's what I want for Caracalla. Someone kind."

Before his mother left, she presented the Cobra with an heirloom orichal dagger, enchantment only shared among family. The whole court recognized the betrothal was official.

Nobody knows where he came from.

Marius did now.

He ascended to the Cobra's receiving room. When the parlour doors opened the Cobra's band started up a jaunty tune. Two women pranced out front and began a dance with shoes that tapped on the floor.

Marius aimed a silver disc at a cymbal with enough force that it spun from under the stunned musician's hands, sending several instruments crashing down before driving its edge into a wall. When a dancer stumbled, Marius caught her in his arms.

"Madam, please take a seat." He dropped her on the conversation sofa.

The dancers exchanged panicked looks. The doors to the Cobra's private chambers burst open with a cascade of gold foil snakes, which the man himself absently shook off his shoulders.

"I'm not in the mood—*Marius?*"

Today's herigaut was thick with bronze as well as gold thread, cinched tight with an elaborate bronze belt. It was a far cry from rags or emblazoned shirts on strange streets. Eric held his head high at all times, but today his jaw was clenched and his dark eyes dangerous as a poorly banked fire. Marius wondered if something had happened.

Eric's face didn't invite inquiry.

Marius folded his arms and made himself look immovable. "I must talk to you."

"I don't have anything to say."

"There's a first."

Eric's lip curled. "I don't think *you'll* have anything interesting to say."

"So you're from another world," said Marius.

The roving glimmer of Eric's gaze froze for an incredibly satisfying moment.

"Guys." His voice went carefully casual. "Lord Marius has had too much to drink. Give us a moment."

The band sidled out, giving Marius wary glances. One singer stopped to tell him he was very strong, which Marius knew already. The Cobra strode to the door to check nobody was listening. Once the spymaster was assured he wasn't being spied on, he turned back to give Marius a nasty look. Then the nasty look was abruptly diverted.

"*Jesus,*" said the Cobra. "What did you do to your hands?"

He clicked his fingers, peremptory, but when Marius surrendered his hands Eric took them gently. He gave a soft exclamation as he saw the wounds from the Oracle's nails.

As always, Eric's priorities were strange. No wonder, from an otherworldly stranger.

"My hands would be healed by now if I hadn't been holding reins."

Eric dropped his hands, turning away. "Sure. Let's pretend that's cool and normal."

Warriors were built to heal fast. Marius shoved away the Oracle's voice saying *throwback*.

"What do you think the Oracle told me about you?"

Eric had been tense since the mention of the other world. Now his shoulders slumped.

"Does it matter if I'm dying in New York by the side of a road or waking up in the gutters of the Cauldron out of my mind with hunger and fear? Either experience would be equally alien to you, *Lord Marius*. As far as you're concerned, I've always been from another world. You were born in a manor. You could heal from being hit by a car. I've never been the main character in any story."

"This isn't a story. This is our lives!"

Eric offered a lopsided, humourless smile. "Maybe it's both."

"In that other world, you were dying. Are you dead?"

Was he a charlatan? Or was he a malicious ghost, puppeting what should be a corpse? There were so many nightmares the Cobra could be.

"I can't be dead," Eric answered. "My mother died trying to get me the Flower of Life or Death. So I have to live, as hard as I can."

"Is that why you did all this?"

The Cobra lifted his chin, eyes glittering defiantly. He'd been glittering defiantly for as long as Marius knew him.

"I did what I must to survive. Then I did many other things because I thought they would be funny, and make me look cool."

Whenever Marius was at his lowest, he went to the Cobra's. Eric always let him in. Once Marius had leaned his head back against the ridiculous sofa and listened to a lullaby-soft song on the gilded piano, pretending to sleep. The Cobra touched his hair, and said, 'Hush.'

If Marius was comforted by lies, what did that make him? A frightened child, a fool, or a traitor?

Trying to work it out, he said slowly, "You were good once. You saved a little girl."

"Look where that got me," Eric retorted. "Now I save myself. What can you do when the story says you don't matter? I have to matter to myself."

"What about Lady Rahela?"

Eric hesitated. "She matters to me too."

Why should she? Marius said sharply, "I've known her for years. She isn't from another world. She's no innocent."

Eric wheeled from the window.

"Do only innocents deserve to be saved? Then put me down for the long list of the damned." To Marius's amazement, Eric's voice broke. He covered his face with his arm. "God, I *cannot* do this tonight. I searched across the palace for you while you were hunting down my secrets."

It was always Marius going to him. He'd never looked for Marius before. Marius's gaze trained on a flying sleeve, seeing a stain on the gold.

"Is that blood?" His own ran cold. Who did he have to kill?

"It isn't my blood," Eric said in a raw, muffled voice. "Somebody died. I had to watch his body get thrown in the ravine."

"Who died?"

"A gutter brat," spat Eric.

Marius was relieved before he remembered the vision of Eric starving in the Cauldron. It had always seemed tragic that beggars died of cold and hunger in the streets. Eric said tragedies were sorrow given distance.

Now that distance was wrenched away.

In a room that seemed an opulent stage set for a character who never doubted or grieved, Eric might be crying.

"Eric." Marius's voice went rough as he failed to sound gentle. "What can I do?"

The shining curtain of the sleeve fell to reveal not tears but fury.

The Golden Cobra snarled, "Kill the king!"

It was the realization of every dark fear that visited Marius at night, waking in cold grey before dawn to the knowledge the Cobra had power over him, and might ask him to do anything.

The Cobra's lip curled. "I know you won't. You'd rather kill me and my friends. Some lives are worth more than others. So kill me, or leave me alone."

Eric had shown kindness and ended up huddled on a street corner with clotted blood coming from his nose and mouth. He'd lied and lied, constructed an elaborate fantasy of a person and become his own creation. Marius didn't know what he deserved and didn't understand him and didn't understand his own uneasy heart.

If the Cobra had never turned him away, Marius could have killed him. And then, every gathering with no voice calling him over, every night silent. Not because the Cobra was angry, but because the Cobra was dead.

He could have killed him.

Marius picked up an abandoned lute, smashing the glass on the Cobra's display case for the Valerius blade.

"Oh, here we go," Eric muttered beneath the sound of glass breaking.

Marius grasped a golden rope cinching a curtain and wrenched it loose so the curtain fell as if signalling the end of a play. He tied a loop in it, and aimed the rope at the broken case. The rope snagged the blade, bringing it in a wide silver arc across the golden chamber. The dagger landed in the Cobra's hands.

"Come here," Marius commanded, imploring.

When Eric started furiously forward, Marius caught Eric's wrist, holding it in place so the blade rested against his own throat.

"There. You're safe. Talk to me."

Blade between them, Eric stared as if Marius was deranged. "Statistically, how many productive conversations are held at knifepoint?"

"Maybe this will be the first."

He could fix the moment, precise as an arrow in a heart, when Eric lost patience. The Golden Cobra shoved Marius up against the wall with an enchanted knife to his throat.

"You said once that I torment you. Do you *want* to be tormented?" Eric demanded.

The blade was sharp and cold against his skin. Marius was fast and strong, but he might not be fast or strong enough. The Cobra might actually be able to kill him.

It was a novel feeling. Marius tilted his head back against the wall, and smiled. "Try me."

Eric threatened, "Let me tell you something dangerous and true. I'm your worst nightmare. I've read every secret of your heart. I know what happened, that last night in the manor when you were seventeen. I know why you ran to the Ivory Tower. I've always known."

Marius had come home unexpectedly, and found his father in a berserker frenzy. The door to the east wing, the only protection for his mother and small sister, was broken down by his father's men. His father's loyal followers had loyally left a woman and a child to face the duke's murderous fury.

He could still hear his father whispering, over seven years.

"This is divine wrath." Firelight had made the duke's face a twisted golden mask. "You feel it too, boy. I know you do."

None could stand against a Valerius. Nobody else could stop his father. Marius had to do it.

So he picked up a sword, and did it. And he swore to never touch another blade again.

"If you'd ever told me that before," Marius murmured, "that's when I would have killed you."

The blade stung, cold edge and hot blood. If Eric was certain Marius would kill him, here was Eric's chance to kill him first.

The Cobra's eyes gleamed, mocking and cruel. "So eager for my truth, but you can't face yours. Want to know another secret, Marius? I could strip you bare."

He laughed.

"Here's the truth. The blackmail never mattered. I trade in knowledge, so you hate me worse than poison. You don't know me. You don't know Octavian. You don't know Lia. You don't know yourself. You're afraid to know. I'm not the coward of the court, Marius. You are."

It was the worst insult Marius could imagine, and the worst part was he could do nothing but listen, dry-mouthed, pulse a tempest. He was able neither to move nor speak, because he was afraid.

"Time to end this," Eric said gently. "I will not be the blade hanging over your head or the blackthorn branch you lash yourself with. I cannot be either your fated doom or your lost gods."

He stepped back and hurled the knife away with enough force to shatter a stained glass window.

Marius stared into the jagged vacancy where beauty and illumination had been. "What do you want me to do?"

"The right thing!"

What a request from a villain.

"The right thing," Marius shouted back, "is to *kill you*."

Every secret he had learned, every drop of what his father called divine wrath, called him to that end.

They stood breathless, with no defence between them.

Defiant to the end, Eric said, "Then don't come back here unless you're ready to kill. Believe me, Marius Valerius. I was never meant to be part of your story, but I always thought you should be the hero. You have to be one now. Or there are no heroes left."

CHAPTER THIRTY-ONE

The Villainess and the Dread Ravine

The godchild's blood spilled and split the earth where it landed. The ravine was his death wound. Our land was cut off from the continent and drenched in divine blood, but centuries passed and even wonders and monsters became routine. People grew accustomed to living near a wound in the world. Fathoms of darkness down, sullen fires burned in the depths, and whatever moved in faraway shadows couldn't reach the outside world.

Until the Emperor. Until the flames rose, and the dead with them.

Time of Iron, ANONYMOUS

ithin days, the dread ravine called to its master up above once more.

Rae leaned on Octavian's arm as they walked through the Ballroom of Sighs under the mirrored ceiling and across the night-dark floor. Through glass doors she saw the sky torn with silent lightning. Stark lines of violet and burning scarlet sliced through the night.

The blaze made her eyes water. Now she believed the world was real, the edges of every facet cut.

After her collapse, Octavian had admitted in a benevolent manner that he'd been ungentlemanly not to escort Rahela from the room before the throat cutting. He liked the idea of aristocratic ladies needing to be sheltered, even the Harlot of the Tower. Rae did nothing to disillusion him. Being considerate kept him from her bed.

People were still calling Lia his princess. Whenever they did, Octavian's eyes darted to Rae.

They didn't know what the Last Hope might have told Octavian about other worlds, or how much Octavian believed. Rae must play along until the Flower of Life and Death bloomed. Then she was blowing this evil popsicle stand. She didn't know what would happen to Rahela's body when she plucked the flower and stepped through the door to her own world. Rae imagined the body slumping dead, being thrown in the ravine. The story was always supposed to end that way.

Rae had only bought herself a temporary stay of execution.

The price was Key's life.

The king and his wicked prophet walked out onto the balcony to acknowledge the gods' will. Wind blasted from the ravine as though someone had opened a vast oven and was about to shove Rae and Octavian inside. The clouds were dyed black and blue as bruises. Crimson lightning turned the cracked moon into a pool of faintly glowing blood. The ground trembled as if the palace was a treehouse and a giant shook the branches. Columns of smoke rose from the ravine to the sky. The ravine opened wide as a hungry mouth.

Smoke stung Rae's eyes. Tremors made her knees unsteady. This world, turned real, was overpowering.

The palace guards had cast Key away like garbage. The Cobra had only been able to close Key's eyes and watch it happen. Nobody knew how far down the ravine actually went. Perhaps Key's body was still falling. Eyes closed, throat cut open, falling forever.

Key had believed in her so much. From the beginning, she'd planned to betray him.

She couldn't change her last words to him or his last thoughts. Once someone was dead, the world through their eyes ended. She would always be the villain in Key's story.

A red lightning bolt made the masked crown a mirror. For an

instant the king wore a crown dipped in blood. A chorus of apprehensive thanksgiving broke from the crowded balconies overlooking the abyss.

Everyone waited for the god to come. Nobody really believed he would.

Octavian gave the devout throngs a regal wave. His voice sounded troubled. "Your prophecy flies from mouth to mouth faster than crows. The people are frightened. My ministers say to calm the populace I must descend to the depths of the ravine, and claim my imperial power."

He wasn't supposed to climb down for years, not until the whole country was in danger and he must risk his life to save it. But the ravine wasn't meant to yawn and smoke for years, either.

She shuddered to think what that meant for Emer and the Cobra, who had to stay in this world. She'd once felt like the only real thing, but now everyone felt true and precious except herself. Her friends thought it was shock. Rae believed she was getting ready to go home. She had to succeed, after what she'd paid for success.

She was so grateful the flower would bloom tonight. She couldn't bear to stay here a moment longer.

People say, *I'll give anything.* The universe listens. But the universe doesn't listen when you say, *Wait, not that.*

From the depths of the dread ravine, she heard the ghouls. Their cry was coming clearer and closer by the hour.

"*Muh – muh– muh. Master!*"

Rae smiled at Octavian. "They're calling for you. Go to them."

She wished she could ask the original Rahela: Were you doing what you felt you had to? Perhaps wickedness wasn't about how you fell, but where you stood and what you saw from there. Perhaps even the worst villains were doing their best.

Octavian believed what he wanted was the most important thing in the universe. Since he was the hero, he was right. Rae couldn't blame him. She'd spent her whole time in Eyam believing what she wanted mattered more than anybody's life.

Heated whispers rose from the ravine. Cold wrapped her like a shroud.

Rae watched the king's beautiful face outlined against a brilliantly broken sky, and knew one absolute truth.

You will never be the hero to me.

She was constantly tired these days. When Emer woke her from an evening nap, Emer's words made exhaustion vanish like a scared ghost.

"The Flower of Life and Death is blooming. His Majesty invites you to join him in the greenhouse."

The Iron Maid clothed Rae in ivory and blood, and slid the enchanted gauntlet onto her hand. As Rae rose from her dressing table for the last time she gave Emer's shoulder a grateful squeeze.

"If I don't come back," Rae began.

Emer's fists closed as though on invisible axes. "Why would you not come back!"

"If I don't, go to the Cobra."

He said he had a getaway bag ready for when trouble came, and if Emer reached him in time he would take her along.

Emer's face set and she stalked from the room. When Lia came running, Rae realized where Emer had gone.

Lia was flushed and tousled from her rush, hair clean moonlight streaming down her shoulders. "I can go in your place. Octavian won't ask anything of me."

She might be an ice-hearted little schemer, but she was loyal. Cold hearts could still be gold.

Rae shook her head. "Do something else for me. Will you go to the throne room and delay Octavian?"

If Rae could reach the greenhouse before the king, she would never have to see him again.

Lia nodded, worried but trusting. Rae did the winding snake gesture to make her smile.

Her stepsister brightened. "Vipers together."

"Vipers together," Rae promised.

Together wouldn't last. Rae was leaving. She wouldn't be there to help when Octavian unlocked his full power. Marius wouldn't help Lia either. Rae had ruined that too.

It would be Lia and the Emperor, alone. Rae shivered as she raced across the battlements under the broken blood moon.

The ravine yawned ever wider, rising fires glowing like lava. The silvery evening sky shimmered with heat haze, and thunder was an avalanche in the clouds. The pounding of Rae's heart and head seemed one terrible drumbeat. The world trembled, waiting for its Emperor.

Lia still shone like the last star in the dark. With Rae's interference ended, surely the Emperor would come to love her the way he had once upon a tale. In Rae's opinion, Lia was easy to love.

A shadow moved towards her on the battlements. Rae's heart tripped and fell with a crash.

Out of the dark walked Prime Minister Pio, hands clasped behind his back. Rae abruptly recalled the man might be plotting her death. At the critical moment in books, the victim always saw their death in the murderer's eyes. Rae couldn't be sure if she saw her death in his eyes. What did death look like, exactly?

Instead of pushing Rae off the battlements, the prime minister inclined his head.

"Return to your bedchamber. The king cannot attend your evening of botany admiration."

"Pity. Just in case, I'll wait for him in the greenhouse."

When Rae tried to get past, Pio barred her way.

"Can't you hear the drums!"

Abruptly, Rae realized she'd been a fool again. The pounding in her ears wasn't her heart or her head. The shaking of the earth came from all sides.

"It's the raiders," Rae whispered.

Everything was happening faster than it should. Why not this too? The balconies were crowded with worshippers praying and singing. The guards weren't at their posts, and let a party of raiders slip through. Just like in the book.

Except that couldn't be right.

From the battlements, Rae could see the city streets seethe with panic.

"Tagar's army is within our walls. Why do you seem so surprised, Lady Rahela?" Pio asked thinly. "Surely you knew they were coming."

"I told Octavian how to stop both battles!" Rae snarled. "I said to keep the guards at their posts when the ravine opened. I said to set a watch on the Tears of the Dead River, that one day years from now the raider army would get behind our walls. Octavian didn't listen!"

This time, she hadn't lied or cheated. She had predicted the future, clearly and precisely, in a genuine effort to save lives and avoid disaster. Only the powerful man she'd told hadn't believed her, and now the city might fall.

Pio's eyebrows climbed high as intrepid hikers while she spoke. "It's unfortunate His Majesty didn't post the guards, but let us not pretend you had no hand in this."

"I didn't!" Rae protested. "When I read the future ... in the stars ... the princess met a band of raiders on her way home. The raiders attacked the city when the populace was on their balconies witnessing the ravine, but it was only a small group. The army comes after we're prepared. Why would the army come now? This isn't meant to happen yet!"

"*Somebody* sent Princess Vasilisa home with a story about her brother dying," said Pio. "The princess sent a message on beforehand. An investigation proved their king was being poisoned. Do you think anyone in Tagar believes in prophecy? They think *we* poisoned him. They are retaliating against what they believe was our attack. As the princess came home, she didn't meet a band of raiders. She met her brother's army. Our guards were at the balconies watching the ravine, not their posts. The raiders slipped in through the rivers. The Ice King's troops are storming our capital."

On the wind Rae heard the crash of a thousand feet and the clash of a thousand weapons. Outside the palace walls, she heard a scream.

In the book, the Ice King died young. Here, the princess had gone home to save her brother. Because of Rae, Ivor lived. Ivor the Heartless, whose metal horrors could fight even the dead.

Rae had called doom down upon them all.

Prime Minister Pio advanced. She didn't know if he meant to drag her back to her chamber, or strangle her with his bare hands. Either way, he barred the way to the flower and her only chance to live.

"This is war, Lady Rahela. It's your fault."

CHAPTER THIRTY-TWO

The Villainess in the Greenhouse of Good and Evil

Lia's body was fastened to her throne with silver thread. Her corpse made the most beautiful puppet.

The Emperor said, "She believed goodness was real, friends could be trusted, and love might be true. She died because she was wrong."

Time of Iron, ANONYMOUS

 ae used her gauntleted hand to shove the prime minister aside, racing desperately down the flight of the stairs to the greenhouse. There was peace here, the leaf-hushed quiet found in deep forests, the air made close, warm and fragrant by green, growing things. There was life here, though it might be crushed. Thick stone walls muffled the sound of oncoming troops and the surge of ravine fires, but the great glass windows shook with the onslaught of a world tearing itself to pieces.

Rae ran until she saw the arch of the stalk bearing the Flower of Life and Death. The Flower had emerged from its green bud like a delicate winged creature from its egg. The outermost petals were moon-white and gorgeously insubstantial, a fringe of Valenciennes lace surrounding a red so dark it was almost black, shading to lilac, to primrose, and finally to the innermost row of petals still unfurling.

When Rae started forward, reaching to pluck the flower, a hand clamped on her wrist. Pio forced her gauntleted fist down by her side.

"This is no time for your tricks!"

"Let me go and you'll never have to see my trickster face again," Rae promised.

"I merely want you safe in your chambers!"

"Why? I know you hate me. You sent ghouls and assassins after me."

"I certainly did not. I'm a politician," Pio snapped. "We kill people through making laws, not breaking them."

"It must have been you!"

"Actually, he argued against sending the assassins. He was overruled."

The new voice was calm with the assurance given by absolute authority. A shadow emerged from under the spreading petals of the Flower of Life and Death. The rays of the blood moon, streaming cold and stained through the greenhouse windows, struck the silver of his gauntlets.

"All bow before the crown," said King Octavianus.

For a long moment, Rae stared at his face, the masked crown pushed back to reveal brilliant green eyes. A guard stood at a respectful distance behind him. Only one. Every man who might be spared must have joined battle against the raiders. Octavian wore full battle regalia, bronze breastplate gleaming, cape bright as the stars lost behind bruised clouds. Her favourite character, and he was nothing but this.

"My beautiful, treacherous lady. I sent assassins and ghouls to test your claims you could tell the future. Could anybody else truly command the royal assassins or drag up my dead from my ravine? How did you imagine it was anyone but me?"

Because she trusted the Emperor.

Octavian had let the ghouls loose and killed a dozen women under his protection. And he'd sent assassins on the night of the ball, not to test if she could tell the future, but because he was having a jealous fit about her dance with the Cobra. He was a spoiled, selfish child.

"You're right." Rae stared him down. "I should have known."

Octavian's charming face darkened. "You used your new powers of prophecy to hoodwink the palace. You seduced the Cobra, and the Cobra's man seduced the princess. You saw with your witchcraft that the King of Tagar was being poisoned. You framed me as you once framed your stepsister. You used the princess to incite the Ice King's wrath, and you planned to steal the Flower of Life and Death to cure him when he stormed the capital. This is a plot to betray our country and marry the Ice King. You were determined to get your revenge, and be a queen. You never will. Kneel to me."

All the pieces fitted together. It sounded a lot more plausible than Rae being a dying traveller from another world, who needed the flower for herself.

Here came the conclusion to her misery and guilt. Villains always did come to a bad end. She might as well face hers with courage.

Rae curled her lip. "You aren't worth kneeling for."

Octavian's hand moved to the hilt of a new sword. This hilt wasn't shaped like a snake. She wondered what he'd done with the other. Thrown it away, perhaps, as he would throw her away.

Her head would be the first revenge the Emperor took against his enemies.

"I feel the ravine's power burning in my blood," Octavian promised. "I will be glorious and terrible, and you will finally be sorry."

A pointed cough sounded. Pio gave his king rather a cold look. "We don't have time for this, Your Majesty. General Nemeth leads the men against Tagar's troops, but their numbers are greater than ours. Though beacon fires have been lit, reinforcements cannot arrive tonight. We need your strength."

"I am already strong!" Octavian snarled. "I'll show you. I'll show *her*. She's the rot at the heart of my court. She even corrupted the pearl of the world."

He stared at Rae with furious contempt.

"I saw through Lia's treacherous attempts to delay me so you could steal the flower. I have her under watch in the throne room. Guard! Keep Lady Rahela in the greenhouse."

The Flower of Life and Death bloomed into incandescent fullness,

Octavian captured under its spotlight. The charming prince his court had idolized, the heroine's true love.

"Evil is always defeated in the end. I will drag Lia here and have her executed before your eyes."

Before Rae could respond, the king swept off with his shining cape and sword, to be the hero of the story. His prime minister followed, with an air that suggested he was starting a migraine. She didn't watch them go.

Every outstretched petal on the Flower caught light like a display of jewels. Pollen danced in the air, grains of sparkling brightness surrounding the flower in a radiant halo. The Flower of Life and Death's heart was luminous silver and gold.

Rae aimed a sultry pout at the guard.

"Let me confess my sin. I carry a knife strapped to the inside of my thigh, but it won't be any use against a big strong man like you. Should I remove the knife myself, or will you do it for me?"

His eyes crossed and his sword lowered a fraction. That was all Rae needed.

When she moved, he let her. The villainess didn't slide up her skirts or produce a blade. She reached up and plucked the Flower of Life and Death.

The flower felt cool in her hand as water in the mouth when she was parched, heavy like carrying her sister as a child and knowing she bore the weight of something precious. She held victory in the palm of her hand. A sound came, faint as a page turning or a pen scratching.

Rae turned and saw a doorway forming. One line of light, then another, was superimposed on the deep dark background of leaves. Bright brushstrokes made on canvas, or cracks opening in a world. Until the door handle hung before her, golden as a ripe apple.

She took a deep breath of the air issuing from the other side. The air smelled sweet as the blossoms in her mother's yard, sweet as a forbidden apple. The light around the door shone like a grail.

All Rae had to do was open the door.

All she had to do was forget Lia trapped in the throne room waiting for death. Forget her friends, trapped in a city at war. She would have everything she wanted, and to hell with anyone else. She would be just like the king.

If she turned the handle, she would live.

Rae reached out with her free hand, and turned the handle. She let the door swing open and the light shine through.

Just a little.

The question was, how did she want to live?

She whispered into the light, "I swear I'll come back. If I can."

On the cusp of hearing, she heard a response. It sounded like her name. It sounded like her sister.

The Flower bloomed for one night. There were hours of night left still that Rae could use before she escaped. Rae turned her back on the door for now, slipped the flower away for safekeeping, and beckoned the dazed guard. "Want to know your future?"

Real alarm touched the poor man's face. On this night of sacred storms and oncoming death, people were inclined to believe in prophecy.

Soothsayer, oracle, witch of legend, Rae let her eyes widen and her voice drop low. "I see your fate. It's terrible."

She punched the guard in the head with her magic-armoured fist. He slid to the floor with a sad long whimper like a deflating balloon.

Rae made an apologetic face. "Told you it wasn't good."

She was still standing over the fallen guard when she heard a crash, and realized the palace gates had fallen.

Rae stooped to steal the guard's sword, then spun and ran, ivory and blood skirts sweeping the stairs, racing along the battlements beside the seething revolt of the ravine.

She found King Octavian standing on the battlements. His living subjects chanted on the balconies, encouraging him to descend and rise to scourge their enemy. His dead army called for him from the abyss. Courtiers clustered about him, including the prime minister, urgently advising.

Octavian wasn't listening to any of it. Nor was he rushing to execute Lia.

He stared into the ravine, red light flickering on the quiver of his mouth. In that moment Rae knew he was afraid. She was wickedly glad.

The First Duke, who had once been the great god, was waiting in that abyss. Rae knew the Emperor would win the battle against his father. But oh, she hoped it would hurt first.

"Hear my last prophecy, Your Majesty!"

The purr of her voice was a roar. She began her villainous stalk towards him.

He had no guards left. The courtiers around the king retreated, in fear of the future.

"You will fall a long, long way. The dead are waiting for you, and a man more terrifying than the dead."

Octavian trembled. Before all the king's ministers, the treacherous Beauty Dipped In Blood lunged.

"When you finish falling," hissed Rae. "Tell him I sent you."

With all her might and stolen magic, she shoved the king off the battlements and down into the dread ravine.

The faithful of the palace broke off their chants and cried out as their king fell. The city witnessed their last king-in-waiting plummet, a ruler one moment, and the next nothing but a dark outline delineated against consuming fire.

Then he was gone.

The abyss screamed as if suffering the pangs of birth. The heavens opened and hell rained down. What fell from the bruise-coloured clouds looked like snow, but the snowflakes were grey and burned when they landed on Rae's shoulders. The sky wept ash. Pillars of smoke and flame struck the surging clouds, forming a dark shape that cast a vast shadow from the palace to the mountains. It was the shadow of a crowned man.

CHAPTER THIRTY-THREE

The End for the Golden Cobra

No ordinary man could have crossed the distance with
a mortal wound, but none could describe the Last
Hope as ordinary. By the time he reached the hawthorn
tree, even his great strength was failing.

He had saved Lady Lia. Was that enough to wipe
away the blood on his conscience?

Summer was gone, it was dark, and Marius was tired.

The Cobra had been so surprised to die. In his dying
moments, he looked young as the boy Marius had met
under the hawthorn tree.

As Marius Valerius's vision dimmed that was what he
saw. The first look, and the last.

The sun rose, but the Last Hope never witnessed its
light. As the storm raged and the city burned, he died
in the dark beneath a hawthorn tree. Rain slid through
the leaves in silver lines, and fell on his cold face
like tears.

Time of Iron, ANONYMOUS

Battle raged outside the palace walls. Marius Valerius had
received his king's command.

When Octavian strode into the library to announce
the raiders were attacking, it felt like a reverse avalanche. Stone upon

stone tumbling off his chest, finally letting him breathe. Marius was made for war.

Scouts were sent, maps unrolled, and Captain Diarmat brought in to consult on the situation. Marius ordered men sent to every palace gate. From the sound without, raiders were trying to break through at several points, and there were already men within the walls trying to let their comrades in. Once one gate was breached, they would flood through. The flood must be beaten back.

He wanted to be outside fighting, but recalled his duty. "Tell me your will, sire."

Gilded by the fires of burning buildings beyond the palace walls, Octavian's profile had looked carved in gold. Only the faintest glint of red sparks spoiled the image.

"My Valerius general. Find Nemeth, and take command. You must lead my army into battle. First, I have business with the traitors who sold us to Tagar. Then I must descend into the abyss and claim my birthright. Fear nothing. I will return with lightning in my hands and the dead at my back."

All through their boyhood Marius always knew Octavian needed someone to believe in him. Marius always wanted to. *Fear nothing,* his king had said. A good man obeyed his king.

I'm not the coward of the court. You are, a voice echoed in his mind, but that was wickedness leading him astray.

"Before you take command, you must do one last thing to prove yourself to me."

Marius had bowed. "Sire, anything."

"Bring me the Cobra's head," commanded his king.

With that, Octavian had departed.

Marius's course was clear. Octavian might have promised to leave the Cobra's fate to Marius in peacetime, but this was war. The Cobra was a liar and a traitor, a criminal corrupted by dark magic. Even if he were noble, his sins called for immediate execution, and he wasn't noble.

Days ago, Marius had gone to Octavian with the Oracle's truth.

Octavian had leaned forward avidly in his throne. "Is the Cobra a corrupt noble of Eyam, or a spy sent by our enemies?"

"He began his life in Eyam on the streets of the Cauldron," Marius began, and the king cut him off.

"So he's riff-raff from the streets. He can't matter at all, and you wasted the Oracle's answer on him. Pity."

Marius's mouth closed on his tale of other worlds. "Yes."

Oh, the pity of it. But his king was right. By any measurement Marius knew, the Cobra was worth nothing. Disobedience meant damnation and dishonour.

Marius should try and do what was right.

"Captain," Marius said quietly. "In the Room of Memory and Bone, set by the memorial of the God-child, is a secret passage into the city. Send men you trust through to hold off the raiders. The palace is not all that needs defending. Our people must be protected."

Diarmat left to execute his orders.

Fire painted the night. The battle raged beyond the palace walls, but the library was quiet. Years ago, Marius had hung his ancestral sword on the library wall. Starving for Blood was the sword's name, and it had drunk no blood in years. Not since the heir gave up war training and knelt on the ice outside the Ivory Tower, swearing he would be a scholar.

Now Marius stood by the hearth listening to the chaos, reflecting the painful turmoil in his own heart. Across seven years, he heard a child screaming. *Deliver me from the monster I might be. Send help, send salvation. Lost gods, find me.* Moonshine and firelight twined in shimmering red and silver ribbons on the bared blade.

At last the Last Hope broke his vow, and took down his sword.

As Marius raced towards the Cobra's manor, the palace gates crashed down. At the noise, Marius's step checked.

He had watched the raiders from the library windows, blood burning for the kill, yet knowing strategy won wars, not strength. Tagar's army was made up of two distinctly different factions. There was no cavalry, only a vast quantity of footsoldiers and bowmen. The footsoldiers were dressed in furs, leather and clanking chains, and they shouted war cries not only to heat their blood but to indicate their position to each other. Smoke eddied through the streets, fire-light edging Marius's vision, but these men were not butchering and burning at random.

He'd seen the movements of their own forces through the city. Commander General Nemeth was flinging troops at the raiders to combat their sheer volume. He'd missed that it wasn't only the Tagar numbers which made them a serious threat.

"The raiders on the ground have a leader," Marius told his captain. "A leader on the front lines, not behind them. Watch how they move, they're following someone." He tilted his head. "Look above to see a different story."

Bowmen, silent and grey-hooded, glided over the rooftops. No pattern or discipline could be discerned in their movements, each finding the position that suited them best. For some, that position was a place of safety in the shadows.

"They don't have a leader, or if they do, they don't trust him," said Marius. "Send men to the rooftops, and—"

Raiders spilled from the broken east gate in an unchecked flood. Where were the king's men who should be on guard here?

"Go," Marius snapped at Diarmat. "Spread the word. Gather our archers, gather pitch and stones. The Tagar army has a weak point. We must strike at it. Lead the soldiers, protect the people, and if you can, come find me."

He waited until the captain was safely gone, then let his control slip. He dared only let it loose by a fraction, as if he held a rein in bloodied hands. The rein might fly from his grip at any moment.

Seeing Marius posed a real threat, raiders pressed in on every side. The Tagar army had well-trained soldiers, strong and brave. It wasn't enough to save them.

Their end was brutal, swift, and messy. Marius barely stopped himself from stabbing a guard of Eyam in the back. He blinked, lashes heavy with blood, and realized how far from the east gate he had come.

On sheer instinct alone, Marius had moved towards the Cobra's manor. The king's men shouldn't be here.

Unless Octavian had sent a strike team to make doubly sure the Cobra died. Unless the king thought the Golden Cobra was that dangerous.

Maybe he was.

Marius hesitated another instant. Then he ran, faster than any ordinary man could. Faster than he had ever run before in his life, except once.

The streets roiled with raiders, soldiers and the terrified citizens of Themesvar. An ice raider made the mistake of attacking a pot boy cowering against a wall while in Marius's line of sight. The raider clawed at Marius's collar and sleeves, gurgling on blood as he died. Marius tore away his own encumbering sleeves, using them to wipe his eyes.

The Cobra's doors had been reduced to splinters, the gold handles already stolen. Footsteps marked in blood led up the grand staircase. Marius ran into the Cobra's parlour.

Soldiers had no time for hesitation or emotion. The Cobra wasn't in his parlour, but other men were. Marius paused to clean his sword on the golden curtains, before heading into the inner chamber. A magically reinforced door that could only be opened with an enchanted key blocked his path. He broke it down.

The Cobra was in his bedroom, hauling a canvas bag, in the process of climbing out a window. He grimaced when he saw Marius.

"I was just leaving. I have a getaway bag. I did my hair in my getaway bun."

He offered Marius a tentative smile. Marius didn't smile back.

"Can't you let me go?" the Cobra asked, without much hope.

Marius said, "I can't."

Eric's gaze slid over to the horizon, buildings burning against the night. Calculation crossed his expressive face, measuring the drop from the window and the likelihood of escape. Marius caught the Cobra's eye and shook his head. There was no chance.

Eric sighed and eased the getaway bag off his shoulder, leaning back against the windowsill with an indolent air. His act wasn't as good as usual, since he was nervous. Marius crossed the lavish, frivolous chamber, and faced the Golden Cobra with his sword in hand.

After a pause, Eric raised an eyebrow. "If you've finally come to a decision? Get it over with."

"This is a solemn moment for me," Marius snapped.

Annoyance flickered across Eric's face, brief as a candle flame or a swinging gold chain. The flash of irritation was gone as soon as seen, replaced with what lay behind the many shows.

Quiet and kind, Eric said, "Don't be hard on yourself later, Marius. If it had to happen, I'm glad it was you."

He turned his head, baring his throat. The light from burning buildings sparked on the tiny gold hoop in his ear. Even running for his life, the Cobra had stopped for his contraband jewellery.

Marius slid to his knees, and set the blade against his own breast. Above him, Eric recoiled in a shocked-back movement.

"Marius, stop!"

Eric always had to be difficult. It was all right. Marius had made up his mind.

This would have been easier if he had a dagger. He slashed a long line on the skin below his collarbone, and felt the hot blood spill.

"'First cut for gods lost in the sky, second for fiends in the abyss. Third cut for me, Marius Valerius. Fourth cut for you, Eric Mitchell. By the sword, I swear to be loyal and true.'"

"You've *got* to be kidding me," whispered the Cobra.

He should know Marius never made jokes. Marius shot the Cobra an exasperated glance, remained at the Cobra's feet, and completed his vow.

"'I swear to love all you love, and hate all you hate. You will feel no rain, as I will be a shelter for you. You will feel no hunger or thirst while I have food to give or wine in my cup. When my name is in your mouth, I will always answer, and your name will be my call to arms. I will ever be a shield for your back, and the story told between us will be true. Everything agreed between us, I will carry out, for yours is the will I have chosen.'"

A last slash, and it was done. He was dishonoured and damned. Marius bowed his head.

The next minute strong hands closed around his arms, pulling him to his feet.

"Get up right now, I think I'm having a panic attack!" Once he was standing, Eric shoved him. "Explain."

"The blood oath is the most solemn thing between sky and abyss. It is the sword that cannot be broken, the word that cannot be unspoken. It is placing your shivering soul into someone's palm, and trusting they will not clench their fist. The oath says for all my days, your life is dearer than my life, and if I can be true to you past death, I will. Anybody who makes this oath lightly is lost."

Eric gave a strange breathless laugh. "Trust me, that I know. What does that *mean*? Do you want to be—warriors in arms?"

"Have your skills in war recently dramatically improved?"

Eric laughed again. This time, it sounded more real. "Are we chivalry bros? I haven't even read the books of chivalry! I don't think I'll agree with them."

"You should read them," said Marius. "I look forward to disagreeing with you."

"What are you planning to do?"

Marius hesitated. "Care for you."

Eric made an expansive and explosive gesture, ending with a hand clawing through his getaway bun. "Give me a second, hang on a minute. I thought the plot was going somewhere completely different."

The city was being invaded, but Eric had asked for time, so Marius would give him time. Marius dismissed the mention of a plot. Somebody at court was always plotting something.

After a moment, Eric lifted his head, a wicked gleam lighting his eye.

"You'll care for me? Thank you, oh gracious lord," Eric purred. "Will you care for my brothel?"

The sky outside the windows went white. Marius thought that was the effect being profoundly scandalized had on his vision, before he realized another explosion of fiendish magic was tearing the world apart.

"Is now the time to discuss—that!"

"Yes!" Eric snapped. "Out in the burning city is a large building full of vulnerable people under my protection. Will you help me?"

Put that way, the matter required urgent attention.

"I will."

"You will?" Eric repeated blankly.

"I took vows," Marius reminded him, vexed. "You were there. It just happened."

The Cobra employed the deep breaths he used to calm himself. The calming breaths went on for longer than usual. "Cool, cool, cool. Let's go out the window, I think soldiers stormed the house."

"I dealt with that."

Octavian had sent a strike force to capture the Cobra. The king doubted Marius's loyalties. He was right to doubt.

Octavian had broken his word first, but that didn't excuse Marius breaking his. Oath breaking was unforgivable. Marius had done it anyway.

Eric shook his head, rueful. "I took too long to run. I was waiting for someone."

"Lady Rahela?" Marius asked sharply. "Lady Lia?"

The snake, or her snake sister?

"Emer," said Eric.

"Rahela's *maid*?"

"How do you know her name!"

"I know fifteen servants' names now." Marius had been asking around.

After a wide-eyed pause, Eric shouldered his bag and headed out of his inner chambers. Marius followed, but the Cobra froze in the middle of the parlour.

"*Marius Valerius!* Why are there twenty dead men in my salon?"

This wasn't an efficient escape from a war-torn city. Why must Eric waste time with questions that had obvious answers?

"They got in my way."

The strike force was there to execute the Cobra. It was Eric's life or theirs.

Eric's gaze flitted from one bloodied corpse to the next, lingering on a young soldier's torn body hurled down on his ripped sofa cushions. Marius groped for understanding. Eric liked things to be pretty. Was he upset about his parlour being a wreck?

Uncertain, Marius righted a chair. He searched across the room and saw Eric leaning forward to close the dead soldier's eyes.

Understanding flooded back, cold as horror. Marius sat, covering his face with his free hand. Battle fury was peace to him. It felt good to be mindless and desperate to kill. Marius had forgotten murdering people should matter.

A hand settled on the back of Marius's neck, cool with rings. Marius looked up, hopeful.

Yours is the will I have chosen.

"Come with me," Eric said steadily. "I know the way."

Marius hadn't known being damned and dishonoured would be such a relief.

Outside the palace, raiders were looting and killing in the streets. The Golden Brothel shone bright as a sun nesting in the city, lit by the fires of war. Heading towards the brilliant dome, they were intercepted by a squadron of ice raiders. Marius glanced at the Cobra.

Eric braced his shoulders to take on a great weight. "Kill."

The sword felt good in Marius's hand, like freedom after years of living bound.

Three bloody seconds later, the Cobra commanded, "Stop."

They moved on.

The lowering clouds were dyed scarlet as if the sky bled. As they made their way through the outer city, Marius saw people kneel in gutters that ran red, praying.

Those Marius had rescued from the raiders followed them. Others noticed the Cobra, the darling of the commons. By the time they reached the brothel there was a long line.

On the street of the Golden Brothel, a red-headed woman threw herself into Eric's arms. She kissed him full on the mouth and clung to Eric's jerkin with her fists gone white.

"Marius," said Eric. "Amelia. Amelia, Marius. You made shocking advances to him in a bar where he was hunting me down for my crimes?"

Amelia nodded impatiently. "What took you so long?"

"A burly lunatic broke into my bedchamber and vowed to protect me."

"I wish that would happen to me." Amelia cast her sparkling gaze on Marius, who receded behind Eric with dignity. "Hello again. You the burly lunatic?"

"I wouldn't characterize myself in that fashion, no."

Amelia laughed. "I love how he talks like a book on manners."

"I know," said Eric, amused. "Always in a whole different genre to everyone else."

Amelia gave Eric a glance of total incomprehension, which Marius felt was more than fair. "You prattle nonsense whenever you're overset."

"The sky is splintering like a mirror with evil red strobe lights over our heads. I can't be the only one who finds that disturbing!"

Eric pointed upward. The sky trembled as though it were a dew-heavy spiderweb touched by a giant's fingertip.

Streets away, a plaintive young voice sang. *"Oh how we adore you, we are waiting for you . . ."*

Steady as the drums of war, issuing from darkened houses and the dust of unloved graves, a chant rose across the city.

"The child of gods is dead and grown
He is coming, he is coming for his throne!"

This land had waited a long time for its Emperor. Marius recalled his father talking of divine wrath.

Marius told Eric, "You're not the only one. But duty calls."

"Duty doesn't know my name," Eric claimed, but he sighed and headed for the Golden Brothel. Marius followed. So did Amelia. The woman had a name from the upper echelons of nobility: Marius couldn't understand why she was dressed and painted so. He'd ask Eric later.

For now, Eric seemed busy. The doors of the Golden Brothel were figured prettily with carvings: birds flying from open cages to trees. Eric gave a complicated series of knocks, and Marius heard the sounds of bolts being drawn back.

Eric shoved open the doors. "Daddy's home!"

"He says that every time," reported Amelia. "We have tried to stop him."

The doors opened into a grand hall filled with people. A little girl ran to the Cobra, who swung her into his arms and returned her to a silver-haired couple who appeared to be her aged grandparents.

"I am far from an expert on brothels," said Marius, "but this doesn't seem right at all."

The Cobra coughed. "Let's say you had information about tragedies certain to occur in the future. Dramatic massacres that would lead to massed heaps of unnamed peasants. Nobody would notice if you scooped a few out of the heap." Eric misinterpreted Marius's stare. He snapped defensively, "*Somebody* had to save refugees from the plot."

"Are you also a prophet?"

"Have you ever seen a more unlikely candidate for holiness than me!"

Marius nodded acknowledgement of this point.

The Cobra continued, "So you're a lord of suspicious origin and even more suspicious character. You require a place to stash people out of the way."

"Hence you built a *giant golden brothel*?"

"It made sense at the time!" Eric glared. "Some people here do entertain guests for a price. Amelia runs that side business."

"It's very profitable," Amelia contributed. "Especially as he lets me keep all the profits."

"Because I'm not a pimp," Eric said shortly. "I use the brothel as a cover for the real business."

Marius thought of Eric's rooms, his plays, even his sleeves. "'Give 'em the old razzle dazzle'?"

The words sounded strange coming from Marius's mouth. Maybe Eric thought so too. It made him smile briefly, in the midst of looking extremely worried.

"Nobody has questions about a Golden Brothel. The answer's in the name."

Eric turned away, calling for everyone to grab their things. Red-haired Amelia caught Marius's eye.

Marius hesitated. "It's not . . . normal to pretend you run a golden den of sin, is it?"

Amelia shook her head. "He's having the most flamboyant and prolonged descent into madness I ever saw. But it says a lot about a man, when the form his madness takes is saving lives."

Marius nodded thoughtfully, and withdrew to help people gather their belongings. Several paled when they recognized the Valerius. Marius left them alone. They didn't need to be any more afraid.

The walls shook with the passage of soldiers and the rising storm. A teenage boy was slipping golden candlesticks into his bag. The Cobra helped him get one down from a high shelf.

The Golden Brothel, the treasure chest of the city. The wicked marquis's hoard was the lives of those discounted as worthless.

Isn't character who you are when nobody is there to see you?

"Oh," said Marius.

Eric noted Marius's gaze. His own eyes went wide with new horror.

"Don't give me that look! Stop right now! I *cannot* believe one of the main characters found out about my well-hidden heart of gold. I'm going to die. I'll get a whole touching death scene. I'll have to think of something witty to say. You'll be sad for about twenty pages before Lia – or your new love interest, I guess – heals your wounded heart with her sweet words. You were always going to be the death of me. You'd better be sad for at least twenty pages!"

Marius understood Eric was frightened, but he didn't feel it had been well judged to take actual hallucinogens to cope with the situation.

No, it was only natural. Eric was a man of courage, but he hadn't received any martial training. The debauched palace lifestyle had made him skittish as a high-bred horse.

"You're not making any sense," said Marius, "I have no interest in ever loving Lady Lia. I—"

Eric put a hand over his mouth.

"Please do not attract the attention of the narrative. Let's escape the burning city with a train of terrified refugees in a low-key way. In a way that should be told in a paragraph. Better yet, a footnote. If you think of any dramatic speeches, keep them to yourself."

He lowered his hand. Marius took this as permission to speak again. "Eric—"

"Maybe I'm a library, because all I want is *quiet*! I need to work out where to bring these people."

"I thought you had a getaway plan?" Marius reminded him. "You have a getaway bag."

One side of the canvas bag had got splashed with blood in the streets.

"I do have a getaway plan! For myself. I have faraway boltholes where I could live out my life in—"

"Humble repentance," murmured Marius. Often he'd dreamed of a place where he could rest and pray.

Eric scoffed. "Have you met me! Luxurious dens where I could live a life of quietly sinful decadence. I had carts to take these people away at the first sign of trouble. They should already be gone."

That was why Eric had raced here the first chance he got? Marius regarded the Cobra with fascination. Was this how people felt watching plays? Marius was most entertained.

"You thought you'd abandon them?" Marius laughed. "Eric. Have *you* met you?"

Eric regarded him with loathing. "Focus instead of making cryptic remarks! I can't stand characters who make cryptic remarks. They're never helpful. Can you be helpful?"

"I can try. Let's take your people to my manor."

For once the Cobra was shocked silent. Outside, fires raged. Eric's eyes were dark and still as the night between the mountains and the manor.

"It might be a good idea," Eric told him softly. "Things go wrong at the manor. Trouble is coming for your sister. Perhaps I could help. But can you bear going back?"

Marius didn't ask how the Cobra knew. Marius couldn't fathom this strange creature from a strange world.

But Marius could take a leap of faith.

He said, "Come home with me."

The refugees from the Golden Brothel made room in their carts for those who had followed Marius and the Cobra through the streets. Somewhat to his surprise Marius's personal guards were still at their posts at the stables, and seemed relieved to receive orders. Marius got as many people mounted as possible.

The Cobra got upset Marius's stable was entirely warhorses. He worried over the war steeds having fangs. Apparently Eric expected people to ride to war on vegetarian horses.

"You saw this horse born," Marius reminded him. "I told you his bloodline could find their way anywhere. You named him."

"That was a joke," said Eric.

Marius didn't see what was humorous. He'd thought it was a nice name.

The Cobra stared at the expanse of the warhorse's arched neck, up to the rolling eyes. "So this is my noble steed, Google Maps?"

Firelight painted the stable red. A simmering moan rose like wind across the city.

"Hurry!" Amelia was handling her steed competently.

Marius reined in his mount. "Ride with me, if you want."

One of the Cobra's people hesitated in the doorway. "My lord—"

He was cut off by a man blundering past in a rush of expensive fabric and panic. The strange minister from the ballroom staggered towards them.

He gasped, "Thank the lost gods there are some of our kind still alive."

Eric frowned. "What do you mean, *our kind*?"

As if in answer, a pack of ghouls crashed through the stable wall. Blank-faced, eyes streaming black tears, they swallowed Lord Zoltan in a dead sea. Blood splashed on the golden hay.

Marius rode for Eric, but Eric was already swinging himself into the warhorse's saddle. He shouted at the carts to get moving. The wheels picked up speed slowly through muck and blood. The sound of marching footsteps echoed past the broken walls. A girl in her teens, no older than Marius's sister and looking thoroughly overwhelmed, gave a faint sobbing cry.

"My family motto is 'Honour in my heart, death in my hand'."

Marius reined in his horse so he could shield the girl, and drew his sword. "On my honour, you are safe."

A force in Eyam's black and blue colours turned the corner, led by Captain Diarmat.

Diarmat saluted. "My lord, the dead are killing the raiders, but also a great many of our own people. I've returned for new orders."

"I've committed treason by disobeying a royal command," said Marius. "Thus, I am a villain fleeing the king's justice. The city burns and the dead rise, so I am taking any who wish to leave under my protection. We head towards the Valerius estate. Try to stop me, if you can."

Marius would have to kill these men.

Captain Diarmat nodded. "Fall in, boys."

"I said I disobeyed the king," Marius said sharply. "Are you loyal until death, or not?"

"I am, my lord," the captain replied. "But not to him."

They rode hard down several streets before Marius drew his horse alongside Eric's. By then Eric was handling the horse smoothly. He always caught on fast.

Something worried Marius. "The ghouls made for his lordship specifically, but why?"

As if coming to a dark revelation, Eric murmured, "Eat the rich."

Marius frowned. Ghouls didn't choose victims. Ghouls answered to nobody and nothing but their own hunger.

The dead were meant to obey the Emperor when he rose, but why would Octavian wish for ghouls to eat lords?

Grey ash blanketed ruined buildings, but the outer walls of the city were in view. More people joined their retinue, fleeing for safety. Marius swung his mount, gesturing to his men to protect the new refugees. As he turned, a rotting woman lunged from the dark and grasped Marius's reins with shrivelled hands. She growled in his ear, dragging him off his horse.

The Cobra's horse came alongside his, riding her down. The sound of bones crunching under hooves made Eric's face turn sick and grim.

They passed the last square in the city. Blood covered the frescoes, so Marius didn't know if there was a god in the painting at all. Another ghoul leaped from a darkened window directly onto Marius's horse. Marius's steed, well trained, didn't startle when Marius cleaved the ghoul in two. When it was done, the horse stepped daintily over one of the bloody halves.

The barbican passage was meant to keep soldiers out of the city. Except the raiders had come in with the river, and the dead had risen from the ravine. Now the barbican had transformed into a stone trap where ghouls or soldiers could lunge in the dark.

The royal coat of arms, the crown atop the mountains, was painted above the central gatehouse passage. Even that blue and silver was stained with blood.

Marius took Eric's reins in one hand as they rode, so he always knew where Eric was. Marius could see in the dark better than the rest. The orichal steel of Starving for Blood gleamed red even in shadow. Marius rode up ahead, holding the blade high, and people followed as though the sword was a torch.

Their party emerged from the shadow of city walls, leaving behind the hungry dead and the living enemy. Eric leaned back in his saddle, checking on the others, then looked at Marius. His face was serious. For a moment, Marius believed Eric would ask him to let go.

Instead, Eric said, "I'll do my best to honour the oath, and you. But I can't work out why you did it."

The road to the mountains was long, but not long enough for Marius to find all the words he needed. He didn't know how to make Eric feel what he'd felt from the broken door to the ice cliffs, to the hawthorn tree and beyond. Marius couldn't trace a line on a map of the realization he'd come to.

Saying *I had no other choice* would be false. He could have obeyed the king. According to the laws of his land, the word of his gods and his own code of honour, he should have. Choosing one person above all else was the act of a monster. Marius had deliberately done evil. He had chosen to be blasphemous, treacherous and monstrous.

Every rule of Marius's world said Eric did not matter. Since that was a lie, they must have new rules. Eric could make up the new rules as they went along. He was good at that.

On the roof Eric had explained, *I love watching how you live.* The Cobra always did know how to find the right words.

"I'm your number one fan," said Marius.

That surprised a laugh out of Eric, bright and startled on the shadowy path to the silver mountains.

At their backs, the ravine howled like a wolf about to swallow the city. Though it was night, the sky was all red sunset. Ferocious in its obscenity, the sound was a discordant scream of hate against nature itself. Faint shrieks of terror and rapture rose from the throng behind them. Eric's face wore a different emotion.

"What are you thinking?"

Eric's compassionate gaze fixed on the burning horizon, as though he pitied the crowned shadow stretching over half the livid sky. "I think Rae made a terrible mistake. I should have known the story couldn't happen the way she claimed, but if I went to her I'd be abandoning everyone else. There's nothing I can do for her now."

His eyes travelled from the people escaping their city, to Marius, to the horizon under a rain of ash. Behind the mountains waited a dark manor and darker memories. Seven years and a long road, but Marius was finally going back.

They set their horses' heads towards home. The Cobra led the way.

CHAPTER THIRTY-FOUR

The Villainess Under Siege

"The strength of bulls cannot stop him. No, he will not leave off," said the Oracle. "Until he tears the city or the enemy limb from limb."

Time of Iron, ANONYMOUS

fter you pushed the king into an abyss before a thousand witnesses, it was wisest not to stick around. Fortunately, the crowd of courtiers and worshippers were distracted. With the sounds of war clashing in her ears and a crowned shadow covering the sky, Rae wrenched herself free from restraining hands and made a break for it. The earth groaned and shuddered like a dying man as she ran, the palace battlements tilting beneath her feet. She saw a pair of hands, mottled green as though gloved in rot, grasp the parapet. As the ravine opened wide and wider, the dead were being vomited out.

Rae clutched a toppling turret for balance, brushed the ashes off her burning dress, and ran on to save Lia. The air was burning and so was her throat. She grasped onto a bush shaped like a swan by the tower for the ladies-in-waiting and drew in desperate lungfuls of air that seemed on fire. Her silk slippers sank deep into morning dew.

Except when dew seeped through slippers, it shouldn't feel warm. The lawn intended for ladies' light footsteps was soaked in fresh gore.

Raiders were in the palace, violent men seeking revenge for the attempted poisoning of their Ice King. Raiders must have come for the king's women.

Before Rae came here, she hadn't known the sound of sharp steel cutting through living meat and bone. She knew it now. She forced her feet to keep moving, though she dreaded what she might see.

She emerged from behind the bush to see Lady Horatia Nemeth, wearing a lacy gown in her favourite shade of pink, sinking a morningstar into a raider who was now meat for the crows. After Horatia was done with him, he might be mincemeat for the crows.

"Take that, blackguard!" said Horatia.

"Stop, he's already dead."

Emer sounded bored, as though she'd been trying to restrain the bloodthirsty aristocracy for some time. She carried an axe over her shoulder like a woodcutter. The steel was coated with a pale red glaze.

Not magic, but blood.

When Rae's gown rustled the bushes, Emer and Horatia turned in a single savage moment like wolves in gowns. Emer's axe swung and stopped with a jerk.

"My lady! Where is Lady Lia?"

"King Octavian imprisoned her in the throne room," Rae answered succinctly. "I pushed him into the ravine. When he returns, he will have ultimate power. We have to break Lia out before then."

Emer glanced at the sky writhing with ominous storm clouds and scorched by lines of eerie lightning, and the crowned shadow over the palace. She shouldered her axe again and went to Rae's side.

Rae bit her lip. "Where will you go?" she asked Horatia.

The weight of this world was heavy on her shoulders. She felt responsible for them all.

The set line to Horatia's mouth suggested anger. She put her fingers in her painted-pink mouth and whistled. Several ladies-in-waiting appeared. One wore a breastplate, sheened with red magic, over her baby-blue gown.

"We're staying," Horatia announced. "The girls have been training since the Court of Air and Grace, when the king failed to protect us. This tower is defensible. Papa loves to tell war stories and they simply bore Fab to tears, so I listened. And now I believe I know tactics?"

"I see," Rae murmured.

Horatia's eyes were the colour of shallow lakes, but grief darkened them into deep pools. "Besides, Hortensia can't leave the tower. I must protect my sister."

She coughed, as if embarrassed by her own emotion.

If not for Rae, ghouls would never have attacked the Court of Air and Grace. Hortensia would never have been hurt. Rae remembered a dying villain in a play saying, *I mean to do some good in spite of my own nature.*

When one had wicked curves, one also had storage options. Rae reached inside her corset, and took out the Flower of Life and Death.

The petals were crumpled like tissue paper, but the fragrance was still sweet. Rae smelled the flower and felt carried back to the apple blossoms in her yard at home. Loss hollowed out her insides. She intended to get home, but just in case she didn't . . .

She couldn't waste a miracle.

Rae laid the flower in Horatia's hand. "Keep this for me. If I don't make it back by morning, give it to your sister."

She hoped to return and live, but she wouldn't act as if she were the only person who mattered in the world.

Wearing her magic gauntlets, Horatia seemed to be cradling the glowing flower in a silver nest to keep it safe. "Are you certain?"

Rae took a step back. "Yes."

"Did you really push the king into the ravine?"

"Yes."

"My dear!" A faint smile curved Horatia's stern mouth. "Treason's really getting to be a habit with you."

Rae left the general's daughter standing in the blood-drenched garden, holding the cure for her sister. She raced towards the throne room with Emer beside her.

When they approached the golden entrance to the throne room, they saw the doors were barred. Four guards were posted outside.

Rae flattened herself behind one of the huge pillars. She pulled Emer in beside her and whispered, "We have to take them down."

Emer spoke in her driest tone. "That shouldn't be a problem."

"What do you mean?" Rae asked, then heard the slithering, shuffling sound of grave-wrapped feet, marching in the relentless unstoppable rhythm of the dead. She risked one look around the pillar and saw the pack of ghouls descend on the guards.

Blood-drenched teeth bared in decaying faces filled her vision. The guards had no enchanted weapons or armour to protect them. They had no chance. Rae withdrew behind the pillar, clutching Emer's iron-cold hand. The marble wall at her back was all that held her up. She scarcely dared breathe.

They waited until the screams faded and the hungry gnawing ceased. The indistinct whispers of the dead scraped and slid along the malachite passageways, in search of fresh meat.

When Rae let out a whimpering breath and forced herself out from behind the pillar, there were two ghouls left. Wraiths with sorrowful faces, ankle deep in blood and tattered flesh. They turned at the sound of her movement, scenting the air, quivering animals eager to hunt. Rae's hand, shaking in her gauntlet, closed hard around her sword hilt. She ran one ghoul through.

The other reached for her, murmuring almost plaintively, "*Rahela.*"

Finger bones sharp as knives grazed Rae's hair. The dead touch almost seemed affectionate.

Emer swung her axe at the ghoul's neck. Black blood spattered on her crisp white apron. With the last ghoul beheaded, Rae and Emer unbarred the doors and rushed inside.

Lia waited on the silver dais, a luminous trembling figure outlined by the sharp-edged brilliance of the jewelled throne. She held out a beseeching hand, bright with the gauntlet Rae had given her, and watched her evil stepsister and her treacherous maidservant sweep into the throne room.

"You came for me." Lia burst into tears.

Rae gathered Lia into her arms, shoulders so impossibly fragile she felt like a baby bird held in Rae's palm. Something small, to be protected. Certainty rushed to fill the hollow places inside Rae. Even if the sky was falling, Rae knew how to be a big sister.

"Stop crying," soothed Rae. "You're already so ugly. Crying is making it worse."

Astonishment silenced Lia, as if Rae had stuffed a sock in her rosebud mouth.

"I'm the most beautiful woman in the world!" Her face fell when she realized she'd forgotten to be modest and humble.

Rae gulped a laugh and kissed Lia on the nose. "I know. We're here to rescue beauty in peril. I have a plan."

"My lady Rae, she's already so distressed," murmured Emer. "Must you make things worse?"

Rae continued with determination, "There's a secret passage from the Room of Memory and Bone down to the Cauldron. Emer will take you. I'll bar the doors once you're out."

Barring the doors wouldn't save Rae, but saving herself was no longer the first priority. As soon as she'd seen Lia, Rae had known she would trade places with her, would make any bargain. Rae tried to let go. Lia clung with her magic-steel fist.

"I'll stay with you. I don't mind dying, if we're together."

"No. Little funnyface, baby sister," Rae whispered. "*He is coming.* When he does, he will be the Emperor. I'm the traitor. I'm the one he hates the most. I can buy you enough time to get away."

"I can't leave you."

Silver trails of tears poured down her moonlight-pure face. Rae had scoffed a thousand times at characters racing to lay down their lives for the perfect heroine. Who cared about saving Lia?

As it turned out, Rae did.

Rae grasped her slim shoulders and shook her. "Why did I come here if not for this? If I can save you, I won't die for nothing. I'll try to live. I'll fight as hard as I can, but if I do die, please let it mean something. I beg you to go."

Let me be your favourite story. Let me be the greatest story you ever heard.

Lia swallowed, nodding. She stripped off her magic gauntlet and held it out to Rae.

"I won't go if you don't take it."

The windows were full of scarlet and shadows. The Emperor would be here soon.

She dropped a kiss on Lia's cheek. "Go live. Tell everyone how brave and noble I was. They'd never believe me, but they might believe you."

Tear-blinded, Lia was even clumsier than usual. She stumbled from the dais. Emer was there to catch her.

"Take care of her," Rae said. "Take care of yourself. And get Lia spectacles, this falling into everyone's arms is ridiculous. Go!"

With an axe in one hand and a beauty in the other, Emer still managed a perfect curtsy.

"My lady Rae. It has been a pleasure to serve."

They vanished away behind the golden doors. Rae barred the doors after them, knowing they weren't safe yet. But when Rae was gone, perhaps the story would show favour to its heroine again. Since Emer was with Lia, perhaps some of that shining fortune would transfer to her. Perhaps they could both be saved.

Rae shut her eyes as if blowing out a birthday candle. She wished them a happy ending.

Scarlet light burned away even the dark behind her eyes. Rae opened them to see the ravine rise, a black cauldron overflowing and spilling its blood-red contents out onto the land. The lost gods and the forgotten past were all returning tonight.

Down in the depths of the ravine, the First Duke waited. The great god in disguise, who had arranged throne, crown and kingdom for the son he'd murdered, as though laying out a sleeping child's clothes in readiness for morning. After the Emperor duelled the Duke in the abyss, the Duke would offer his son a cursed jewel. The Emperor should refuse the jewel and slay the Duke for love of Lia, but Rae couldn't imagine that happening now.

What would happen?

Nothing good.

Her mind could hardly encompass the immensity of the disaster rushing down on her head. It was as if a galaxy would swallow her.

Grey twisted hands scrabbled in the space under the golden doors. Dry as dust the susurration rose, and from dead throats issued a hissing and a byword. Every ghoul in the palace was whispering her name.

Windowpanes rattled like bones with the coming of the Emperor. The thunder of a ghoulish army, using their bodies as battering rams, boomed against the throne room doors. Against the livid clouds, the falling ashes were dark tattered shadows like ghosts swooping to claim her.

Rae had always known she would face the end alone.

In the throne room echoing with dead voices, soaked with light like blood, Rae raised her head high. Villains had no time for tears.

Who can believe the wicked? The wicked could believe in themselves. The world was hard and cruel. It bore down and broke you into a thousand pieces. When nobody believed in you, when even you couldn't believe, you must arrange your broken pieces into a terrifying new shape. You could believe in the fantastic recreation of yourself.

In the end, she was lucky. She'd been granted her dying wish.

If the ending couldn't be happy, at least it would mean something. She would do something great before she died. She would be an unforgettable part of the story.

The golden doors shook like someone in their death throes. Rae raised her sword. The doors crashed down and the Emperor stood framed against an army of the dead.

CHAPTER THIRTY-FIVE

The Lady's Guide to Escape

"I want someone to believe in so badly. I know it's not wise to believe in you," murmured Lia. "I will anyway."

Time of Iron, ANONYMOUS

mer and Lia ran down the secret tunnel out of the palace. Frantic sobs erupted from Lia's throat, but Emer pulled her along. She wouldn't betray either of them again. This time, she wouldn't let Lia go.

"Wait," Lia gasped, through her sobs. "Behind us!"

The light at the end of the tunnel was the eerie burning sky. Emer dragged her another few paces, but Lia wrenched herself free with a burst of strength.

"My lady, we *cannot* go back!"

As Emer spoke, the ghoul lunged. Emer hurled herself in front of Lia, shielding Lia with her body. The ghoul knocked them both down. In life, he must have been a big man. He was heavy atop Emer, huge cold hands tugging at her wrists as if he was a child trying to pull her along on the playground. Lia screamed and scrabbled backwards in the debris of the tunnel, rolling out from the tangle of limbs and away. When the ghoul opened his mouth, there was no breath, only the scent of decaying innards.

"*Rahela,*" the ghoul crooned.

Lia grabbed the ghoul's rotted collar and yanked him off Emer. Moss-tipped fingertips left cold slimy traces like slug trails on her skin, but he didn't succeed in grasping Emer before she scrambled to her feet. Once Emer was up, she raised her axe and gave the ghoul as many whacks as it took to keep him down.

"He wasn't trying to bite you," Lia whispered. "He was trying to drag you back."

For whatever punishment the Emperor had in mind. Emer shuddered and headed determinedly to the mouth of the tunnel.

Their great escape had led them to a roof overhanging the Cauldron, that notorious den of sinners and thieves. The battle seemed to be over, though Emer didn't know whether the raiders had surrendered or been killed. Perhaps both living armies had been torn to pieces by the dead. The blood-slick streets were hushed, lost under a red haze of magic. Faraway sounds of eerie rejoicing mingled with the clotted muttering of the dead.

Beyond the Cauldron lay the remnants of the ravine's rising. Among rocks blackened as burned-out coals in a grate, the dead were teeming.

For a fleeting moment Emer thought she saw Lord Marius, but even at this distance there was something wrong with his eyes. One instant he seemed a tall powerful man with ice-and-night hair, the next a shadow, the next a flame, until she began to doubt if she saw anything at all. Beside the shifting presence walked a young man with fox-fire hair, his snow-pale face strangely familiar. Keen-eyed though she was, Emer's vision blurred as though she stared too long into the sun. When she blinked, there were only shadows and the dead.

Beyond the grey city walls was a long line of people escaping to the mountains. She and Lia could join the refugees. It wasn't a future Emer had pictured for herself, fleeing the city with the fairest of them all. If anyone had ever told Emer this would come to pass, she wouldn't have believed them. Now that future lay before her like a bright road.

When she turned to Lia, Lia's shining face was clouded.

"That ghoul said '*Rahela*'," Lia mused, in her sweet clever voice.

"I heard the other ghouls outside the throne room door. Emer, they were all saying her name."

Her lady Rae had said, *He is coming. When he does, he will be the Emperor. I'm the traitor. I'm the one he hates the most.*

He hated her enough to put her name in the mouths of hungry ghouls. His rage was splitting the sky. Emer was terrified for Rae, but Emer had been terrified and helpless before.

Emer said roughly, "She's as good as dead."

"All I ever wanted was a family," Lia said. "Now she's my family. She's willing to die to prove it. I won't let her! I know how men think. He won't kill her. He'll keep her to torment. I can rescue her."

Emer was suddenly furious. "There's no need to always be good and forgiving! She betrayed you. So did I. She's being punished. That's how it should be."

She'd never let herself shout at Lia before. She was ashamed to even face her, and now she realized that somewhere in the back of her mind she'd believed the story everyone told about Lia: that she was too fragile, that real emotion would make her crumple to pieces.

Instead, Lia's eyes reflected the strange lightning in the sky. Twin blue fires burned in the pearl of her face.

"Thus, I should never trust anyone?" demanded Lia. "Then she dies alone, and someday so do I. If I believe she's my sister, if she believes it, doesn't that make it true? When you pretended to care for me, I believed in you. Did you ever believe in me?"

Emer had built a cage for those memories, locked the door, and refused to let them out. Now with a soft question, the memories escaped like unchained monsters. Sharing a bed, sharing secrets, knowing she must betray one woman she cared for or the other. How Emer had hated herself, and hated the whole world.

She'd refused to let herself even look at Lia. Now, Lia gazed up at her. Emer's lies burned away under the clear light of those eyes.

The fairest of them all. The irresistible one. Emer believed every story men told about her, because Emer felt that way too.

Emer confessed, "I didn't want to be a fool like everyone else. I wanted to be iron, but you were the only thing that made me a fool. You're the only story I ever believed in."

The smile that touched Lia's mouth was magic, making her impossibly more beautiful. She cupped Emer's face in her lily-petal lady's hands and drew her down into a soft kiss that left Emer more dazed than the hardest of blows.

Even in the darkest night and the scarlet storm, Lia made it seem like sunlight would return.

"She saved me. Now I'll save her. Come," murmured Lia. "I know someone in the Cauldron who will help us. I have a plan."

Hand in hand, they found a way down from the roof together. The iron maid and the pearl went hunting through streets of sinners and thieves.

FIRST & LAST CHAPTER

The Villainess and the Emperor

Everybody needs something to reach for. Even the dead.
Given a light to follow, we can drag ourselves from the pit.
   All the dead and damned are climbing towards you.
I am reaching for you with the hands of an army. They
cannot stop me. The dead outnumber the living.
   I am coming for you ten thousand souls strong.

Time of Iron, ANONYMOUS

he Emperor broke into the throne room. In one hand
he held his sword. In the other, the head of his enemy.
He swung the head jauntily, fingers twisted in blood-
drenched, tangled hair.

A scarlet trail on the hammered-gold tiles marked the Emperor's
passage. His boots left deep crimson footprints. Even the ice-blue
lining inside his black cloak dripped with red. No part of him was
left unstained.

He wore the crowned death mask with the First Duke's jewel
burning dark on his brow, and a breastplate of bronze with falling
stars wrought in iron. The red-gleaming metal fingers of his gauntlets
tapered into shining claws.

In one lethal iron claw, he held another jewel. Small as a teardrop,
red as blood.

Her ruby earring.

When he lifted the mask, fury and pain had carved his face into new lines. After his time in the sunless place he was pale as winter light, radiance turned so cold it burned. He was a statue with a splash of blood staining his cheek, like a red flower on stone. She recognized him at last.

He was the Once and Forever Emperor, the Corrupt and Divine, the Lost and Found Prince, Master of the Dread Ravine, Commander of the Living and the Dead. None could stop his victory march.

She couldn't bear to watch him smile, or the shambling dead behind him. Her gaze was drawn by the hungry gleam of his blade. She wished it had stayed broken.

The hilt of the re-forged Sword of Eyam was still a coiled snake. On the blade an inscription glittered and flowed as if written on water. The only word visible beneath a slick coat of blood was *Longing*.

The sword's name was Longing for Revenge. She understood it now. The girl with silver hands trembled, alone in the heart of the story.

The Emperor approached the throne and said,

"You lied to me."

His step echoed like the tolling of a funereal bell.

"You betrayed me."

Giving up without a fight wasn't in her nature. Evil and treacherous to the end, Rae swung her sword. The Emperor laughed.

"You left me to die."

As soon as Rae's blade kissed the Emperor's, her stolen sword shivered and broke into a thousand pieces. The hilt fell from her hands. Silver dust eddied down to the gold mosaics. Rae had expected nothing less. His was the blade no enemies could withstand. Nothing stood between him and his richly deserved revenge.

"Thank you," murmured the Emperor. "For teaching me how to please you."

The Emperor tossed his enemy's head at her feet. Rae stared at the bloody stump where the neck had been, and the still-beautiful hair. The head rolled until it touched her slippers. Eyes green as lost summer, already glazing over, stared up at her. It was the head of Octavian the king.

"I am only beginning. I will destroy worlds. I will kill gods."

This wasn't the beautiful singing voice she loved to hear calling for her. This was the Emperor's voice, the stone on stone of a tomb scraping open. He was hoarser than the call of crows or ravens, because when she tried in her arrogance to fix the story, she made it worse.

His voice had changed when they cut his throat.

"When I woke broken in the pit, I remembered your face like the worst sin ever committed against me. I held the thought of you as close as a grudge, my lady."

When Rae tried to run, the dead caught her. A dozen hands grasped hold, fingers sharp bone protruding from ragged flesh, or spongy with rot. They held her so tight she was forced into absolute stillness. Her heart didn't beat, but shuddered. Terror shook her as if she were a rag doll in the grip of a demon child.

"*Master,*" the ghouls crooned, in a rotten lullaby.

In another world, her sister had told her, *Even when you get everything wrong, you believe you're right.*

At every turn, she had failed him. She knew the sing-song voice the ghouls used to call her name. The sky had raged when he watched his beloved in danger at the Queen's Trials. The future Emperor had always moved too quickly, healed too fast and fought with divine fury. He had even cured her bite, but every time he displayed his power she never noticed. Because in books people often healed with convenient speed or fought better than ten men. In the story before she broke it, he was the one who suggested heating iron shoes over a fire to kill Rahela, horrifying both the Cobra and her sister. The Cobra asked, "*Octavian what?*" when Rae said Octavian became the Emperor, because he expected it to be someone else. The Cobra feared the Emperor, but never the king.

In the story before she ruined it, Lord Marius and Princess Vasilisa loved the king but hated the Emperor. The Emperor, who Rae had always loved and never been able to see in Octavian. The evidence had been staring her in the face all this time. Octavian, who discarded one sister for another, was not loyal past death. Octavian frequently removed his gauntlets, and Rae knew the Emperor hated taking them off.

King Octavian and the Emperor weren't the same person. They never had been, not in any version of the story. The Emperor was always Key.

Even now, seeing his face in a flash of lightning made her heart leap with joyous revelation, followed by the long fall into despair. Her favourite character. She'd always thought if she met him, she would understand and believe in him as nobody else could.

When she met him, she didn't even recognize him. She betrayed him. Her schemes got his throat cut.

She'd wanted to believe the story could be fixed, the sick could be healed, and darkness transformed into something beloved. She knew the heroine belonged with the guy in the crown, remembering only the figure he cut when he first entered the throne room as the Emperor. She had filled in the spaces where the story should be with what she believed already. Rae had looked at costumes and thought she saw truth.

She forgot the clue of his name.

Key. The key to the narrative. The hero of the story. Enough blood and tears could buy a life. After centuries hurling sacrifices into the ravine, finally the payment was enough. Yet when the Emperor returned, nobody noticed.

Everyone looked to the king, though they were warned the crown was not his to keep. Octavian was simply the child of the king and queen. The child of the gods had been reborn from the abyss, a miracle raised not in a palace but the gutter. The ravine woke not when Octavian was crowned, but when Key was born.

The Emperor said, "Be terribly afraid. I come to swear love undying."

Lightning made the sky shiver without cease. The hollows under his eyes were dug deep as graves. His eyes were red-rimmed from centuries of smoke.

The line where they cut his throat was a braided scarlet ribbon wrapped around his neck, twisted thread still too raw to be scar tissue. He was an uncanny and awful creature, a glorious ruin of what could have been. Her eyes were dazzled. He had died so young.

He had come back so wrong. He should have lived years longer, should have chosen to climb down into the pit. She had ripped his choice away. She had done worse. He needed time under Lia's gentle protection, learning goodness. Instead he had the vipers. Emer, coldly telling him words changed reality, the Cobra laughing as he spoke of blood and circuses, and Rae. The Beauty Dipped In Blood, the woman who lied and betrayed and killed.

She had taught him how to please her.

The Emperor made a gesture of command to his ghouls. "I love you as a knife loves a throat," he murmured as the dead overwhelmed her. "I crawled out of hell to fall at your feet."

Dead fingers crept across her skin as if they were worms and she already in her grave. Elaborate chains draped and chilled her as she stood violently helpless. Cold hands fastened the jewel around her throat, twin to the one shining darkly in the crowned mask. He gave her the Abandon All Hope Diamond.

He spoke of love, but she knew him. He called her 'my lady' when he was furious. She knew him, and he was a nightmare and a catastrophe, doom she could not hope to control.

With the Emperor's rage came ruin on the world and blood on the moon.

"The burning city is mine, and I am yours. I changed the story for you. So tell me the lie that you love me."

There was brutal tenderness in the hoarse love song of his voice. His promises grated like stone on gold as the ghouls dragged in the marble throne. The seat for a dead queen, intended for Rae now.

The ghouls placed the queen's pale chair on the shining dais beside the Emperor's throne with its darkly brilliant wings. He made a gesture of invitation towards their thrones, courtly as if he were raised to be a gentleman.

She dropped her burning gaze to the dust. She couldn't bear to see what she'd done.

He reached out.

The blade was hot with blood, the steel beneath cold as the grave. The Emperor used his sword to lift her chin, so they stood staring at each other before the black and white thrones.

"Be happy. Be my evil queen."

The horror was relentless. So was she. At the edge of desperation, all she needed was to live long enough to craft one last scheme.

Stolen silver made her fingers shine cold and glowing pale as a ghost's. The Emperor's armoured claw closed, heavy as a cage, on her gauntlet when she offered him her hand. A monster, clinging to a shade.

Rae vowed, "I will."

When they ascended their thrones, she held her head high on the dead queen's stone seat. He sprawled with insouciant grace, one leg hooked over the throne's arm, still looking at her.

The Emperor's eyes had once been the grey of ashes, but the ash had woken to burning new life. Fire and smoke rose in the dark red imperial gaze. A crimson ravine yawned wide. She stared into the abyss, and saw her death in his eyes.

Key smiled. "Evil wins at last, my lady."

The story continues in...

TIME OF IRON: BOOK TWO

ACKNOWLEDGEMENTS

They say it takes a village.

It certainly takes a lot of people to carry someone through late-stage cancer, and back to being someone able to write a book. And that is why these acknowledgements are so horrifically long, and come in two parts: during and after.

How do I say 'thank you for saving my life'? To Dr Claire Feely at Ballybrack Medical Centre and her amazing team, who got me diagnosed. I know, it's always bronchitis, Dr Claire. And to Dr Kamal Fadalla, and his unstoppable team at St Vincent's Public Hospital, who got me chemo. Thank you. For saving my life.

My family. My parents took me back in when they didn't expect the eldest-in-her-thirties to need to be nursed like a baby. I was driven to every appointment despite the price of hospital parking and brought breakfast in bed. My brother shaved my head. My sister and little brother travelled to be with me. My cousins, aunts, uncles checked in all the time.

My friends.

Chiara Popplewell, who never failed in the trips down to see me, no matter how weird they got. Rachael Walker, who brought every baked good and watched *Goblin* with me. Susan Connolly, who made up all the excuses to fly in from England, and who tried to burn the year with me that New Year's.

Joanne Lombard, Stefanie O'Brien, Jessica Barrett, Aileen Kelly, Zoe Cathcart, Karen Pierpoint, Emma Doyle, Clare Lynch.

Especially for that time I had to call Joanne and say, don't visit me if you're pregnant, I'm currently radioactive.

For the angels who came from America for me: Kelly Link, Cassandra Clare, Holly Black, Robin Wasserman, Maureen Johnson, Marie Lu, Ally Carter and Elizabeth Eulberg. I haven't forgotten, and I won't forget.

Libba Bray, Megan Whalen Turner, Suzie Townsend, Cindy Pon, Eleanor Doyle, Kristin Nelson, Carrie Ryan, Sarah MacLean, Amie Kaufman, Jay Kristoff, Barry Goldblatt, Rachel Toomey, Fran Moylan: who sent letters and gifts and remembered me in a time I was forgotten.

And perhaps most of all, for those who fought the same fight I did, no matter the outcome, and who stay in my thoughts like light. Philip O'Keeffe, Natalie O'Brien, Claire Lynch, Michael Brennan, Breda Morrisroe, Nora de Burca, Emmet Burns, Roy Esmond, Ted Kenny, Rachel Caine and May. I never did get your last name, but the dark chocolates are always for you.

The second part of these acknowledgements is for those who saved me through recovery, and my return to writing. Recovery is a tricky concept. There are so many parts to recovery. Recovering from cancer to find out you're chronically ill. Recovering your ability to write, and only later your self-confidence in that ability. One is discovering you won't ever recover, really: not who you were before. I was privileged to find those who loved me through all my transformations.

Jenny Mulligan, who saved a room for me when we didn't know if I'd live to come be her flatmate. Lovely living with you, Jens, though considering I just did a reading at your wedding, I hope we won't do it again!

Leigh Bardugo, Holly Black, Elizabeth Eulberg and Robin Wasserman for the Covid check-ins, the zoom calls, the catch-ups, the encouragement, the wisdom, the shared pressure to write and shared joy when something good happens with your work. You are stars who deserve the universe.

Susan Connolly, who did both the far and near parts of writing with me, including travel. I might never have finished the rewrite without the Barbie-pink room in the German enclave, or the sexy cave dinner.

Rachael, who lived with me through Covid, and with Binx and Jadis. Sorry Binx bites you! He's a demon baby.

Chiara, who braved Covid living in a new country. My birthday trip with you to Italy gave me Castle Aragonese at Ischia, the main inspiration behind the Palace on the Edge.

C. E. Murphy, who had a Covid office with me and put up with the absolutely deranged time when I was making up the musical, and Ruth Long who does lovely writing Fridays with me now. Seanan McGuire, who sang outside my door at the convention when I still wore a wig and was scared.

C. S. Pacat and Beth Dunfey, for still wanting to work with me in the after times, and never making me feel I'd come back wrong.

Natasha Walsh and David Bates, for the honour and the dark edits. Katie Morrisroe, Gwen Billett, Caitriona de Burca, and Shalini Columb, and Sinead Keogh and Paul Quigley, and Kate Lorigan and Ashling Lynch and Pinelopi Pourpoutidou, and Carol Connolly for the laughter.

For my family, all those mentioned above, but also the new members who brought even more joy and love into my life – my new brother and sister Eric and Jess, my goddaughter Romey, my nephew Ryan and my niece Lia (my sister and I came up with the name independent of each other. Just sister things).

I don't believe any book is an island. We're all part of a system of inspiration and influence, talking to those who came before and will go after, and this book is especially a monument to the stories that made me. Shakespeare's Edmund and Richard III, and Milton's Lucifer, the first villains to compel me. Josephine Tey's Richard III, who made me realise how easy it is to be villainised. Anne Rice's *The Vampire Lestat*, which had me truly considering evil as a point of view. C. S. Lewis's *The Voyage of the Dawn Treader*, which first made me think of going to another world through art so beautiful it seemed alive. *Howl's Moving Castle*, *Labyrinth*, *The Phantom Tollbooth*, *Pleasantville*, *The Chronicles of Thomas Covenant*, *Stranger than Fiction*, *Pan's Labyrinth*, *Lost in*

Austen, Extraordinary You, Carry On, Galavant, Rosencrantz and Guildenstern Are Dead, Thursday Next, *Inkspell* and *The Romance of Tiger and Rose,* all made me think about the many different ways of stumbling into a story.

Inspiration comes from all over the world, and while I couldn't write a traditional *isekai* I was influenced by the subgenre and am grateful: a favourite is Mo Xiang Tong Xiu's *The Grandmaster of Demonic Cultivation.* I hope many more get translated so I may read them.

Thank you to all those who showed me new ways of weaving a portal fantasy, like Seanan McGuire's *Every Heart a Doorway,* Alix Harrow's *The Ten Thousand Doors of January,* and (hear me out!) Greta Gerwig's *Barbie.* Those who lit new paths to writing fantasy, with irreverence, genius, and sympathy, especially Leigh Bardugo's *Six of Crows,* Scott Lynch's *The Lies of Locke Lamora,* Naomi Novik's *Spinning Silver,* Shelley Parker-Chan's *She Who Became the Sun* and Tamsyn Muir's *Gideon the Ninth.*

I can't inflict a whole bibliography on top of all this, but Max Adams's *Aelfred's Britain,* Stephen Greenblatt's *The Swerve* and Catherine Nixey's *The Darkening Age* were invaluable reference points.

Everyone writing fantasy today owes a debt to Tolkien's The Lord of the Rings and George R. R. Martin's A Song of Ice and Fire. I owe an even greater debt to their readers, and many from other fandoms. I read endless essays on the internet about other worlds, about the nature of evil, about love stories that should be, who was the favourite and why, about the maligned and misunderstood. Those who believe in stories are always changing my mind about tales I thought I knew, casting illumination on liminal spaces, waking new love in me. Nobody goes through the same story twice, but sometimes we walk through different stories holding hands. Seeing you love stories reminded me that I do too, and filled me with inspiration and hope. You believers build all the ways to the other worlds.

And for those who made my dream project a published reality…

Flowers for my agent Suzie Townsend, who signed me up like a week before I was diagnosed and stuck with me all the way through up until I said "Hey, those two books we planned? Here's a book that's neither of them about EVIL!" and stayed even then, and Sophia Ramos, Pouya Shahbazian, Olivia Coleman and the amazing team at New Leaf Literary.

For my UK editor Jenni Hill, who gave me the genius note for the Viking invasion of York, and who – even more vitally – believed in me and wanted me when I truly thought nobody ever would again. For my US editors Nivia Evans and Tiana Coven, for choosing and carrying me through. For all the folks at Orbit: Nazia Khatun, for excellence and excellent kdrama recs. Angela Man. Aimee Kitson. My copyeditor Sandra Ferguson. Blanche Craig. Angelica Chong. Ellen Wright. Alex Lencicki. Natassja Haught. Paolo Crespa. Rachel Goldstein and Rachel Hairston. Jessica Purdue and Zoe King and the rest of the fabulous rights folks. Tim Holman, our captain!

For Syd Mills, the artist extraordinaire, and Ben Prior, designer likewise. Rebecka Champion, who made my wonderful map.

For Venessa Kelley, who first put my evil imagination into beautiful art.

For my Fairyloot box, a dazzling honour, thank you to Bon Orthwick's stunning artistic talent, and thanks especially to Anissa de Gomery for choosing me and Evil. And to Jessica Dryburgh and Nicole Cochrane.

For you, beloved reader, if you're reading this. Thank you for believing in my story. For a while, I couldn't believe in my story or myself.

I do now.

extras

meet the author

Edel Kelly

SARAH REES BRENNAN was born in Ireland by the sea. After world travel and surviving stage four cancer, she settled there in the shadow of a three-hundred-year-old library. Writing young adult fiction, she was a Lodestar, Mythopoeic, and World Fantasy Award finalist, Carnegie Medal nominee, and *New York Times* bestseller. *Long Live Evil* is her first adult work.

Find out more about Sarah Rees Brennan and other Orbit authors by registering for the free monthly newsletter at orbitbooks.net.

if you enjoyed
LONG LIVE EVIL

look out for

THESE DEATHLESS SHORES

by

P. H. Low

Gorgeous and devastating, P. H. Low's debut fantasy is the richly reimagined tale of Captain Hook's origin, a story of cruelty, magic, lost innocence, and the indelible power of stories.

Jordan was once a Lost Boy, convinced she would never grow up. Now she's twenty-two and exiled to the real world, still suffering withdrawal from the addictive magic Dust of her childhood. With nothing left to lose, Jordan returns to the Island and its stories—of pirates and war and the cruelty of youth—intent on facing Peter one last time, on her own terms.

If that makes her the villain . . . so be it.

Chapter 1

Nine years after leaving the Island, Jordan still hated the city heat.

She shoved her duffel bag back behind her hip, breathed through the soup of air that stuck her shirt to her skin. Sweating spectators jostled and leaned toward the ring below, where two fighters in similar gear jabbed and blocked and danced.

An otherwise equal match, except one of them was going through karsa withdrawal. Even from up here, Jordan could see him shaking.

"Are you really the Silver Fist?"

She looked down. A boy of about ten stared up at her, grubby fingers clenched around a fried dough stick. No parents or siblings that she could see—and he was thin and wary looking in a way that reminded her of Peter, of the Island, of crawling through forest underbrush with Baron, senses pricked for the rustle of a pirate or a Pale or a hungry feral boar.

An aspiring fighter, then. Or perhaps one already.

She wondered if he'd ever dreamed of the Island. If he'd ever read the Sir Franklin novel or watched the many movie adaptations and thought it, for a moment, real.

"No," she said, serious. "It's just a costume."

The kid cast a long look at her hands. She spread them: the prosth on her right a glove of metal, the click of uncurling fingers masked by the crowd. "Pretty convincing, huh?"

"Sure," said the boy, but he did not shuffle away to his seat. As Jordan turned back to the match, he hovered on her periphery, gnawing his lower lip; stayed until her focus broke like a wave against stone.

"You should get out," she said finally. Smiled with all her teeth. "While you still can. Don't let them use you."

He backed away then, the stick of fried dough in his hand untouched.

The match below was not going well. Third rounds in general tended to be where the most bones broke, fighters both exhausted and amped on their drug of choice, but the karsa addict had fallen to his knees; when his opponent kicked him in the shoulder, he crashed backward and lay twitching on the sand.

As the referee raised his arms, a roar went up through the stadium, half triumph, half protest. This late at night, after the rookie matches and the polite international ones, the spectators hungered for fast punches and faster bets, snapped wrists and broken backs.

This late at night, they wanted a show.

And the addict had failed to provide.

As the medical team—not all of them certified—carried him out, Jordan caught a couple men in suits moving through the stands, wireless headsets hooked around their ears: syndicate muscle, most likely, deployed to ensure a quick disposal of the man's body. The karsa had rendered him useless as a fighter, but they couldn't have him shouting valuable intel in dark alleys, no matter how convincingly it came off as an addict's ravings.

"Pity," the man standing beside Jordan muttered to his friend. A dragon tattoo snaked down his shoulder, wrapped his wrist in flames. "I've been watching Gao Leng since I was in primary school."

"Happens to all of them. They're uneducated, desperate—" The friend's gaze flicked to Jordan. "Hey, isn't that—"

Jordan ducked toward the aisle, their eyes pressing into her shoulder blades.

Two purple cubes of karsa burned in her own pocket. She had deliberately kept her doses as low as she could stand, these past nine years, and not just because Obalang was a stingy arse who would withhold her next canister the moment she missed a rent payment. Karsa tore up your nerves and digestive system; spend too much time in its grip, and withdrawal would leave you vomiting and convulsing until you regretted the day you were born.

But she could not regret the choice she'd made, nine years ago. Not when the alternative, withdrawal from the Island's Dust, would have killed her.

Not when it might still.

As she shoved into the locker room below the ring, a hand clamped down on her shoulder.

From anyone else, it might have been a gesture of encouragement. From Obalang, it was anything but. Jordan rested her right palm casually on top of his tobacco-stained fingers; felt them quivering there, hot and trapped. In a single twitch she could crush his bones so finely he would need a prosth to match hers, and for a moment she reveled in that, even if he held sway over the rest of her pathetic little life.

"You owe me," he said.

Jordan's eyes narrowed. Her landlord-dealer's black eyes were jittering, thin lips parted in suppression of ecstasy. The eejit was sharp on his own drug.

"I said I'd run your errand in the morning."

"What, and count that as payment for a four-ounce can? It's a small deal. Weak stuff. I'll barely get enough to cover the cost of transport." His grip tightened; she shifted back.

"Then why didn't you ask Alya to do it?"

Obalang scowled. His breath smelled of scorpion curry and the rotted sweetness that came with karsa chewing. A hint of the same, she knew, tinged her breath as well. "You're replaceable, girl. I can find a dozen kids on the street quicker and hungrier than you. Don't forget that."

Jordan nodded at the stadium above. Ads for energy drinks and foreign cars blazed across the walls in four different languages, but beneath, the chant had gone up, faint but unmistakable: *Silver Fist. Silver Fist.* "Tell it to them."

Obalang's mouth twisted. It was his word that opened the Underground doors to her every Fifthday night, his karsa that kept her from melting into a drool-mouthed wreck.

Even so, it was not every day that one of his tenants made him big among the ringside betting circles.

"Make sure you win all three tonight," he said as she shrugged off his grip and made for the locker room. "Or I'll give that job to Alya after all."

As the door swung closed, she flipped him a two-fingered salute.

The locker room was, if possible, even hotter. She shoved her bag in her graffiti-encrusted compartment as fast as she could get it off her; fished out a near-empty tube of ointment, which she smeared over her arms and face to keep her skin from breaking.

Then she downed the two karsa cubes dry, and the world sharpened, sweet and slow: the bone-rattling thump of eedro music, the shift of a thousand sweat-slicked bodies, the gleam of her opponent's smile as he prepared himself in an identical room on the other side of the ring. Shitty karsa, this—withdrawal would leave her sluggish and achy in thirty minutes, dry-heaving a couple hours after that—but she'd run out of the stronger stuff she'd nicked off errands, and she would ride this high for as long as she could.

And if her right arm prickled a warning beneath the prosth, if the very weight of her bones and blood simmered with the echo of pain—

Through the walls, a chime sounded. Jordan rolled her shoulders, shoved in her mouth guard, and pushed open the door.

The sound almost blasted her back into the room. She'd hovered at the outer edges of this crowd all night, but here at its center, the spectators' fury washed over her like a tide. Her heart was an adrenaline pump, her body electric. As she raised her arms—at once a V for victory and a giant *up yours* to Obalang, who stood, arms crossed, in the front row—the screams swept her up, drowned her, coated her veins in titanium and glowing ore. Two words, pounded into chests and rusted benches.

Silver Fist. Silver Fist.

She fought to pay for the karsa, yes, and for a rat-infested closet Obalang called a room. Fought to keep her other addiction, her Dust addiction, at bay. But as she rolled onto the balls of her feet, felt the slow hard stretch of muscle and joint, she also felt *alive*.

She was a burning star, hungry and inexorable, and she would not be broken.

A pale silhouette sliced the opposite doorway.

Jordan did not blink. She had stayed up nights to study this fighter in the Underground's video archives: his predator's gait, the kicks he snapped like mouthfuls of scorpion pepper. As the ref raised his arms, she mouthed along to the name that blasted from the flat, tinny speakers.

"Gentlemen, I present to you—the White Tiger!"

Jordan's opponent loped across the sand, his white-blond hair shining beneath the lights, and the crowd *howled*.

The White Tiger was the darling of the Underground, tall and lanky and arrogant—*and Rittan*, people whispered loudly behind their hands, as if in explanation. Jordan had fought him twice since she'd first shown up at the back gates of the arena. The first time, he'd knocked her out in seconds. The second, he'd snapped two of her ribs and whispered, as the medics carted her away, that he went easy on little girls.

But Jordan had come back. She'd wrapped her broken bones, iced her bruises. Learned to throw a punch with the full weight of gravity dragging her down, to stay light on her feet even when no Dust from the Island kept them in the air.

All in all, she'd gotten decent at fighting on sand.

And tonight, she would win back her pride—and her next week's worth of karsa.

As they bowed to each other, the Tiger's eyes locked on hers. His irises were giveaway Rittan, the cold pitiless blue of movie stars and senators' sons, and at the sight of them, an old heat seared across Jordan's chest.

"Pity you think you've already lost," he said, the words crisped by his accent. "It might have been a good match."

"Pity you're an arrogant kweilo," Jordan countered. "It'll be fun to beat you."

They stepped apart, and the scoreboard clock flicked into a countdown, digits burning red against the faded wall paint.

Ten seconds.

At the edge of the arena, Obalang flicked a cigarette. *Three for three.*

He did this sometimes, when someone big had bet on her and he was behind on rent or drugs or whatever increase in tribute money the Hanak were demanding from him that week. These days it was usually two for three, minimum, or that she hold out for a certain length of time—which gave her lower audience ratings, but fewer broken bones.

In the past few months, however, she'd been losing him fewer bets. Had even thrown a few matches on purpose.

Six.

The Rittan's white tank top was a paper ghost. The memory of his video matches sketched across the backs of her eyelids: the dancer-like lift of his back foot before a kick, a phantom gap between raised hands. She just had to catch him in real time.

If only it were that easy.

Three.

Fists raised, a meter and a half apart, they crouched as one.

Two.

She needed this, she told herself. A hundred times more than he did.

One.

if you enjoyed

LONG LIVE EVIL

look out for

HOW TO BECOME THE DARK LORD AND DIE TRYING

Dark Lord Davi: Book One

by

Django Wexler

Groundhog Day *meets* **Guardians of the Galaxy** *in Django Wexler's laugh-out-loud fantasy tale about a young woman who, tired of defending humanity from the Dark Lord, decides maybe the Dark Lord is onto something after all.*

Davi has done this all before. She's tried to be the hero and take down the all-powerful Dark Lord. A hundred times she's rallied

445

humanity and made the final charge. But the time loop always gets her in the end. Sometimes she's killed quickly. Sometimes it takes a while. But she's been defeated every time.

This time? She's done being the hero and done being stuck in this endless time loop. If the Dark Lord always wins, then maybe that's who she needs to be. It's Davi's turn to play on the winning side.

Prologue

Life #237

It takes me two weeks to die, locked in my own dungeon.

Not for lack of trying on my part, mind, but orders have come down from the Dark Lord that the Princess isn't allowed to pop off early. I found a bit of chicken bone in my soup once, but the spoilsports got to me before I could choke on it.

On the plus side, to the extent that there is a plus side to being tortured to death, I don't have to see what's happening out in the city. I assume it's bad. It's usually bad. If I got into therapy and unloaded half the shit I've seen, Dr. Freud would take a running leap out the nearest window. So not having to actually watch is kind of a relief.

I hear Artaxes coming, the *clank clank clank* of his rusty iron shitkickers. When he opens the door, I give him a little wave with my fingers. This is all I can manage, since I'm manacled to a wooden contraption that raises my arms like I'm in the middle of a cheer routine.

"Morning, chief!" I sing out. "What's the haps?"

I keep hoping being cheerful will annoy him, possibly enough to rip my throat out, but so far no joy. It's hard to tell how anything lands with Artaxes, since he wears his iron armor like a second skin.[1]

"How do you poop?" I ask him. "Just between us. I won't tell anybody."

He gives a grunt and steps aside. There's someone else in the doorway. Tall and gaunt, black robe hanging limp from her bony shoulders, mouth full of long curving teeth. Sibarae. She looks me over and raises her scaly eyebrow bumps.

I'm naked at this point, modesty provided only by a crust of dried blood and matted hair. For all that matters to Artaxes, I might be a side of beef on a hook. I mean, maybe he has a raging hard-on inside his rusty codpiece, but I doubt it. I've seen Artaxes serve as the right hand of the Dark Lord more times than I can count, and he always goes about his business with the dumb brute efficiency of a buzz saw. You get exactly what you expect with him. It's comforting, in a way, although obviously not when he's tearing my fingernails out.

Sibarae is a whole other kettle of snakes. She's practically drooling at the sight of my gory tits. Her tongue comes out, long and forked, to taste the air. I briefly contemplate what it would be like to get head from a snake-wilder,[2] but I have let's say a premonition that this is not on the agenda.

---

1 He seriously never takes it off. How does he poop? *I have to know how he poops.*
2 The tongue would be fucking weird, right? Dunno. Maybe I'm into it.

"Look, clanky," I tell Artaxes, "I realize you're worried about not...you know, getting the job done anymore, but you can't just introduce a third wheel into our relationship without talking to me about it. We have something special together, I don't want to spoil it."

"My master worries that you may become accustomed to the conditions of your imprisonment," he says. His voice is as cold and dead as his armor.

"And I *begged* him to be allowed a turn," Sibarae says. "I've always wondered what a princess tastes like."

This is *not* a sex thing, trust me.

"Sorry, scaly. I only date girls with tits."[3]

"Those bulbous mammalian things?" She glides forward. "So soft and...vulnerable. Like the rest of you. *Skin*." She pronounces the word with a contemptuous flick of the tongue.

"Remember our lord's instructions," Artaxes admonishes.

"Oh yes," Sibarae hisses. "I'll be sure to show...restraint."

He clanks out, shutting the door behind him. She gets on with the business at hand. Which, let's not put too fine a point on it, fucking sucks. You think you'd get used to this shit after a while, but nooooo, when someone bites your finger off, your body's gotta be all like, oh no, someone bit my finger off, pain pain pain! I know, okay? I was fucking there, you don't have to remind me.

So I scream a lot and piss myself, which is breaking character a little. Cut me some slack. Artaxes at least doesn't *bite*. In between screams, I amuse myself planning how I'm going to kill her next time we meet. Rusty, jagged metal will be

---

3 This isn't really true. I'm just trying to piss her off. No offense to my flat-chested sisters!

involved. There may be, like, a little corkscrew bit on the end, possibly some kind of barbed flanges. I'll use my imagination.

Eventually I pass out, thank God. When I wake up, there's a teenage girl in the uniform of the palace healers, the glow of green thaumite leaking between the clenched fingers of her shaking hand. A small pool of vomit by the door marks where she lost her lunch at the sight of me. I wonder what the wilders have threatened her with.

She grows back most of my missing bits, but leaves me with a few open wounds just for shits and giggles. Dark Lord's orders, presumably. Fucker likes to twist the knife, figuratively and distressingly literally. At least when he killed Johann, my poor beautiful himbo boyfriend, he didn't have time for any of this sadistic bullshit.

Now that I can think without being *completely* submerged in white-hot agony, I'm getting pissed off. I know you're thinking, Davi, *just now* you're getting pissed off? And it's true, this anger has been building for a while. It's taken some time to bubble to the surface, but it's been stewing down there in the acid swamps of my subconscious.

To put it bluntly: I am about done with this shit. The whole being-tortured-to-death thing, *obviously*, but also the rest. Finished. Kaput. No more. Fuck every last little bit of it. I have a new plan and it's time to get started.

Fun fact: Did you know that snakes lose their teeth and constantly grow more, like sharks? Actually I have no idea if snakes do that, what the fuck do I know about snakes, but snake-wilders do. I know this, as of today, because I have one of Sibarae's fangs embedded in my palm.

The healer has grown the skin back over it, but it's merely the work of an excruciatingly painful eternity to dig it out with my fingernails. The fang has a nice curved shape and a vicious point, and I grip it between two fingers and press it against my wrist, right on the artery. I don't have much leverage, so the best I can do is work the point back and forth, sawing through the skin. Hurts like a motherfucker, but sometimes a girl's just gotta die, you know?

When the artery finally pops, the spatter of blood hitting the floor is like music to my ears. I keep tearing at the cut, opening it wider, willing my stupid heart to pump harder and get my whole blood supply out before someone notices. The fang slips through my fingers about the time my vision starts to go gray, but by then I can taste victory. Also blood.

I slip into the sweet embrace of death with a contented sigh. So long, #237. Go fuck a porcupine.

Life #238

"Well now." The voice is frustratingly familiar. "That won't do at all."

Chapter One

I sit up out of the cold water of the pool, gasping for breath. Again.

Twelve seconds.

Done done *done* with this shit, for real. No more.

Still naked, of course. Death, birth, nudity, very mythic. Frankly if it has to be that way, I'd rather die in bed during an epic fuck[1] than bleeding out after weeks of torture in my own fucking dungeon, but beggars, choosers, you know.

Ten seconds.

Anyway. Naked in a rancid pool of chilly water at the top of a hill. Edge of the Kingdom, right up against a wilder-haunted forest. I'm healthy and hale of limb once again, and also about three years younger, with a lot less muscle tone and a ghastly sort of pixie cut. Same as always. I figure it's what I looked like when all of this kicked off, when whatever happened happened and I got here from Earth some-fucking-how.

Six seconds.

I focus on breathing. Calm and centered, that's me.

Four seconds. Sound of someone scrambling up the rocks.

Take a deep breath. Hold it. Let it out.

Two. One.

"My lady!" Tserigern says. I mouth the lines with him. My timing is perfect. "So it's true, then. Gods preserve us. We have a chance."

I look over at him with my best expression of doe-eyed innocence. He climbs the last few feet, dusts off his motley robe, and approaches reverently.

Tserigern is a wizard, a very old and famous one. Everyone says he's the most powerful wizard in the Kingdom, but *frankly* I've never seen him do magic for shit. Light the way in caves and get cryptic messages, that's about it. You could replace him with a flashlight and a walkie-talkie. But he at least looks the part: He's a bony old motherfucker with a beard you could lose a sheep in, like Santa Claus after a debilitating illness. He has

---

1 Managed it once!

kind, crinkly eyes and a sly grin, a weathered, avuncular voice perfect for laying out the mysteries of the universe for an awe-struck young naïf. Just the guy you want on your side when you wake up all nudie in a weird fantasy universe with no idea what the fuck is going on.

He bends to one knee and offers me his gnarled hand.

"My lady," he says as I wrap my fingers around his, "I—"

He doesn't get to finish, because I grab the back of his head with my other hand and slam his face into the fuck-ing rocks. I hear his nose break with a *crunch*, and my heart sings, it's so goddamn cathartic. He lies out flat and I swing astride his back, both hands in his hair, and start pounding his stupid fucking face into mush against the stone edge of the pool.

Seeing as how he's a little occupied, I say his lines for him.

"I know you must be frightened"—*crunch*—"but I swear to you, I mean you no harm"—*crunch*, you fucking liar—"I have hoped against hope for your coming, and I thank the gods my reading of the texts was true"—*crunch*, they didn't pre-dict this, did they, motherfucker?—"you must come with me, the fate of the Kingdom is balanced on the blade of a knife"—*ca-crunch*.

Holy fuck, it's better than sex. I don't stop until long after his legs have quit kicking and bits of blood and brains are float-ing in the water.

"I'm done," I tell the body, leaning back and breathing hard. "Hear me? Done. I'm not some holy savior here to protect your fucking kingdom." I've been doing that for, hold on, let me check my watch, *fucking ten centuries*, and where the fuck has it gotten me? A fucking snake-woman eating my goddamn fin-gers, that's where.

I strip off his nasty-ass robe and wrap myself in it. He's

452

wearing trousers, too, but I'm not touching them without a hazmat suit.

"What am I going to do instead?" I say in response to an inaudible question. "I will tell you what I am going to fucking do. We have an expression back home concerning what course of action to take if you find yourself under no circumstances able to beat 'em. I intend to follow its advice."

I tie the corners of the robe under my chin, plant my hands on my hips, and let it flap behind me like the cape of an extremely inappropriate superhero.

"I," I announce to the world, "am going to become the *fucking Dark Lord.*"

Follow us:

/orbitbooksUS

/orbitbooks

/orbitbooks

Join our mailing list
to receive alerts on our
latest releases and deals.

orbitbooks.net

Enter our monthly
giveaway for the chance
to win some epic prizes.

orbitloot.com